P9-CIV-385

DATE WITH DEATH

The figure stood before her, no more than four feet away. The same figure who had cut her months before, dressed in a cassock-like robe of coarse brown cloth, a large hood pulled forward hiding the face.

"Sylvia," a voice hissed within the hood. "Now."

The voice sent sudden rage surging through her. The scream in her throat turned to a moan, and Sylvia threw herself at the hulking figure, fingers formed into claws.

A blow to her chest knocked her back. But the attack had made the hood fall way. She stared into the face she had feared for months. Her head shook back and forth. "No. No."

The figure straddled her, head nodding as if reading her thoughts, then slowly lowered itself until their faces were only inches apart.

"Yes, Sylvia. Yes. And now it's time, Sylvia. Now it's time to pay the piper."

Sylvia was not the first victim. And despite all Paul Devlin could do, she would not be the last. The question was, how many more? . . . and would the horror ever stop? . . .

SCARRED

Also by William Heffernan
Broderick
Caging the Raven
The Corsican
Acts of Contrition
Ritual
Blood Rose
Corsican Honor

William Heffernan

SCARRED

A SIGNET BOOK

SIGNET
Published by the Penguin Group
Penguin Books USA Inc., 375 Hudson Street,
New York, New York 10014, U.S.A.
Penguin Books Ltd, 27 Wrights Lane,
London W8 5TZ, England
Penguin Books Australia Ltd, Ringwood,
Victoria, Australia
Penguin Books Canada Ltd, 10 Alcorn Avenue,
Toronto, Ontario, Canada M4V 3B2
Penguin Books (N.Z.) Ltd, 182-190 Wairau Road,
Auckland 10, New Zealand

Penguin Books Ltd, Registered Offices:
Harmondsworth, Middlesex, England

First published by Signet, an imprint of Dutton Signet,
a division of Penguin Books USA Inc.

First Printing, December, 1993
10 9 8 7 6 5 4 3 2 1

Copyright © Daisychain, Inc., 1993
All rights reserved

Cover illustration by Don Brautigan

REGISTERED TRADEMARK MARCA REGISTRADA

Printed in the United States of America

Without limiting the rights under copyright reserved above, no part of this
publication may be reproduced, stored in or introduced into a retrieval system,
or transmitted, in any form, or by any means (electronic, mechanical, photo-
copying, recording, or otherwise), without the prior written permission of both
the copyright owner and the above publisher of this book.

PUBLISHER'S NOTE
This is a work of fiction. Names, characters, places, and incidents either are
the product of the author's imagination or are used fictitiously, and any resem-
blance to actual persons, living or dead, events, or locales is entirely
coincidental.

BOOKS ARE AVAILABLE AT QUANTITY DISCOUNTS WHEN USED TO PROMOTE PROD-
UCTS OR SERVICES. FOR INFORMATION PLEASE WRITE TO PREMIUM MARKETING DIVI-
SION, PENGUIN BOOKS USA INC., 375 HUDSON STREET, NEW YORK, NEW YORK 10014.

If you purchased this book without a cover you should be aware that this book
is stolen property. It was reported as "unsold and destroyed" to the publisher
and neither the author nor the publisher has received any payment for this
"stripped book."

This book is for Parker,
who arrived too late to get his name
in the last one. And, again,
for Stacie, whose love brought
him to us.

Prologue

Sylvia Grant stared at the blinking cursor on the computer screen, the steady, rhythmic heartbeat of the electronic beast. She raised her hands, fingers poised above the keyboard, then let them fall, trembling, back into her lap. The cursor continued to blink. Her mind flashed to a teacher she had had in grade school, a rigid, sour-faced woman, the very epitome of the aging schoolmistress, arms folded, one foot tapping an impatient tattoo on the floor as she awaited an answer from a dull child.

Sylvia stared at her trembling hands, then at the small stack of papers to her left, the few miserable chapters she had managed in the past two months. A tear formed, broke free, and slid slowly down her cheek. The words had been there each day. They had formed in her mind, waiting to be transported by the fleet movement of her fingers. Then the past horrors had come rushing at her, pushing their way in, and each time her hands had begun to tremble, and the words had shattered like delicate crystal. Gone. Irretrievable.

Sylvia stared at the screen again, the blinking cursor, the foot tapping impatiently, awaiting performance she was unable to give. Her jaw tightened. Then her hand reached out and touched the power switch. The screen flashed with a fast-fading green blur, then turned black, dead, lifeless. She swiveled her high-backed chair away from the machine and sank back into the plush leather. One hand unconsciously stroked the glove-soft material, the first indulgence she had given herself when her last book had made its very brief appearance on the best-seller lists. Her eyes roamed the room, taking in the other indulgences that had followed. The wall of books rising from floor to ceiling, shouting out literacy and comfort and security. The framed jackets of her three novels. The last—the lone success—placed in the center, and beneath it *The New York Times* best-seller list that had proclaimed that achievement. The room itself. A true study rather than the desk stuck in a corner from which most writers worked. All of it, even the building. A renovated brownstone on Manhattan's West Side, which the bank had allowed her to buy based on the substantial advance she had received for her next book, along with the promise she would turn the upper two floors into income-producing apartments. And now it was all useless, because no new book would ever come. Not unless they caught the madman who was going to kill her.

One small fist slammed against the arm of the chair.

"Dammit, you can't do this to me. You've done enough. I won't let you do more."

Sylvia struggled to her feet and walked unsteadily across the room to the ornate mirror that hung beside the door. The mirror was draped with a cloth, and she reached out and pulled the covering away. Her face seemed frozen in the glass: dark blue eyes, wide and fearful, staring out between the soft brown hair that fell along each cheek. She turned her head to the left and brushed the hair back, exposing the right side of her face, the fine, delicate features marred only by the dark smudge of sleeplessness beneath her eye. She turned her head again and repeated the gesture, uncovering the left side of her face. Her jaw tightened in shock and revulsion as the ugly red scar jumped out at her. It was there, just as it had been an hour before, an undulating line that began under her ear and moved across the whole of her cheek—like the trail of a snake across soft sand.

Just as it's been there for more than two months now. Still as unbelievable, as foreign as when the doctor first removed the bandages. Her hands curled into fists. She could still hear the plastic surgeon's confident, self-satisfied voice assuring her the disfigurement was correctable, in time, by simple surgery.

But what of the other scar, the one that cut so sharply into her mind, her very being? And what about the letters and the telephone calls that had begun almost at once? The clumsily printed words and disembodied voice that had promised her a slow and painful death. Phone calls that continued even when her number was changed, even when she fled to the weekend house she rented in the Hamptons.

The police had come, had taken the letters away. They had provided protection. Two policewomen had stayed with her in rotating shifts. They had monitored her telephone for three weeks, only to have the calls abruptly stop as soon as they arrived. And, from the start, the detectives with whom she had dealt had seemed almost annoyed with her, angry that she couldn't describe the hooded figure who had hovered above her bed. They had brought in a consultant, a wonderful woman, a psychiatrist who had hypnotized her. But it had been useless. She simply hadn't seen a face.

Sylvia leaned her head against the mirror and drew a deep breath.

"Oh, God," she whispered. Now the police were gone and the phone calls were coming again. But now, this time, only one word. Spoken in a wheezing, rasping, unidentifiable voice. *"Soon."*

She straightened. Turned back toward the desk. Stared at the telephone. At least Gabrielle hadn't abandoned her. She'd been there for her throughout it all. Ever since that first session when she'd hypnotized her. Three times a week she'd sat with her, talking it through, trying to help her overcome the immobilizing fear, the uncontrollable terror. A tic came to the corner of her right eye, and she rubbed it, trying to force it away. Gabrielle. Call her now, dammit. Call her. Talk to her.

Sylvia moved quickly across the room and picked up the phone. She hesitated, staring at the small antique clock next to it. It was almost midnight. Too late. She started to replace the receiver when her eyes fell on a large kitchen knife that lay in the center of the desk. The knife she carried with her throughout the house now, even into her own bathroom.

"You can't live like this," she hissed. "You can't."

She raised the phone again and punched out Gabrielle's number, waited as it began to ring. After the fourth ring an answering machine came on. Sylvia closed her eyes and lowered the phone.

"Damn. Damn."

She drew a deep breath and stared at her lifeless computer, willing herself to try to work again. She shook her head and started for the door, then stopped abruptly and returned to the desk for the knife.

Upstairs, in her bedroom, she went immediately to the window and peeked out through the heavy, drawn curtains. It had been raining and West 67th Street was slick and wet, its dark surface reflecting the glow of the streetlights. A cab sped past, sending up a plume of water in its wake. Then nothing. She glanced at her watch, then looked back at the street, waiting, waiting. Finally, a blue-and-white patrol car came into view. It slowed almost to a stop before her door, and she could see the face of the cop in the passenger's seat as he scanned the front of her building. He seemed so young. Too young. She looked at her watch again. Twenty minutes had passed since she had gone to the window. It was the "protection" they had promised, and it was useless.

The creak of a floorboard behind her made her jump, spin around, the knife held out at arm's length like a protective barrier. Her breath came in rapid gasps and she could feel her heart pounding in her chest. There was nothing there. Nothing. Just the creaking of an old house.

She moved to the center of the room, arms and legs still trembling, and suddenly she felt a dull pain in her hand. She stared at it. The hand was wrapped tightly around the handle of the knife, and it had left the fingers white and bloodless. She went to the dresser, laid the knife down, and massaged the hand, forcing herself to concentrate on the pain, determined to keep all other thoughts from her mind. Slowly she began to remove her clothing, her mind fixed on each item, on the systematic ritual of undressing. When she had finished, she looked into the dresser mirror, the only one in the house she had left uncovered. Naked, her body jumped out at her. It was a body she no longer recognized. Ribs pressed through tightly drawn flesh; collarbones protruded. Even her breasts seemed smaller, almost delicate, like those of a pubescent child, not a thirty-year-old woman.

You don't sleep; you don't eat, she told herself. What do you expect?

She turned away from the mirror. Go to sleep. Go to sleep and hide.

The thought of closing her eyes, of surrendering to darkness, produced a sudden wave of terror, and she looked quickly at the bedroom door to be certain the heavy steel bolt had been slid firmly into place.

You've turned this house into a fortress, she told herself. No one can get to you. No one.

She took a nightgown from a dresser drawer, pulled it over her head, and felt it fall loosely about her body. There was a sudden screech of tires, and she jumped at the sound, heart pounding. Then she caught hold of herself and moved cautiously toward the window. Outside, a woman climbed out of a small car, leaned back in the open door, and spoke angry words Sylvia couldn't hear. She watched as the woman marched furiously across the street, each step slamming the pavement like a shout. The car sped off with a squeal of rubber.

Sylvia turned back toward the bed. Her body stiffened, frozen in mid step. It was as though she had struck a hidden wall. Her muscles tightened, became rigid; a scream rose in her throat, caught there, and quickly died.

A figure stood before her, no more than four feet away. It was the same. The same figure who had cut her months before, dressed in a cassock-like robe of coarse brown cloth, a large hood pulled forward, hiding the face in deep shadow.

"Sylvia," a voice hissed within the hood. "Now, Sylvia. Now."

The sound of the voice sent sudden rage surging through her. The scream that had caught in her throat turned to a wild, animal growl, and Sylvia threw herself at the hulking figure, fingers formed into claws, reaching for the face, the hidden eyes.

A blow to her chest knocked her back, but the force of the attack had made the hood fall away, and she stared into the face of the madman she had feared for months. Her head began to shake back and forth.

"No. No."

Pain exploded in her chest. Pain where she had been struck, driven back. She looked down and saw the blood slowly spreading across the front of her nightgown. Her face registered disbelief, and she looked back at the figure, at the bloodstained knife held firmly in one hand.

All strength seemed to drain from her body, and she sank slowly to the floor. The figure moved forward and hovered above her as Sylvia stared into the now smiling face.

Her mind screamed at her. Dear, God. No. Please, God. It can't be like this.

The figure straddled her, head nodding as if reading

her thoughts, then slowly lowered itself until their faces were only inches apart.

The voice hissed; sour-smelling breath washed her face:

"Yes, Sylvia. Yes. And now it's time, Sylvia. Now it's time to pay the piper."

Sylvia Grant started to scream as a glove-covered hand seized her throat, killing off the sound.

Eddie Grogan stood quietly, staring at the body, as a young assistant medical examiner went about his preliminary examination, carefully jotting notes on a clipboard that rested on one knee. The kid's name was Blair. Michael Blair. He was new and Grogan had never worked with him before, so he had decided to watch him, make sure he didn't screw things up. Especially not this case. Behind Grogan, men from the police forensics unit also waited for the M.E. to finish so they could begin their own work.

"Do we have any ID on the victim?" the young M.E. asked without looking up.

"Sylvia Grant," Grogan said.

"You sure?"

"Yeah, I'm sure."

The M.E. glanced at him, then made a note on the clipboard. "You knew her?"

"Yeah. From a previous case."

Grogan continued to stare at the corpse. There was a small puncture wound in the chest just above the left breast. And there were dark bruises on the neck, indicating strangulation. Grogan drew a deep breath. Sylvia Grant's face was twisted in pain and fear. The eyes were open, filmed over to a dull blue-gray. Her tongue protruded between her teeth. Her legs were spread obscenely. The bloodstained nightgown had been ripped, or cut open, exposing a pale, flaccid body which looked strangely frail and vulnerable, almost like a kid's. One who had been in a bad accident. But Sylvia Grant was no kid. She had just lost weight since the last time he had seen her. A lot of weight for a small woman.

"My guess is she was raped," the M.E. said. "But I won't be sure until I do the post."

"You won't find any semen."

The M.E., who was blond and boyish, stared up at Grogan, wondering if he should just dismiss the remark. The man came across like an aging, overweight rummy in his baggy brown suit and rumpled shirt and tie. His face looked as though someone had stepped on it, and his unruly gray hair gave the appearance of having been combed with a rake. And now this battered old hump was telling a trained pathologist what he would or wouldn't find.

"You're sure of that, are you?" There was a hint of a smile on the M.E.'s lips.

Grogan looked at himself in the dresser mirror. He looked like shit, he thought. But then, he always looked like shit. At fifty-two—after thirty-one years as a cop, twenty-six as a detective—he had no illusions about himself or the job he did.

"Yeah, I'm sure, kid. You'll find penetration but no semen."

The M.E. bristled at the word *kid*, but decided to let it pass. "Well, failure to ejaculate isn't all that unusual," he said.

Grogan turned away and started for the door. "Make sure you bag her hands," he said. "I need the whole shot on this one. Scrapings under the fingernails, the works."

There was no response, and he stopped and looked back over his shoulder. The M.E. was glaring at him, his face red with anger.

"You hear what I said?" Grogan asked.

"I heard you."

"Good." The corners of Grogan's mouth turned up. Almost a smile. "Don't take it personally," he said.

When Grogan reached the bottom of the stairs, a uniformed cop came toward him from the front door.

"You got a suit outside. Claims he's FBI. Says he wants in. I told him I hadda check with you."

Grogan nodded, then glanced into a nearby room. A middle-aged woman sat on a sofa, her nose and mouth buried in a handkerchief.

"That the one who found the body?" Grogan asked.

"Yeah. Says she's the victim's agent. Came by when she couldn't get an answer on the phone. Claims the door was open, so she just came in."

The cop raised his eyebrows as if to say: Believe that and I got another one for you. He looked well past forty and his gut hung over his gun belt. A "hairbag" who'd been on the job so long he wouldn't believe the fucking pope, Grogan decided.

"You the first unit on the scene?"

"Yeah," the cop said. "Me and my partner. He's on the door outside."

"You question her? Get an ID or anything?"

"Naw," the cop said. "I just told her to get her ass in there and wait. Then I called it in and secured the area."

The cop seemed pleased with himself, but Grogan couldn't tell if it was because he thought he'd done a good job, or had gotten away with the minimum required of him. Grogan nodded and heaved his bulky body toward the front door, where a certain FBI sonofabitch was cooling his heels. Then he stopped and turned back to the uniformed cop.

"How long you been on the job?" he asked.

"Been wearing this blue bag for twenty-three years," the cop said.

Grogan grunted; the hint of a failed smile returned to his lips. "Retire," he said.

He stepped out the front door onto the stoop of the aging brownstone. Matthew Mallory stood there in a slight drizzle, red-faced and angry. There was another agent with him, a woman whom Mallory didn't bother to introduce.

"This your idea, Grogan?" Mallory snapped.

Grogan motioned the cop stationed at the door down to the sidewalk below; then, ignoring Mallory, he extended his hand to the woman.

"Eddie Grogan," he said.

The woman seemed nonplussed, uncertain if friendliness was permitted. She hesitated, then finally extended her hand.

"Special Agent Wilson," she said.

"You got a first name?" Grogan asked.

"Wendy."

Matthew Mallory and Wendy Wilson. M. M. and W. W. He grinned at the thought of it.

"Cut the shit, Grogan," Mallory hissed. "Did you tell that blue suit to keep us out?"

Grogan offered a contrite look. Mallory headed up a team from the FBI's Behavioral Science Unit, the Quantico-based hotshots who tracked serial killers throughout the country—a unit that had been brought in at the specific request of the mayor, and put in charge of what was supposed to be a *very quiet* investigation. Early on Grogan had decided he was also a flaming asshole.

"I told him to keep everybody out until he checked with me. We don't want some reporter, claiming he's a fed, waltzing into all this."

Mallory's jaw tightened. It was a square jaw, just like the rest of his facial features, framed in close-cropped brown hair and punctuated by cold gray eyes. He was well over six feet, and towered over Grogan's five-eight. He was about forty, and Grogan had decided he was becoming a bigger asshole the older he got.

"Well, now that we know it's not *The New York Times,* can we go inside?"

Mallory had forgotten his raincoat, and the steady drizzle was quickly melting the press of his dark blue suit. Grogan smiled at him.

"There's a woman inside—the one who discovered the body. Better we talk out here for now."

Mallory's eyes brightened. "She have anything for us?"

"I was just about to start with her when you showed up."

"We'll let Wilson deal with her." Mallory's voice had dropped an octave, filled with sudden authority. "We find women do better dealing with other women."

Grogan glanced toward Wendy Wilson—W. W. as he now thought of her. She appeared to be in her mid-twenties. Probably fresh out of law school. Yeah, Grogan thought. Who needs a hump detective who was doing this shit when she was in diapers?

"Yeah, well, I'd like to talk to her first."

"Listen, Grogan—"

The detective suddenly flared, months of repressed anger hitting its flash point. "No, you listen. You can stand out here in the fucking rain until I finish, or you can come inside and wait. Me, I don't give a fuck."

"You're pushing it, Grogan." Mallory's eyes were hard, as threatening as he could make them; the muscles in his jaw were pulsing.

"You already got what you wanted. You got another stiff," Grogan snapped. "It's not going anyplace."

"What's that supposed to mean?"

"Hey, I gotta draw you a fucking picture? You guys work from the crime scene. You gather it all up and run it through your voodoo science shit. And when you hit a brick wall, you wait for another stiff so you can start again. Keep adding it all to your 'profiles.'" Grogan spoke the word with contempt. "Then, when you've just about got it together, some rookie cop in East Jesus makes a traffic stop and accidentally nails your guy for you."

Grogan's face was red now, and he wanted to reach out and grab Mallory by his Countess fucking Mara tie and choke him.

"You're still pissed we called off the in-house protection, right?"

There was a cold smirk on Mallory's face, but, sur-

prisingly, it didn't fuel Grogan's anger. It soothed him.
His voice became calm.

"Hey, me? Pissed? What for? It's like you told us.
We don't scare this fuck off. We don't create another
Ted Bundy, who's running all over the fucking country,
and who's maybe gonna take years to nail once he
starts moving. We let him feel safe and keep him right
here. We don't tell the public there's a maniac fucking
loose on the streets. We don't want that kind of publicity. It might shake this guy up, make him feel insecure.
Shit, we don't even tell the next woman whose face he
carves up. God forbid she should know what she's up
against. That she's staked out like a fucking goat at a
tiger hunt. She might jump on a plane and get her ass
out of the country. And then what would we fucking
do?"

Mallory's smirk had grown wider, more menacing.
He glanced at Wilson, then turned his gaze back on
the rumpled, and to his mind, useless detective.

"You are really pushing it, Grogan. You're pushing
me. You're pushing your goddamned pension."

Grogan threw back his head and let out a short,
harsh laugh. "Hey, Mallory. Fuck you. I'm a detective
first grade, with thirty-one years on the job. I put in
my papers tomorrow and draw three-quarters pay for
the rest of my fucking life. Right now I work it your
way. To a point. Because that's what the bosses at
headquarters say I gotta do. And me? I'm a good cop.
I follow orders." He grinned. "Most of the time. Even
when they come from a bunch of empty suits who sit
around the Puzzle Palace and shit their pants every
time they get a call from that cocksucker of a mayor."
Grogan inclined his head toward Wilson, offering an
apology he didn't mean.

He turned back to Mallory and smiled. "That should
be enough to have me up on charges. So tomorrow I
put in my papers. And you know what I do then? I trot
down to see this guy I know at the *Daily News*, and I

tell him a tale they're gonna love on Forty-second Street, but maybe not so much down in Quantico."

Mallory's face became harder but suddenly paler. He put a hand on Grogan's shoulder, only to have it shrugged off.

"Just calm down, Eddie." The voice was suddenly smooth, consoling.

"Hey, Mallory. I'm calm. You're the boss here. I'm just a dumb cop who wants to do his fucking job."

"Eddie, that's all I want. You go talk to the woman." He offered a smile that was even falser than Grogan's. "And I'd like to get out of the rain."

"Hey. Come inside," Grogan said. "This rain, it's no good for your suit."

1

Adrianna Mendez came through the gallery door with her hand pressed over her mouth. She was fighting back laughter that moments before had threatened to escape and create an outlandish scene. On the sidewalk she turned and pointed an accusing finger at the man who stumbled out behind her.

"You're determined to get me sent back to a filthy garret, aren't you?" she said.

Vincent Richards brought his fingers to his chest in mock surprise. "Madam, you obviously have me confused with another."

She began to giggle. He was doing it again, a perfect prissy imitation of the gallery owner to whom she had just been speaking. *Her* gallery owner, the man who had catapulted her paintings into the public eye.

"The man is going to make me a famous artist, *and* a wealthy woman," she said. "Unless you screw it all up."

Vincent offered a look of mock contrition. "I never, ever would." He wiggled his eyebrows, then put on his prissy voice again. "Besides, the way my last play flopped, I may need a wealthy woman to support me."

Adrianna wanted to laugh again, but settled on a quick shake of her head. Looking past Vincent's shoulder, she could see Umberto standing far back inside the gallery. He was staring out at her, and his lips were pinched together in what could only be described as incipient disapproval. She smiled and waved to him.

21

Vincent, catching the gesture, turned and did the same. The gallery owner simply nodded, then turned abruptly and walked off among his paintings.

"Bye-bye, Umberto," Vincent said through grinning teeth. "We'll miss you. You pompous little twit."

"Stop," Adrianna snapped. She grabbed his arm and began walking him away.

Earlier, as she had talked with Umberto about her upcoming show, Vincent had stood beside him, slyly and outrageously imitating his gestures and mannerisms. And Umberto had never noticed. At least she prayed to God he hadn't. No, she thought. If he had, there would have been a scene. A memorable one. Umberto took himself far too seriously to broach any disrespect. Especially within the walls of his own lofty domain.

But it had been funny. And deserved. And Adrianna knew she needed it, if only to keep her perspective amid all the pomp and pretension that made up the world of big-money art. All the bullshit, as her Uncle Eddie would have described it.

"Umberto's not that bad. He's actually rather sweet," she said, goading Vincent just a bit.

Vincent stopped and turned toward her, placing his hands on her shoulders. He leaned forward for emphasis. He was a strikingly handsome man, Adrianna thought. Tall and slender, with wavy brown hair and the bluest eyes she had ever seen. Looks that belonged onstage—where he had once tread as an actor—not hidden behind the scenes in a director's chair, a role he claimed to infinitely prefer. She wondered if that was true.

"Umberto is worse than bad," Vincent said. There was a mischievous look in his eyes. "He's a pompous little poof."

"He is not," Adrianna said. "He plays at being flamboyant because it's what his clientele expects. It sells."

"Well, if he's not, he belongs in my business," Vincent said. "Besides, anyone who grows up in the Bronx and changes his name from Hubert Walsh to Umberto, then insists"—he raised his chin and looked down his nose, again doing a perfect take on the gallery owner— "no last name is required, is about as pretentious as anyone I've ever encountered. And since I make my living on Broadway, that's a real stretch."

"You're just jealous because he's a better actor than you were, Vinny boy."

"Everyone's a better actor than I was," Vincent said. "And don't call me Vinny boy. It gives away your Brooklyn roots. If *Umberto* finds out about them, he'll dump you like a sack of wet laundry." He took her arm and continued along West Broadway.

Adrianna pulled herself against him, momentarily resting her head against his shoulder. It was mid June and the night still held a slight chill.

"He already knows I'm from Brooklyn," she said. "What he doesn't know is that I know *he's* from the Bronx. Besides, if he ever tries to dump me, I'll send my Uncle Eddie to see him."

"Ah, yes. Uncle Eddie. The infamous detective."

"The large, mean infamous detective," Adrianna said. "And you better not *ever* say infamous around him. *If* I ever decide to introduce you."

"Don't you think he'd love me like the son he never had?" Vincent teased.

"He's a cop. He'd think you were trying to get into his godchild's knickers."

Vincent offered a grunt and a mock shiver.

"You're lucky my father isn't alive. He was a cop, and he was Cuban. He would have known you'd already been there."

They turned east on Spring Street, leaving the lights and glitter of Soho's gallery-strewn main thoroughfare behind. Across the street two rough-looking black kids huddled near a darkened doorway, as if waiting for easy game. Vincent ignored them and pointed to a wine bar a few doors down the block.

"Let's stop and toast your upcoming one-woman show," he said.

"It's still a month away, and all the paintings aren't even finished yet," Adrianna said.

"Then let's toast the fact that it's a month away, and all the paintings aren't finished." One of the kids said something indistinguishable that made the other laugh. Vincent threw them a quick, steady look that cut the laughter short.

She smiled at him, flashing even white teeth that seemed to jump from her sallow complexion. She had been with men who became edgy around street punks—a sure way to gain even more unwanted attention. Vincent understood the streets, and she liked it that he did.

Vincent took time to run his hand through her hair. He loved looking at her. Her nose was just ever so slightly too large, her mouth a bit too wide, and her light brown eyes were too much in contrast to her thick, black hair. A casting director would have rejected her at once, Vincent thought. Yet to him, she was among the most striking women he had ever seen.

The wine bar was typical Soho, designed to favor the yuppies who had flooded the area years earlier. They made their way through potted ferns and hanging plants, past the long mahogany bar, to an area of cast iron tables and chairs set atop a patterned tile floor. It was a Wednesday night and crowded with customers, but little about art was being discussed. Snatches of conversation revealed talk about the markets—real estate, stocks, commodities—and the patrons tended more toward Brooks Brothers and L.L. Bean than paint-spattered jeans and T-shirts.

"I feel out of place here," Vincent said, pulling on the lapel of his corduroy jacket, complete with scuffed elbow patches. He gave Adrianna an appraising look. "And you look like someone from central casting, who the owners hired to make everyone think real painters come here."

Adrianna was dressed in jeans and well-worn Reeboks, topped off by a red-and-black-checked hunting shirt that had picked up a few errant drops of paint. He had pulled her away from a canvas several hours earlier and forced her to have dinner with him. He had refused to let her change, fearful that some new inspiration would strike and send her irretrievably back to her easel.

"Real painters do come here," she said. "They just don't admit it to one another."

The waiter brought a bottle of Pouilly-Fuissé and poured a small amount in Vincent's glass for the ritual tasting. Vincent waved him off, took possession of the bottle, and filled both their glasses.

Vincent raised his glass. "To the upcoming one-woman show, and the paintings yet to be finished."

Adrianna mimicked the gesture. "And to your new play. May the start of rehearsals next week be everything you hoped for." She narrowed one eye. "Almost everything. May the actresses also decline all your offers of comfort."

He shrugged, smiled, then reached out and took her hand. "Are you excited about your show?"

"I'm flying," she said. "And I'm scared to death, too. I still can't believe the prices Umberto is asking. And that he's already had requests for private viewings. From people who want a chance to buy *before* the show. I've waited so long for this to happen."

Vincent smiled at her. "You're thirty-two. There are painters who waited their entire lives to be where you are now, and who went to their first major show in a wheelchair."

Adrianna looked into her glass, then back at him. "I know. But I'm greedy. And, besides, you're only thirty-five and you've already had a hit on Broadway."

"And a flop."

"Everybody has a flop," she said.

"But they better not have two in a row," he added quickly.

Adrianna raised her glass again. "You won't. And neither will I. Our stars are in the ascension."

"That's terrible English."

She offered up a dazzling smile. "I know. But I'm just a little Cuban girl from Brooklyn."

Vincent leaned across the table. "I always wanted to seduce a little Cuban girl from Brooklyn."

She gave him a coy look, then unfastened one button of her checked hunting shirt. His eyes widened and his mouth fell open. "Ply me with more wine, and you may get your chance," she said.

He filled her glass to the brim, and offered her his best acting-class leer. "You know, what you really need is some publicity that will make you a public curiosity," he said.

Adrianna shook her head. "I'm not very good at self-promotion."

"Then you could always die. That's sure to bring out the art buffs, checkbooks in hand."

She made a face. "Tell me your other ideas."

He leaned forward, smiling.

They moved together under the ceiling fan, the gentle breeze not enough to keep the sweat from forming on their bodies. Vincent buried his face in her neck, kissing her, licking the salt from her skin. Adrianna arched against him, enjoying how impossibly hard he felt, reveling in her ability to excite him. He moved down her body, and she lost all sense of her surroundings, her mind filled by what he was doing, the way his lips seemed to be feeding off her flesh.

She felt his tongue linger at her breast, circling, teasing. Her breath came faster, and she closed her eyes with the pleasure of it. He moved lower, pausing briefly at her stomach, his chin brushing lightly against her pubic mound.

Her fingers entwined in his hair, anticipating further movement; her legs began to part, almost with a will of their own. And then he was there, his fingers spreading her gently, his tongue searching, then finding her clitoris, sending a wave of pleasure and excitement coursing through her body. Her back arched and a groan of pure joy that bordered on pain escaped her lips. Her fingers tightened in his hair, urging him on until the first wave of orgasm struck, filling her mind with near oblivion. Her mouth opened involuntarily, teetering on the edge of a scream; her head began to thrash back and forth, hair tangling against her face. Then a second wave struck, forcing her to arch her back impossibly high, her muscles shuddering, imitated by her breath, her mind telling her she couldn't possibly stand more, but knowing she wanted it, needed it to continue, a greedy child bordering on the edge of control.

She felt him move away, and she looked down the length of her body, eyes imploring for even more of him. He began to move up to her, his own eyes filled with urgency, and she knew what her mind demanded was coming now, and her body opened to it, called out for it. Then he entered her, filling her, a sensation suddenly foreign, suddenly everything she had wanted. He moved against her, thrusting smoothly, eagerly, and she caught his rhythm, bucking beneath him, against him, her mind whispering with sudden shame, not caring, dismissing it.

Another wave struck and she felt her entire body shudder, starting at the center of her being and moving out through every limb, every part of her. She heard him gasp, barely recognizing the sound, her own pleasure so intense she thought it might be herself. And then the warmth of him shot into her, spreading, and her legs tightened about him, the muscles of her vagina pulling him even deeper, until she thought she would swallow him.

Vincent collapsed against her, his breath coming in rapid pants. Adrianna's hands moved along his back, feeling his sweat play against her fingers, her own

breath as fast as his, her nostrils filling with the scent
of them, the residue of what they had done.

She tried to speak, found she could not, waited, then
tried again.

"Oh, Vinny boy. That was so sweet. You should do
this for a living," she whispered.

"Don't call me Vinny boy," he said, voice hoarse, still
breathless.

"I'll call you Vincenzo," she said.

A short laugh escaped him, little more than a gasp.
"That's worse," he said. "Even more Brooklyn than
Vinny boy."

He slipped down beside her, and she stroked his
hair, brushed her lips against his forehead. They lay
together, then dozed, their bodies loose and spent.

Later, she wasn't sure how long, she felt his hand
against her cheek, and she opened her eyes and found
him smiling down at her. A sigh of languorous satisfaction spoke of simple contentment, and she closed her
eyes again and smiled.

"I have to go," he whispered.

She looked at him, smiled again. "I know," she said.

He turned her face to the side and gently brushed
her hair away. One finger traced the outline of her
ear, then moved slowly, barely touching her, across her
cheek.

Adrianna looked up at him again. His eyes were
closed; there was a faint smile on his lips.

"I love the way your hands touch me," she said.

He bent to her, his lips tracing her cheek as his
finger had done moments before. "I'll call you tomorrow," he said. "I have an early meeting with the playwright. I'll call when we finish."

Adrianna hummed assent.

"Sleep," he said.

She hummed again.

Adrianna was dreaming about her father. He was
younger, the way he had been when she was a child.

He was standing above her, dressed in shirtsleeves, wearing the shoulder holster he always put on before he left for work. She couldn't see herself, but she could feel her own presence, and she knew she wasn't a child in the dream, and that felt wrong, somehow out of place.

Her father seemed to be shouting at her, berating her about something. His lips moved, but there was no sound; she couldn't hear his voice. Ridiculously, she wondered if he was speaking English or Spanish, as he sometimes did with her. It would tell her how angry he was.

She felt herself move beneath the sheet, her mind lingering between sleep and consciousness. The vision of her father disappeared, replaced by only a sense of presence, something indistinguishable hanging over her.

Adrianna's eyes fluttered—opened momentarily, then closed again. A shadow had seemed to hover above her, partially obscuring the faint glow of the streetlights that filtered in through the windows. Her mind dismissed it, urging her back to sleep. Then it jolted her awake, screaming out danger, threat, an alarm of sudden fear.

The figure loomed above her, draped in dark, heavy, hooded cloth. A gasp flew from her lips, and she struggled to push herself back, away. A fist lashed out, striking her just above the ear, stunning her, sending flashes of light across her eyes. She felt a heavy weight straddle her body, pressing it down into the bed. A cloth suddenly engulfed her nose and mouth, and a cloying, pungent odor invaded her nostrils. She held her breath, refusing to inhale the noxious fumes, and forced her body to go slack, concentrating, willing herself not to breathe.

The cloth slipped away and her head was pushed to one side. Out of the corner of her eye she saw a flash as light glittered on the blade of a knife moving toward her face.

Adrianna brought her knee up sharply, driving it between the legs of the figure. She felt it sink into soft flesh, heard the grunt of sudden pain, the expulsion of breath that washed over her face. The knife flashed past her cheek, and a sudden sharp pain seared her shoulder. She brought her knee up again, then a third time, the last bringing forth a weak, strangled gasp.

The figure rolled off her and fell to the floor. She forced herself up, reached back, and grasped a baseball bat leaning against the wall—a bat her father had taught her always to keep beside her bed, ever since she was a child.

Adrianna jumped from the bed as the figure rose, staggering slightly. She swung the bat back.

"Fucker," she screamed as she swung the bat with all her strength.

The bat connected high on the shoulder, and the figure staggered, then fell back.

"Fucker, fucker, fucker," she screamed again, stepping forward and drawing back the bat again.

The figure turned, staggered again, then lumbered across the long, wide room toward the door. Adrianna hesitated, then let out another scream and raced forward, bat held high above her head. The figure pulled open the door and spun away down the hall.

Adrianna followed the fleeing form, now only a blur of heavy brown cloth. She stopped in the hallway as the figure turned into the stairwell. She was naked, and her breath came in heavy gasps. She could feel her heart pounding in her chest, and she stepped back inside and shut the door behind her.

Pain suddenly seared her shoulder again, and she looked down and saw a wash of blood spreading across her chest.

"Oh, my God," she gasped, falling back against the door. Slowly she sank to the floor.

2

Eddie Grogan pushed his way through the mass of bodies that filled the emergency waiting room of St. Vincent's Hospital. It was early Thursday morning, and the city's regular weekend butchery was off to an early start: the room already reeked with the stench of poverty and fear and mayhem. Grogan eased past a woman leaning against one wall, a blood-soaked towel pressed against her head. A small child, no more than three, clung to her leg, soothing its own terror. Grogan's face was unusually pale and tense, the stubble of his beard making his features seem even whiter, almost sickly. Less than an hour ago he had received a call from the First Precinct, telling him his godchild—the daughter of his long-dead partner—had been slashed by a man wearing a hooded robe. The words had cut through him like a second knife.

Grogan pushed his way to a large glass-enclosed counter that kept the admitting nurse safely out of reach of the victims she was there to help. Her head was bent, intent on the papers before her. Grogan leaned down to a small opening in the glass.

"My name's Grogan," he said, loud enough to startle her. "*Detective* Grogan, NYPD."

The nurse looked up, took in the large, disheveled hulk, studied the stubble on his face, and narrowed one eye. A tough old bird, Grogan decided.

"You got some ID?" she snapped.

Grogan wanted to shove his arm through the opening, grab her, shake her. Instead he pulled out his gold

31

shield and aimed it at her face. "You got a woman here. Adrianna Mendez. Stabbing victim. Just tell me where I can find her."

The nurse's face softened. "Sorry. But we get all kinds here. Claim they're everything from a U.S. senator to the mayor's brother-in-law."

"Yeah, I know how it is." Grogan felt he was about to jump out of his clothes. "Just tell me where she is."

The nurse punched the name into her computer terminal. "They already took her upstairs. So she must be okay. Room 423."

Grogan found the uniform he had requested already standing guard outside Adrianna's door when he reached the fourth floor. He flashed his shield, told the blue suit to stay where he was, and went quickly inside.

Adrianna's bed was elevated, and she lay there with her eyes closed. There were no tubes, no support systems, only the bulge of a shoulder bandage beneath her hospital gown. At least the cop hadn't lied when he said the wound was superficial. Her eyes opened as he moved toward the bed.

"How you feeling, kid?" He ran one large hand lightly over the top of her head.

"Lousy. They said I lost a lot of blood. But there was no serious damage. I just want to go home." Her voice was weak, almost frail. He wasn't sure if it was caused by the medication or the wound.

Grogan pulled a chair next to the bed and sat. "You stay a while. Let the insurance company give back some of your premiums."

Adrianna glanced toward the door. "When the nurse came in before, I saw a cop outside. How come?"

Grogan offered a small shrug. "Hey, I ordered it. Special treatment for my old partner's kid."

Adrianna studied his face. "Tell me what's going on, Uncle Eddie."

He wanted to tell her to rest, that they would talk

about it later. But he knew the clowns from the behavioral science team would be swooping down on her.

"Listen, it's complicated," he said. "You gotta listen to me, and you gotta do what I say." He saw concern creep into her eyes, and he tried to soften what he had to tell her. He took her hand, dwarfing it in both of his. "By the way, I'm proud of you. The cop who called me said you sent that hump's voice up a couple of octaves, then took a Louisville Slugger to him. Made him beat feet like somebody torched his tail."

She was watching him, studying his eyes. "I thought he was trying to rape me. But now you're saying it's complicated. What's so complicated about an attempted rape?"

She was a hard lady—had been even when she was ten, Grogan thought. He twisted in his chair, but continued to hold her hand. "Look, this is more than attempted rape. A lot more." He shook his head and looked away, trying to keep her from seeing the fear in his eyes. But that was stupid. She had to know. He gave up and faced her again. "I ain't supposed to tell you about it, but I'm gonna. I just couldn't live with myself if I didn't and . . ." His jaw tightened. "Shit, you gotta promise me you'll do what I say."

"Uncle Eddie, please. Just tell me what's going on." Adrianna's lip began to tremble; the concern in her eyes had turned to fear, and Grogan realized he had blown it badly.

He released her hand and bit down on the tip of his thumb. Adrianna recognized it as something he did only when anxious or nervous. He leaned close to her and lowered his voice, as if afraid someone would hear him through the closed door.

"Look, kid. This is the most screwed-up investigation I've ever worked. You wouldn't believe the political crap that's flying around this thing. And there's no way to change it. It runs too deep, and too many heavy hitters have their tails on the line. If you even hint you know what's going on, it ain't gonna take them five minutes to find the connection between us. And when they do, they're gonna bounce my ass so fast, I'll think Michael Jordan is using my head for a basketball."

He leaned closer to her, the heat in his eyes holding her like a hypnotist. "Honey, I don't give a shit what happens to me. Hell, I got thirty years in, and I plan to toss in my papers when this is over, anyway. But I want this sonofabitch. I want him more than I ever wanted anyone in my life. And, even more important, I can't protect you; I can't keep you alive unless you do what I say."

Adrianna's lips moved for several moments before the words came. "Eddie, you're scaring the hell out of me. What's this all about?" She reached toward him with her good hand, then tried to force a smile. "What is it? Some hack from the mayor's office? Some politician's kid who's gone around the bend?" She forced the smile wider.

Grogan recognized what she was doing. She was grasping at straws. Praying it would turn out to be something simple. He rubbed his face with his hands. He hadn't slept in two days and he was beat.

"I wish it was like that." He watched her face surrender to the fear again. "The guy who attacked you is a serial killer. And we've been hunting the bastard for more than a year. He just keeps running circles around us."

The shock hit her like an electric charge. "He was there to kill me?" She stared at him, waiting for him to dispel the idea. "To kill me?" she said again.

Grogan shook his head. "No, not this time. But soon. This time he was there to mark you."

Confusion flooded her face. "I don't understand."

"I told you, it's complicated." Grogan began chewing the tip of his thumb again, thinking with it. "This is the craziest bastard I've ever come across. And the most sadistic. He picks out a target. We think from newspapers and magazines. Then he stalks them." His jaw tightened, not wanting to tell the rest. "It's always women. All fairly young, all beautiful. And each one has just had a first big taste of success. Each one is an up-and-coming star in her field."

"What field?" Adrianna asked. Her stomach was churning, and she fought to keep her voice steady. She couldn't let herself break down, couldn't give in to her fear.

"Always the arts," Grogan said. "Acting, dancing, writing." He hesitated. "Now painting."

Adrianna stared at him, as though trying to make sense out of what he had said. "There have been three?" she said at length. "He attacked three women before me?"

"Attacked them and then killed them," Grogan said.

She shook her head, struggling to reject the idea. "But you said they were famous. That's not me, Uncle Eddie. I'm just—"

"They weren't famous, kid. Just on their way. Just starting to get the kind of recognition they needed to get there." He took her hand again, but she pulled it back, still shaking her head. "Look, you fit the pattern," Grogan said. "I wouldn't be telling you this if you didn't. You've had one big show. Very successful. I know. I went to it. Remember?" He reached for her hand again, and this time she let him take it. "Your paintings are bringing heavy prices. Now you've got another show coming up, and it's already getting play in newspapers and magazines." He squeezed her hand lightly. "And you saw the guy, just like the others did the first time he came. It's him, kid. No doubt about it."

He felt her hand tremble; felt her tighten it into a fist; fight it off. "You said he comes twice. The first time to mark them." Her voice had become steady, as if she had willed it. "I don't understand."

"Neither do we. It's the craziest part of the whole thing." He released her hand and sat back, told himself she could handle it. He'd give it to her straight.

"Look, most serial killers don't work like this guy.

Usually they limit their exposure. They pick their target. Maybe it's random, maybe it's somebody they've watched a long time. Then they make their move; do their thing. Rape, murder. Maybe the whole shot. If they've got some little quirk—something they gotta do—they do it then." He shook his head. "But this guy, he goes after them twice. First time he gets into their apartments—we're not sure how, but we think it's when they're out. He hides, waits for them. They come home, fall asleep, and then he makes his move. He attacks them, uses chloroform to knock them out. Then he cuts them." Grogan raised his hand, touching his left cheek. "Puts his mark on them. Here. A wavy line, like a goddamned snake. Then he just goes away. No rape. No messages left behind. Zilch. He just does it and, bang, he's gone."

Anger flashed in Grogan's eyes. "A couple of weeks go by. He lets them live with what he's done to them. The way he's scarred them. You can imagine what it's like for these women. He lets us finish our preliminary investigation, waits for us to give up on any protection we've set up. Then the telephone calls start. And the letters. He tells them there's more. That he's coming back. That this time he's gonna kill them.

"So we go back. We put in a team to protect them. We tap the phone. And suddenly everything stops. It's like he's watching us. Like he's sitting in some apartment across the street, waiting for us to give up. We checked that. But the women all lived in different parts of town. And there's nobody new across the street. Or upstairs, or downstairs. At least nobody who's moved from place to place.

"So eventually we pull out. We shouldn't, but we do. And we start running a loose watch, which ain't worth shit. And right away it starts again. Like he's been waiting. Cat and mouse. So we go back. This time we sneak the surveillance teams in. We do it perfect. No way anybody can tell. Bang. It stops again."

Grogan rubbed his eyes, shook his head. "Then,

when we're gone again, he comes the second time. Same M.O. But this time he rapes them. Kills them." His eyes glowed with hatred. The case had driven away the detachment he had learned to maintain over the years. "But it's not just us he's playing with," he continued. "He lets weeks go by before he makes his first call, sends his first letter. It's like he wants to make sure they suffer. Make them live with the scarring. Then torture them again about what they still have to look forward to. Let it sink in that the cops can't protect them."

Adrianna's eyes were wide, her mind filled with what lay ahead if Eddie were right. She shook her head. "So this time you don't pull your surveillance." Her mind immediately clicked in, telling her what her life would then be like. "Oh, Jesus," she whispered.

"And what if he just waits?" Grogan asked, misunderstanding her final words. "What if he moves on to somebody else, then comes back a year later?" He let out a short, frustrated breath. "But even that won't work. We don't have the manpower to keep protection going that long."

Adrianna just stared at him. He was presenting a picture so hopeless, it was beyond comprehension. Grogan looked away, suddenly embarrassed.

"Look, it gets worse." He paused a moment. "Even if we had the people, we couldn't use them. The NYPD ain't running this investigation. We're just a bunch of fucking gofers doing the shit work."

"What are you talking about? Who's running it?"

"The FBI. Their hotshot Behavioral Science Unit." Grogan ground his teeth. "The mayor called them in on the Q.T. Ordered the bosses at the Puzzle Palace to let them take charge."

"And they agreed?" Adrianna was staring at him as though he were speaking Chinese.

"Hey, you're a cop's kid. You know what they're like. The mayor growls, they all get so uptight, they couldn't count past twenty without opening their flies. Yeah, they agreed. The chief of detectives, that asshole, he's ready to kill somebody. But officially he keeps telling us how lucky we are, how they're the only experts on serial killers." Grogan let out a snort. "So who'd they ever fucking collar, except in the fucking movies? Sure, they put together great profiles that tell you what you're looking for. Maybe. They provide the best lab work you can get. But in the end, some mooch cop nails the guy because some junkie snitch passed on something he heard on the street. Or, like Son of Sam, some smart detective thinks maybe he'll check out parking tickets that got handed out around the scene of the last murder."

Grogan stopped himself, realizing he had gotten carried away with his own frustrations. And that wouldn't help. It would only give Adrianna reasons not to do what he wanted her to do. He shrugged, forced a smile.

"So you're gonna ask me why the Fibbies don't provide protection when they've got people sitting around Indian reservations playing with themselves." He drew a breath. "It's the same reason the lid's on so tight. Why you haven't seen squat in the newspapers. They don't want to scare this guy off. They don't want him to hit the road for Chicago, or San Francisco, and pick up his trade there. They know that sooner or later he's gonna get caught by some cop. And they want him caught here, where they're in charge. And then they can say: Hey, look, we finally caught somebody. And then Jodie Foster can do another movie, a real-life fucking adventure this time. Or they can all get their mugs on Sonny Grosso's Top fucking Cops show." Grogan's hands balled into fists. "And the mayor's playing along, 'cause it's just the way he wants it. Quiet. He's already on everybody's shit list, and there's an election coming up. He don't need all his rich white, liberal buddies in the silk stocking district to suddenly get scared because crime is hitting too close to home. Hell, they might hide under their beds, and take their fucking checkbooks with them."

Adrianna sat forward slowly, grimacing at the pain the movement brought to her shoulder. Her eyes were wide, disbelieving. "What are you telling me? That these FBI experts are going to let me sit there? Use me as bait, and not even protect me because they're afraid they'll scare him off?"

"What I'm telling you is they work from crime scenes. From forensics. From what they find *after* a crime is committed. It's the *only* way they work. What I'm telling you is that two feds are gonna be around to see you today. They won't offer you any protection. They won't even tell you they're feds. They'll just say they're cops investigating the attack. One's name is Mallory, a big hump with a square head and the personality of a fucking fish. The other's a woman named Wilson. Right now they got a forensics team going through your place with toothbrushes. But they won't tell you that either. What I want you to do is tell them everything you know. Everything. Then I want you to get the hell out of here. Out of the city. Out of the state. Out of the fucking country." Grogan held her eyes, the look unflinching. "Let me get you a phony passport. Then you haul ass down to some island in the Caribbean without telling anybody where you're going. And you wait this thing out. Rent a house. Take somebody with you if you can. Or hire some live-in help. But just get out, make yourself as secure as possible, and make sure nobody can follow you."

An array of emotions fled across Adrianna's face. Then her mouth tightened into a narrow line. "I can't," she said. "I can't leave."

Grogan's face turned bright red. "Whadda you mean, you can't? You deaf or something? This guy is gonna kill you. No two ways about it."

She shook her head. "I've got the show. In one month, and all the paintings aren't even finished yet."

"So you postpone the show. So you finish the paintings on Virgin Gorda. What, you can't paint you see a fucking palm tree?"

Adrianna lowered her head, shook it. "I can't post-pone it. The gallery has spent too much time, too much money. They'd write me off forever if I did that. And the show's in a month. I couldn't pack everything up, go somewhere; paint, then have everything crated and shipped back. There isn't time. And even if there was, it would be like leaving a trail of bread crumbs right back to where I was. It just wouldn't work." She looked up, her eyes suddenly hard. "And dammit, Eddie, I'm not going to let this bastard destroy my life. Destroy everything I've worked for. I can't. I won't."

Grogan let out a long breath, rubbed his palms against his thighs. "Okay," he said. "Plan B." It'll stir up more political shit than either of us ever saw. But maybe it'll work."

He hesitated. He knew this plan would produce even more resistance, and he wanted to word it so he left her no choice but to accept.

"Look, kid. I'm good at what I do. You give me a straight murder case, and if the sonofabitch can be had, I'll find him and put his ass in the slam. But I don't know squat about these serial killers. Almost no-body does. Mostly they get caught from blind-ass luck and time. That's just the way it is. And as far as you're concerned, we ain't got time, and we can't just sit around and hope we'll get lucky. Not if you're gonna still be alive and kicking when it's all over." He paused, holding her eyes again. "But we got one shot. Only one, if you're not willing to do a disappearing act." He drew a breath and continued to stare at her. "I know this guy, used to be a detective here. I worked with him a couple of times. He's out of the job now. Retired. But he broke two of these serial cases. One here. One up in Vermont after he put in his papers. He's the only guy I know who's done that."

Adrianna stared at him. Her expression was suddenly rigid, her eyes hard despite the fear. "Who are we talk-ing about?" She knew the answer. She had followed the man's career in the newspapers, knew what he had done, what had happened to him in the ten years since she had last seen him. But she wanted to hear Eddie say it.

"Paul Devlin," Grogan said.

Adrianna lowered her eyes and began shaking her head back and forth. "No," she said. "No, I can't do that. I can't."

Grogan leaned forward and fought to keep his voice calm. "Listen, dammit. You ain't got a lot of choices. You can get the hell out; go hide somewhere. You can help me get Devlin into this to catch this sonofabitch. Or you can sit back and wait for this fucking psychopath to kill you. And, believe me, that's just what he's gonna do. You can make book on it."

Adrianna looked away toward the window, her fists tight in her lap. "Uncle Eddie, I walked out on him ten years ago. I was in love with him, but I couldn't stand the idea of spending the rest of my life with a cop." She shook her head again. "I knew what it was like, and I didn't want it." She turned back to Grogan and he could see tears beginning to form in her eyes. "He wouldn't listen to me, told me it wouldn't be the way it was with my father. Insisted it would work for us." She lowered her head again and brushed the corners of her eyes with the back of one hand. "I just walked away from him and never looked back. Never answered his calls, his letters, anything."

"He's still our only shot," Grogan said. "And it's been a long time. He's been married, had a kid, and been widowed since then. And I don't think he's gonna let some psychopath ice you just because you treated him like shit back when he was just a kid."

Adrianna felt the sting of the words. "He was twenty-five," she said. "And I was twenty-two. We weren't kids. And he didn't deserve what I did to him. I just couldn't help it." She stared at him. "What makes you think he'll come?"

Grogan shrugged. "You." He hesitated, letting the word sink in. "And he owes me a big one. I'll put the arm on him." He watched her shake her head. "We'll go up and see him as soon as you can travel. I got a couple of days coming, and we can drive it in six, seven hours."

Adrianna shot forward, then fell back as the pain hit her shoulder. "We. Why do you want me there?"

Grogan stood and stared down at her. "I want all the pressure I can get. I wanna make sure he can't say no."

She began shaking her head again, but Grogan would have none of it. "Look, it's the way it's gotta be. Either you jump on a plane and head for some palm trees, or you and me are taking a quick trip to shit-kicker country. Even if I gotta handcuff you and throw you in the trunk of the car."

The room was shuttered against the early morning light. Faint streams filtered in, illuminating dust motes that seemed to hover over the bare wood floor. The figure sat in a darkened corner, body hunched, an occasional whimper the only sound to break the silence.

His testicles ached where she had kneed him repeatedly. And his shoulder, where the baseball bat had crashed into him. Nothing was broken. He had checked, was certain of it. But he would be in pain for days, perhaps even a week or more.

She would have killed him with that bat if he hadn't run. There was no question of it. Or he would have had to kill her with his knife. Just to stop her. And he hadn't gone there for that. He had gone to mark her. To mark her for her crimes, her sins.

She was worse than the others. Far worse. He hadn't realized it before, but there was something intrinsically evil about her and it frightened him. He was certain she would try to bring about his downfall, and that others—just as evil as she—would now help her.

But she had been marked. That was the important thing. Not as she should have been. Not on the face.

With the sign. But his blade had cut her shoulder, drawn her blood, marked her body.

"It's enough. For now it's enough," he whispered.

"No, it's not. There must be more. More!"

His hands began to shake. Then his arms, his shoulders.

"Yes. There will be more. I promise. But I have to wait. Wait until things are better. Safer. Then . . . Then I'll go back."

"No! Now!"

His hands trembled. He drew a deep breath. Then he began to nod his head.

3

Paul Devlin swung the ax, cleaving the log perfectly, sending each half flying in opposite directions from the chopping block. He was dressed in jeans and a black T-shirt emblazoned with the name Moody Blues. It was a gift from his eight-year-old daughter, Phillipa. She had come across it at a garage sale, and although she was too young to remember the once popular rock group, she had thought it suited him; she had bought it for twenty-five cents.

A blue sedan pulled into the driveway, a battered Chevy that Devlin immediately recognized as a New York City car. It had too clearly suffered the ravages of parking on the city's streets. He was expecting the car and the man in it. Eddie Grogan had called, had said he needed to see him, needed his help. And Grogan was a man he owed big time. Years ago, when Devlin had been a young, inexperienced cop, Grogan had saved his life in the filthy hallway of a Harlem tenement.

Grogan climbed out and lumbered toward him, shaking off the stiffness of a long drive. There was a big, sneering grin on his face. "Hey, Paul Devlin," he said. "Shit, you look like Paul fucking Bunyan. Either that, or Lizzie Borden in drag. I can't make up my mind which."

Devlin drove the ax into the chopping block, then moved forward and took Grogan's hand. "Watch your mouth, Eddie," he said through his own grin. "I've got an eight-year-old running around here someplace, and

44

I brought her to this paradise just so she wouldn't grow up hearing people like you."

"Jeez," Grogan said. "My passenger's been yelling at me for seven hours about that. Now you. What's the matter, everybody forgot how colorful I am?"

He hadn't mentioned a passenger when he called, and Devlin looked past his shoulder as a woman exited the car. She was tall and slender, with raven-colored hair that hung past her shoulders, and she still had the most striking pale brown eyes Devlin had ever seen. He felt a tightness in his stomach and looked quickly back at Grogan.

"What is this, Eddie? What's Adrianna doing here?"

Grogan inclined his head to one side in a half-hearted shrug. "She's the reason I need help, Paul. And believe me, kid, I need it bad."

Devlin looked past Grogan again. Adrianna was coming toward him. She was dressed in a loose-fitting violet blouse that still managed to cling to her, and off-white slacks that seemed to flow with her movements. And she still moved beautifully, Devlin thought.

Adrianna came up to him, and now he could see a hint of nervousness in her eyes. She hesitated, appeared to fight it off, then warmed him with a smile that seemed to leap from her face. He immediately felt grubby, very much the country bumpkin, and he suddenly wished he had postponed splitting firewood, or had it least put on a decent shirt.

"Thanks for seeing us, Paul," she said. "It's been a long time." She lowered her eyes, then looked up at him again. "Eddie said you wouldn't mind, but I wasn't sure you'd want to see me again."

"Of course I would." Devlin felt the tightness intensify, and he wondered if what he had said was true. He forced a smile of his own. "Look, let's go inside." He was still looking at her, couldn't stop himself. "After all that time listening to Eddie curse every jackrabbit that crossed the road, you must need a drink."

"I could use a beer," Grogan said, falling in behind. "Hey, Paul. Whadda you do for excitement up here? Collect moose patties?"

Devlin threw him a look over his shoulder. "I catch bad guys, Grogan. Cattle rustlers. Sheep molesters. Just like in the big city."

They entered the old post-and-beam house that Devlin had bought three years earlier when he had fled New York, and found Phillipa carrying a pitcher of iced tea across the living room.

She stopped, taking in her guests with a self-confidence that belied her age. "I fixed a place on the deck," she said, playing the lady of the house. "Dad likes to show off the view of Blake Mountain."

"Any mountain lions up there?" Grogan asked.

Phillipa grinned impishly. "No, Mr. Grogan. Only an occasional elephant."

Grogan barked laughter. "You remember me, huh, kid?" he said. "I didn't think you would. You were only a little squirt last time I saw you. Now you're a big squirt."

Phillipa's eyes danced playfully, and Devlin held his breath, awaiting her reply. She had a quick mind, an even faster tongue, and few adults were ever ready for the seemingly innocent barbs that erupted from that eight-year-old brain.

Surprisingly, she only widened her grin, then turned to Adrianna. "Hi," she said. "I'm Phillipa."

"Hi, I'm Adrianna. Don't pay any attention to Eddie. I never did, and I grew up with him. Besides, I don't think he's ever seen a mountain."

Phillipa gave her a conspiratorial grin that said she understood completely.

"Jesus," Grogan said. "Are we having fun yet?"

Phillipa turned and led them toward the deck. Adrianna watched her with a mixture of pleasure and regret. She was a bright, beautiful child, with blond hair tied back in a ponytail and a field of freckles spread below vivid blue eyes. She was still very much a little girl, not having reached that stage of prepubescent awkwardness, and Adrianna could see her father's handsomeness in the bone structure, only softer. She could have been her child, she told herself, then immediately pushed the thought away. Still, she hoped she'd have a chance to sketch her before they left.

They took seats on the wide deck, and Phillipa fetched a beer for Grogan, then retreated inside to a sofa near an open window. She turned on the television set, but Devlin knew she'd be listening to every word, then would offer her critique and counsel later.

He turned to Adrianna. "Eddie said he had a problem. Said he needed some advice. I guess it involves you."

Grogan leaned forward. "A little more than advice, Paul. I need your help. We both need it."

Devlin noted that Grogan had smoothly shifted the need to include Adrianna. He's calling in an old chip, he thought. And now he's adding her to the pot. Grogan knew about their old relationship, and now he was using it. Devlin didn't like the sense of emotional blackmail, but found he couldn't generate too much umbrage. He kept looking at Adrianna, and realized that whatever it was, he hoped it was something he could do. The degree to which he wanted it surprised him.

Grogan began to fill Devlin in on the details of the case he had been working for more than a year. Adrianna listened, feeling surprisingly detached, removed from the madness. When Grogan reached the part about the attack in her studio, Devlin's eyes snapped back to her, and she saw a sense of shock and anger and concern. She felt her breath catch, then a wave of emotions that ran the gamut from gratitude to pure pleasure.

Adrianna continued to watch Devlin's face as he absorbed the details. She liked the way he looked. He seemed more solid and at ease with himself than he had ten years ago. He still had the same wavy black

hair and deep blue eyes she remembered so well; he
was still handsome in that rugged, unhandsome sort of
way she had always loved. But now there was a two-
inch scar on his left cheek, almost like a dueling scar.
It had given her a start when she had first seen it,
making her mind flash to the scar the madman they
were discussing had intended for her. But it seemed
insignificant now, unrelated, something that added a
touch of world weariness to his face.

There was another scar on one arm, longer, more
serious. She recalled reading about him being wounded
in something the newspapers had called the Ritual
case. And later, how he had been forced to retire from
the NYPD. She had wanted to call him then, but had
stopped herself.

She continued to watch Devlin's face, to study it
both as a painter and a woman. When Grogan had
mentioned the words *serial killer*, momentary fear had
flickered across his eyes. He had masked it quickly,
but it had been there. And the fact that it had hit
home. If the reality of it all frightened him, then perhaps she did belong here. She stood suddenly, sensing
it would be better if they were left alone.

"I think I'll go in with Phillipa. If nobody minds."

Devlin stood as she did. Grogan remained seated,
looking from one to the other, amused. Adrianna had
always liked Devlin's gentlemanliness. She had forgotten it, remembered it again now, and was pleased to
see he hadn't changed. She found herself wondering if
he had changed in other ways.

"If you need anything, just ask Phillipa," Devlin said.
"I hate to admit it, but she runs this place a lot better
than I do."

When Adrianna had left, Devlin walked to the railing
and stared out across his rear yard to the woods
beyond.

"What you've got, Eddie, sounds like political quick-
sand," he said. He turned to face the older detective.
"I don't know what I can do for you."

"What I've got is a death warrant for Adrianna," Grogan said. "And right now I can't protect her. And I can't fight my way through the political bullshit and nail this perp without help. I need an expert. And you're the only one I got."

"I'm not an expert," Devlin protested. "No one is with this kind of creep." He shifted his weight nervously. "You work a case like this, it's like waking up in the middle of a nightmare that doesn't make any sense." He shook his head. "Except the nightmare's still going on after you're awake. But the perp understands it. He's the only one who knows what it's all about. And all you can do is try to think like him. And that's hard enough without all the political crap and interagency games you're dealing with."

"Like it or not, Paul, you're the only expert I got," Grogan said. "You've solved two of these things, all by your lonesome." He grinned at Devlin. "Maybe you're just nuts enough to think like these guys. I don't know. But you're the only cop I ever heard of who's batting two for two."

Yeah, and with all the mental scars to prove it, Devlin thought. Two men dead. Two friends. First the Ritual case. Then the other one—a year ago—the one the papers had dubbed Blood Rose, owing to the withered rose the killer had left behind in the blood of his victims.

He didn't need another one, Devlin told himself. No one in his right mind needed even one. He drew a long breath. "The worst thing about this is the FBI. Their Behavioral Science Unit is good. But only from a forensic standpoint, and in developing psychological profiles. They're not street cops, no matter what Hollywood says. They're a think tank, designed to collect evidence, analyze it, and feed information to the cops working the case. All the mayor did by putting them in charge was handcuff everybody." He took a few steps along the deck, then stopped. "He obviously knew they'd jump at the chance. It's a no-lose situation. If they screw it up, nobody knows. If they nail this bastard, it's a high-profile win, and they're out front with the TV cameras rolling. But somebody should have told him it wouldn't work."

"Hey, I'm sure Cervone told him. But the mayor hates his guinea ass. He wouldn't believe our beloved chief of detectives if he said there was a fucking snake in his bed."

Devlin grunted, found himself agreeing with the mayor. At least on that. He knew he would never trust anything Cervone said, would never turn his back on the man. Experience had taught him that years ago.

"I still don't know how I can help, Eddie."

"I need you to come to New York," Grogan said. "I need you to work the case privately, away from all the bullshit. I'll help you. So will other guys on the task force. And I need you to help keep Adrianna alive. Live with her when you're not working. Protect her. I'll find a way to have people watching her when you're not there."

Devlin stared at him. "She knows about this?"

"About you coming down, yeah. I ain't told her about you staying with her and playing watchdog."

Devlin shook his head. "She'll never go for it. You forget, she doesn't like cops. Doesn't like all that macho authority bullshit she grew up with. And to her all cops are the same." He looked away momentarily, remembering the way it had ended between them. "And there's one cop in particular she doesn't like. I found out about that ten years ago. I'm not sure I want to deal with it again."

"Then she's dead meat, Paul. No two ways about it." Grogan stood and came over to him, put one beefy hand on his shoulder. "She'll do it, Paul. She ain't got a choice. She may not like it any more than you do, but it beats all hell out of a pine box." Grogan paused. "Paul, you ain't seen what this guy does."

Devlin's eyes hardened. "That's dirty pool, Eddie."

"Yeah, I know. But I'm that desperate."

Devlin turned away and stared out into the rear yard and the woods beyond. "I don't know, Eddie. I have to think about it." He turned back to face Grogan. "If I do it, the department can't know about it. The bosses, the FBI, can't have a clue about what I'm doing. It won't work if they do."

"Hey, you got my word. Not the department, not the mayor, not the fucking FBI. Not for as long as we can keep it quiet."

"This is crazy, Eddie," Devlin said.

Grogan nodded. "Yeah, I know. But it's the only shot I figure we got. *If* we're gonna keep her alive."

Devlin looked away. "There's a better way. Just get her out of town," he said. "Hide her until it's over."

"I tried. She won't go," Grogan said.

Devlin turned back and stared at him; he watched Grogan shrug.

"Won't let herself be run off by some nut case." Grogan pulled out a cigarette, lit it. "And I hate to admit it, but in a way she's right. Better to fight this guy on your own turf than take a chance he'll follow you somewhere you got no support."

"It's his turf too," Devlin said. "And it's his game, his ball, his bat."

"Yeah. There's that too," Grogan conceded. "So, will you let me call in a chip?"

Devlin turned away again. He wanted to escape the man's stare. "I'll think about it. Sleep on it. Then I'll talk to her. I've got a job here. And I've got Phillipa. And I can't just go running off and do something that isn't going to work." And you've got more than a month in time off coming, a kid who just started her summer vacation, and a sister in Queens who'd kill to have her stay there, Devlin told himself. And you owe Eddie Grogan. He suddenly wanted to laugh. He was just running one big con job on himself, avoiding the real reason he wanted to do it. He turned back. "I've got to be honest with you," he said. "The idea of doing this scares the living hell out of me."

Grogan nodded. He wouldn't blame the guy if he said no. "Hey, so you'll sleep on it. You'll talk to her. And you'll tell us tomorrow," Grogan said. He grinned. "That means you gotta cook me breakfast."

When Devlin entered the house he found Phillipa sitting in a chair, hands in her lap, looking like a demure young lady. Adrianna was seated across from her, sketch pad in hand. He walked up behind her and stared down at the remarkable likeness of his daughter. She had captured every nuance of the child. Not just her features but the vitality, the impishness that spewed from her.

"That's wonderful," he said.

"It's for you," Adrianna said. "For putting up with us."

Grogan walked out into the rear yard, stopping at the first line of trees that edged the property. He stared into the forest that rose into the foothills beyond.

"Shit, they probably got bears in them woods," he mumbled. He tugged on his belt, readjusting the revolver that rode on his hip. The feel of it made him think about Devlin, about that last time they had worked together. They were in Harlem, after some doped-up militant who had decided he was going to shoot it out. Grogan shook his head and grinned at the memory. Christ, it was like fucking World War III. Bullets flying everywhere. Devlin was in a hallway, and he had run out of ammo. The fucking jambone, he steps out of a doorway, and he's got a fucking Uzi pointing at Devlin's head. Grogan grinned as the scene replayed itself in his mind. Devlin was dead meat—the crazy bastard was ready to blow his head off—and Devlin just stares at the sonofabitch and then spits in his face. That was when you blew the bastard away. And Devlin, he just turns around and says: "Thanks, Eddie." That's it. Grogan shook his head. He started to laugh. "Shit," he said aloud. "Deader than McGilby's balls, and he spits in the fuck's face. And then, when it's over, and his ass is still standing there, he says: 'Thanks, Eddie.' How's that for fucking balls?" He turned and started back toward the house. Now all he had to do was get the man's ass back to New York. And that still wasn't a done deal. Adrianna held the key to that little problem. He just hoped she was smart enough, or scared enough, to see it.

Before Devlin went to bed, he entered his daughter's room and found her still awake, awaiting his nightly visit.

"You're supposed to be asleep," he said.

"I couldn't," she said, her eyes barely open.

He stroked her hair.

"Are you going to help Mr. Grogan?" she asked.

"You were listening."

"Yup. Are you?"

"I owe him a favor," Devlin said. "A big one."

"How come?"

"He saved my life a long time ago."

"Then I think you should help him."

"You do, huh?"

"Yup. And Adrianna. Did you know her before?"

"Yes, I did. We were friends a long time ago. Before I met your mom."

"Do you still like her?"

"Sure."

"Then I think you should help her."

"It's a hard favor, honey. I have to think about it."

"I know," she said. "I know it scares you."

He knew that she did. She had lived through the last one. He stroked her hair again. "Sleep tight, honey."

"You too, Dad."

He bent down and kissed her forehead.

Early the next morning Devlin found Adrianna sitting in the small sun room he used as a study. She was dressed in white shorts and a white T-shirt, and she was nursing a cup of coffee. She looked very young, and very fresh, and very beautiful. Just as he remembered her.

"That's funny," Devlin said. "You don't look like a soon-to-be famous artist. You look like a graduate student I used to date."

Adrianna smiled at him. But beneath the smile she seemed uneasy, uncertain. He knew exactly how she felt.

"Everyone was still asleep, so I came in here to look at your books," she said. "I hope you don't mind."

"Not at all." He took a chair opposite her.

She picked up a book from her lap, weighing it in her hand. *"The Psychology of Pleasure in Killing,"* she said, reading the title. "Pretty grim stuff."

He nodded. "At the time it was useful."

She stared at him; he found her eyes almost mesmerizing. "Are you going help us?" There was a hint of nervousness in her voice. But no fear, Devlin noticed.

"Is that what you want?"

"I suppose." She hesitated. "Yes. Yes, it is. Eddie says it's the only way we can stop this maniac. I just feel as though I don't have the right to ask you."

"You don't," Devlin said. He softened the words with a smile. "But I'm glad you did."

"So, you're going to help?" Relief suddenly washed over her, and Devlin realized the fear he hadn't seen had been there. She had just done a damned fine job of hiding it.

"I have to make some arrangements," he said. "It will take a day or two, and I'll want you to stay here and drive back with me."

Adrianna grimaced. "God, I have so much to do. I—"

Devlin stopped her. "Look, we have to work some things out. First, we have to agree that when I tell you to do something, you do it. No questions. No discussion." He saw her eyes flicker with momentary resentment.

"I'm not saying that to be macho," he explained. "I've just got to be confident that when I tell you something

I need you to do, I don't have to look over my shoulder to make sure it's happening." He stared at her, but tried to keep any sense of threat from his voice. "This could get dangerous for both of us. And we stand a better chance if we're sure of each other."

She nodded, then smiled. "You know what I'm like. But I'll do my best."

Yeah, I know what you're like, he thought. "It's important," he said. "It won't work unless we play it this way. And, one other thing. Eddie wants me to stay at your place. He wants you to have live-in protection. And he's right. I know it will be awkward. But we're not kids anymore. We can make it work."

Varying emotions flashed across her eyes, and Devlin wasn't sure what they were, or what they meant.

She drew a breath. "Yes, Detective," she said. Then she smiled. "How's that for being a compliant citizen?"

"It's great," Devlin said. "But I'm not a detective anymore." He returned her smile. "Now I'm a chief of police."

"That's funny," Adrianna said, imitating his earlier words. "You don't look like a chief of police. You look like a guy I used to date."

The figure moved through the loft in erratic bursts of energy. He seemed to charge from place to place without any plan, or sense of purpose, guided only by the muted light from outside street lamps. He had gone first to the sleeping area, one hand deep inside the pocket of his robe, clutching the chloroform pad he had hidden there. But her bed had been empty, just as he had feared.

He had begun watching the building as soon as she had left the hospital. Two days now. Just to make sure there were no police, no traps waiting to be sprung. He had thought she would be inside, afraid to come out, or simply nursing her wound. But she was gone. She was hiding from him. Hiding from the work he had to do.

Her absence had thrown him into a rage. He had gone to her desk, searched it for some clue about where she had gone. He had grown angrier with each passing minute, and he had taken her papers and books and appointment diary, and had thrown them wildly about the massive room. He had searched her dressers and her closets, and had scattered clothing across the floor. Now he stood among her paintings, seething with uncontrolled anger and frustration. He wanted to destroy the filth he saw displayed before him, but knew he could not. She would be back. She had no choice. And destruction of her work might be the final blow that would drive her away forever. It might remove the one compelling reason that forced her to stay. And he needed her here. Here where he could see her suffer.

He turned and started for the door, then stopped, his eyes riveted to a small painting hanging on a far wall. He moved closer and stared into a face that was burned into his mind. His hand reached inside the robe and withdrew a long knife from a sheath attached to his belt. He raised it and stepped toward the painting. His eyes blazed and his lips trembled with anticipation. It would do for now, he told himself. But only for now.

4

The door opens slowly, quietly, the back lighting presenting the figure only as a dark, looming shadow.

The child lies in the bed watching, knowing what is about to happen, remembering past nights, recalling sensations that will soon be felt again. There will be fear—already it is beginning to grow—a fear approaching terror, but one that will gradually dissipate as pleasure slowly overwhelms it, though never driving the fear completely away. Is it fear, or is it guilt—some childlike understanding that it is wrong, sinful?

There is a slight trembling beneath the covers. Fear? Or anticipation? Perhaps both, mixed in a mind unable to differentiate.

The door closes, returning the room to darkness. Now there is only sound. Movement coming closer, closer. The slow sag of the bed as the figure sits, then the soft, soothing, whispered words, the hand reaching out and gently stroking the brow. Now the hushing sounds as the hand drops to the covers and slides beneath.

The child can feel the hand tremble slightly, and there is a sense of power barely understood yet instinctively felt. Then a sudden exhalation of breath as coarse hands touch soft flesh.

Now a barely audible whimper. The child? It is impossible to tell. It is obscured by the eagerness of movement, the uncertain yet unquestionable response. Lips come down in the darkness, caressing the cheek, the shoulder. Hot breath and the unmistakable smell of liquor wash the air. The child's eyes squeeze shut and visions of a backyard playhouse fill the mind. Playhouse? Whorehouse? Playhouse? Whorehouse?

Adrianna Mendez was jolted awake as the car stopped suddenly for a traffic light. She let out a small grunt, and Devlin turned in the driver's seat and offered a mumbled apology. She looked out the window. Soho. Her street. Only a block from her building.

"God, how long have I been asleep?"

"Forty-five minutes. We were only five minutes away from my sister's house when you conked out."

They had gone to Queens to get Phillipa settled in, and they had decided to stay rather than continue on to Manhattan and arrive at the loft late in night. But despite the long, wearing drive from Vermont, Adrianna had not slept well. She never did in a strange house. She laid awake, watching the unfamiliar shadows—like a small child afraid someone, or something, would come to her in the night.

She turned to face him, but his eyes were now roaming the street. He's looking for something, she told herself. Something out there waiting to hurt me. She sat up and adjusted her clothing, then looked back outside. It was nine o'clock, Sunday, and Soho had not yet come alive. That would not happen for another two hours, when the brunch crowds and gallery browsers slowly began to fill the streets. Now only a few people moved about, headed to newsstands for the Sunday *Times*, and to delicatessens that would provide the morning's bagels and rolls and cream cheese. Just what you'd be doing if everything were normal, she thought.

A young man moved toward them down the sidewalk. He was unshaven and his clothes were rumpled, his face puffy and slightly pained from a long, liquid night. Making his way home from an unplanned visit to someone else's bed, Adrianna thought. She had done that once herself, years ago. It was after she had driven Paul away and realized she had done it too well, that he was not going to yield to her demands, was never coming back. She had gone home with a man she had met at a party—back to his apartment—then had changed her mind at the last minute, and had barely gotten out the door without having her clothing torn from her body.

She stared down the street, realizing she had suddenly begun to hate the neighborhood she had made her home. There was something false about it, something contrived. Even the highly prized iron-fronted buildings, with their decorative designs and columns, exuded an aura of chichi fraudulence. Soho had once been an area devoted to light industry—glove factories, paper merchants, small warehouses. Then artists had discovered the large lofts and had rented them from failing businesses. Then the realtors had discovered the artists and had begun moving the yuppies in—at inflated rents that drove most of the artists out. Next came the galleries and wine bars and antique shops. And suddenly Soho was gentrified, which meant no nonmonied person could afford to live there. Now, what was once a quiet commercial street had taken on the look of a neighborhood grocer all dressed up for Sunday Mass, out of place and character in his blue suit and gaudy necktie.

Devlin pulled into a parking place and turned in his seat. "Let's go up and leave the bags in the trunk. I'll get them later, after dark. I don't want anyone watching to know you have a live-in guest." His voice was different now. Cold, hard and methodical.

The sound chilled her. Being back chilled her even more, but she struggled to hide it. "James Bond stuff, huh?" she said.

"Yeah," Devlin said. His eyes were like his voice. "But this isn't a movie. Okay?"

"Sure."

Adrianna stopped short and gasped as she stepped through the door. Her eyes darted around the loft, then grew wide, first in disbelief, then with a sudden rush of anger, and finally an almost paralyzing fear. She began to back away, eyes still fixed on the large, open space. Her mouth began to move, but no sound emerged.

Devlin stepped in front of her, shielding her body, his hand moving instinctively to the revolver on his hip. He pushed her back toward the hall. "Get out, and stay there until I call you," he snapped.

He pulled the revolver, extended it in his right hand, grasping the wrist with his left, and moved into the loft, the weapon pivoting with him as he scanned the room. Everywhere he looked drawers hung open, some pulled out completely and overturned; clothing and books and papers lay strewn across the floor as if caught by a sudden blast of wind.

He moved quickly but cautiously, checking behind every door, behind and under every conceivable hiding place. There was no one there. He turned and found Adrianna standing in the center of the loft.

"I thought I told you to stay in the hall," he snapped.

She stared at him as though he were speaking a foreign language, then pointed at a framed canvas that had been propped up against a supporting column. He came to her and stared down at the picture. It was a self-portrait of Adrianna, the eyes pensive, the lips drawn into a moody, distant pout. It was an unflattering visage, and especially now, with an undulating gash cut into the left cheek.

Adrianna pointed at a far wall. "It used to hang there," she said. Her voice held a tremor, and Devlin saw that her hands were shaking.

He went to the door, closed it, and shoved home a steel bolt. Then he took her arm and led her to a sofa.

"We'll get new locks," he said. His eyes roamed the room again. "Locks for the windows too. Who else lives in the building?"

She shook her head. "No one. The third floor is empty. It's for sale. The art-supply store downstairs is open during the day. Monday through Saturday." She shook her head, as if trying to drive the madness away. "It's one of the reasons I bought this place. I thought it would be so convenient having it there." Tears began to form in her eyes, then her mouth grew hard and angry. "Damn him. Damn that rotten son of a bitch."

Devlin gave her a moment, then reached for her hand. He wanted to talk to her about the way she had ignored his order to stay in the hall. But he knew it would be better done later. "Let's look around. See if he left any other presents. But touch as few things as possible. I want Eddie to have the place dusted for prints." He withdraw a handkerchief from his pocket. "Anything you have to touch, use this."

They covered the loft slowly, methodically. There were no other surprises. Adrianna's bedroom was the last stop. It was on an elevated platform one step above the living area, with a railing rather than a wall separating it from the remainder of the loft. When they reached it they found the dresser drawers opened, and clothing scattered across the floor.

Adrianna bent down and picked up a pair of bikini panties, then realized who had last touched them, and let them fall back to the floor.

The answering machine next to her bed was blinking furiously. Devlin took the handkerchief and punched the button. They sat on the edge of the bed and listened.

There were three messages from someone named Vincent, and it was clear to Devlin that he was more than a casual friend. There were four other messages interspersed, each becoming increasingly didactic as they progressed. Someone who identified himself as Umberto with self-assured importance, and who demanded to know why Adrianna had missed a scheduled meeting and "lacked the good grace even to call and explain."

Devlin moved to a chair across from her. "Tell me about these people," he said.

A tinge of color came to her cheeks. "Everything?" she asked.

"Afraid so."

She began hesitantly, starting with Umberto. "He owns the gallery that represents me," she said. "Which means he pretty much controls my destiny." She offered up a helpless smile. "Which means I better get my tail over to see him lickety-split if I'm going to have any destiny at all."

"Tell me about him personally. What he's like?"

She laughed. But there was no humor in the sound. "You're just going to have to meet him. Words don't quite work for Umberto."

"And Vincent?"

She drew a breath and shrugged. "Boyfriend, I guess."

"Guess?"

"Boyfriend."

"What else should I know?"

Adrianna looked down at her shoes, studied them. "He's a director on Broadway. I've been seeing him for about six months. Pretty exclusively." She offered another small shrug without looking up. "But only on my part. He sees other people," she said as though it didn't matter. "I just don't have the time to see a lot of men. And he's entertaining. Fun to be with." She hesitated, then looked up. "And . . . I guess you should know he was here that night . . . before I was attacked. I can't tell you what time he left. I was half asleep, and he let himself out." She looked at her shoes again. It wasn't embarrassment, Devlin decided. Just discomfort at having to discuss intimacy with someone who had once been her lover.

Devlin felt a momentary pang of jealousy, but pushed it away. "So he could have left the door open and come back. Or left it open for someone else," he said.

Adrianna stared at him incredulously. He offered a regretful smile. "I've got to think that way," he said.

"You don't. But it might help if you did. Both in keeping you safe and in finding out who this person is."

Adrianna digested it, then nodded. "It's not going to be fun, is it?"

"No. It's going to be dangerous. Every minute of every day." He was staring at her. All traces of gentleness had left his voice. He inclined his head toward the door. "A little while ago I told you to get in the hall and stay there. You ignored me. Don't do it again."

Her face registered shock, then her eyes grew hard as anger began to take over. The sound of the doorbell cut off her reply.

Adrianna jumped from the bed and grabbed the baseball bat that was leaning against the wall. Devlin was halfway to the oversize metal door when she caught up to him. His revolver was in his hand again, held next to his leg.

He motioned her away, and this time she did as she was told. He moved to the door and looked out through the spy hole and saw Eddie Grogan's enlarged face behind it. He slipped the revolver back into its holster.

"It's Eddie," he said. He noticed the baseball bat for the first time and grinned. "Was that for whoever was behind the door? Or me because I yelled at you?"

She stared at him, fighting off her own smile. "I hadn't decided," she said.

When the door swung back Grogan stepped inside, then stopped and let out a low whistle. He turned to Devlin. "Our boy? Or did we entertain one of the city's renowned B&E artists?" he asked.

Devlin pointed at the picture leaning against the column, and Grogan went immediately to it.

"Sonofabitch," he said.

There had been a woman standing off to Grogan's right, who had not been visible through the spy hole. She stepped inside now and moved quickly to Grogan's side.

He jerked his head toward her. "This is Gabrielle Lyons," he said. "She's a consultant with the department. A shrink. And she's here officially." He bent down to get a closer look at the painting. "And unofficially," he added. "Thought she could help us wade through all that voodoo shit those behavioral science clowns keep throwing at us."

The woman shook Devlin's hand, surprising him with the strength of her grip. "You found this here when you got back?" She watched Devlin nod, then turned to Adrianna. "This must be very upsetting for you," she said.

"Why did he come back?" Adrianna demanded. "Eddie said he always waited weeks, months even, before he came back."

Gabrielle moved to Adrianna's side and took her arm. "He came back because you frustrated him when he attacked you. So he came back and scarred your picture."

Adrianna stared at her. "But he was coming to do it to me, wasn't he? Not the picture. Me."

Gabrielle started to guide her across the room, toward a cluster of sofas and chairs. "We can't be sure," she said. "Let's sit down and try to talk it out."

The woman's voice was remarkably soft—almost melodious—and Devlin could sense how well it would work with someone in need of comfort. He watched them retreat into the living area. The woman had been there a scant few minutes and had already taken charge, but so smoothly it was barely noticeable. She was in her late thirties, he guessed. Tall—about five-eight or -nine—with a large-boned yet quite attractive body. At first glance a man might not find her particularly appealing. But the proper use of makeup could easily change that. She wore none. It was like her hair. It was a dull brown, and cut severely short. Her clothes were another matter, though. She wore a well-tailored suit—with pants rather than a skirt—and the cut fit her perfectly, and had obviously put a heavy dent in her checking account. She looked *professional*, Devlin decided. And she obviously worked at the image.

He turned back to Grogan. "So what's with the shrink?" he asked softly.

"Department brought her in," Grogan said, keeping his own voice low. "She's been on their consultant list for a couple of years. Worked mostly with cops who were getting a little too violent, a little too often." He shrugged, as if to say: What the hell do they expect?

"She's also worked with some rape victims. Hypnotism. To help them remember stuff. That sort of shit. And she's done some work with cops' widows, kids, whatever."

"You ever work with her before?"

Grogan shook his head. "Not until this case. Cervone assigned her—or somebody told him to—to help us understand all the psychological crap the FBI keeps throwing at us. And to work with the victims. See what she can pry outta them that they don't even know they know. But she understands the game here. And she's willing to help us on the Q.T. I think she's gotten a little pissed at the way the fucking feds are using these women as bait."

Devlin nodded.

Grogan glanced back at the painting. "Whadda you make of this?" he asked. "You read the reports. He ain't done this before."

"I think the shrink was right. She frustrated him, and he's not used to that. He needs to do what she stopped him from doing, and he can't stand the idea of being outwitted, or outmaneuvered."

"So maybe it's pushed him to a point, he'll make a mistake," Grogan said.

"Don't count on it, Eddie. The only thing we can be sure of is that it's made him more dangerous."

Grogan looked back at the painting and shook his head. "I really feel like I'm in over my head on this," he said. He looked back at Devlin. "You want forensics to go over the joint?"

"As soon as you can get them here." Devlin doubted they'd find anything. But then, they might get lucky.

He held out a business card that had been stuck in the door when they arrived. It gave the name Matthew Mallory. But it was an NYPD card, not FBI.

"The phony fucks," Grogan said.

"Try to find somebody who'll do the forensics on the Q.T.," Devlin said. "We don't need the Fibbies coming in like gangbusters."

"You got it," Grogan said.

Devlin glanced toward the women. They were going through some of Adrianna's smaller paintings which were lined up against one wall. They seemed remarkably at ease with one another, and Devlin attributed it to Gabrielle Lyons' professionalism. The lady was obviously good at what she did, and he decided she could probably afford a closet full of the expensive suits she wore.

Gabrielle turned and smiled as he approached. "Have you seen Adrianna's work?" she asked.

He shook his head. "Haven't had time yet."

"You must. She's an extraordinarily talented young woman."

Devlin noted that Adrianna didn't demur. She knows she's good, he thought. She's heard it before and accepts it as her due. He liked that. He had always thought that false modesty was just that. False.

"We need to talk," Devlin said. "About the case, and about what we're going to do."

Gabrielle nodded. "Of course. Then, later today, I'd like Adrianna brought down to my office. It's in the Village. We have some work to do that would be easier in neutral surroundings."

Devlin gave her a questioning look.

"Hypnosis," she said. "The department wants it, and I believe in it. It might bring out memories of the attack Adrianna doesn't even know she has." She smiled at Adrianna, then looked back to Devlin. "I've discussed it with her, and she's agreeable."

Devlin glanced at Adrianna and noted the tension in her eyes. She might be agreeable, he told himself. But she sure as hell isn't thrilled with the idea. He offered her a consoling look. She'd just have to live with it. He wondered if she'd be able to live with everything else she'd have to do.

He turned back to Gabrielle. "That's fine," he said. "We're bringing in a forensics team, and I'd just as soon we're out of here while they're taking the place apart. The fewer people who know what we're doing the better."

Adrianna sat quietly, curled up at the end of the sofa as she listened to them review the evidence of the previous attacks and murders, then finally her own attack. She offered nothing. She had already told Devlin and Eddie everything she knew, and Gabrielle Lyons had said she did not want to hear anything from her prior to the hypnosis. She didn't want her perceptions colored by what Adrianna told her beforehand. It felt awkward. It forced her to remain mute, like a voyeur to her own assault, an outsider here in her own home.

"The reports don't give a clear picture of how the perp got in." It was Devlin.

"Not in the murders," Grogan answered. "That's the screwy thing. In each case, when the initial assault happened, there were signs of forced entry. A door, a window. But the second time, when he killed them, the entry was clean. Like they had let him in."

"So he had a key. Either stole in extra or made an impression from one he found the first time. While the women were unconscious." It was Devlin again.

"Possible for the first two," Grogan said. "But not the last one. Not Sylvia Grant."

"Why?"

"Because we didn't tumble to this thing until after the second murder," Grogan said. "The first two happened in different parts of the city. Different precincts, different cops handling it. And there was months between the assaults and the murders, so different cops handled each incident. It was only after the second murder that we put it together. Knew we had one perp. So the last one, we told her to change the locks." He glanced at Adrianna. She shouldn't be hearing this shit, he thought. It ain't gonna help her sleep.

"And she changed them?" Devlin asked.

"Yeah. Sylvia Grant I'm positive about, because I changed them myself. The one before her—Monica Wells—I just don't know."

Devlin stared across the room, thinking. "The others probably changed them as well," he said at length. "They were getting phone calls, threats. They'd have been crazy not to."

"Yeah," Grogan agreed. "But we don't know for sure."

Devlin was quiet again. "So they let him in. Somebody they knew, or felt safe with." He looked at Grogan. "Somebody posing as a cop, maybe." He hesitated. "Or a real one." He glanced at Adrianna, making sure she had heard, had picked up on what he was implying.

"Jesus," Grogan said. "That's a scary thought."

"It's possible," Gabrielle interjected. "Police officers are as prone to madness as anyone else."

"But they're watched," Grogan objected. "Observed by other cops every day."

Gabrielle offered a patient smile. "You'd be surprised, Eddie, how difficult madness is to see. Even psychiatrists miss it in patients. Sick people don't always walk the streets talking to trees. But Paul's suggestion doesn't necessarily mean a cop working the case. It could be someone who's not connected to it in any way, or even someone who's left the job. Someone who's retired, or who was forced out, but managed to get his hands on a badge. Perhaps even the child of a cop."

"Or it could be anyone in authority who you'd normally let in," Devlin added. "A fire inspector. Somebody claiming there was a gas leak. A meter reader." He paused. "But if it was me, and I was as scared as these women should have been"—again he glanced quickly at Adrianna—"a cop's the only one I'd let in. He'd be the only one I'd be happy to see. And then only after I'd seen his shield. Either that, or someone I knew well. Somebody I really trusted."

He turned to Gabrielle. "Did you find any hint of a connection between these women and a third party?" he asked. "However remote."

The psychiatrist stared off at nothing for a moment, searching her memory, then slowly shook her head. "I only saw the last one," she said. "But outside of moving in the same social circles—the arts, visits to the Hamptons to varying degrees—there was nothing obvious. Certainly no specific person. They all attended similar charitable functions that attract people in the arts." She smiled. "Some I even attend myself. AIDS, the homeless, environmental causes, social concerns of that sort. But the police haven't—to my knowledge—been able to place them all at any one particular event." She glanced at Grogan, who shook his head, confirming her statement. She leaned forward, as if to emphasize what she was about to say. "But if that's the connection—contact through some social function—it doesn't have to be *direct* contact. The killer simply could have been in the same room with the victims, or stood nearby, listening to them speak." She shrugged helplessly.

"Tell me about the FBI profile."

Again the shrug. "Some of it's fairly obvious," Gabrielle said.

"So you don't put a lot of value in it?" Devlin asked.

"Oh, no, not that. I'm just not sure I agree with it all." She dismissed her own statement with a wave of her hand. "But they're the experts." She was interrupted by a snort from Eddie Grogan that caused her to smile.

"First, we have a man with an extreme hatred of women. Not one particular woman—perhaps a certain type of woman—but more likely women in general, who our victims personify as some exaggerated example of their sex. The FBI believes he was sexually abused as a child. Abused *by* a woman. I agree with the sexual abuse. But not necessarily that a woman was the perpetrator. The abuse may have left *him* feeling like a woman. And perhaps he enjoyed that feeling, and the act itself, and suffered extreme guilt over the pleasure he took from it. So now he perceives women—who also enjoy that act—as sinful. People who lead other men—just as he once did—into committing such acts." Gabrielle raised her hands, then let them drop back into her lap. "Anyway, he's between thirty and forty, which makes him slightly above the norm for a serial killer; is well educated and probably working in, or aspiring toward, a respected profession. He's athletic, or was once so. He lives alone, or if with someone, a person with whom he does not have an intimate relationship, although he once might have had. And he becomes sexually impotent at the time of the attacks." She leaned forward. "As I'm sure you've seen in the reports, it's believed the rape is done with an object— probably some type of dildo or similar device—and that his gratification comes solely from the mutilation and the killing."

Gabrielle raised her eyebrows and let out a long breath. "That's essentially it," she said, sitting back.

"And what about it don't you agree with?" Devlin asked.

Gabrielle leaned forward again. "First, that it has to be a man." She looked at each of them in turn, enjoying the mixture of surprise and confusion on their faces. "That also may be why the FBI has concluded the killer's abuser was a woman."

She raised an index finger, then grasped it with the other hand. "The FBI has never encountered a case of serial murder—including both those they've been involved in, and those they have not—in which the killer, when caught, did not turn out to be a man." She raised a second finger and grasped that as well. "But we know that only about ten percent of the suspected serial killings have ever been solved. Is it possible that some—even one—of the remaining cases could have been committed by a woman? Of course. But the FBI insists not. Is it possible some of those cases have not been solved because the FBI, and the police who listen to them, have dismissed all women as potential suspects?" She shrugged, then smiled. "It's an interesting form of sexual discrimination. Believing that women could not do these things." She glanced at Devlin. "And a frightened woman just might let another woman into her apartment."

"The person who attacked me was a man," Adrianna said.

Gabrielle shot Adrianna a sharp look as if silently admonishing her for speaking out of turn. Devlin saw Adrianna's eyes harden under the rebuke, then watched as Gabrielle quickly softened it with a smile.

"Do you base that on the fact that you kicked him in the testicles?" she asked.

Adrianna seemed momentarily confused, suddenly hesitant. Gabrielle had thrown her off stride. "Yes," she said. "I . . . guess so."

"Have you ever been kicked in the vagina?" she asked.

Adrianna shook her head. "No, I haven't."

"I assure you it can be as painful—or very nearly as painful—and almost as debilitating as it is to a man." Gabrielle reached over and took her hand. "It just isn't that common to us," she said. "We seldom play the type of contact sports where it happens frequently. Nor do we commonly get into childhood street fights. It's not an injury that's in our realm of common experience."

Adrianna shook her head; the line of her mouth had hardened again. "I'm still certain it was a man," she said.

Gabrielle released her hand, and forced another smile. "Let's save that for later. For the hypnosis," she said.

Devlin caught the look in Adrianna's eyes; knew she

found Gabrielle's attitude patronizing. So did he. His opinion of the psychiatrist went down a notch.

"Did the last victim tell you anything that made you think the killer was a woman?" Devlin asked. He had decided to push the point.

Gabrielle sat back and steepled her fingers before her face. "Nothing definite," she said. "It's just a feeling I can't quite pin down." She shook her head thoughtfully. "Perhaps it's a man with certain female characteristics, or someone—because of what happened to him, as I said—who strongly identifies with women."

"Homosexual?" Devlin asked.

"That's too simple," Gabrielle said quickly. "At least I feel it is. But don't ask me why. I simply can't tell you yet."

5

"I want you to close your eyes and concentrate only on my voice."

Adrianna did as she was told. She was lying on a sofa in Gabrielle's office, her head resting on a small pillow. The shades were drawn, leaving only a faint glow of light, and the sounds of a running stream played softly on a concealed stereo. She felt surprisingly relaxed.

The office was large and comfortable, plush by any standard, and Adrianna knew it was intended to produce a feeling of confidence. But it was not intimidating. The furniture felt soft, inviting, the color scheme equally soft and muted. Even the desk—that intended symbol of power—looked gentle and unobtrusive. It was a Louis Quatorze with rounded, flowing lines.

Gabrielle and Adrianna were alone, despite Devlin's initial objections. He had wanted to hear firsthand what she had seen and heard and smelled the night she was attacked. But Gabrielle had been pleasantly adamant. Things could come out that were private, privileged. And Adrianna had to feel assured they would remain so if the technique was going to work. Adrianna was pleased it would be that way—she did not not want to feel like some laboratory animal, watched and studied while unconscious. And she wasn't frightened. Paul and Eddie were in the waiting room, only a few feet away.

"I want you to free your mind of all thought, and concentrate only on the parts of your body you are trying to relax." Gabrielle's voice was smooth and soothing, barely louder than a strong whisper. She was seated in a chair, out of sight behind Adrianna's head, and the words seemed to blend with the sound of the running stream that filled the room.

"We will start with your legs. Each muscle is relaxing now. Each becoming soft and pliable, all the tension draining slowly away, like water flowing down a gentle stream. . . ."

Grogan lit a cigarette, spat a bit of tobacco from his tongue, then blew a stream of smoke toward the street. He and Devlin were standing on the sidewalk outside the building, a large high-rise at the southern end of Fifth Avenue, only a few steps from the rising arch that marked the entry to Washington Square Park.

Grogan had wanted to smoke—something Gabrielle did not allow in her office—and they had stepped outside. The office was on the ground floor, its door clearly visible through the glass-fronted entry, and they knew no one would get past them without being seen.

"Tough broad, our shrink, huh?" Grogan said.

Devlin smiled. "No question she would of thrown me out physically if I'd tried to force my way in there," he said. "No matter how softly she spoke."

"She could do it too," Grogan said. "I took her arm once. It was like a rock. Told me she's into bodybuilding, lifts weights three times a week."

"Weights?"

"I know what you're thinking. But she ain't no dyke. The department checks out its shrinks pretty good. If anything, the lady ain't into sex at all. Doesn't do anything but work." He inclined his head back toward the building. "She lives in an apartment upstairs. Christ, some days she probably doesn't even leave the building. Real heavy into charitable stuff, on top of her regular patients. Volunteers her time with the homeless, AIDS patients, stuff like that. Doesn't charge them a fucking dime." Grogan shook his head at the incredulity of it.

"How's that. A fucking doc who does somethin' on the arm. Probably costs her thirty, forty big ones a year in her time. It ain't fucking natural."

Devlin looked toward the park and smiled. And she probably still knocks down two fifty to three hundred thousand a year, he thought. Shrinks in New York, especially those with a good Manhattan practice, could command one fifty to two hundred bucks an hour. The great benefit of a profession. He should have listened to his mother. Worked his ass off and become a doctor, or dentist, or lawyer. No, not a lawyer. He'd rather sell used cars.

Devlin looked at his watch. They had only been here half an hour, and Gabrielle had said it would take at least double that time. He glanced down the street. He and Adrianna had both taken graduate classes at New York University, whose buildings fronted much of Washington Square Park. They had met there and become lovers, and had spent hours sitting on the rim of the fountain at the park's center, or watching the old men play cutthroat games of chess at the fixed concrete tables at its southwest corner, oblivious to the derelicts and junkies who prowled the narrow walkways. Later, they would go to the still hip coffee houses—the Cafe Reggio or Patisserie Lanciani—and sip steaming, sugar-rimmed glasses of caffè Romano, while they whispered and held hands and laughed together. He knew now he'd like to take her back to those places again. But those days had been a lifetime ago. And they had ended painfully. The only greater pain he had ever known had come when his wife was killed in an auto accident years later. But the way it had ended between him and Adrianna had been bad. Bad enough that he didn't want to risk repeating it. Or so he kept telling himself.

Devlin turned to Grogan, forcing his mind back to the killer, to the reason he was there. "I think the FBI might be right. About these women being picked out of newspapers and magazines." He offered a grimace.

"I know that's the worst-case scenario, but it's the one solid thing I keep coming back to." He shifted his weight, squinted his eyes against the sun. "All the victims had major press coverage before this goon cut them," he went on. "They were all a specific type of woman, and according to the reports, they had all had their faces plastered across newspapers or magazines a month or so before they got sliced. It's the only constant we have."

"What about the charitable gigs Gabrielle mentioned? You think he could be picking up on them there and following them home? He has to find out where they live."

Devlin shook his head. "I don't think he's had to. Take them one by one. He follows the dancer home from a rehearsal or performance. Same with the actress. The last one, the writer, Sylvia Grant, was doing book signings, TV interviews. And all those things had been publicized somewhere. Trade newspapers, magazines, whatever. Hell, they might as well have given him a timetable of their movements."

"Same with Adrianna," Grogan said.

Devlin nodded. "Yeah, the reports had a copy of that big piece that ran in *The Times* about a month ago. All about her meteoric rise in the art world. And it mentioned the show she had coming up, and had a picture of her in her 'Spring Street loft.' All our perp had to do was stand around Spring Street, with all the other mopes and street trash, and wait for her to waltz by."

Devlin knew he was right. Most—hell, almost all serial murders involved random selection of victims. There was always a type—prostitutes, teenage girls who frequented shopping malls, street people, drifters, whatever. But it was usually a specific type the killer wanted for his own reasons. And he seldom had to expose himself to find them. He simply identified his target, found a means for an approach, then acted. Quick and clean. It was a technique that lowered the risk of witnesses. So much so that the killers were usually caught only after a potential victim escaped and could give police specific information that identified the perp. And the arrest, Devlin knew, seldom came from physical evidence at the scene. That was gathered to tie the perp to the crime *after* he was caught. And, unlike most murder investigations, serial killers were seldom found because somebody dropped a dime on them. They were essentially loners, who didn't travel in the low-life circle of street criminals, who gave cops most of their information. They avoided unnecessary contact, both with their victims and people outside normal daily functions. And that was what was most puzzling about this killer, Devlin thought. He confronts his victims; he cuts them, and then he goes away and comes back later. He exposes himself when he doesn't have to. And the reason why he acted that way could be the key to everything. He turned back to Eddie.

"You think this could be two perps?" he asked. "One who scars them? Then one who comes back later and finishes the job?"

"Connected?" Grogan asked. "Working together?"

Devlin nodded. "Yeah, connected. A copycat wouldn't work. The physical evidence makes it impossible."

Grogan lit another cigarette, then jabbed at Devlin with it. "Connected. Jesus, I don't know. Two guys working together just increases the chances of fucking up. And this guy ain't fucked up. Not once. Not even close."

Grogan jabbed his cigarette again, sending a clump of ashes onto Devlin's shoe. "You're right about it not being a copycat. It'd have to be a fucking miracle if it was. 'Cause they'd both be wearing the same type robe, made from the same fucking coarse brown cloth. Like the reports said, forensics pulled threads from the scenes, after the attacks and after the murders. So unless they're both fucking Capuchin monks . . ."

Devlin turned back toward the park. "I don't know,

Eddie. There's something about this that screams two people to me. Let's just keep that idea floating around."

"Hey," Grogan said, "you're the fucking expert. We'll play it however you want."

Devlin glanced at his watch. "I want to get back inside," he said. "If I remember right, there's a hardware store over on Sixth that's open seven days a week. I'd like you to pick up a new lock for the front door and all the windows. There are eight of them."

"You got it," Grogan said. "See you back here in about twenty minutes."

He grabbed Eddie's arm, stopping him. "One other thing. I know you checked all the theatrical rental outfits on this robe our perp wears. But I want you to do it again. This time under a specific name."

Grogan thought a moment. "Adrianna's boyfriend? The fucking director?"

"The director," Devlin said. "It's a long shot, but he's the only person we have who had easy access to that kind of costume. Or two of them," he added.

"I am going to count to ten now, and when I finish you will awaken. You will feel refreshed and relaxed, and your mind will be free of everything you saw and heard while you slept."

When Gabrielle finished counting, Adrianna opened her eyes, blinked several times, then sat up.

"How do you feel?"

"Like I've had a full night's sleep," she said. She made a face. "One that was filled with dreams I can't quite remember."

"I told you to forget them," Gabrielle said. "You relived the experience. Quite vividly. And there's no need to endure that stress twice." She patted the notebook on her lap. "I have it all here."

"What did I say?"

Gabrielle smiled. "You saw everything quite clearly. There was nothing new, I'm afraid. Nothing major, at least. But you were right. It was a man. You remembered the scent of his cologne. Even that it was a good one, not the cheap, drugstore variety. And you recalled the roughness of the beard on his cheek. Your hand brushed his face during the struggle."

Adrianna shuddered involuntarily. "I don't remember that happening."

"Not consciously," Gabrielle said. "But your subconscious remembers. You mustn't forget, you were fighting for your life. Your conscious mind was filled with that. Not small details."

"Was there anything else?"

"Just that he was thin, and not terribly strong. At least you didn't think he was. And he let out a yelp when you kicked him. High-pitched rather than a grunt. Like a man who was not used to being hit."

Adrianna shook her head. She didn't want to hear any more. "Let's go outside," she said. "I need some air."

"Of course," Gabrielle said. She went to the window and drew back the drapes. The window opened on a rear alley. Far from an imposing view, Adrianna thought.

"Just let me gather my notes," Gabrielle said. "I'm sure Paul will want to review them."

Adrianna noted a lilt in Gabrielle's voice when she mentioned his name. Earlier, when she had arrived at the office, she had also noticed that the woman had put on makeup she had not been wearing before. She wondered now if it was for Devlin's benefit. She suddenly disliked the idea it might be.

Gabrielle started around her desk, then stopped. There was a second door in the office, and someone was rapping lightly against it.

"That's strange," she said. "That door leads to the hall. It's for patients to use after their sessions. So they don't have to go back through the waiting room." She stared at it for a moment, then shrugged. "Perhaps Paul and Eddie went outside, and accidentally locked themselves out."

She went to the door and opened it. A figure loomed before her, encased in a coarse brown robe. The large hood was pulled forward, hiding the face in deep shadow, making it seem more like a specter than something of flesh and blood.

A hand withdrew from the folds of the robe, and the long blade of a knife flashed in the light. The figure took a step forward.

Gabrielle had seemed frozen in place, but now she moved quickly. She slammed the door, throwing her weight against it. The figure crashed against the other side, shaking the door in its frame. She looked back at Adrianna. "Help me," she shouted.

Adrianna ran to the door, shouting for Paul as she reached it. She threw her weight against the door, helping Gabrielle hold it.

Devlin rushed in from the waiting room, revolver in hand.

"It was him," Gabrielle said. "He was wearing the robe, and he had a knife."

"Get away from the door," Devlin snapped.

He moved to the door in a low crouch, the revolver extended out in front of him, then reached for the handle and pulled the door open. There was no one there. He stepped into the hall, quickly pivoting in both directions, still in a crouch, the revolver still out in front. No one.

"Stay here," he said. "And lock both doors behind me."

The second door led into a short hall, around a corner from the main entrance to Gabrielle's office, which opened on to the lobby. He raced to the lobby but found only the doorman, his mouth and eyes suddenly wide at the sight of the weapon.

"Police," Devlin snapped. "Did somebody come out here? A guy in a brown robe?"

The doorman shook his head. His eyes were even wider now, and he seemed unable to speak.

"Is there another way out of that hall?"

The doorman began to stutter, then caught himself. "There's a service entrance that leads to an alley. Just that and the stairwell."

"Watch Dr. Lyons' door. Both of them. If anyone tries to go in, call for help."

Devlin raced back down the hall, reached another corner, and spun into it, staying low, his revolver again out in front. There were two doors. One to a stairwell and a second leading to the alley. The second door stood open.

Devlin stepped into the alley and spun in each direction. To the rear, the alley ended at an eight-foot cyclone fence, then continued along another building to the next street. He turned and ran to Fifth Avenue, looked north, then south, toward Washington Square Park. Eddie Grogan was just rounding the corner, his arms loaded with packages.

"Eddie," Devlin shouted. "He was here."

Grogan broke into a run, turning into the alley behind Devlin and following him back through the service entrance.

Devlin pulled up at the stairwell. He turned to Grogan and quickly told him what had happened.

"I'm gonna search the basement and the stairs," Devlin said. "Check on Adrianna. Make sure she's okay. Then get back here in case he slips by me. And keep an eye on that damned back door to the office," he said.

Grogan had dropped his packages in a heap on the floor, his own revolver out now. "You oughta have backup," he said.

"The important thing is to keep him out of there," Devlin snapped. "Just do it. I'll be all right."

Devlin emerged from the stairwell fifteen minutes later, his face tight and angry. "Nothing," he said. "He must have made it over that fence in the alley." He let out a long, frustrated breath. "The sonofabitch must have followed us. Unless Gabrielle told someone we were coming here."

"I asked her," Grogan said. "She said she didn't tell anybody. They're okay, by the way. A little shaky, but okay."

Devlin didn't seem to hear. He was staring past Grogan, his eyes fixed on a blank wall. "Fucker," he snapped. "What kind of game is this bastard playing?"

6

They sat across from each other, eating Chinese food delivered from a nearby restaurant. It was a Sunday night ritual for Adrianna, and she had refused to alter it, despite the madness that had marked this first day back in her loft. Devlin had spent the previous two hours changing the lock on the front door and adding security locks to each of the windows. But Adrianna had consciously ignored him. She had placed herself before a new canvas and painted furiously, and Devlin had correctly assumed she was using it to blot out her fears, to beat back the day's repeated assaults.

Even now she seemed distracted, struggling to make conversation, and he wondered how much more of it she could take. The way this perp was playing, he was certain he'd find out.

"What do you think of Gabrielle?" Adrianna asked.

The question had come out of the blue. The chopsticks were halfway to his mouth, and it froze them before they reached his lips.

"I think she handled herself real well this afternoon," he said. "I also think we're going to have a small battle of wills. But other than that, I like her fine. I just don't know yet how much she's going to help."

"Sort of a male-female competition?" Adrianna asked.

"I don't think so. I hope not." He laid the chopsticks down. "I just have to be in control of this situation if I'm going to get this guy. And keep him away from you. Maybe I'm pushing too hard to make sure I am."

"She is aggressive, in a quiet, sneaky sort of way."
She was smiling. Devlin wasn't sure if she had meant
it in a derogatory way.

"Assertiveness," Devlin said.

"Mmmm. But not a straightforward assertiveness.
Maybe it's because she's a shrink. A part of her technique. Making people think they *want* to do things her
way."

"Did you know she lifts weights?"

"No. Really?"

"Eddie Grogan told me. But he says she's not gay."

"No, she's not."

"You can tell?"

"Sure. There's always a hint of sexual tension with
gay women. Like there is between a man and a woman.
It's not as strong. It's very faint, actually. But it's
there." She hesitated, used her chopsticks to push her
food around her plate. "Besides, she likes you too
much."

"What the hell are you talking about?"

"Didn't you notice that she put on makeup for our
afternoon session?" She smiled at him. "She didn't
have it on in the morning. And I noticed the way she
looked at you after you ran that madman off. She was
impressed. I think she fancies you."

"Weren't you impressed?"

The question caught Adrianna off guard. She had
been trying to question him about Gabrielle without
revealing any latent jealousy, and he had suddenly
turned the tables on her.

"I was too frightened to be impressed," she said. She
wanted to change the subject, get away from dangerous
ground.

"You should have been." He stared at her for several
moments. "Stay that way. It will help keep you alive."

Adrianna could feel herself stiffen under the words,
but she fought it off, tried not to let it show. He had
mentioned how well Gabrielle had handled herself that
afternoon. Not her, just Gabrielle. Now she had admit-

ted just how terrified she had been. She had done it to change the subject. Now she regretted that she had. She had no intention of showing any further weakness.

Devlin resumed eating, then stopped again. "Are you going to get back to Umberto and Vincent?" he asked.

She nodded. "I have to. Why?"

"I want to meet them both tomorrow."

She stared at him. "Because they're suspects?"

"I need to meet the people who've had access to you. Who are going to continue to have access."

"So they're suspects," she said.

He tried to make light of it, raising one finger for emphasis. "Everyone is suspect," he said, using his best Hercule Poirot accent.

She forced a smile. "Just like in the movies," she said.

Devlin noticed that the smile didn't quite work.

He listened as she spoke to Vincent Richards. Even hearing only one side of the conversation, he realized her absence had caused concern. But, as agreed, she gave little information over the phone other than to assure him she was well and would explain more fully when they met the following day.

"Where are we meeting?" Devlin asked when she had finished the call.

"At the theater where he's holding rehearsals."

He nodded. "Perfect." Perhaps he'd even get a chance to look in the room where they kept their costumes. "That wasn't too bad, was it?" he asked.

She rolled her eyes. "The next one will be."

"Umberto?"

"Umberto."

Adrianna had no sooner identified herself than she was stopped short by an obvious tirade on the other end of the line. She held the phone away from her ear, and Devlin could hear a voice ranting across the line. She waited for it to subside, then tried again, only to be cut short a second time. Finally she blurted out her message:

"Umberto, please listen to me. Someone broke into my apartment and attacked me." She threw Devlin a look of regret, listened, then hurried on. "Four days ago. The night I left the gallery." Another pause. "No, I'm fine. Really." She waited, listening. "No, the pictures weren't damaged. Everything is fine. I'll be there first thing in the morning. Ten o'clock. And I'll explain everything." Again a pause. "Thank you, Umberto. I know you're concerned, and I adore you too."

She replaced the receiver and turned to Devlin. "I'm sorry," she said. "He was in a full-fledged snit. He was even threatening to cancel my show." She let out a breath. "The man holds my future in his hands. I just couldn't afford not to tell him."

She slumped into a chair across from Devlin. He thought she looked shaken by the conversation.

"Is he always that volatile?"

She shook her head, then smiled. "No, usually he's pompous." She became serious again. "It's the business climate," she added. "All gallery owners are a little crazy right now. Galleries are closing all over the city. Not a lot, but enough to make them all a bit panicky. The bottom's fallen out of the art market, and all the expansion they did in the eighties is like an anchor around their necks now. The rents, especially for the uptown galleries, are murderous. Up to sixty dollars a square foot."

"Is Umberto in danger of closing?" Devlin asked.

"No. At least I don't think so. He's one of the lucky ones. He owns the building he's in. But one of the other galleries he rents to may be. And it's made him nervous. It'll cut into the cushion he has for his own overhead." She offered a helpless shrug. "It'll be all right when the big-money people regain confidence in the economy. Then they'll start spending the big bucks again. Just like they did in the eighties."

"But Eddie told me your work's selling like crazy," Devlin said.

"Yeah, but I'm hot right now. And comparatively cheap next to the big boys. A gallery can get several hundred thousand for a picture by an established, recognized painter. And one picture can take care of a lot of rent for a long time, especially since the gallery's take is fifty percent. But Umberto has to sell a lot of Adrianna Mendez to do that." She offered a self-deprecating shrug. "He's doing that right now. But he also knows how fast interest can fade. So he wants to get all he can out of this show." Her look became more serious. "And so do I, damn it. That's why I can't let some maniac keep me locked up like a frightened rabbit."

Devlin lay on the sofa bed, struggling for sleep. He had called Phillipa earlier and told her he would try to see her the following day. He knew it was doubtful, but he would try anyway.

His pistol lay on the table next to the bed, within reach. He could see its shadowy outline in the dim light. He turned over and stared at the window, listened to the almost forgotten street sounds he had once lived with every day—the nightly cacophony that was part of sleeping in New York. But the noise wasn't keeping him awake. He tried to tell himself that it wasn't Adrianna, either. He could handle a woman he had once loved lying in a bed only fifty feet away. It was hard, but he could deal with it.

He drew a deep breath, thinking about her. They had changed for bed as discreetly as possible, each retreating to their own corners of the loft. But it was still awkward, uncomfortable. And he knew he would much prefer to be lying fifty feet west. But that would only confuse things, make everything he was here to do more difficult.

You have enough problems, he told himself. He

pounded the pillow, trying to make it more accommodating.

The sound at the door woke Devlin at three o'clock. He swung out of bed, instinctively grabbing the pistol from the bedside table, then moved quickly across the bare wood floor. The sound stopped when he was half-way to the door, and Devlin thought he could hear someone moving away.

Adrianna was already there when he reached the door, and despite the absence of light, he could see the anxiety in her widened eyes. He motioned her away, then flattened himself to one side. Pistol up be-side his head, he reached out and turned the new dead-bolt lock, then swung the door back and stepped into the opening. The revolver was out in front of him; his hands were sweating. There was no one there.

He stepped quickly into the hall, weapon extended, and turned rapidly in both directions. It was a repeat of the afternoon. The hall was empty. He turned back and looked at the door to the loft, searching for some sign of an attempted forced entry. A key sat in the lock. Devlin glanced at Adrianna, then back at the key. He reached out and, touching only its edges, turned it. It didn't work, didn't throw the bolt. Still holding the edges, he removed it and went back inside, straight to the old lock he had left on a kitchen counter. He slid the key in. It turned easily, throwing the bolt.

"I need a small plastic bag," he said. "I want this checked for fingerprints."

Adrianna quickly got one.

"Did anyone have a key to this place?" Devlin asked. "Vincent Richards, anyone?"

She shook her head. She was twisting her fingers, trying to fight the trembling. She was dressed only in a long T-shirt that just barely covered her. Devlin could tell there was nothing beneath. She didn't seem to notice.

"No. No one's ever had a key," she said. She let out

a long breath. "But I carry my keys in a big carryall-type bag, and I'm always leaving it around where anyone could get to it."

"Stop doing that," Devlin said.

"I will. Believe me, I will."

He placed a hand on her arm, felt the bed warmth that still held to her body—felt a faint tremor brought on by renewed fear. "Go back to sleep," he said. "I'm going to sit up awhile. Just in case."

She nodded and walked back toward the elevated sleeping area. Devlin tried not to watch her move away, but found he could not.

He slumped down in a chair and stared at the door. What kind of game was this sonofabitch playing? He knew now that the perp hadn't been trying to get Adrianna that afternoon. He had known she wasn't alone then. And he had known she wouldn't be alone tonight.

It isn't just that she frustrated him. Not anymore. He knows you're here, and he's playing with you, Devlin told himself. It's become part of his game.

7

The two men drummed a staccato beat on the macadam walkway. Sweat ran down their faces and into the towels wrapped around their necks. Their jog was far from strenuous, or athletic, but the full running suits they wore guaranteed perspiration, even in the cool early morning air. Off to their right the chaos of Monday morning traffic could already be heard along the FDR Drive, mixed with the occasional horn blast from the barge hauling tugs that plowed regular paths down the East River. One of the runners glanced behind him at the two uniformed cops who followed in a golf cart. The sight always amused him. He was probably the only running black man in the entire city who cops protectively followed rather than chased. But then, he told himself, he was a different class of nigger. Even to these two red-faced micks. It would not bode well for their careers if the mayor of New York—and only the second black to hold that position—was mugged in Carl Shurz Park within the shadow of his official residence. And especially not when he was running with the city's police commissioner. Christ, it would be the final blow to a city whose reputation was already on its knees.

Delong Norris pulled up and bent over, hands on knees, then drew several long breaths.

"You okay?" Andrew Dalton pulled up beside him and huffed out the words. His own lungs felt as though they were about to burst. He was fifty-two, six years younger than the mayor, but right now felt ten years older. The mayor ran twice a week, each time with a different commissioner. For Dalton it was a term in purgatory for sins yet to be committed.

"I hate this shit," Norris said, straightening and stretching his back.

"Then why do you do it?" Dalton asked. And why in hell do you make me do it? he added to himself.

"It's a requirement of the times," Norris wheezed. "Politicians have to show how youthful and vigorous they are. So they run around like a bunch of panting basset hounds. What the public should ask is how many times we get laid each week. Then they'd find out their governments were being run by a bunch of limp-dicked old bastards who can't get it up without masking tape."

The mayor started forward again. "Can't nobody see us now. Let's walk a bit."

Dalton was grateful for the reprieve, but knew what was coming. Now the questions would begin without the restriction of labored breathing. The questions, especially the hard ones, always followed whenever the mayor put that black street twang in his voice. It was like a warning bell to anyone who worked for him.

"So what's happening with the case?" Norris asked.

The case, Dalton knew, meant one investigation and one only. It was the lone matter before the police department in which the mayor had any serious interest.

"The latest victim"—Dalton paused and searched his memory for a name—"Adrianna Mendez, has gone missing."

"That much I know," Norris snapped. "That white-bread sonofabitch from the FBI called me last night harping about it. Said she talked to him in the hospital, then split without warning. Thinks our beloved chief of detectives has stashed her away so he can cut them out and run his own little game. Catch the killer himself and take the bows. Frankly, I wouldn't put it past the guinea prick."

Neither would I, Dalton thought. "I doubt that's the

case, but I'll find out," he said. "It's more likely she just freaked out and ran for cover."

The mayor stopped and turned toward Dalton. Norris was only five-eight and slender, except for a slightly protruding paunch, and his wiry hair was liberally flecked with gray. His face looked old, covered with loose, pliable flesh. But his eyes were hard, young even, not filled with the world-weariness the television cameras always managed to project.

"Did you know this Mendez woman is the daughter of a dead cop?" Norris asked. "A detective first grade, according to the FBI."

Dalton felt a tinge of color come to his cheeks. "No, I did not," he said stiffly. He fought for some semblance of authority, failed to find it.

The mayor looked off to his left. " 'Course, it could be somebody who knew her father told her to take a dive under the bed." *Christ, now I'm even thinking up his excuses for him,* the mayor thought. "But it wouldn't take me a lot of looking to conjure up Mario Cervone's footprints all over this thing."

"I'll find out," Dalton said.

You won't find out shit, Norris thought. *Not from that hard-assed dago bastard.* He jabbed a finger toward Dalton's long, WASPish nose. "You just tell our chief of detectives that if he's done this, and it comes down to a pissing contest, that I've still got the biggest dick in town. And if he thinks his friends at the archdiocese are going to cover his guinea ass, he better remember I have some pretty good rabbis over there myself."

The mayor started walking again, his hand on Dalton's back in a gesture of false affection. "Look, Andrew, you know what the political situation is. We have an election coming up, and the wolves aren't just nipping at my heels. They've chewed my legs all the way to the knees. That little racial incident your cops created out in Queens a few months back has got the black community ready to kiss *this* black ass good-bye.

And now I've got a half-dozen pricks in my own party ready to jump into a primary fight if I even appear to stumble one more time." Norris stopped again and took Dalton by one elbow. "All I've got right now is my nice, rich, liberal, uptown friends, who are still willing to throw a shit load of money at their favorite house nigger to ease their well-deserved guilt. And that'll be just enough to beat back any opposition. *Just* enough. Providing I spend those sonofabitches into oblivion."

Norris shook his head. "But I've also got something else. I've got three dead white women. All moderately prominent. Three unsolved murders that the press has played up, and then forgotten. Thank God it happened over a two-year period. And thank God we've been able to sit on the evidence, and nobody has put it all together. Because I'll tell you one other thing, Andrew. All that guilt money would disappear like a ten-dollar whore if those uptown liberals found out that those successful, young, talented white women got their tickets punched by a serial killer. One that *my* police department can't do jackshit to stop. Their guilt just won't survive bein' scared shitless. You got that?"

The mayor stopped again. "Andrew, the reason I asked the FBI to take over this investigation is that I knew they'd keep their mouths shut until we caught this bastard and could *afford* to let the public know. And it's why your department has been limited to a handful of detectives working directly out of the chief's office. That way any leaks are on his head, and his head alone. And that dago prick knows I'll cut it off if that ever happens."

Dalton drew a long breath, summoning courage. He was a pleasant-looking man with bland, slender features and soft gray eyes that showed none of the many years he had spent in the district attorney's office as first assistant. But then, he had always been an administrator, never a courtroom shark. "There are some who feel the FBI might be using these women as bait." He gestured awkwardly with his hands. "Perhaps now that a cop's daughter is involved—"

"I don't give a damn who's involved," Norris snapped. "And I am not about to second-guess the FBI's Behavioral Science Unit. They're in charge, and we—read your police department there, Andrew—will play this investigation their way, no matter who likes or dislikes the way it's being run. Understood?"

"Completely," Dalton said. "And it's not that I disagree . . ." He paused. "But if it ever came out that we hid this investigation from the public for political reasons, and that we allowed the FBI to use these women as bait—"

The mayor cut him off again. "I appreciate all that, Andrew. But it's not going to come out. That's why the FBI is running the show. We know they'll keep their mouths shut. They have a penchant for reticence. And if something does go wrong, they might even make convenient scapegoats. And frankly, Andrew, if you did disagree, I'd have someone else sitting on the fourteenth floor of One Police Plaza. Reluctantly. But he'd be there. This is that crucial to me."

"I realize that, Mr. Mayor," Dalton said stiffly.

The mayor resumed a slow jog. "Let's run again, Andrew. Somebody might be watching."

They rounded a bend and turned back toward Gracie Mansion. In the distance they could see a television crew setting up before the wide front porch. Dalton felt a chill. Something had happened and now the vultures were descending.

The mayor seemed to read his thoughts—like some jungle animal sensing fear. "Nothing to worry about," he said. "It's just a little TV bit about the mayor running his black ass around the park. Get me some of that yuppie vote. You just worry about Cervone and finding this woman. That's where our asses are gonna get burned."

"Consider it done," Dalton said, not in the least bit sure how he would make good on the promise.

They pulled up ten feet from the TV crew—the mini-cam already rolling—and Dalton quickly shook the mayor's hand and beat a speedy retreat to his waiting car. The mayor immediately moved forward, a broad smile creasing his sweat-covered face.

Cass Walker stepped into camera range, her microphone poised like a weapon. She was a tall, willowy blonde with a perfect model's face and pouting lips that had produced more than one fantasy among her male viewers. But it was her bright blue eyes that elicited comments from her peers—strikingly clear, almost innocent on camera, but holding the glint of a carnivore when the TV lights went out.

"Mr. Mayor, does the presence of Commissioner Dalton indicate some police problem we don't know about?" Cass lunged right in, hoping to make something major out of "this piece of shit story" they had handed her. She had suggested they film it with her jogging alongside the mayor, certain the sight of her in shorts and a T-shirt would have guaranteed more air time. But the little fag on the assignment desk had nixed the idea. But maybe, just maybe she had lucked out after all.

Norris' smile widened, his soft brown eyes hiding an instinctive sense for menace. Cass Walker had a rising reputation as a cutthroat bitch who would chew your balls off if given the chance. She worked for the local CBS station, but made no secret of her lust for network news. But not by climbing over my sweet ass, Norris told himself.

The mayor let out a small laugh, then spread his arms wide, taking in his surroundings. "What could be wrong on a day like today?" he intoned. "The commissioner's just here for his regular run with me—just like all my commissioners." He patted his sucked-in belly. "Like to keep my team lean and mean," he said, winking at the camera.

Cass' enthusiasm wavered, but she caught herself and pushed on with the jogging story she had been

sent to cover. When the interview ended, she watched
the mayor climb the steps to Gracie Mansion, then
turned to the camera and did her stand-up to close out
the piece.

When the lights blinked off, her expression darkened
and she glanced quickly at the closed front door of
the mayor's residence. Shit, she thought. Twenty-seven
years old and still covering crap like this. She turned
back to her crew. "Let's pack up and get the hell out
of here," she snapped. "Maybe we'll luck out and some
maniac will blow up a school."

The Lincoln Town Car that chauffeured Andrew
Dalton about the city pulled into the ramp that led
to the underground garage beneath One Police Plaza.
Dalton's driver—a uniformed sergeant—gave only a
perfunctory nod to the lone cop manning the guard
booth, then pulled the car into its designated space.
Dalton jumped out immediately and headed for the
private elevator that led to his fourteenth-floor office.
His driver hurried behind, carrying a garment bag and
a pair of black wing-tipped shoes.

As the elevator opened, Dalton strode across his spa-
cious outer office barely acknowledging the string of
greetings that followed him like morning prayers. He
offered a cursory nod to the two uniformed chiefs who
sat in the reception area awaiting their scheduled appointments, speaking only to his appointment secretary, a uniformed lieutenant who occupied a desk
outside his office.

"Tell Chief Cervone I want him in my office forthwith," he snapped, then pushed through the double
doors that bore his name, trailed by his driver, who
resembled an African gun bearer, toting the clothes his
master would wear that day.

After dismissing the driver, Dalton stood in the center of his office, gathering his thoughts before heading
toward his private shower. Goddamned Cervone, he
thought. The man had plagued him ever since his ap-

pointment as commissioner four and a half years ago. Four and a half years. Only six months to go to have his full sixty months in, which would qualify him for a commissioner's pension. He let out a long breath. Then he could claim the judgeship he'd been promised, and he'd have all the financial security he would ever need. And with it, all the prestige he wanted. Christ, why couldn't the man just lay back for six months?

He stared out the large window that overlooked the East River and the imposing stone towers of the Brooklyn Bridge. It was no secret Cervone wanted his job, no secret he'd been thoroughly pissed when he didn't get it four and a half years ago. And in six months he could have the damned thing. But not if the mayor had his way.

He thought about their conversation that morning. Norris was wrong if he thought they'd survive public disclosure of what they were doing. Oh, the mayor would do everything he could to weather the storm. But the FBI wouldn't be the only scapegoat. Dalton knew his name would be second on that list. But he'd be damned if he'd go down alone. If it happened, the judgeship would be gone. And he sure as hell wouldn't keep his mouth shut and quietly fall on his sword.

Dalton stared down at the heavy desk that dominated the large office. It had been Teddy Roosevelt's when he had served as the city's police commissioner, and was one of the most coveted seats in the country. Christ, if they only knew the bullshit and intimidation that went with it. If they knew how your balls got roasted every time some maniac decided to ply his trade. And in a city of eight million maniacs. Hell, the way he despised Cervone, he could think of nothing better than to personally put him behind that desk. Let him deal with Norris and his jive-ass street talk. Or whatever other egocentric sonofabitch took his place. But not until you get yours, he told himself. Then you can sit up on the bench in black robes and break the

balls of every pissant lawyer who stumbles into your
court.

Dalton moved toward his private bathroom. "You bet
your ass," he mumbled to himself. "It damn well is
better to give than to receive."

Mario Cervone arrived outside the commissioner's
office fifteen minutes after he had been summoned. A
"forthwith" call from any superior within the department was ignored only at one's peril. And there was
only one person who could issue that order to Cervone.
The incompetent asshole who occupied the office he
himself deserved.

Cervone took a seat in the reception area, knowing
the P.C. would keep him waiting at least thirty minutes
just to let him—and everyone else—know he was
pissed about something. He offered a regretful nod to
the chiefs of patrol and administration, who would also
be kept waiting so the P.C. could make his point. Who
gave a fuck that the department ground to a crawl
while the game was played? It *was* the game, and he
had played it himself more times than he'd ever admit.

Cervone eased back in an intentionally uncomfortable upholstered chair, crossed his legs, and began
thumbing through a well-worn copy of *People* magazine. At fifty-five, he had been a cop for thirty-four
years, a detective for thirty, and chief of detectives for
ten. If he had learned one thing to perfection, it was
how to wait.

He glanced across the reception area at the glass-
enclosed office that housed the commissioner's three
secretaries and other staff. One of the secretaries was
about thirty, with blond hair and one of the best set
of tits he had ever seen. He wondered now, as he had
before, if the P.C. was balling her. Naw, he told himself. That wimpy-assed little shit wouldn't know what
to do with stuff like that. But you could bet the entire
department pad that he'd have her knickers down

around her ankles fifteen minutes after he took over as P.C. Oh, yes indeed.

The secretary looked up and caught his eye and smiled. Cervone smiled back with teeth that had been capped ten years ago when he had been appointed chief. He was not an exceptionally handsome man, but he knew he exuded power. And that was a quality, he had found, that attracted some women like flies to shit. He was five-nine with a once muscular body that was slowly going to fat. His hair was black, obviously dyed, and combed straight back, accenting his hard brown eyes. He wore hand-tailored suits at fifteen hundred dollars a pop—not that he paid that price, or anything close to it—and his life was just about everything he could hope for. He had a wife who was happy to be ignored, and a mistress, fifteen years his junior, stashed in an apartment in Queens. There was a son at Columbia on a scholarship he had arranged. And a married daughter on Staten Island who had given him two granddaughters whom he adored, but chose not to publicly acknowledge. There was only one thing he still wanted, and he would have that as well, whether that nigger bastard wanted him to or not. And he felt certain his friends at the archdiocese would see to it. He had attended enough goddamned communion breakfasts, and submarined enough priestly peccadillos to grease the skids. The only thing in his way now was the fucking FBI. And if he wasn't a match for those pompous little pricks, he didn't deserve the shot.

The appointment secretary broke his reverie and told him the P.C. was ready for him. Cervone stood, straightened his coat, then gave the large-breasted secretary one more smile. Fifteen minutes, shit, he told himself. Ten minutes, tops.

Dalton was waiting, grim-faced and stern, when Cervone entered his office. The P.C. was seated behind his desk, rays of light from the row of floor-to-ceiling windows giving off glints of silver in his otherwise brown hair. Behind him the Brooklyn Bridge and the

East River offered a tableau that reeked of power. It gave Cervone a near sexual rush of desire.

"I just left the mayor," Dalton began without preamble, other than to point Cervone toward a chair. "You might be interested to know the FBI was climbing his tail last night over this Mendez thing."

Cervone extended his arms and offered a helpless shrug. "You know how the Fibbies are. It doesn't take a helluva lot to get their noses out of joint."

Dalton leaned forward, his gray Brooks Brothers suit coat moving effortlessly with him. "But apparently it doesn't concern you that a victim has disappeared for five days—a victim we were hoping would lead us to a serial killer?"

Cervone held up both hands, palms forward, as if casually warding off a blow. "We're certain nothing has happened to her. She called one of my men. Said she was getting out of town for a couple of days. Wouldn't say where she was going. But she's been in touch by phone. And I'm told she's coming back. Maybe today." Cervone offered a regretful smile. "We can't hold her prisoner, even if it is for her own good."

"Which of your men do you get this from?" Dalton asked.

"Eddie Grogan."

Dalton leaned back in his chair, fighting with only partial success to keep a smirk from his lips. It was rare for him to catch Cervone—he wasn't sure he had ever done so. But he knew he had him this time.

"You know, of course, this Mendez woman is the daughter of a detective who died in the line of duty?" The momentary look in Cervone's eyes confirmed he was had. Dalton pushed some papers around his desk, looking for a name he already knew. "Rick Mendez, a detective first, killed ten years ago." He leaned back again and watched Cervone offer another helpless shrug. "And do you know who his partner was back then?"

Cervone's jaw tightened. He hadn't known. At least not until this moment. "Eddie Grogan," he said.

"That's right. I checked this morning. I thought somebody should."

Cervone bristled, but controlled the rage he felt building in his gut. It was the other thing he had perfected in his years as a cop. Use it, don't lose it.

"Seems I haven't been told some things I should have known," he said. The bitter taste of the words almost choked him. He offered a smile that could chill blood. "Thanks for bringing it to my attention."

"Or perhaps it's something you should have checked yourself," Dalton snapped. He couldn't resist twisting the knife. Who knew if the opportunity would ever come again?

Cervone's cold smile remained fixed as he nodded in agreement. It was bullshit, and the unctuous little prick knew it—knew he didn't have time to check out every detail that might rise up and bite him on the ass. But he knew someone who'd pay for this one, unless he had one fucking incredible excuse. "You're right, Commissioner. It won't happen again," he said. Right now all he wanted was to shoot Eddie Grogan. Then come back and blow Dalton right out his fucking power window.

Cervone entered his own office in a whirlwind of rage. He stopped before the desk of his own appointment secretary and spat out three words: "Eddie Grogan! Forthwith!"

8

She's back. The figure paced the bare wood floor. Faster. Faster. A deep breath. Another. Have to get control. Yes, you must have control. Because now she's back. Finally. The one who likes to hurt people. To cause them pain. And now she thinks her new little lock will keep her safe. But it won't. And neither will the man—the one who likes to chase people with his pathetic little gun. Sudden laughter filled the room, then stopped as abruptly as it had begun. He's just like her. Evil. Stupid. A fool. And you'll show him. Show them both. Nothing will protect her. Nothing at all. Not ever again.

Umberto Walsh walked quickly across his bedroom, turned, and marched back. He was puffing on a cigarette, and the movement was reminiscent of the actress, Bette Davis. The pale satin dressing gown with its feathered collar only added to the image.

"Inconsiderate little bitch," he mumbled to himself. "Couldn't take the time to call and let me know she had left town." He crushed the cigarette in a large silver ashtray, then glanced at the diamond-studded woman's watch that adorned his wrist. It was nine o'clock, time for him to change and get down to the gallery. She would be there in an hour, all regrets and looking for sympathy. Never thinking about all the trauma she had caused.

He ground his teeth, then looked at the blue blazer and sharply creased gray slacks that hung on the wooden valet. He still had to select a shirt and tie, and he really didn't feel up to it. He had gotten only three hours' sleep, and now he would have to make it through the day dragging his ass around like a whipped puppy.

He slipped out of the dressing gown and carefully hung it in an ornately carved armoire that held his second wardrobe, the one he could never trust anyone else to see. And that was a shame, he thought, as he often had. He looked so good in those clothes. Especially the one ensemble he wore only on those very special occasions.

But it couldn't be helped.

Slowly, almost delicately, he slipped out of the lace bikini panties and tossed them onto the bed. He grimaced as he gingerly removed the tape that held his penis and testicles up between his legs. Finished, he let out a sigh of relief. Then he walked quickly to the shower.

Adrianna waited at the front door of the gallery, just as Devlin had instructed. Across the street, one of the detectives who had followed her from the loft nodded as Devlin reached her, then turned and headed off with his partner.

Adrianna could feel the sweat in her palms. It had been safe, just as he had assured her it would be. But the fear had been absolute, nearly overwhelming. It was the only time she had ever felt that way, walking down a city street in daylight. She felt a shiver move along her spine. If it was going to be like this, she wasn't sure she could handle it. Wasn't sure she wanted to.

Devlin had set up the tail with Grogan. He had left the loft first, slipped inside a flower shop, and watched. No one had followed her; no one had paid her undue attention.

"I hate this," she said. "I hate being scared, and I hate being followed by cops." She wanted to tell him she didn't hate him being there. Only the rest of it. But he was a cop too. Would always be one. Just like her father. And she didn't know how to explain the difference. Even to herself.

Devlin didn't respond. He simply took her arm and guided her inside.

The gallery, which had once been a commercial insurance agency, was now a single open space. In what had been a rabbit warren of smaller rooms, walls had been torn down and replaced by occasional Ionic supporting columns. Everything—walls, ceiling, even the floor—was painted white, almost blindingly so, and track lighting cast spots of illumination on the paintings that hung from every perpendicular surface. Dotted about the center of the room, pieces of sculpture stood on white pedestals. It was like a small, exclusive museum, Devlin thought. Very pure. Very rich. An intended image, designed to lure checkbooks from pockets.

The atmosphere seemed to have calmed Adrianna. She was in her element, he decided. One not overrun with cops and killers. He wished the part about cops didn't exist. But he knew from past experience it always would.

A woman approached them. She was tall—reed-like would best describe her, he thought—dressed in an expensive tweed skirt and pale silk blouse, and her walk was loose and slightly arrogant. Her hair was long, flowing to her shoulders, and while she was not remarkably attractive, she seemed to be. It was something exuded by a sense of confident disdain, he decided.

"Oh, Adrianna, I didn't recognize you," the woman said, stopping a few feet from them. She eyed Devlin as though he had wandered in looking for a men's room.

"I'm here to see Umberto," Adrianna said.

The woman smiled, as though it were both an effort and a favor. "Of course. I'll tell him you're here."

Devlin watched her move back toward the rear of the gallery. "Friendly," he said.

"It's her job to make the browsers feel uncomfortable. Drive them way, if possible," Adrianna said.

"Why? Doesn't the owner want to fill the place with bodies, make it look like his paintings are practically jumping off the walls?"

"Just the opposite," Adrianna explained. "He wants the gallery to look exclusive. *Too* exclusive for the plaid pants set. Reserved for those who can appreciate *and* afford fine art." She rolled her eyes. "Believe me, if a skid row bum walked in with a large roll of bills in his grimy little hand, Umberto would snatch up the money in a second." She let out a small laugh. "It might cause him pain, and he might put on gloves before he took the money. But he'd be on his way to the bank before the bum got out the door."

Devlin shook his head and glanced around the room. "It's good to be back in New York," he said. "It's nice to have an easily attainable denominator of acceptability." A small smile played across his lips. "In Vermont it's how well you can use a hunting rifle. Here it's much simpler." He patted the wallet in his hip pocket.

"You seem nostalgic . . . for New York," she said.

"It's the egalitarianism," he said, his eyes still roaming the gallery. "It gets to you. Captain of industry or pickpocket, it's all the same here. As long as you've got the gelt."

Devlin turned to the sound of leather heels striking the highly polished white floor. The man coming toward them was tall and slender—almost frail—but he walked with a sense of elegance that made the mere act of arriving an entrance. Adrianna had briefed Devlin about Umberto—a.k.a. Hubert Walsh, as Devlin now thought of him—and her description had been on the money. Umberto seemed about forty, but could easily be older, given the availability of face lifts, tanning salons, health clubs, and hair colorists. He had a thin, almost pinched face, outlined by a well-defined bone structure that accented the line of his jaw and cheeks. His hair was reddish brown, short and neat and possibly dyed, Devlin thought. His clothing was impeccable and striking. A double-breasted blue blazer over gray slacks, set off by a pale violet shirt and deep purple necktie, all of it starched and pressed as though the creases had never been in contact with a chair. The tasseled loafers outshined the high gloss of the floor; their small Gucci emblems gleamed.

When he stopped before them, Devlin realized the man wasn't tall at all, but little more than average height, the affect achieved by the slender body and cut of clothes. Umberto ignored him, moving straight to Adrianna. He offered her what passed as a hug, hands on her shoulders, his body remaining a full foot away, as he leaned his head forward so their cheeks could touch momentarily. Not one crease in his clothing was ruffled. Almost like offering an obligatory gesture to a leper, Devlin thought.

"So, you've returned," Umberto said. He pivoted his head, acknowledging Devlin for the first time, his eyes roaming the corduroy sports coat and jeans, the buttoned-down blue-checked shirt, the well-worn brown boat shoes. "And you've brought a friend." His voice had a nasal quality to it, and his lips remained pursed as he spoke.

Adrianna offered a quick introduction, keeping to the script they had agreed upon earlier. "Paul's a neighbor and a friend," she said. "He's keeping me company when I go out. Until my nerves quiet down."

"Yes. The break-in. It must have been dreadful." Umberto offered her a look of regret, nothing more. "We are surrounded by savages," he added, then turned to Devlin. "And what do you *do*, Mr. Devlin? Something in the arts?"

"Nothing so exciting," Devlin said. "I work for a brokerage firm. I write stock analyses for their newsletter."

"Ah. And you can afford to stay away from Wall

Street." Umberto narrowed one eye, offering either skepticism or open suspicion.

"I work at home. On a computer." Devlin said. "Writing about companies losing money doesn't require me to be there."

The line produced an immediate dismissal from mind, just as Adrianna had predicted. Umberto viewed the loss of money as something potentially contagious, and therefore chose to keep carriers of that disease distant.

"Well, I suppose we should get to matters at hand," he said, turning to Adrianna. "Shall we go to my office?"

"Is it all right if Paul comes too?"

Umberto's lips pinched, and he flicked his gaze back at Devlin. "Do you know much about the workings of the contemporary art world, Mr. Devlin?" he asked.

"No, very little. But after seeing some of Adrianna's work I'm anxious to learn."

Umberto let out a short, slightly exasperated breath. "Very well," he said. "Shall we?"

He led the way to the rear of the gallery, to a door that was literally a part of one wall. The door had no doorknob, only a key pad set off to one side. Umberto punched in a numbered code, and the door popped forward several inches with a loud click. "Security," he said. "The code is changed several times a week," he added, as if Devlin might be a potential burglar who needed warning off. "We store valuable art inside, as well as the documents of provenance."

Adrianna had told Devlin that Umberto lived in an apartment that occupied the entire third floor of the building, and he wondered if the tripping of an alarm would bring him down, weapon in hand. He also wondered if he'd be dressed in the robes of a Capuchin monk.

They passed through a small storage room filled with paintings and sculpture, past a freight elevator that led, Umberto explained, to a basement storage area equal in size to the entire first floor, then through a carved mahogany door that took them into a large private office.

Umberto gestured toward a soft beige sofa, then took his place behind an antique partner's desk. Unlike the gallery, the office had soft beige walls and a rich oriental carpet. But, like the gallery, the walls were hung with contemporary paintings, and one enlarged photograph which Devlin found particularly disturbing. The photo showed a young girl—perhaps twelve years old—who was clearly from a third world country. South or Central America, Devlin guessed. But the child was dressed in the ostentatious clothing of a street walker, and she was looking at a soldier whose back was to the camera. The look on the child's face—especially in her eyes—left little doubt about her intentions. It was a mixture of pure innocence and blatant lasciviousness. Devlin thought it was the most discomforting picture he had ever seen of a child.

He dropped his eyes from the photo and found Umberto watching him closely. "Are these also for sale?" he asked.

Umberto steepled his fingers before his face. "Everything in the gallery is for sale, Mr. Devlin. Does something catch your fancy?"

"The photograph," Devlin said, nodding toward the picture.

Umberto continued to stare at Devlin. "I should have qualified that. All *paintings* are for sale. I do not represent photographers, although there is little question the work of some definitely qualifies as art." A faint smile flitted across his lips, then quickly faded. "But that, I'm afraid, is a rather common street scene. I took it myself. It's a hobby, or a self-indulgence, if you wish." He looked up at the photo. "I call it: The Whore of Panama." The small smile momentarily reappeared. "I'm flattered you find it appealing."

Umberto sat forward, dropping his hands, and turned his attention to Adrianna. "Now, I think we should get down to business. I'm becoming concerned that all the new work may not be in house by our agreed-upon deadline. We have slightly less than a month, and a postponement is definitely out of the question."

Adrianna twisted nervously. The veiled threat that cancellation of the show was *not* out of the question had not been lost on her.

"I understand," she said. "This last week has just been—"

"I know. I know," Umberto said, cutting her off. "But you must also understand that I have my own reputation to consider. I have promised a major exhibition of *new* work, and that leads people, and reviewers, to believe that it will be a sizable quantity of work. And we are still several paintings short of what I consider a sizable quantity."

He leaned back and again steepled his fingers before him, this time lightly tapping them together. "As I told you," he continued, "we have already had requests for private viewings by some rather select clients, and I fully expect a considerable number of your paintings to be sold *before* the opening. And nothing—I repeat, nothing—must be done to make these clients feel that I am showing the work of an artist whose talents and creative abilities are waning. I can think of little that would close their checkbooks faster." He pursed his lips, then continued. "As you know, these people buy primarily as a potential investment, and as such, they are only interested in artists whose stars are ascending, not declining."

Adrianna was wearing a long red cape, and she had it pulled about her now like a huddled child. "I assure you, the paintings will be here on time. At least five more."

Umberto shot forward in his chair. "Splendid," he said. "And that raises another question." His flicker of a smile returned, more avaricious this time. "As I said, I expect a considerable number to be sold prior to the opening, and, of course, others during the show itself. Now, normally we insist that work that has been sold remain in house until the show has ended. But in this case it would not surprise me if, after a time, we found ourselves with only two or three pictures still available for purchase. Should that become the case, I intend to allow some buyers to remove their paintings, and will ask you to make others available to replace them."

Umberto saw an objection coming, and moved quickly to defuse it. "Now, I'm not suggesting that you work madly to prepare for that event. But I know that you, like most artists, have work you have never offered for sale. Simply because you are too attached to it. What I'm suggesting is that some of those paintings be available, if needed."

Adrianna nodded. "I could do that."

"Good. Then I'd like to arrange a time when we can privately"—he glanced quickly at Devlin—"look over that work and select what would be most suitable."

"Whenever you wish," Adrianna said.

"Good." Umberto brought his hands together in an affected clap. He smiled—as warmly as possible for him, Devlin thought—then stood, and moved quickly around the desk. "Then why are you here? Why aren't you home slapping paint on canvas?" He turned toward Devlin. "Nice meeting you, Mr. Devlin." He slipped his arm around Adrianna and guided her to the door.

It was a dismissal. Pure, simple, and completely straightforward.

"Nice meeting you too," Devlin said to his back.

They had two hours to kill before they were due to meet Vincent, and Adrianna took time to show Devlin some of the paintings in the gallery—including two of hers, which Devlin decided was the real purpose of the impromptu tour.

After about fifteen minutes, he glanced at his watch. "Let's head uptown," he said. "I'll buy you some coffee at Sardi's." He smiled at her. "It isn't the Cafe Reggio, but . . ."

Adrianna returned the smile, pleased he remembered their old coffee house. Pleased he had thought of it now.

As they left the gallery, an old man stepped from behind one of the columns and watched them turn north on West Broadway. He was wearing a tattered raincoat, and a broad-brimmed hat hid most of his face.

He hurried out of the gallery, then turned into the street behind them. The sidewalk was crowded as people moved in and out of the shops, and several threw him curious glances as he weaved between them. He was walking too fast for an old man, and it was drawing attention. He slowed his pace and struggled to keep them in view.

He was a dozen steps behind when they reached West Houston, and Devlin suddenly stepped into the street and hailed a passing cab. He stood there in frustration, teeth clamped together, as he watched the man help the slut inside. And he thought he might scream as he saw the cab slowly pull away. The old man's hand was in the pocket of his coat, opening and closing repeatedly, then finally settling into a firm grip as he fiercely clutched the handle of the knife.

The cab headed uptown toward the theater district, where Vincent's rehearsals were due to start in half an hour. The cab moved through Greenwich Village, then on into Chelsea, and Devlin found himself looking for buildings where cases he had handled had begun. It was the bane of a homicide detective, he thought. The city developed its own landmarks for you. Places where you had gone to stare at the remains of murder victims, others where you had hunted or caught the people who had committed that ultimate crime. When you traveled any distance through the city, it was disquieting to realize how many streets held those unwanted memories.

They were on Eighth Avenue now, in what was

known as Hell's Kitchen, and they were passing a well-known Italian delicatessen. It had a large plate-glass window hung with cheeses and salami and the severed heads of several pigs—a special delicacy for those whose stomachs could abide it.

He had caught a murder there years ago. A *capo* in the Gambino family had taken a shotgun blast to the face. It had blown him, and what was left of his head, back through the window, and when Devlin had arrived, he had found the gangster sprawled across the window display platform, his legs dangling outside. The blast had jarred loose one of the pig heads, and it had come to rest on the shoulders of the dead *capo*. Either that or the killer, or one of the uniforms first on the scene, had put it there. He had never found out which. They had been forced to dust it for prints. It was probably the first and last time the head of a pig had gone through a forensics lab.

"Tell me about Vincent," he said, as much to dispel the memories that held him as his need to know.

Adrianna stared out the window, keeping her eyes on the passing streets. "He's talented, handsome, and utterly charming," she said.

Devlin felt a tinge of unwelcome—and undeserved—jealousy. "And?" he prodded.

"And . . . sometimes I wonder why I keep seeing him."

"Is he married?"

"Separated. For a long time, and working toward a divorce." She laughed, but it was brittle again. "Like all the attractive straight men in New York. The working toward a divorce part, I mean." She looked at him and smiled weakly. "Vincent's a bit of a playboy. No, more than a bit. He's a confirmed playboy." She leaned her head back against the seat. "If my father were alive, he'd kill me. Or Vincent. Or both of us. But he's fun to be with and—in case you hadn't noticed—New York isn't exactly overrun with interesting, eligible men. There's an incredible number of interesting gay men.

But they don't quite meet the requirements." She laughed again, a little more loosely this time. "There are self-centered jerks galore, and an endless supply of conquest freaks." She smiled at him. "We're rather low on chiefs of police from Vermont right now, but we're working on it."

Devlin was pleased by the compliment. He wanted to say so, but was afraid it might be taken the wrong way and rebuffed. "What about Vincent's work?" he asked instead.

Adrianna looked out the window again, momentarily disappointed. "He's extremely talented, as I said. But also enormously insecure about it. But I suppose that goes with the territory. Stars rise and fall on Broadway faster than anywhere else. I think he sees himself directing television commercials some day, and it scares the hell out of him."

"What about his relationship with his wife? Or soon-to-be ex-wife?"

She laughed again. "He seems to have a healthy dislike for her. Healthy from the viewpoint of the women he dates. He says she reminds him of his mother, whom he despised. Other than that he has a *very* healthy interest and attitude toward women."

"Any quirks, kinks, or anything else I should know about?"

Adrianna stared at him for a moment, wondering if the question was sparked by jealousy. She decided to make a joke out of it and rolled her eyes, mocking him for his intrusiveness. "No," she said. "Nothing that I've noticed."

Devlin felt his cheeks redden slightly. "Sorry," he said. "I had to ask."

No, you didn't, she told herself. But you wanted to know.

9

The woman brought the script against her thigh with a light slap, then let out a long breath.

"Vincent, dear. This line simply doesn't work for me. I love the play, and I adore the character, but I'd like her to sound reasonably intelligent. Just some lines I can do justice to."

Melissa Coors was thirty-five, a full ten years older than the character she was playing. Vincent Richards had bedded her off and on for the past two years, and he decided now that he would never again allow a woman he had fucked to play a lead in one of his plays. He smiled at the thought. And you may never get laid again, he told himself. Either that, or it's all-male casts from now on.

Vincent slipped on his reading glasses and looked at his own copy of the script. They were standing at the side of the stage, speaking in hushed tones, so the playwright, who was seated nine rows back in the orchestra, would not overhear their conversation.

"Melissa. Dearest. I simply cannot find a thing wrong with the lines. Morgana is a young woman. Barely twenty-five. And a *young* twenty-five. She is from a small southern town, and now she finds herself in a situation she can't even begin to fathom. She is trying to appear worldly, and is failing miserably. She is naive, and everyone around her knows she is naive. That is the part. As it is written. As it will be played."

He looked up from the script; Melissa's beautiful, finely boned face was pinched now. There was a hint of red in her cheeks; her dark blue eyes glittered with simmering anger.

"Are you saying I'm too old for the part?" Her voice was noticeably restrained, and he could almost hear the screech that was waiting to escape.

Vincent smiled at her. He knew it was his most engaging feature and he used it now. "Darling, you were too old for this part when you were eighteen. You're a worldly woman, have always been one. But you're also an excellent actress. And I know you can bring life to the character. Challenge yourself. For me. Please." He watched the incipient anger subside. She let out a long breath. "Shall we try it?" he asked.

Vincent returned to his seat next to the playwright, fell into it, and let out his own weary breath.

Brenden Brooks leaned toward him. "What's the problem?" he asked, keeping his own voice low.

"The stupid cow doesn't like the lines. They're not sophisticated enough for her taste." He pinched his eyes between finger and thumb. "It's her latest thing. She thinks all women should sound like Gloria Steinem. Some sort of Jane Fonda complex."

"Ask her if she wants to play the part of the older sister," Brooks suggested. "I think she'll suddenly decide these lines are brilliant."

Vincent let out a short, harsh laugh. "Yes, I'm sure she would. The sister's thirty-five. If I ever suggested that lovely Melissa play a woman her own age, they'd have to take her to her analyst in an ambulance." Vincent turned his attention to the stage. "Let's begin," he called, then rested his head against the back of his seat.

He listened as Melissa Coors delivered her lines flawlessly. He looked at her legs, and thought of times they had been wrapped around him so tightly he could barely breathe. When the scene ended, he stood. "That was terrific," he called up to the stage. "Perfect. Now let's try the opening scene in Act Three. Melissa, you're not in that, so you're free to go. I'll call you tonight."

Vincent sat back in his chair and turned to Brooks. The man was short and plump and fifty, with wispy hair that was heavy only over his ears. He looked like an aging Puck, Vincent thought. Even more now with a wry grin on his lips.

"She *was* good," Brooks said.

"She's an excellent actress," Vincent said. "Just crazy as a shithouse rat. Like all of them." He returned the grin. "She'll drive us crazy. All through rehearsals and during our out-of-town run. But when we open here, she'll bring people into the theater."

"So we'll live with it," Brooks finished for him.

"Of course. Then you can call an ambulance to take *me* to my analyst."

Brooks tapped the side of his nose with one finger, a British gesture taken up by American stage people who had worked there. "You've got to stop sleeping with every actress in town. Then you won't need an analyst," Brooks offered.

"I have," Vincent said. He smiled at Brooks. "As of today." He laughed softly at himself. "The shrink I've been seeing says I don't even like them that much. Claims all that frolicking in bed is just a power feed."

Brooks squeezed Vincent's forearm. "That's a game, I've found, that women always win."

Vincent turned to him, his eyes becoming harder. "Not always, Brenden. There are games, and there are games." He softened the look with another light laugh. "Besides, it hones my once proud acting skills."

"Faking orgasms again, eh?" Brooks teased.

"Always, Brenden. As the guy in *Dr. Strangelove* said, never surrender your precious bodily fluids."

"A neat trick, if you can pull it off. But the woman always knows."

"Ah," Vincent said, winking at the older man. "A condom and a little whiff of amyl nitrite, and the woman *never* knows."

"You're joking, of course." There was a hint of incredulity in Brooks' voice.

"Of course." Vincent glanced up at the stage. "All right, everyone. Places, please."

Devlin and Adrianna entered the Lenox Theater through the stage door, which was located off Lenox Alley, a one-block pedestrian walkway that runs between West 44th and 45th streets. There was a bronze plaque on the side of the building that intoned: "Lenox Alley, dedicated to all those who glorify the theater and use this thoroughfare." The adjacent Booth Theater, a bar, and an office tower took up the remainder of the narrow walkway.

As they stepped inside, an old man with the pallor of a prison lifer checked Adrianna's name against a list hanging from the wall of the closet-sized cubicle he occupied. He eyed Devlin suspiciously, but finally agreed he could accompany Adrianna inside.

"Except for the search, it's easier to get into Attica," Devlin said as they moved away. He was surprised by the size of the backstage area. It was small and cramped, and ten long strides from the stage door would practically put you center stage. He hesitated. Off to his right was a small, barren room. The "quick change" room, Adrianna explained. When the play opened it would be filled with costumes, she said, and used by actors who had to change clothes and get back on stage in minutes.

Devlin took her arm, keeping her from moving ahead. "Where are the rest of the costumes kept?" he asked.

"All over the theater when the show's running," she said. "There's the girls' changing room." She winced. "Their word, not mine. The boys' changing room. They're both in the basement, along with the room the wardrobe mistress uses. That's where the costumes are now." She nodded toward an iron stairwell off to their left. "It's down those stairs. Upstairs are the principal dressing rooms. The principal players get their costumes delivered." She smiled. "But you'd be amazed how tiny their dressing rooms are," she added. "The largest is about ten feet by six. More like a prison cell. Nothing like Hollywood portrays them, jammed with dozens of people after a show. And not one of them has a window. Vincent told me that a few years back, a producer lured Katharine Hepburn to Broadway, and that her one request was to have a window in her dressing room. So they put one in. It's now the only dressing room in all the theaters on Broadway that has a window. And it only offers the view of another theater."

They started walking again, Adrianna leading the way, her red cape flowing out behind her. Lines and cables hung along the sides and rear of the stage, and above them hovered the fly gallery, a narrow walkway that allowed workers to get to the lights and the mechanics that operated much of the scenery. On the far side of the stage, the shell of an automobile was suspended twenty feet aloft on heavy cables. And all around them, men in work clothes moved about, attending various tasks.

"Is it always so crowded?" Devlin asked.

"Even worse during a performance," Adrianna said. "When the actors are moving around, getting in position for entrances, or heading to changing rooms, everyone's practically falling all over each other."

"But there are so many people *now*," Devlin said.

"There's a lot to do. And there are union rules. Whenever the theater's open—whether it's rehearsals or a performance—the entire crew—stagehands, prop men, electricians, carpenters, custodians, whatever—they all have to be here." She smiled. "And be paid for it." She shrugged. "It's one reason orchestra seats cost sixty-five dollars a pop. If Vincent comes in alone—to study the sets or work out changes—then only Charlie—he's the old fellow who guards the door—has to be here. And that's for security. Vincent said he had four bag ladies wander in when he was rehearsing a play last winter," she said over her shoulder. "Apparently they saw actors arriving, and decided it would be a good place to get warm."

"Did they get parts?" Devlin asked.

"Maybe they did," Adrianna said. "The play folded after four days."

She opened a door that led to a short set of stairs that went down into the orchestra, and they could hear an actor reading lines, his voice thin and nasal in the empty theater.

Adrianna slipped through the door, Devlin right behind, then moved up the side aisle until she was abreast of the row where Vincent and Brenden Brooks sat. Vincent turned to her and smiled as she moved quietly down the aisle. Then his eyes settled on Devlin and his face registered surprise, curiosity.

They took seats across the aisle from Vincent and Brooks, and turned their attention to the stage, where a young actor continued to read from a hand-held script. To Devlin he looked small and underfed, and the sheer size of the stark, barren stage appeared ready to swallow him whole.

"That's fine. Great," Vincent called out. "Let's take lunch and be back at two. We'll run through the scene one more time and call it a day." He stood, stretched, then turned and walked to where Adrianna and Devlin were seated.

He leaned down and kissed her cheek. "Where in heaven's name have you been?" he asked, consciously ignoring Devlin. "I thought you'd been kidnapped by gypsies."

"It's a long story," Adrianna said. She turned to Devlin. "This is Paul Devlin, a new neighbor and new friend," she said. "Paul, this is Vincent Richards."

Vincent nodded to Devlin. "I didn't know you had neighbors. I thought the third-floor loft was empty."

"Paul's just taken it, and started moving in."

Vincent narrowed one eye. "That's pretty quick. I thought the place was a shambles."

"It is," Devlin said quickly. "But I'm living in the

clutter while I fix it up." He shrugged, improvising as he spoke. "A recent divorce."

Vincent tilted his head to one side in an apparent gesture of sympathy. "War is hell," he said, then smiled down at Adrianna. "Let's eat. I'm starved. And then you can tell me all about your mysterious disappearance." The smile returned. "I want to make sure I'm sitting down. Just in case it turns out you eloped. If you did, you get the check."

"Nothing so romantic," Adrianna said.

"Well, in that case, lunch is on me."

They arrived at Broadway Joe's, a popular show business eatery two blocks north on West 46th Street, and were ushered to "Mr. Richards' regular table" by a maître d' who obviously knew and favored the director.

It must be nice, Devlin mused, to have your patronage so valued that a table was set aside for you each day. When he had been a detective, he and other cops had eaten in the same restaurants regularly. Although they were known and treated well, he had always suspected that the owners had groaned inwardly over the drinks and occasional meals they felt obligated to provide "on the arm."

"You come here every day?" he asked Vincent.

The man smiled at him, with a touch of condescension, Devlin thought. He immediately regretted the question.

"I call if I'm *not* going to use the table. That way they can give it to someone else."

He turned away from Devlin with a sense of dismissal and smiled at Adrianna. "Now tell me about this sudden disappearance."

Vincent listened as Adrianna related the details of the attack. She kept to the basics, as Devlin had instructed, and avoided any mention of an ongoing threat. Devlin watched Vincent's face—especially his eyes—and noted that his emotions seemed to run the gamut of disbelief to open concern. He reminded himself the man had been trained as an actor. When Adrianna explained that she had fled for several days to the weekend house she rented in Bridgehampton, Vincent simply nodded in understanding, then reached across the table and took her hand in both of his.

"You should have come to *me*," he said. His eyes momentarily flashed to Devlin. It was an unspoken message that he was no longer needed.

"I didn't want to cause any problems," she said. Now her eyes flashed to Devlin. It was because of the reference to Vincent's estranged wife, he told himself.

Vincent picked up on it too. Especially the needed look at Devlin. "It wouldn't have been a problem," he said. "It's not an adversarial situation."

Adrianna looked down at the table. "It just seemed better."

"Well, you must let me come and stay with you now," he said. "You shouldn't be alone at night."

Devlin knew the offer was real, but he suspected the man was also probing—trying to find out if Devlin had taken on that role.

"I'm fine," she said. "And I really have to work. And Paul's just upstairs if there's a problem."

Vincent turned to Devlin, his face expressionless. "You don't work during the day?" he asked.

"Yes, but I work from home," he said, offering up the cover story. He was grateful Vincent didn't push it further by asking which brokerage house employed him. The story had no prearranged backing, and wouldn't survive a simple telephone call.

"Well, it seems I won't be seeing much of you for a bit," Vincent said, turning back to Adrianna.

She offered a regretful shrug. "No one will. At least not until I finish the paintings for the show. We just left Umberto"—she smiled as Vincent rolled his eyes at the mention of the gallery owner's name. "He was a bit adamant about what he expected, and when."

"You mean, didactic," Vincent offered.

"Let's just say he was Umberto."

Vincent's face suddenly brightened. "Listen, I have

a splendid idea. Actually, it's one of the reasons I've been calling. There's a party tonight. Some very heavy money people on Park Avenue who you could lobby for your show." He hurried on before Adrianna could object. "It's a typical fund-raising sort of thing. To benefit a homeless shelter run by this little priest I know. In fact, he's the one who called and invited me. Even asked me to bring a date. I think he's afraid no one will come." He offered a wide smile. "But that won't happen, and it should be a good group, and it might even be fun." He raised his hands, holding her off. "I know you're in seclusion. But this might help ease some of the tension. Bring you back into the world a bit."

Devlin nudged her foot under the table, and gave a quick nod of his head outside Vincent's line of sight.

"It sounds like fun," Adrianna said. She glanced at Devlin, then back at Vincent, offering him an unspoken message.

Vincent let out a short breath, then turned to Devlin. "You're invited too, of course. If you're not working, that is." The offer was blatantly disingenuous. Either Richards wasn't as good an actor as Devlin suspected, or he wanted to make sure his message was clear.

Devlin smiled, enjoying himself now. "Actually, I'm quite free," he said. The smile widened.

They took a cab and headed back to Soho.

"What did you think about Vincent?" Adrianna asked after they had gone several blocks.

"He makes me feel inferior. Like somebody who doesn't belong in his league."

"I think he tries to make people feel that way. *You* shouldn't." Saying it, she realized she meant it. "Why the party?" she asked.

Devlin stared out the window. "Just felt like going out," he said.

She felt suddenly chilled. "Or you think it's the kind of place this monster picks out his victims." The idea shook her, and she knew she had to lighten the conversation, just for her own sake. "Or maybe you just want to see a little more of Vincent."

Devlin turned to face her. "Some of the above. All of the above." He shrugged. "And I also want it to appear that your life is back to its old routine."

Adrianna stared at him. "So I'm more attractive . . . as bait?" she said at length.

"It's the way it has to be," Devlin said. "If we're going to catch him. I'm sorry."

Adrianna turned to the window. "Jesus," she said. "I guess I knew that. I just didn't admit it to myself."

Back at the loft, Devlin went straight to the telephone and reached out for Eddie Grogan. When he finished, he returned to the living area and took a seat opposite Adrianna.

"I'm meeting Eddie at seven o'clock. There's something we're going to check on." He hesitated, knowing Adrianna would not like what he would say next. "Eddie is sending someone to take you to the party. It starts at eight, but don't get there before eight-thirty. I should already be there, or will be within minutes. Eddie's guy will just take you up to the apartment and then take off. I know you don't like being herded around by cops, but it has to be that way."

Adrianna looked at the floor, but this time let the subject of yet another cop pass. "What are you and Uncle Eddie going to do?" she asked.

"I'll let you know later," Devlin said.

10

Eddie Grogan looked down Lenox Alley. Well-dressed people seemed to be everywhere, all rushing to restaurants for a quick bite to eat before the eight o'clock performances began at the various theaters. They moved with neat precision, dodging around the street people and beggars who flocked to the district every night, each one intent on his or her own entertainment, ignoring all else, not wanting to confront anything that detracted from the glitter of what they were about to enjoy. Along West 44th and 45th streets limousines were illegally parked and double-parked, and what was left of the roadways were clogged with taxis and cars fighting their way through.

"So whadda we expect to find in this fucking mausoleum?" Grogan asked, nodding toward the stage door.

Devlin stared at the eighty-year-old theater. "I want to look in every crack in the wall. If Vincent is our boy, this would be the perfect place to lose some costumes he doesn't want anyone to find."

"Capuchin monks, huh?" Grogan said.

Devlin nodded. "Later, I want you to take a look at Vincent's apartment. See how hard it'll be to get into when he's not home. Then check out Umberto's gallery. He lives upstairs, and I'd like to get in both places when they're empty. There are alarms there, so you'll need somebody who can tell us how hard it'll be to bypass them."

"You're turning me into a fucking thief," Grogan said.

"You're a cop," Devlin said. "Everybody knows cops are bent."

"That's what Cervone thinks," Grogan said. "He hauled my ass in on a 'forthwith' this morning. Then chewed it up and spit it out."

"Over what?" Devlin asked.

"The little temporary disappearance we pulled. Seems a little bird told him who Adrianna's old man was, and how we used to be partners. Shit, I thought that was old enough he wouldn't dig it up."

"So?"

"So I played my dumb act. Blamed it on her. Said she was rebellious, didn't like cops." He raised his eyebrows. "Hey, it ain't far from the truth. Then I told him I found her in a beach house she rents in the Hamptons, and convinced her to drag her ass back to the city so we could protect her."

"He bought it?"

Grogan rolled his eyes. "Just barely. It helped when I called her a smartass little spic. You know what a racist bastard Cervone is." He offered a small shrug. "But he'll be watching my rosy red ass like a faggot at a Boy Scout jamboree. I'll just have to do a little sleight of hand with the bastard."

Grogan looked back at the theater. "I'll check out Umberto's and Vincent's places. But you better hope whoever they got as a security guard in *this* joint is an ex-cop, not an ex-con. Or some old mooch who's afraid for his job. Otherwise we ain't even gonna get in *here*."

The security guard turned out to be young and dumb and, like many of his ilk, enamored with the idea of one day being a cop himself. His eyes glittered when Grogan flashed his gold shield and began his tap dance about what he wanted to do. The only difficulty proved to be keeping the guard from going with them. And he happily promised to be deaf, dumb, and blind to the fact they had even been there.

"The little shit didn't even ask us not to take nothin'," Grogan said as they headed down the stairs that led to the wardrobe room. "Some fucking security."

The wardrobe storage area proved to be two rooms—two long, stark rectangles, illuminated by a series of bare bulbs under green metal shades.

"It's lit like a fucking pool hall," Grogan said.

They were standing in the doorway between the two rooms. The first held a desk and a long, L-shaped sewing table, and there were wardrobe boxes along one wall. The second room was little more than rows of costumes hanging from rods and covered in heavy plastic. Devlin decided to start the search there.

He started on the first rack of clothing, and realized his hands were sweating. Neither the lighting nor the place itself conjured up images of a pool hall. It reminded him of another search years before. One in the storage rooms of the Museum of Natural History. It had been as forbidding as this theater. Filled with the same labyrinth of hallways and dark storage areas. A place where another serial killer had lunged out at him, cutting him with an obsidian knife. He was glad Grogan was with him. It kept him from having to do it himself. Alone.

"Nothing," Grogan said half an hour later, closing the last of the trunks.

"Nothing here either," Devlin said.

"Hey, you can't expect to hit a home run first time at bat."

"Why not?" Devlin asked.

"That ain't the way this case works," Grogan said. "Trust me."

The boys' and girls' dressing rooms proved equally fruitless, as did the various work and prop rooms. They moved into a large, central room directly under the stage. In one corner a computer console fitted with a half-dozen television monitors was in the process of being set up. From there one man would control all the lights and curtains—the various mechanics of the stage—reading from scripted instructions, while the TV monitors allowed him to watch the performance on the stage above.

There was a carpet runner taped along the floor, crossing the room to another set of stairs that led back to the stage. Actors would use it to get from one side of the stage to the other—racing down one flight of stairs, across the basement, then up the other side—always staying on the carpet to keep their costumes from snagging on the men and equipment that would then fill the room. The remainder of the room was now filled with props and furniture, which would be moved to other locations later, when dress rehearsals began.

Devlin glanced at his watch. It was almost eight. He could still get to the party in time if he had luck with a cab.

"What a fucking spook house," Grogan muttered as he moved around the room. "Look at that," he said, pointing at a far wall where a coffin stood propped on end. "What show they doin' here? Fucking *Dracula*? That door swings open, and I start blasting. No two fucking ways about it."

"You'll get the security guard in trouble," Devlin said. "And he likes you. Thinks the policeman is his friend."

"Fuck him," Grogan said. "He's old enough to know better."

They began searching behind the sets and furniture—Devlin took the inside of the coffin. It was like rummaging through someone's cobwebbed attic, the possessions of family members long dead and forgotten. In the rear of the basement was a second room, holding the theater's heating system and a work area jammed with tools. Even a chainsaw, Devlin noted. In one corner there was a large roll of burlap. Devlin walked to it and fingered the material. He motioned Grogan over. It was heavy, and brown, and coarse.

"This stuff just made me think of something," he said. "There's no reason that somebody—the wardrobe mistress, or one of her people—wouldn't have made a costume."

"So you want me to talk to them. See if Vincent put in a special order," Grogan said. "Good thought. But our killer started wearing this rag two years ago. So I gotta find out what play he was doing back then, and who his wardrobe mistress was."

Devlin nodded. "Actors' Equity, or some outfit like that, ought to be able to tell us. Theatrical people are in one union or another. And unions keep records."

"I'll get somebody on it tomorrow. We about finished here?"

"Yeah, I think so."

A pipe clanged overhead, and Grogan gave a sudden start. He covered it with a weak smile and a shake of his head. "Fucking spook house," he said. "Give me dark Harlem tenements any day."

It was quarter to nine when Devlin exited the elevator of the Park Avenue building. It was a massive old structure with elaborate exterior decoration, an interior courtyard, and a large lobby of pink Italian marble. In the ninth-floor foyer, where he stood now, there were only two doors, indicating there were only two apartments occupying the entire floor. That would mean about five thousand square feet per apartment, he told himself. At New York prices that was very rich living.

There were two coat racks outside one door, one already full, the other well on its way. A uniformed maid stood beside them. You could rent anything in New York, he mused. And if you were wealthy, you didn't toss your guests' coats in the master bedroom like normal people did.

He approached the maid, explained he was Ms. Mendez's date and had been delayed. She nodded, eyes blank. I don't care if you're Jack the Ripper, the look said. She took his coat and nodded at the door. Devlin wondered if he was supposed to tip her. His knowledge of etiquette at fashionable soirées was decidedly limited. The hell with it, he thought. He'd watch what people did when he left. And play monkey.

Inside the door was another foyer fashioned in the same Italian marble used in the lobby. It glistened, mirror-like, reflecting the underside of a large, round table at its center. He could hear soft music coming from an adjacent room, and less than soft conversation, broken by occasional laughter. He crossed the foyer, wondering if his leather heels would scratch the glistening marble. It reminded him of the few visits he had made to the convent of the Catholic grammar school he had attended. Everything there had been highly polished, and inordinately clean and well ordered. Whenever he went there he had always feared spreading some kind of dirt in his wake, something that would bring a pack of angry nuns down on his neck.

The adjoining room was large and crowded, and at first he had difficulty spotting Adrianna. But she was there, two-thirds of the way across the room, talking with Vincent and a tall, striking woman who wore a dress cut so low, it would have gotten her arrested in Vermont.

He made his way toward them, angling through knots of people, picking up a glass of wine on the way, and wondering how much theater dust still clung to the blue suit he was wearing.

Adrianna smiled when he reached them. So did the other woman. Vincent did not.

"Sorry I'm late," he said. "And forgive any dust. The loft is still a construction site."

"You have a loft. How wonderful. I've always wanted one. But all the good ones are so far from the theater district." It was the other woman, who was quickly introduced by Adrianna as Melissa Coors, an actress who would be in Vincent's new play.

She moved closer to Devlin, the décolletage of her dress only inches from the drink in his hand. She was very beautiful, and she understood the fact, and knew how to use it. Devlin wondered if she was Vincent's date for the evening—some retribution for Adrianna's subtle insistence he be invited.

"What do you do, Mr. Devlin?" Melissa asked.

"It's Paul. And I do stocks," he said. He went through the cover story, ending with the recent divorce and the resulting new loft in Soho—in Adrianna's building. He noticed that Melissa threw a quick, smirky glance at Vincent, indicating she knew of his relationship with Adrianna—or suspected it—and enjoyed the idea that he had competition.

"We've all been through divorce, I suppose," she said. "Or are working toward it." Another glance at Vincent. "These days it's all part of a well-rounded life experience."

The statement seemed appropriately jaded, and Devlin let it pass. He had never thought of his own life that way. Divorce was something he had never contemplated. It had taken years to recover from his wife's death, and each time he looked at his daughter, he still wished she was there, watching and helping Phillipa grow into a young woman.

"Tell me about your play," Devlin said.

"Ah, the play." Melissa smiled. "It's wonderful. And Vincent is directing, which makes it even better." She bowed slightly in his direction, and Devlin thought she was already a little drunk. Vincent returned the bow, as though it were his due.

"It's about a young man who goes to officer training at an army base in the South. He meets a young woman there"—she held one hand to her breast, indicating the young woman was she—"and falls in love. But, alas, there are problems. The young man has been abused as a child. Sexually abused. And this causes deep problems, which the naive young woman"—again the hand to her breast—"is unable to understand." She raised her chin. "The play's marvelous." Her eyes darted to Vincent. "Although the dialogue does need some work."

"Dialogue always needs work," Vincent interjected.

"That is why we have brilliant actresses playing leading roles."

Melissa looked back at Devlin. "Never buy anything from this man," she said. "He cannot be trusted."

The conversation was interrupted by a middle-aged woman whose dress was as stunning as Melissa's, only a bit less revealing. Her name was Rachel Barrows, and it was her apartment, her party, her night. There was a tall, almost sickly-looking man with her, somewhat out of place in an ill-fitting blue blazer, a bit shiny at the elbows, and a red turtleneck. Rachel Barrows introduced him as "Father Jim," the guest of honor.

Father Jim, she explained, was a Catholic priest who ran a shelter for the homeless in the theater district—a shelter that was desperately in need of support. There was little question what kind of support she was alluding to, and Devlin wondered if his very limited wallet was soon to receive a severe dent.

"I know Father Jim well." It was Vincent, stepping forward and taking the priest's hand. He glanced in turn at Adrianna and Melissa. "He started doing some street theater with his people a few years ago, and from time to time has come to me for some help, some costumes"—he grinned—"whatever."

The "whatever" had obviously been cash, Devlin decided, but Vincent was too modest to say so. He just wanted everyone to know.

"Well, I hope you all brought your checkbooks," Rachel Barrows said. "I'll leave Father Jim with you, then come and collect him in a bit."

The woman smiled at each of them, then turned and headed off to another group. It was the smile of a well-turned-out shark, Devlin thought.

"I haven't seen any of your street performances. Tell me about them." Melissa had moved in on the priest, her décolletage now attacking *his* drink.

The priest was in his mid-thirties, Devlin guessed, and he had the haunted, vulnerable look that some women were instantly attracted to, a man who needed to be comforted, mothered. But Melissa didn't seem the mothering kind, and the priest was clearly ill at ease. He brushed back his sandy-colored hair in a nervous gesture, and struggled to keep his pale blue eyes away from the exposed breasts that loomed up before him.

"It's not much as performance," he said. "But it does give our people some purpose, and some sense of themselves."

"Father's right," Vincent interjected. "They'll never make Broadway." He paused for effect. "But he could." He let the words sink in, ignoring the priest's protest. "About a year ago they involved me in a skit. It called for a part of an old woman. But they didn't have one in the shelter at the time." He jabbed a finger at the priest. "So Father Jim played the part. A little makeup from one of my people, and no one—including myself—could believe they weren't watching some old harridan of a bag lady. The man's a natural-born actor."

Father Jim blushed and shook his head. "But they say that about all priests, don't they?"

"Don't dismiss it," Melissa said. "Vincent *never* praises actors . . ." She cast a narrowed eye at the director. "Unless they're extraordinary, and it can't be avoided."

"Hello."

Heads turned to the sound of the new voice, and found Gabrielle Lyons smiling back.

"Gabrielle," Adrianna said. "What a surprise."

The psychiatrist slipped her arm into Father Jim's. "This is one of my favorite people," she said. "I always show up when he's beating the bushes for money."

The priest smiled at her. He seemed relieved to have someone he knew at his side. "She does much more than that," he said. "She works with our people. Counsels them; helps them overcome their despair. She's named for the archangel Gabriel. God's messenger. And aptly so."

Gabrielle waved a hand, dismissing the words. Adrianna quickly introduced her to Vincent and Melissa. Then to Devlin, who she pointedly identified as a new neighbor in her building.

Gabrielle played dumb, showing no sign she had ever met Devlin before. He was surrounded by actors, Devlin thought. Even those who weren't supposed to be actors.

Gabrielle gently maneuvered the priest away from Melissa's assaultive breasts, and placed him in front of Adrianna. The man seemed relieved. Adrianna's sedate silk blouse and slacks obviously made her less difficult to deal with.

"We've met before," the priest said. "But you probably don't remember."

"I'm afraid I don't," Adrianna said.

"I'm not surprised," the priest offered. "It was at another party, and you were with Vincent and a large group of people. I just passed by with my alms cup. Unofficially, that time." He turned to Devlin. "I guess I've seen all of you before"—he nodded to Melissa— "Miss Coors on the stage, of course." He looked back at Devlin. "Except Mr. Devlin." There was a hint of something in the priest's eyes. Suspicion, Devlin thought. It struck him as odd.

"I'm new to the scene," Devlin said. "The functions I usually get invited to are far less glamorous."

Melissa Coors slipped her arm in Devlin's. "Adrianna's just been hiding you," she said. There was a slight tightening in Vincent's jaw. Devlin wasn't sure if it was the mention of Adrianna or Melissa's aggressiveness toward him. "But we won't let her keep you all to herself," Melissa added. She continued to hang onto Devlin's arm, and he wasn't sure what he could do about it. Or if he wanted to do anything at all.

"Ah, there's Brenden," Vincent said, doing a neat side step of the scene Melissa was playing. He waved toward Brenden Brooks, caught his eye, and motioned him to join them. "Brenden's the author of my new play," Vincent explained to the priest. "You certainly can get some money out of him. We all smell hit with this one."

Brenden Brooks waded into the circle. His face was slightly flushed and his eyes glistened. It was obvious Rachel Barrows' wine had taken a heavy hit.

"We're hearing wonderful things about your new play," Gabrielle offered.

"A lot of the credit goes to Vincent, I'm afraid," Brooks said. "Much of the original story idea was his."

Adrianna moved to Devlin. "Come with me a minute. There's someone I want you to meet." She smiled at Melissa as Devlin moved from her grip, then turned and started away. A hand reached out and took her arm.

Adrianna turned quickly, as if the hand had hurt her. Her eyes met the priest's and he quickly loosened his grip.

"I just wanted to say that I read the article about your upcoming show," he said. "I wanted to wish you success."

"Thank you. And I hope you do well here tonight."

Adrianna led Devlin away, through the knots of people clustered in small and larger groups.

"Who did you want me to meet?" Devlin asked.

"No one. I just wanted to get away from Brooks. He gives me the creeps. Especially when he's been drinking. He always looks at me like he's writing a sex scene in his mind."

"Well, you seem to have made a hit with the priest," Devlin said.

Adrianna let out a small shiver. "He's a bit on the creepy side too," she said. "God, maybe it's just me. But when he grabbed my arm just now, it felt like someone was attacking me."

"Too strong?"

"Much too strong. Like he wanted to stop me from leaving. I mean really stop me, not just hold me up for a final word." She shook her head. "It must be me. Nerves, I suppose." She smiled at him, offered a small, regretful shrug. "At least *you* made a hit." Her look was steady, then became coy. "With Melissa Coors."

"I think that was for Vincent's benefit," he said. "I think he brought her because you brought me. And I think she sensed it and was working him over a bit. Did they see each other once?"

"I think so." Adrianna shrugged again. "Maybe they still do. Who knows?"

She began to look past Devlin, as though searching for someone in the room.

He turned and followed her gaze.

"I'm looking for Umberto," she explained. "I thought about what Vincent said. About doing some lobbying for my show. So I called him after you left and suggested he come. I can't bring myself to do that sort of self-promotion. So I asked Umberto to come and do it."

"When you throw a party like this, do all your guests turn around and invite a half-dozen other people?" Devlin asked.

"Oh, the hostess doesn't mind. It's expected," she said. "As long as they're the kind of people who'll open their wallets before the evening's over."

"How big a check do they expect you to write?" Devlin asked. There was a hint of nervousness in his voice.

"Oh, there he is," Adrianna said, ignoring his question. "I have to go over and thank him. Do you want to come?"

Devlin glanced at Umberto. He was dressed in a fawn-colored jacket that looked like silk even from a distance, a dark blue shirt, with a fawn ascot at his throat. Foppish to a fault, Devlin thought.

"I think I'll just wander around and survey the scene," he said. "Like a good detective."

"You just want to avoid Umberto," Adrianna said.

"Well, there's that too. And, he wasn't too thrilled to see me this morning. No sense overloading his circuits. He might hold his breath and explode."

Adrianna closed her eyes and gave a small shake of

her head. "You're mean," she said. Her face broke into
a wide grin. "Try to stay away from women with low-
cut dresses," she warned, then turned and began weav-
ing her way toward the gallery owner.

Devlin watched. When Umberto saw her he opened
his arms like a mother hen receiving a favored chick.
The sternness of the morning was gone, but Umberto's
version of a hug was the same. He clasped her shoulders, keeping his body a full foot from hers, then extended his cheek to Adrianna's until they touched. He
was a man who definitely didn't want to get too close,
Devlin thought.

He turned away and began circulating through the
room, which was larger than the entire first floor of
his house in Vermont. It was a monied existence at its
costliest, he told himself, one that probably included a
large house in the Hamptons and another in some
warmer clime. It was no wonder the poor despised the
rich. There was something blatantly corrupt about extreme self-indulgence, while so many scratched for sur-
vival. And the inevitable charity didn't ease the distrust,
it only deepened it. Even the poor knew these people
weren't providing shelter for the homeless. They were
entertaining themselves with a party. One that was
fully tax-deductible. Yet, without it, the true poor
would have even less. And that, Devlin thought, was
something that only deepened the hatred. A self-styled
largess that was based on whim, and personal pleasure,
and a need for public recognition rather than concern.
He decided the city's homicide detectives were lucky
the poor didn't read the society pages.

He wandered among the knots of people, studying
faces, body language. It was a handsome, well-attired
group, pleased with who they were. He wondered what
he would be like if he were suddenly dropped into
this world, as Adrianna had been. Or the seemingly
vulnerable priest he had just met. He questioned if it
would change his needs, his priorities. The things that
mattered to him. He decided he was lucky he would

never find out. He had always been a sucker for temptation.

He took a glass of wine from a passing maid, wondering what she thought of it all as she rode a filthy and dangerous subway home. He wondered if Mrs. Barrows worried about the maid getting home safely, or if she even knew where she lived.

He looked past the people and studied his hostess's possessions. Modern paintings covered the walls, and he thought he recognized a Jasper Johns, one of the few contemporaries he knew anything about. To his left was a glass-enclosed case that held what looked like pre-Columbian figures. He knew from an earlier investigation that they could command outrageous prices if real. He also knew that most of the figures bought at those prices were fakes. The rich didn't have to be smart, he thought. They only had to be rich.

"You look like a man visiting the zoo for the first time."

He turned and found Melissa Coors' décolletage hovering in the attack position. She had apparently given up on the priest, or had sent him scurrying off to safeguard his celibacy.

"That obvious, huh?"

"I thought you'd be making the rounds, ferreting out information about failing companies." She offered up a knowing look. "If that's what you really do. Writing about stocks, I mean."

"Actually, I'm a cat burglar casing the joint," Devlin said.

"That's probably closer. Vincent doesn't believe you're a business writer, you know."

"Vincent's directed too many plays. What happened to our priest? Did he shake everyone down?"

"No, that comes later. Our hostess will take center stage, get everyone's attention at once, and urge them to whip out their checkbooks." Melissa smiled. "It works better that way. Provides a little social pressure."

"I wonder how many of the checks bounce," Devlin said.

"From this group? I doubt if any do. It's too important to them to be invited back."

Devlin glanced toward Adrianna, and saw that the priest had now joined Umberto's little group. "It looks like our priest is cutting in on Umberto's sales pitch," he said.

"Umberto doesn't have a prayer," Melissa said. She grinned. "Mmmm, not a bad pun," she added. "But the priest is selling a tax deduction. All Umberto has to offer is an investment in a soon-to-be-famous—*maybe*—young artist. In today's economy the sure thing always wins. Just ask anyone trying to get backers for a Broadway play."

"Sounds like you know Umberto," Devlin said. "I just met him for the first time this morning."

Melissa shrugged. "Art dealers, theater people, writers, whatever. They all move in the same circles, or try to. You go where the money is, or get dragged along because someone else thinks you should be there." She looked around the room, as if studying it herself. "And the people who have it like to have you around from time to time. You provide an interesting curiosity. Being a patron of the arts is very in these days." She tossed her hair back with a flip of her head. "So we all stumble across each other from time to time. Can't be helped."

"What do you think of him? Umberto?"

Melissa laughed. "I never trust latent homosexuals or celibates," she said. "They confuse the issue and strip me of any advantage."

Devlin fought off a smile, refusing to rise to the bait. He couldn't imagine the woman being unwillingly stripped of anything. "You can't be that jaded," he said.

Melissa slipped her arm in his, and began walking him toward a buffet visible through a doorway to an adjoining room. "Honey, you haven't even seen jaded yet," she said. "Let's eat. I'm starving."

*   *   *

Devlin lost Melissa in the buffet line. She was spirited away by an older, more distinguished-looking man who appeared more inclined toward her cleavage than anything the hostess had laid out for her guests. As Devlin left the line, plate in hand, he found himself suddenly confronted by another woman. She was tall, blond, and striking, with the face of a magazine model. He recognized her immediately. Cass Walker had just begun to make her mark in New York television when Devlin had fled the city years earlier.

"You look incredibly familiar to me," Cass said. "Have you been in the news recently?"

Devlin felt an uncomfortable chill. As beautiful as the woman was, it was still an unpleasant way to have a very thin cover blown. "It's the face," he said. "I look like one of those people who are always waving their hands behind the cameras."

Cass cocked her head to one side and studied his face. "No, you don't," she said. There was a hint of recollection in her eyes. They were the same vivid blue he had seen on the tube, but they lacked the touch of innocence and wonder she projected there. Now they were distinctly tough. "I can't place you," she said. "But I will." She laughed. Partly at herself, he thought. "Anyway, you're a delicious-looking man." She smiled at him. "How's the food?"

Devlin had the distinct feeling he had suddenly turned into an interesting side dish. "I haven't tried it yet," he said.

Cass plucked a shrimp from his plate. "Let me taste this," she said, almost as an afterthought. She bit into the shrimp with a hint of the lascivious, then smiled at him again. "I will place you, you know," she added. It seemed a challenge, the way she said it. "I always do." She paused a moment, her arresting blue eyes slightly playful. "Speaking about doing. How about you? What you do, I mean?"

"I write about stocks," Devlin said. "For a brokerage newsletter. Very boring."

"Which brokerage house?"

Devlin struggled to find a name. "Merrill Lynch," he said. It was the first to come to his suddenly empty mind, and one large enough, he hoped, that she'd find his claim difficult to verify.

Her eyes became playful again. "Got a good tip?" she asked. Her lips curved up slightly at the intended double meaning.

"Buy short, sell long," he said.

She pursed her lips, as if pained by the mundane answer. "I like long," she said, still playing. "But you look too . . ." She paused, seeking the right word, then gave up. "Too . . . something, to be a business writer." She began to turn away, then cast him one more look over her shoulder. "But I'll get you," she added. "I always do."

And then she was gone.

Melissa's predictions proved correct. When everyone had eaten, the hostess brought the priest forward, formally introduced him as their honored guest, Father James Hopkins, and offered a brief but glowing synopsis of his work with the homeless. There was genteel applause, which Rachel Barrows seemed to take as affirmation of her choice in charities. She smiled widely, then launched into her plea for "generous support."

Checkbooks flew to hand, and expensive pens scratched in amounts. Devlin sighed inwardly as he wrote in a one, followed by two zeros. It was more than he could reasonably afford, given the expense of a growing child. But it wouldn't break him, and he was certain it would be among the smallest of the checks received. Certainly not generous enough to warrant a return invitation. But still an expensive way to maintain a cover story that already had its doubters.

Devlin watched as a maid collected the checks on a silver tray. Like a church service with cocktails, he mused. Even the priest seemed mildly uncomfortable.

He stood next to the hostess, shifting his feet, making eye contact with various guests and forcing a smile. It was a tough way to make a living, Devlin thought. High-class panhandling. He hoped Father Jim raked it in tonight. Being able to spread it around to enough needy people might make it all worthwhile.

It was midnight when the party began to peter out, early for a New York gathering. They had all come together again—Umberto, Brenden Brooks, Vincent, Melissa, Adrianna, Gabrielle, and Devlin—and they were watching Father Jim thank Rachel Barrows and pocket the loot.

"He's a wonderful man," Gabrielle said. "Very committed. Working every minute for the people who come to him."

"He told me once he had worked in the archdiocese," Vincent offered. "He must have been a real up-and-comer to be brought into that den of papist pros at such a tender age. I always wondered why he left."

"I didn't know that," Gabrielle said. "But I suppose he wanted to commit himself to a greater good."

Father Jim joined them, his face slightly flushed.

"A good take, Father?" It was Brenden Brooks. His words were slightly slurred, and no matter how much his donation had been, Devlin doubted it would cover the wine he had drunk.

The priest only smiled, but Melissa pressed him. Her breasts were again in the assault mode, and she was enjoying the discomfort they were causing. "Tell us how big it is, Father," she urged, the play on words obviously intended.

There was momentary silence, everyone too stunned or uncertain how to react. Umberto recovered first. His lips pinched together and his eyes blazed at Melissa. But he could do little more than let out a short, angry huff of displeasure. Melissa ignored him. She continued to stare at Father Jim.

The priest shook his head, his own eyes off to one side, away from the view she was offering. "I really don't know. I haven't counted it. But Mrs. Barrows' gift was ten thousand, so whatever the total is, it will help us do a great deal for our people."

Gabrielle calmly suggested they all be on their way.

Umberto took Adrianna's arm and led her off, leaving Devlin with Brooks. Vincent and Melissa were behind him, and he suddenly heard hushed but angry words.

"You use that drunken mouth of yours like some goddamned street walker."

Devlin turned just as Melissa's hand moved toward Vincent's face. Her eyes were wild, her mouth twisted. Vincent caught her wrist and began twisting it.

Devlin reached out and grabbed Vincent's arm. "Let her go or I'll hurt you," he hissed. He held Vincent's eyes. The small scar on Devlin's cheek had whitened, something that happened only when he was close to violence.

Vincent released Melissa's wrist, then pulled his arm away. "You might be biting off more than you could handle," he snapped.

Devlin gave him a cold smile. "It would be fun to find out, asshole."

Melissa straightened, shook herself as though shedding her anger. "I'm all right," she said. "Chalk it up to artistic temperament. For both of us."

Devlin nodded, his eyes still hard on Vincent. Then he turned and walked away. Brooks immediately faded from his side, joining Vincent and Melissa. He obviously hadn't made a friend there, either, he decided.

One by one everyone stopped by the door, thanked their hostess, gathered coats in the outer hall, and headed for the two elevators. Devlin noted there was no tipping of the maid at the coatrack. Benevolence obviously did not extend to paid servants.

They reached the lobby still in one group, and Devlin wondered if Vincent's macho would return and force him to try to see Adrianna home. He doubted the man would risk a rejection. Not in front of Melissa. Not after what had just happened upstairs.

Devlin took Adrianna's elbow and guided her through the lobby. As he moved away, he heard another whispered exchange. He didn't hear what Vincent said, but he heard Melissa's whispered reply: "Fuck off, Vincent." He glanced back and saw they were glaring at each other again. But this time Vincent's hands were firmly at his sides.

The doorman was in the street, hailing cabs for a queue, and Devlin quickly joined it. Adrianna was wearing the same red cape she had worn that morning, and a heavy breeze blew it out, then back around her; it whipped her dark hair about her face. He thought she looked very beautiful.

The queue moved closer to the curb. Vincent and Melissa were just behind them now, and Adrianna—unaware of what had happened upstairs—had just started to turn toward him. Suddenly Devlin felt her stiffen. He looked at her. She was staring up and across Park Avenue. He followed her gaze. Standing under a streetlight, on the opposite side of the avenue, was a figure in a brown, hooded robe.

"Him?" he asked.

"I don't know. I think so," Her voice was trembling.

"Get back inside," Devlin snapped.

He left the queue, and in three quick strides was in the street. He hesitated momentarily to check the traffic, then raced across the first section of the divided roadway, and vaulted the low iron fence of the median divider. The figure in the robe seemed surprised by the suddenness of the assault, and for a moment he stood transfixed. Now he turned and ran.

Park Avenue, even more than most New York streets, is a constant raceway of flying traffic. But Devlin ignored it. He jumped the second low iron fence and darted into the street. There was a screech of brakes, the blast of a car horn, but he kept moving. He hit the sidewalk full tilt and turned south.

The figure rounded the corner at 73rd Street, headed west, only ten yards ahead now. Devlin turned the corner and stepped up his pace. His pistol was in an ankle holster, and the thought of stopping, getting it, flashed through his mind. He rejected it, pushed himself harder, hoping the knife the killer had used on the women wasn't already in his hand.

Devlin was almost abreast of the fleeing figure when he pushed out hard with both hands. He caught the man squarely in the back, and the force of the blow sent him flying forward, crashing face first on the sidewalk.

Devlin reached down and pulled the pistol from its holster, then stood and kicked the man viciously in the thigh.

"Move, and I'll blow your fucking head off," he snapped.

The man's hands were stretched out in front of him, and Devlin could see they were empty. "Roll over," he growled.

"Don't fuckin' shoot me, man." The voice was a terrified plea, ragged and phlegm-choked. "I didn't do nothin'. Don't shoot me, man. Don't."

"Do it!" Devlin snapped.

The figure rolled slowly onto his back, hands held out in front of him, as if pleading or hoping to ward off a blow. "Please, man. Please."

Devlin stared into the face. It was haggard, unshaven, hollow-eyed, the trembling lips strewn with sores. A trickle of blood oozed from a cut on his forehead. It was a face Devlin had seen thousands of times as a cop. One of the city's endless supply of street junkies.

Devlin squatted before the man, keeping the snubnosed pistol clearly in his line of vision. "Who told you to stand there?" he snapped. "Tell me, or I'll blow your fucking head off."

"I don't know, man." The junkie's body shook, visible even under the heavy robe. "It was just some old dude. Gave me twenty bucks to wear this thing and stand across from that building until somebody saw me and looked shook up about it." The hands were back toward his face now, palms up, pleading like his voice.

"What did he look like?"

The head shook back and forth. "I don't know, man. Just some dude. Had on a gray beard that looked fake, ya know. Like it wasn't real." The hands trembled violently. "All I saw was the twenty, man. He said there'd be more if I did it. And more jobs too. Said he'd be watching to see if I done what he said. Man, all I wanted was the fuckin' bread, ya know?"

"And he sent you down to the Village yesterday. To the doctor's office. Right?"

The junkie seemed confused. "No, man. What are you talkin' about?"

"The Village," Devlin snapped. "An apartment building near Washington Square. You didn't go there wearing this thing?" Devlin jabbed at the robe with his pistol.

The junkie shook his head. His eyes were wild and frantic. "No, man. Just here. No place else. Honest."

Devlin glared at him. "You lie to me, I'll blow your fucking eyes out."

The junkie kept shaking his head. "Honest, man. Honest. Just here. That's all."

Devlin didn't want to believe him, but saw no reason for the man to lie. He decided to change tactics. "Where was he gonna give you the rest of the money?" Devlin demanded. The revolver had inched closer to the man's face, turning his voice into a babbling near screech.

"He said he'd find me. Just like the first time. I hang in the park, man. Near the Strawberry Fields. That's where my connection hangs. I'm there every day. Rain or fuckin' shine. Any time after noon."

Devlin stood, took a step back, and lowered the revolver to his side. "Take that robe off and leave it," he said. He thought of asking for some ID, but knew it would be useless with a stone junkie. But he'd be able to find him. If his connection worked the west side of

Central Park, the man would be there. Just like he said. Rain or fucking shine. "What's your name?" he snapped.

"They call me Juice," the man said. He was up now, stripping off the robe.

Devlin reached out and snatched it from him. "You go there tomorrow. Wait for this guy," he said. "You don't, I'll find your fucking ass."

The man, who Devlin saw now was only in his early twenties, and skinny, was bouncing from foot to foot, anxious to be away but afraid to try to run.

"You a cop, man?" he whined.

"I'm your worst fucking nightmare," Devlin said. "I'm a cop who'll blow your fucking ass off, you don't do what I say. You got that?"

"I got it, man. I'll be there. You can take it to the bank."

The man was practically hopping now. Devlin let out a long breath. "You're not there, I come looking for you," he said. "Now, get out of here."

He watched the junkie move down the street. He was walking as fast as he could short of a run, uncertain if running still might not get him shot. Devlin turned and walked back to the corner, rolling the robe into a ball as he did.

At the corner he stopped at a pay telephone, fished a quarter from his pocket, and dialed the home number Eddie Grogan had given him. Miraculously, Grogan answered.

He explained what had happened, told him he had the robe, and Grogan agreed to pick it up the next morning and take it to the lab for tests.

"His street name is Juice," Devlin said, describing the man. "You should have some men at the Strawberry Fields by noon. Find him and stake him out," he said. "It's probably useless, but you never know."

When he got back to the lobby, he found Adrianna inside with Vincent, Brooks, and Melissa.

Devlin held out the balled-up robe. "Lost him," he said. "He dropped this and ran like a rabbit."

"Do you really think it was him? The man who attacked you?" It was Melissa. She was staring at Adrianna, excited to suddenly find herself in a real drama. Devlin realized that Adrianna must have explained to the others, had had little choice but to do so. He moved quickly to cut off further conversation.

"We should get you home and call the police so they can get this thing and test it." He momentarily held out the robe, then extended his other hand to Adrianna.

Melissa turned to him. "You're a very interesting business writer, Paul." She was smiling at him.

"That's what I told him."

He turned to the sound of the voice. Cass Walker had just exited the elevator. "What's this about the police?" she asked. There was an eagerness in her eyes.

"Purse snatcher," Devlin said. He took Adrianna's arm and moved her quickly toward a waiting cab. Cass Walker watched them go, and a quick look back at her told Devlin she hadn't bought a word of it.

He told Adrianna what had happened as the cab headed west, crosstown.

"So somebody sent him. It wasn't him. Just some sick game of his. I . . ." She shook her head. "I guess I was hoping . . ." She let the thought die.

There was nothing Devlin could say to console her. He allowed the silence to play out between them.

"Why can't he just go away?" she finally said. "Go to another city, another state. Take his madness with him." She was staring at the cab's glass partition, but Devlin doubted she saw it, or anything beyond it.

"We don't want him to go away," he said, keeping the words as gentle as he could. "We want to nail him. If he fades into the woodwork, you'll be left sitting and wondering if he'll ever come back." He reached out and took her hand, squeezed it lightly.

Adrianna slumped against him, burying her face in

the hollow of his shoulder. Her hair brushed his cheek, and the light, clean scent of it filled his nostrils. He stroked her shoulder, keeping her against him.

"I don't want him to disappear either," she said at length. "I don't want him to go somewhere and hurt someone else. I just want it over with. When you went after that man, tonight, I thought . . . I thought . . ."

"Yeah, I know. So did I," Devlin said. "But, like Eddie keeps telling me, nothing's easy in this case."

Devlin entered the loft first, pistol in hand. It was something he had explained when they had returned to New York. Something that would be done as a matter of course. Each time they returned to the loft, he would search it. And he would do it armed.

When he had finished, he went to the kitchen counter, then turned back to Adrianna. She was still next to the closed door, just where he had told her to stay. "I'll fix you a drink," he said. "It will help you sleep."

She came across the loft, slipped her arms around his waist, and laid her head against his chest. He held her, and they stood there without speaking.

"Last night I was thinking about you," she finally said. "Wondering how you felt about me. If you felt anything at all." She looked up at him. "When I saw you run out into the street tonight, I knew I didn't have to worry anymore."

Devlin ran his hands along her back. She had removed the cape, and his fingers caressed the soft silk of her blouse. He could feel there was nothing beneath it, and the thought of her naked, next to him, filled his mind.

She raised her head, looking up at him. It was as though she had read his thoughts. Her eyes, he decided, said everything he wanted to hear.

"Come to bed with me, Paul," she whispered. "Please, come to bed with me."

11

Melissa Coors stood under the shower, allowing the water to beat against her neck, hoping it would drain away the tension. Her neck and shoulders felt as if they'd been fused, and she knew she'd never be able to sleep until the muscles relaxed. Vincent, that bastard. He had caused it. Flipping out the way he had, when all she had done was have a bit of fun with that psalm-singing little priest. She tilted her head back, letting the water pound the top of her head. Father Jim. Who did he think he was kidding? His eyes had latched on to her tits like a hungry young wolf, then darted away every time he thought someone would notice. And he really played that vulnerable act to the hilt. Looked a little like that old silver screen idol Montgomery Clift. The same doe-like eyes, always looking like he needed someone to hug him. She smiled. Old Clift had melted the ladies' hearts as they sat in the audience, munching their popcorn. And they never suspected he liked little boys better than little girls. Melissa let out a short laugh. Probably the same thing here. You could never trust anyone who claimed they were celibate. Probably wished he had tits himself, then spent half his time masturbating in dark corners.

She turned and allowed the water to fall against her face, then down along her breasts. She tilted her head back and squeezed the water from her hair, then shook her head, making the long, wet strands fall free about her shoulders. And Vincent. Suddenly playing holier than thou. What a joke *that* was. She'd show him at rehearsal tomorrow. She'd give him a day he'd never forget.

But maybe it wasn't the priest. Maybe it was just a holdover from watching his new little chippie artist play up to *her* new friend. Vincent didn't like to be upstaged. It made him crazy. Really burned his buns. The small, short laugh came again. And maybe he didn't like seeing *you* flirt with him either, especially when you'd walked in the door on *his* arm. Fuck him. He just brought you there to tweak little Adrianna's nose. So he deserved whatever he got. And, besides, that Paul Devlin was an interesting piece of goods. One that might be worth looking into. But business writer, your ass. The man had cop written all over him. And that raised some interesting questions about what was really going on with sweet little Adrianna. Melissa reached down and turned off the water. Tune in tomorrow, she told herself.

She reached through the shower curtain and plucked a towel from a towel bar, then wrapped it around her head. Now she stepped through the curtain, took a second towel, and began patting herself dry. She glanced to her right. The massive mirror that dominated most of the opposite wall was fogged, and the entire room was filled with steam from the shower. She had forgotten to turn on the bathroom fan. It annoyed her that she had. She liked to look at herself when she emerged from a shower, her body wet and glistening. Her body was still good, and she liked to see it. It reaffirmed that she wasn't already losing it, even if she was pushing into the second half of her thirties. And, God, she told herself. These days a woman needs all the affirmation she can get.

She stepped through the bathroom door and into a small dressing room. A three-sided, full-length mirror covered one wall, allowing her to get three different views of her body. A long row of clothing hung behind her, but she didn't see them now. She saw only her body, and she began turning to each side, taking pleasure in each visage that came back at her.

The clothing behind her parted, and she froze in mid-turn as the hooded figure filled the mirror behind her own image. She screamed and jumped back, hands held out before her. But the figure was already rushing forward, the glint of a knife, held in one gloved hand, flashing in the bright light of the dressing room. A low feral growl filled the room as the figure crashed into her. The knife slashed down across her chest, the force of the assault sending her back against the mirror, a spray of blood splattering across all three sides of the glass. Melissa stared in disbelief, then slid slowly to the floor as a wash of color exploded across her eyes. She felt sudden pain in her chest, but it subsided quickly as her head began to swim, her vision blur, then fade. She heard one shouted word, but it seemed to come from great distance. "Bitch." But her world turned black before she ever realized it was the final word she would ever hear. The only other sound was the dull thud of the blade hitting her flesh again and again. Then only the gentle drip of water from the shower head in the adjoining room.

Adrianna lay quietly, watching the early morning light filter in through the windows. Outside, she could hear a gentle rain beat softly against the glass. The sound was soothing, and it held her pinned to the bed, unwilling to move.

It was the time of day she liked best, a time when she usually arose and began to work. But her mind was too somnolent, her body too languid. Movement seemed impossible. She could hear Devlin breathing as he lay next to her. And she could feel the warmth of his body beneath the covers. She turned toward him, her hand sliding up and across his chest, her cheek buried in the soft down pillow. His body felt strange, new. Even though she had known it so well all those years ago. But it was soothing too, like the sound of the rain. He had been a gentle, patient lover, she told herself. So much better than he had been ten years ago. He had never allowed his own eagerness to overshadow the need to give her pleasure. And he had done that. So beautifully, so softly. She could still feel his hands, the fingers caressing her, playing with her. His mouth moving slowly over her body, lingering over every secret part, flooding her mind with pleasure until she was certain she would cry out in sheer ecstasy. A small shiver of pleasure moved through her body now, and she could almost feel him inside her again. Her mind drifted, drowsily, as she clung to the feeling as long as she could, until sleep returned, claiming her again.

The telephone brought her back sharply, crudely. It was on the small table on her side of the bed, and she reached out weakly and pulled the receiver to her. The clock, next to the phone, read eight-thirty, and she realized she had slept another two hours. The light in the loft was brighter now, stronger, confirming the clock, and her mind registered the fact that the rain had stopped.

"Hello," she said, hearing the sound of sleep in her own voice. A voice barked back. It was Uncle Eddie, asking for Paul. She turned and nudged his shoulder with the phone, then watched as he took it and sat up. Then she closed her eyes again.

"Yeah," Devlin said, his own voice heavy with sleep. He rubbed the heel of his hand into one eye.

"Whadda ya do, sleep at the foot of her bed like a fucking watchdog?" Grogan's voice was sharp, caustic.

Devlin ignored him. "What is it?" he said.

"We got another victim." Grogan's voice had grown heavy. "Actress by the name of Melissa Coors. Seems she was about to be in a play your buddy Richards is directing. But not now. Chopped up real bad. Looks like our boy really lost it this time."

"Shit," Devlin said. He swung his feet out of bed, wide awake now. "You sure it was our guy?"

"No question. He did the scar, everything. Just didn't wait to enjoy it this time."

"She was at that party we went to last night. She came with Richards. Left with him too," Devlin said.

"Well, isn't that interesting. We haven't even had time yet to check out her movements yesterday."

"Who found her?" Devlin could feel Adrianna sit up behind him.

"Cleaning woman," Grogan said. "Came in a little before eight, and found things a little messier than she bargained for. Thank Christ the 911 operator spoke Spanish. This woman lost any English she ever had."

"You got there fast."

"Heard the call when I was driving in to the precinct. Sounded like it could be one of ours. Woman. Murdered. Good neighborhood. So I came over. Got here just as the sector car was pulling up." Grogan paused. "Glad I didn't have breakfast. This one was bad, Paul. Worst one yet."

"FBI on their way?" Devlin asked.

"Not yet. But they will be. Thought I'd call you first." He paused again. "If she was at the party with you, it's gonna be hard to keep your name outta things. Vincent or somebody is gonna mention it."

"Yeah. I know," Devlin said.

"We'll do what we can," Grogan said. "But it don't look good. Listen, let me get rid of the Fibbies, and finish up here. Then I'll come over for that robe, and fill you in more."

"Yeah, I'll wait for you," Devlin said. "And let's find a way to have Gabrielle Lyons take a look at the body. I want to know what she thinks this means. The way he lost it. The change in the way he kills."

"I'll see what I can do," Grogan said.

Devlin turned and handed the phone back to Adrianna. Her eyes were wide, and her face looked drawn and suddenly pale.

"Who?" she asked. She had heard enough of the conversation to realize what had happened.

"Melissa Coors," he said. "Eddie said it was the same perp. She was scarred. But this time he didn't wait and drag it out."

"Oh, my God," she said. The phone dropped from her hand.

Grogan arrived shortly after noon. He had Gabrielle Lyons with him. The woman went immediately to Adrianna, hugged her, and asked her how she felt.

"Shaky," Adrianna said.

"You wouldn't be normal if you didn't," Gabrielle said.

"I picked her up on the way," Grogan explained. "I'm going to take her to the autopsy, then back to Melissa's place. She says she needs to see everything to get a good picture of what happened with our killer. You wanna come too?"

"Yeah," Devlin said. "I want to get the same picture. But won't the feds be there?"

"They're still finishing up at the house. And they'll be a little late for the autopsy. I fudged the time it was supposed to start. Missed it by an hour." He grinned. "Must be age creeping up on me. You got that robe you told me about? I wanna drop it off at the lab on the way."

Devlin took Grogan to the robe, which was now stored in a plastic garment bag. Grogan reached inside and fingered it. "You have Adrianna feel this thing?"

"She says it's similar, best as she can tell. But nothing definite."

Grogan nodded. "By the way, I checked the lab. No prints on that key you gave me."

Devlin nodded. He hadn't expected to be that lucky. "What time is the autopsy?"

Grogan looked at his watch. "In two hours, according to the M.E. In three hours, as far as Mallory and his clowns are concerned." He grinned again.

"Who am I supposed to be?"

"Officially, one of my men. He'll be here, baby-sitting Adrianna." Grogan offered a wistful smile. "But the Fibbies are already on the scent. You can expect them banging on the door later today. They already went with one of my people to talk to Vincent. I expect your name to come up."

"So do I," Devlin said. "I don't think Vincent likes me very much." He shrugged. "Hell, we knew this game wouldn't last forever."

The medical examiner's office was on First Avenue, adjacent to Bellevue Hospital. They entered through a side loading area, where the meat wagons, as cops called them, disgorged the steady flow of unattended deaths that occurred in the city each day. Every death not attended by a physician had to be reviewed under law by the medical examiner, who then determined if an autopsy was needed. The constant influx of bodies kept the autopsy tables full, and gave the building's work area the look of a human butcher shop. And the pervading smell of putrefying flesh, mingled with formaldehyde.

Devlin had not been in the building in years and, like most cops, would have preferred never to be there again. But it all came back quickly. The dull, once white tile walls, the bodies left uncovered on gurneys, as though someone had forgotten them, and the smell. Always the smell.

He followed Grogan down a long corridor that led to the autopsy rooms. Gabrielle was at his side.

"Have you been to one of these before?" he asked.

"Not since school," she said. There was a tight, uncomfortable look on her face. "Pathology was never a favorite subject."

"Yeah, I know what you mean," Devlin said.

Grogan glanced through the small glass panels set in the autopsy room doors, until he found the one he wanted. He turned to Devlin and Gabrielle before entering.

"The M.E. on this is a kid named Michael Blair," he

said. "He handled the Sylvia Grant autopsy, so I asked for him on this one. The two cases are so close together I thought it'd be easier for him to spot any similarities." Grogan grinned. "But I ain't his favorite person." He shrugged. "Who can account for taste?"

"Perhaps if you stopped calling him kid, he'd grow to love you, as we all do, Eddie," Gabrielle said.

"Hey, what can I tell you? Everybody under fifty looks like a kid to me." He winked at the psychiatrist. "Especially you."

They entered the autopsy room, which had three tables working at once, and moved to the one where Michael Blair had already begun dictating vital statistics—height, weight, age, physical condition—into a microphone suspended above the stainless steel table.

Melissa Coors lay before them, her eyes partially opened, lips stretched into a rictus. A gaping, bloodless, undulating scar filled her left cheek. She was no longer beautiful, Devlin thought. And the body she had so proudly displayed only last night looked flaccid now, the muscles slack and sagging in death. He looked at the slashing wounds across her breasts, the multiple punctures that had been made throughout her torso. He didn't need a shrink to tell him uncontrolled rage had been at work here. Only someone temporarily or permanently mad could kill this way.

"Dear Lord," Gabrielle said. "I hope the first wound killed her." She closed her eyes momentarily.

"Who are these people?" It was Blair and he was staring at Grogan, asserting his authority in this, his sanctum.

Grogan nodded toward Devlin, giving him the name of one of the detectives working the case, one he was certain Blair had not met. "And this is Dr. Gabrielle Lyons," he said. "She's a police psychiatrist who's helping us."

Blair nodded to Gabrielle, realizing some professional courtesy was required. He ignored Devlin, which was okay. No footprints, no foul, Devlin told himself.

Blair was short, stocky, built like a baseball catcher, Devlin noted. He was in his early thirties, blond and boyish-looking—undoubtedly only a few years out of residency—and impressed with the job he had landed himself. He probably believed cops weren't especially bright, Devlin thought, and was now forced to deal with Eddie Grogan, who knew more about murder than he would learn in the next twenty years.

"We need your help, Doc," Devlin said. He wanted to inflate the man a bit. Get him past any intimidation he felt dealing with Grogan. "We have to know if this is the same perp who killed Sylvia Grant."

Blair drew himself up slightly, gave a curt nod, and tapped a gloved finger against Melissa's chest. The gesture seemed suddenly obscene. Devlin could still see her the night before, taunting everyone with her low-cut dress. Now all that was left was a butchered husk. "The knife wounds should tell us," Blair said. "If he used the same knife. All knives have their own telltale pattern."

Devlin shot Grogan a quick look to silence any comment. Every cop knew what the M.E. had just said—they learned it early, back in their academy training. "That's interesting," Devlin said. "I guess you could also tell from anything you found under the victim's nails? DNA? Stuff like that?"

"Certainly," Blair said. "Very astute of you, Officer." He shot a quick look at Grogan, who was making a point of studying his shoes. Blair inflated himself a bit more. "Shall we begin?" he said.

He took a large, butcher-like knife and began his opening Y-shaped incision, starting at the pubis, then cutting up to the sternum and across to each shoulder.

Devlin turned to Gabrielle. "There's no need for you to watch this," he said. "If you want, I'll wait outside with you."

Gabrielle nodded and turned away.

"We'll meet you outside," Devlin said to Grogan. He

threw him a cautioning look, silently ordering him to behave himself with Blair. Grogan grinned at him.

Devlin took Gabrielle's elbow and started toward the hall. At another table, a pathologist had begun removing viscera from the body cavity of a young man. He lifted the man's liver and plopped it in a scale so it could be weighed. Devlin averted his eyes and continued toward the door.

Outside, he leaned against the fender of a morgue wagon and drew a deep breath, enjoying air free of the fetid odor he had left behind.

"You don't much care for those little mortality plays either, do you?" Gabrielle asked. She was looking at him closely, studying him, Devlin thought.

"Never did," he said.

"That's something most cops wouldn't admit," she said. "That it bothered them."

"They do among themselves," Devlin said. "They just don't admit to any weakness when there are civilians around."

"Civilians are the enemy?" Gabrielle suggested.

"Something like that," Devlin said.

Gabrielle took a cigarette from her purse, and quickly filled her lungs with smoke.

"Thought you didn't like those things. Didn't allow them in your office," Devlin said.

She smiled. "So I'm a fake," she said. "And they do get the smell of that place out of your nose." She extended the pack. "Want one?"

Devlin nodded, took one, and filled his own lungs. He hadn't smoked in years, but now he wanted to.

"You were good in there," Gabrielle said. "It was obvious our young doctor was intimidated by Eddie, needed to play king of his own court. You helped him do it. That was very perceptive of you. Clever also."

She was dressed in another expensive suit. This one with a skirt instead of pants. And Devlin noticed her legs were quite attractive. He also noticed she was wearing makeup again, and that she seemed to be flirting with him.

"Just wanted him to help. And not get all caught up in any dick-waving contest," Devlin said.

Gabrielle let out a short, pleasurable laugh. "He'll help now," she said. "If only to prove you right in your perception of his abilities." She laughed again. "Men are easy that way. But it's usually only women who know that. You should have gone to shrink school."

Devlin blew a stream of smoke toward the rising red brick facade of Bellevue. "There are a lot of people who think I'm a better candidate *for* the couch," he said.

"Because you're able to think like a serial killer?"

Devlin shot her a quick glance.

"It's what Eddie thinks," she said. "And if it's true, it's a unique talent. But if our killer knew, you'd become the contest for him. Every bit as much as Adrianna is."

Devlin looked away. "Maybe I already have. At least it's starting to feel that way."

"Then I hope you're up for it," she said. "It's a very dangerous game. With a very ingenious opponent."

Eddie Grogan came out the side entrance half an hour later. There was a big grin on his face. "Our genius says his preliminary exam indicates it was the same knife. He's gonna run some tests on the scrapings he took from under her nails. Looks like cloth from the robe. That should confirm it was the same perp." The grin widened. "Ain't science grand," he added.

Grogan pulled the unmarked car in front of a fire hydrant a few doors from Melissa Coors' house on West 85th Street. He tossed a card on the dashboard that stated the car was on police business. It was intended to keep meter maids from issuing parking tickets, but invariably had the opposite effect. It seemed to draw them like flies to fresh excrement.

They climbed the front steps of the renovated brownstone. There was a band of yellow crime-scene tape across the front door, and two uniformed cops stood on the stoop guarding the entry.

"The Fibbies gone?" Grogan asked one of the uniforms.

"About half an hour ago," the cop said.

Grogan glanced back at Devlin. "Must be on their way to the autopsy," he said. "Hope they're not disappointed." He was grinning, enjoying the game he was playing.

Melissa Coors' choice of where to live surprised Devlin. West 85th Street between Columbus and Amsterdam avenues was a good neighborhood, but not the address he'd expect a Broadway star to choose. It was a neighborhood that had undergone gentrification almost twenty years ago. Then many of the once elegant brownstones—which had become little more than rundown rooming houses—had been bought up and returned to their former grandeur. But the neighborhood hadn't been fully transformed. Fine shops and restaurants had sprung up on Columbus, and the hookers who had once plied their trade there had vanished. But the odd drug dealer still worked the streets. And the area still lacked the high-priced prestige and security of a Central Park West, or the more fashionable areas of the upper East Side. Devlin mentioned it to Grogan as they made their way past the two uniformed cops and ducked under the yellow tape.

"Yeah, I talked to some neighbors about that," Grogan said. "Seems she bought the place about five years ago. Right after her first big hit on Broadway. It was all she could afford then, and she told people she wanted it as a sort of security blanket, given the way stars rise and fall in her business. But then there was another hit show, and her name became big box office. But she stayed." He shrugged. "Who can figure? According to her agent, they talked about her taking her act out to Hollywood and testing the waters there. I think she waited a little too long for that too."

The interior of the house had been restored to its original Victorian style, and that surprised Devlin as well. It didn't seem to fit the woman. The high ceilings and walls had been painted in the dark colors favored at the turn of the century, and the rooms had been furnished in the delicate, uncomfortable furniture of the time. There were potted palms scattered about and heavy drapes covering the tall windows. In all it looked like a house better suited to an aging maiden aunt than a well-known Broadway star.

Grogan nodded to the long stairway opposite the front door. "It happened upstairs. In a dressing room just off the master bathroom on the next floor," he said. "Let's have a look, then get the hell out of here. This one's got the media drooling, so I wanna be in and out before one of them vultures comes back to shoot some footage of the outside of the building. It was a real circus here this morning."

They climbed the stairs, moved down a long hall back toward the front of the building, then entered a large master bedroom that faced the street. Here the furnishings were more modern, more in keeping with Devlin's perceptions of the woman. The room was dominated by a queen-sized bed. There was a reading area set before the windows, with a chaise longue and a large, comfortable-looking chair. The table between them held a number of scripts that looked well thumbed.

The walls were brighter here, and the room had more a sense of being lived in. Devlin glanced at the still made bed. The dress Melissa had worn the night before lay haphazardly across it, her pantyhose and shoes on the floor beside it.

Grogan followed his gaze. "We figure she came in, undressed, and went straight to the shower," he said. He indicated the adjoining room with his chin. "Our boy caught up with her in the dressing room right after she finished. She never made it back out," he added.

They moved toward the dressing room, Gabrielle a

bit reluctantly, Devlin thought. "You want to wait here?" he asked.

She shook her head. "No. I should see it if I'm going to help."

"Welcome to the butcher shop," Grogan said as they crowded into the smaller room.

The room was brightly lit by a row of lights above the full-length mirrors, adding to the grotesqueness of the scene. The mirrors and the floor were splattered with dried blood. Clothing had been ripped from the rack opposite and lay in crumbled heaps on the floor. There was a taped outline of where Melissa's body had been found, legs spread obscenely, arms at right angles as if awaiting crucifixion. And there were traces of excrement and dried urine, the body's inevitable final offering in death.

"Why haven't they cut away the carpet yet?" Devlin asked.

"They're flying in a special forensics team from Quantico," Grogan said. "I guess they don't trust our boys to do it."

He turned, gesturing with one hand, taking in the small, cramped space. "We figure our perp attacked her right after she came in here," Grogan said. He pointed at the blood on the mirrors. "He cut her here first, probably one of the slashing wounds on her chest, based on the blood pattern. Then he drove her back and started the serious cutting. We think she died pretty quick. There ain't a lot of blood on the carpet, so we figure her heart stopped pumping after a few minutes." He made a rueful face. "The M.E.'s report will tell us how much blood was left in her body."

"Our killer was frantic," Gabrielle said suddenly. "He couldn't contain himself, couldn't wait to get to her."

"Why do you say that?" Devlin asked.

"It's confining in here. A more difficult place to strike out. More difficult to do the other things he likes to do."

Devlin glanced at Grogan.

The older cop nodded. "Yeah, she was sexually assaulted. But again, no sperm. Blair still thinks some artificial device was used."

"He just couldn't wait for her to come out into the bedroom," Gabrielle said. "The rage was too intense. It would have been better for him in the bedroom. He would have had more room." She gave a small shudder. "To do the other things. To make that very precise scar that seems so important to him. And the sexual molestation." She glanced at Grogan. "The body stayed here? He didn't move it?"

He nodded.

"No, he just couldn't wait. The need to kill her was too overpowering."

"Why?" It was Devlin again.

Gabrielle shook her head. "Perhaps because he can't get to Adrianna and he fears he won't be able to for a long time. Maybe he senses you're there, what you're doing. And this frustrates him. Or perhaps it was something that Melissa did, or that he perceived she did."

"At the party last night?"

"It could be. Or perhaps it was something she did long ago. She may be one of a long list of victims he has in mind."

"Why do you think it might have come from something at the party?" Grogan asked.

"She was being aggressive, sort of flaunting her sexuality," Devlin said. "It was just a game, but it could have set somebody off." He stared at the taped outline. "And it fits with the junkie. Whoever sent him knew Adrianna was going to be there. Maybe arranged to be there himself. Richards only told her about it that afternoon—around noon. And she called Umberto later, told him about it."

"We better find out who else she told," Grogan said. "And if anyone called the hostess and asked to be invited at the last minute."

"Adrianna told me," Gabrielle said. Both men looked at her. "I called her yesterday to see how she was. She told me about the party. I didn't tell her I was already going. I didn't want to discourage her. Make her feel she was going to be surrounded by all of us again." She shook her head. "I urged her to go. I thought it would be good for her to get out. Perhaps she told others as well."

"Sounds like she spread the word around pretty good," Grogan said.

"We also have to find out who Richards told," Devlin said. "Brenden Brooks was at the party, and he was at the theater. Maybe Richards told him about it, told him Adrianna would be there."

"Who's he?" Grogan asked.

"The playwright of Richards' new play."

"And who knows who the fuck he told. Or Melissa Coors for that matter," Grogan added.

"But it narrows it down a little. I think our perp made a mistake, hiring our friend Juice," Devlin said. "He gave us a little peek at what he knew, and when. And Juice saw him, heard his voice."

"Yeah," Grogan said. "But like you told me, Juice needed a fix. The guy coulda been the fucking president of the United States, and Juice wouldn't have recognized him." He tilted his head to one side. "And he said the guy was wearing a phony beard and all."

Devlin nodded. "But we better bring him in. Have him look at a couple of people on the Q.T."

"He won't be hard to find," Grogan said. "I'll have him stashed at the Seven-Eight in Brooklyn. We can talk to him there without having to worry about the Fibbies showing up. Those assholes don't even know where Brooklyn is."

"I'd like to interview him," Gabrielle said. "Perhaps even try hypnosis to see what his subconscious can recall."

"I thought hypnosis didn't work with alcoholics and addicts," Devlin said.

"Not always, no. But it is worth trying." She stared

at the bloodstained mirrors again, then closed her eyes. "I think I'll wait in the other room."

When she had left, Devlin pushed the door closed and spoke to Grogan in a lower voice. "I want to find out about this priest too. Father James Hopkins. He runs a shelter for the homeless somewhere in the theater district. He was at the party, and Melissa pushed him hard. Kept shoving her chest in his face. It upset him. And he's the one who invited Vincent, and told him to bring a date. And he knew Vincent was seeing Adrianna."

Grogan nodded toward the closed door. "Why don't you want her to hear this?" he asked.

"She seems to know this Hopkins, and I don't want her becoming defensive about any suspects we're considering. I think we're going to need her to find this guy, and I don't want to do anything that's going to make her hold back on us." Devlin hesitated, thinking. "How did the perp get in?" he finally asked.

"Front window on the garden level," Grogan said. "Those old bars on the windows aren't worth shit. More for show than protection. He just pried them back far enough to be able to squeeze through, then cracked the window, and Shazam, he was in."

"How big was the opening?" Devlin asked.

"Not real big. I doubt you or I could get through. Why?"

"The priest is thin," Devlin said. "Pathetically so. But Richards and Umberto aren't heavyweights either. And our boy Vincent had a little tiff with Melissa last night."

"You don't say." Grogan grinned. "When the Fibbies find that out, they'll be all over him like holy on the pope."

"Couldn't happen to a nicer guy."

Devlin decided to make a quick trip out to his sister's house in Queens. He wanted to see his daughter before they rounded up Juice, questioned him, and had Gabrielle attempt hypnosis.

Gabrielle asked if she could accompany him, explaining that she would very much like to meet his daughter. "I could use some normalcy right now," she said as they climbed into a taxi on Columbus Avenue. "I cleared my calendar for the day when I heard about Melissa's murder. I suspected our killer had hit some new plateau, and I thought I'd better be available." She shook her head. "After seeing her body and the crime scene, I'm afraid my suspicions were correct."

Devlin sat back and looked out the window. The taxi had turned east and was about to enter the roadway that cut across Central Park. It appeared so quiet and peaceful, a glade in the heart of the city. And yet he had begun so many murder investigations there. Including the last one he had worked in New York. It was one case he preferred to forget. One that had ended with the death of another cop. A cop who'd been his friend, one whose blood was on his hands.

He closed his eyes momentarily, then turned to Gabrielle. "What are the odds that Melissa's actions at the party last night pushed our boy over the edge?" he asked.

Gabrielle tilted her head to one side as if weighing the idea. "As opposed to being on some kind of list he keeps?" She pursed her lips. "I would say they're very high."

"Why?"

"The junkie, for one. His planned appearance, and then Melissa's selection as the next victim, make it very likely the killer was at the party," she said. "The two would be too much a coincidence otherwise." She watched Devlin nod in agreement. "Given that, I'd also have to conclude that Melissa was a random choice, one made at the spur of the moment. *Because* of something she did to enrage him. Otherwise it would be too complicated." She began tapping her fingers against her knee. "The killer obviously wanted to frighten Adrianna with the junkie. And I think he wanted to see and savor her reaction." She hesitated a moment, staring at him. "Perhaps yours as well. And why bother with that if he was already stalking Melissa?" She looked down at her hand, stopped the tapping. "Our killer, you see, is obsessed, and he would have been fixated on one or the other. Adrianna or Melissa. To be doing both doesn't make sense." She shook her head. "No, I think Melissa was a sudden choice, brought on by a sudden, uncontrollable rage." She stared at Devlin. "I think the way he killed her supports that."

"So it was something she did, or said to the killer," Devlin said.

"Not necessarily to the killer," Gabrielle said. Her voice sounded insistent about it. "He could just have observed her. Even from a distance. You have to remember that his mind undoubtedly plays out a very specific scenario about his victims. He believes he knows *what* they are. Perhaps even from just reading about them. Serial killers seldom have personal knowledge about their victims. They just *know* them. In their minds. And that's quite enough."

"And it was her sexual aggressiveness that provoked him?"

"Undoubtedly." Gabrielle turned in her seat and her eyes seemed to soften. "She *was* just a bit blatant," she said. "And in a way our killer was sure to notice. I believe he hates sexual women."

"Is that why he uses a device for penetration? Because he can't stand to do it himself?"

She thought about that a moment. "Or is incapable. We can't rule out that possibility." She sat back. "You have to remember that rape—and this is definitely rape—is not a sexual act. It's an act of power and control over the victim. The rapist is saying: 'See what I can do to you, or make you do to me.' That's where the gratification comes from, not from sexual stimulation and satisfaction."

"So you think it was payback time for Melissa. He was saying: 'You wanted it. Well, here it is.'"

A look of discomfort seized Gabrielle's face. "I want to say yes to that. But something tells me it's too simple an answer. That the real answer may be something even worse."

"Like what?" Devlin asked.

She shook her head. "I don't know, Paul. I just don't know."

Phillipa was playing outside when the cab pulled up in front of the house. She broke away immediately and ran to her father, who scooped her up in his arms.

"You're getting too heavy for this," he groaned. "I told your Aunt Beth to put you on a diet, but I guess she didn't listen."

"You're just getting old," Phillipa said, planting a big kiss on his cheek before he returned her to the ground.

He introduced Phillipa to Gabrielle, who beamed at the child in wonder, almost as if seeing some rare new species for the first time. She asked the child her age, her grade in school, and how she liked being back in New York. They were pro forma questions, but asked with a genuine sincerity, a true interest that Phillipa immediately picked up on. She seemed to like the woman right away, and was intrigued when Devlin explained she was a psychiatrist who was helping on the investigation.

"What do you do to help?" Phillipa asked. They were seated on the front steps of the house. Devlin had gone inside to tell his sister he was there.

"Well, I study what the killer's done," Gabrielle explained. "And I try to figure out why he's done it the way he has. From that, I try to develop an image of him. How old he is, what his background was probably like. Things like that. Then I try to predict how he's going to react next. What he might do, and why he might do it."

"Does it work?" Phillipa asked.

"Surprisingly well, a great deal of the time," Gabrielle said.

"But how can you say what someone is going to do?" The child was watching the older woman closely, open skepticism in her eyes.

"People react to things in certain ways," Gabrielle explained. "And their reactions are based on who they are; how they were raised; what happened to them in their own lives—the good, the bad." She stopped, reached out and stroked Phillipa's cheek. "The bad, most of all, I'm afraid. Often times people we consider bad were victims themselves at one time. And it changed the way they thought, how they reacted to certain things. In some cases to the extreme."

"We had a man in Vermont like that," Phillipa said. "Something bad happened to him when he was small, and later, when he was older, he started killing people." She seemed to think about it for a moment. "I liked him. He was very nice. Except for what he did."

"How is he now?" Gabrielle asked. "Was anyone able to help him?"

Phillipa shook her head. "He's dead." She looked sad about the fact. "They had to kill him."

Gabrielle sat quietly for a moment. *Had to kill him.* The sad look in the child's eyes seemed to indicate she understood the rationalization in the statement, or was beginning to. It never ceased to amaze her, the things children could intrinsically comprehend.

Devlin came out of the house. "Got time for a walk to the ice cream parlor?" he asked.

Phillipa started to smile, then caught herself and pointedly looked at the Mickey Mouse watch on her wrist. "I think I can squeeze it in," she said.

"Good," Devlin said. "Gabrielle told me she really had a craving for a cone, so I thought I'd bring you along if you had time." He took her hand, and they started down the street. "You remember the old ice cream place?" he asked.

"Sure," she said. "I've only been there a million times."

"I forgot," Devlin said. "I've only been there half a million."

They continued down the sidewalk, Gabrielle taking up a position on the other side of the child. Taking hold of her other hand.

"How's the case going?" Phillipa asked. She sounded very mature, more like a peer ready to offer advice. It made Gabrielle smile.

"Hard," Devlin said.

"You always say that," Phillipa intoned, her voice very sure of what she was saying. "But then you always catch them."

"Is what Phillipa said true, Paul?" Gabrielle asked. "Do you always catch the people you're after?"

They were in a cab headed back to Manhattan, and Devlin had been staring out the window, thinking about how much he hated leaving his daughter behind.

"She thinks so," he said. "She's a great support system."

"She's extremely bright. Beautiful too."

"Thank you." He looked at her. "You don't have any children?"

She shook her head. "No, I never married. Too wrapped up in my work." She offered a regretful smile. "And, unfortunately, I don't work with children, so I see a great deal less of them than I'd like."

"Did you come from a large family?"

Again, Gabrielle shook her head. "No, I was a foster child. I never knew my real parents."

The subject seemed mildly painful, and Devlin decided to drop it.

"I don't know what I'd do without Phillipa," he said at length. "She's the one person I'd do anything for."

Gabrielle reached out and put her hand on top of his. "It's the way it should be, Paul. Unfortunately, many children don't have parents who feel that way.

For too many they're a nuisance most of the time. They provide the parent with occasional pleasure, and then are dismissed." There was a trace of anger, or vehemence, in her voice, Devlin thought.

Her hand was still on top of his, had remained there far longer than necessary. Gabrielle seemed to read his thoughts and glanced down at her hand, then slowly removed it. But not before she smiled at him.

Devlin dropped Gabrielle off, told her they'd pick her up later for the interview with Juice, then returned to the loft. The detective who had been left to guard Melissa met him on the sidewalk.

"The Fibbies are upstairs," he said. "Thought you should know before you waltzed in there."

Devlin raised his eyebrows in resignation. "It had to happen sooner or later," he said. "You better let Eddie know. It could cause him some problems."

Devlin opened the door with his own key. There was no point in playing hide-and-seek any longer. It was only a matter of hours before the feds discovered who he was and what he was doing. But he wouldn't make it easy for them, he decided. He'd only tell them what he had to. And let them work for the rest.

Matthew Mallory and Wendy Wilson turned to the sound of the door. They were seated across from Adrianna, and now Mallory stood, stared at Devlin, then looked back at Adrianna.

"Who's this?" he asked.

"The name's Paul Devlin," he said as he crossed the room.

"You live here?" Mallory asked.

"Just visiting."

"But you have a key."

"Very observant," Devlin said. He walked to the sofa and took a seat next to Adrianna. "You know who I am. Now who are you?" he asked Mallory.

"NYPD," Mallory said. "We're investigating a murder. Lady named Melissa Coors. And—"

"Why don't you tell the lady the truth?" Devlin said, cutting him off. "You're FBI. Behavioral Science Unit. And you're investigating several murders. Four, I think."

Mallory glared at him. His square face had become suddenly red, and Devlin wasn't sure if it was from anger or embarrassment. He didn't really care.

"Who the hell are you?" Mallory snapped.

"Ex-NYPD. Detective. Homicide." He smiled. "Retired now. I'm an old friend of Adrianna's father. He was a cop too."

"You know Eddie Grogan?" Mallory's eyes had narrowed. The woman—Wendy Wilson—seemed to catch the look and imitated it.

"I've met him once or twice," Devlin said.

"You at this party last night?"

"Yeah, I was there. Good party." Mallory's face was growing redder. It was anger, Devlin decided.

He looked back at Adrianna. "You didn't tell us that. About him being there."

"I forgot," she said.

Mallory continued to stare at her, then turned back to Devlin. "You see some kind of argument between Melissa Coors and a guy named Vincent Richards?"

"Wasn't much of an argument," Devlin said.

"Somebody told us he tried to smack her, and some guy stopped him. You know who that might have been?"

"Your witness got it backward. She tried to smack him. He stopped her."

"You didn't answer my question."

"Best I can do," Devlin said.

Mallory stood, allowing his size—the bulk of his square body—to hover over Devlin. "I want to know what you're really doing here," he said.

"Visiting," Devlin said. "And making sure I'm the only visitor."

Mallory's head snapped back to Adrianna. "This is a bad idea," he said. "A very bad idea."

Adrianna's eyes suddenly blazed. "Why?" she said. "Are you afraid I'm going to scare your killer away? Make it harder for you to use me as bait?" Her lips were trembling. But not with fear. "You even lied to me about who you are. Why should I believe anything you say?"

Mallory started to speak, but Devlin cut him off. "I think you better get out of here. Before the lady decides to call the newspapers and tell them a little FBI bedtime story."

Mallory's jaw tightened, the muscles dancing along the bone. "That would be disastrous for her," he snapped.

"Could be you're right," Devlin said. "But it wouldn't be a walk in the park for you either."

12

Juice sat in a chair, twisting his hands. He was pale
and sweaty. There was a tic at the corner of one eye,
and the side of his mouth imitated it with uncontrolled
jerks.

Detectives had kept him under surveillance for two
hours while he waited for his connection in Central
Park. They had watched him make his buy, then had
followed him as he hurried off to find a secluded spot
to shoot up. No one else had approached him, and
they had grabbed him, as Grogan had ordered, before
he had been able to pump more heroin into his veins.
Now he was even more of a human wreck than he had
been all those hours ago. He was ready to do anything.
He would sell the clothes on his back for five minutes
alone. But the cops wouldn't give it to him. They had
locked him away in a holding cell in Brooklyn's Seven
Eight Precinct. They had even watched him when he
pissed. Then, finally, they had opened the cell door,
only to lock him away again. This time in an interrogation room.

Devlin watched him, feeling a sickening pity for the
man. He looked different than he had the previous
night—even more helpless, more pathetic. His face was
gaunt and haunted, with dark smudges beneath his
eyes, which darted about the room like a caged animal.
His hair was filthy and matted, so much so its real
color was a mystery, and Devlin could smell the putrid
odor that rolled off his body from a distance of eight
feet.

Devlin had brought Adrianna with him, but had left her downstairs with one of the detectives and a cup of bad coffee. Her face had registered distaste when she entered the precinct house, saw the dirt-encrusted walls, the scarred and battered furniture, the floors covered in stains no amount of cleaning would ever remove. It was what cops lived and worked with every day, and she had hated even the sight of it. He looked around the interrogation room he now sat in. It was a microcosm of every precinct he had ever worked in. Barren, battered, and roach-infested. Juice looked as though he belonged there. Devlin knew he did too.

He leaned forward, put a hard edge in his voice. "Let's pick up where we left off last night, Juice. I want a description of the man who approached you. Everything you can remember."

Juice twisted in his chair. "I gotta go to the bathroom, man," he pleaded. His voice was high and whiny and begging. "Please, man, I gotta go." They had allowed the man to keep his drugs as an inducement to talk—a silent promise that he would be able to go his way, do his thing, *if* he cooperated. He wanted them now.

Devlin nodded toward one of the detectives who had brought Juice in—a hard-faced mick named Mike Milligan, a man who looked like he'd enjoy beating the hell out of somebody. "Sure. But he goes with you."

Juice's eyes darted to Milligan, then he slumped in his chair. "Never mind, man. I'll hold it."

"So, tell me," Devlin said.

"Man, it's like I said last night, the dude was old. Gray beard an' all. He gave me twenty, that's all I looked at."

Grogan's eyes were boring into the man, and he looked like he was ready to leap from his chair, grab him by the throat. He was playing the bad cop, to Devlin's bad cop. There was no good cop in this game. Juice kept glancing at him, then at Devlin, then back again.

"Older, like him?" Devlin asked, nodding toward Grogan.

Juice shook his head. "Man, I don't know. Maybe he wasn't old. Maybe it was just the beard and stuff."

"What stuff?" Grogan snapped. His eyes were getting wild now, and the sound of his voice made Juice jump in his chair.

"He had on a big, wide-brimmed hat, ya know? An' dark glasses, like somethin' was wrong with his eyes."

"Why'd you think that?" Devlin asked.

" 'Cause it was already gettin' dark, an' he didn't need 'em, ya know?" He shook his head again. "Shit, man, it coulda been a broad for all I know."

Gabrielle shot forward in her chair. Her eyes were suddenly intense. "Why do you say that? *Could* it have been a woman?" Devlin recalled her earlier argument that the FBI never considered women in serial murder cases. She had thought it a major flaw in their approach.

"Man, I don't know," Juice said. "He didn't show me his dick."

"Watch you mouth," Grogan snapped, halfway out of his chair. Devlin held out an arm, urging him back.

"So it could have been a woman?" It was Devlin, taking control again, his voice soft, prodding Juice on.

"Man, it coulda been the fucking. . . ." He glanced quickly at Grogan. "It coulda been the pope for all I know."

"Tell us about the voice," Gabrielle urged.

Juice twisted in his seat again. "It was raspy. Ya know? Like it was fake too."

"What about the wrists? When he handed you the money. Were the wrists thick, like a man's? Or thin." Gabrielle was still leaning forward, eager to pursue the line of questioning.

"Thin, I think. Shit, I don't know. All I saw was the bread. That's all I wanted to see."

Gabrielle sat back and glanced at Devlin. "I'd like to

try to put him under," she said. "If I can, I'm sure there's more he'll recall."

Devlin nodded. "But *we* stay. This time we don't have to worry about patient confidentiality."

"No, we don't," Gabrielle said. "But it won't work." She glanced at Milligan and Grogan. "He's too frightened. I have to do it alone."

"He'll be out that door as soon as we're out of it," Grogan said.

Gabrielle smiled. "I assure you, I can stop him. And I'll only want you just outside." She reached across the interrogation table and took hold of the junkie's wrist. The man winced with sudden pain. "Do you feel how strong I am?" she asked. There was a hard, unforgiving look in her eye.

Grogan and Devlin exchanged looks. Their faces registered surprise, almost shock. They each kept it to themselves.

Gabrielle opened the door twenty minutes later. She raised a finger to her lips and gestured toward Juice, who was still seated in his chair, his eyes now closed.

"He's still under," she said softly. "I wanted to review what he told me before I brought him back. Just in case there are any follow-up questions. I'm not sure I can put him under again."

"What did he give us?" Devlin asked.

Gabrielle stepped closer, her face only a few inches away. It was almost too close, Devlin thought. She kept her voice low, just slightly above a whisper. "Whoever it was, and he's certain now it was a man." She hesitated; there was a hint of regret in her eyes, Devlin thought. "Well, he's sure the man was wearing some kind of makeup. Something that severely changed his appearance. He remembers the smell of it."

"Theatrical makeup?" Devlin asked.

"It's possible," Gabrielle said. "But he wouldn't know one type of makeup from another. A woman's makeup, properly applied, could do much the same thing," she added.

"But he's sure it was a man?"

"Yes, he is."

"You think there's anything more to get from him?"

"I don't. But I'm willing to ask anything you suggest."

"Can you plant something in his mind? Tell him we're going to show him pictures later, and that he'll be able to remove the beard and makeup in his mind, and see the person as he is without them? Be able to tell if it's someone in one of the pictures?"

Gabrielle nodded. "I can't tell you if it's going to work. It would depend on how creative his mind is. I just don't know how many gray cells the man has left." She smiled. "And a posthypnotic suggestion won't work unless it's something the person would normally do, would want to do. I've already given him one. That he go to a methadone clinic and seek help. But he'll never go unless he truly wants to."

Devlin nodded. "Let's take a shot." He held her eyes. "Since he's already under, I guess we can go inside while you do it. I don't imagine we can scare him now."

Gabrielle seemed surprised at first, then regarded him coolly. "Of course, Paul," she said. "Whatever you like."

The car sped across the Brooklyn Bridge, the tires hissing on the iron-mesh roadbed. Up ahead One Police Plaza loomed like a squat red brick box. Behind it stood the pale white tower of the Municipal Office Building, and slightly to the south, the majestic spire of the Woolworth Building, perhaps the most beautiful and forgotten of New York's skyscrapers.

Adrianna, Devlin, and Gabrielle sat in the backseat, Grogan and Milligan in the front. The plan was to drop Adrianna at the loft in Milligan's care, then Gabrielle in the Village, after which Devlin and Grogan would head uptown. They had telephoned Rachel Barrows from the Seven-Eight, and she had agreed to see them that evening.

Adrianna had been silent ever since she had learned about the latest "baby-sitting" plan. Devlin knew she was angry. He had recognized the signs, had remembered them from ten years earlier.

He leaned toward her, keeping his voice soft and low. "You okay?"

She stared straight ahead. "No, I'm not okay," she said. "I'm tired, and I'm hungry, and I'm thoroughly pissed."

Devlin had forgotten the time, had forgotten all about food. He started to apologize, but Adrianna wasn't finished.

"I'm tired of being dragged all over creation, so you and Eddie can talk to junkies, or whoever the hell you have to talk to. I'm not getting the work done that I need to get done. I can't even go out of my goddamned home to buy the art supplies I need without having a cop three steps behind me. And people come in and out of my home like it was a damned office building." She turned and glared at him. "No, Paul. I'm not okay. And tomorrow morning I'm going out to buy what I need. And, if anyone follows me, I'll . . . I'll . . ." Adrianna snapped her head forward and stared out the window.

Devlin let out a breath and remained silent. Gabrielle looked out the window, intently studying the East River below.

"So how do you like family life Cuban style?"

Eddie Grogan was grinning from behind the steering wheel as they headed uptown. They had dropped Gabrielle off and were moving up Sixth Avenue in light traffic. The psychiatrist had seemed cool and distant between Soho and the Village.

"Jesus," Devlin said. "She really blew, didn't she?"

"You pissed her off," Grogan said. "Hell, you pissed

both of them off." He started to laugh. "You're batting two for two again, hotshot."

"Thanks for telling me," Devlin said. "You really know how to pick a guy up."

Grogan laughed. "Hey, you got one more shot, tonight. One more woman. Bet even you can't go three for three."

It was eight o'clock when they arrived at Rachel Barrows' building. Two well-dressed men in their late fifties were waiting for the elevator. The briefcases in their hands indicated they had just returned home from work, and Devlin wondered if their wealthy wives or girlfriends also bitched about their work habits. They rode up with the men, Grogan in his rumpled suit, Devlin in sports shirt and jacket, and both received openly curious looks. Equality stopped with the wives and girlfriends, Devlin decided. Maybe.

A uniformed maid let them into the apartment, and into the large room that had held more than a hundred people the night before.

"Some joint," Grogan whispered. Devlin noted he had left out the usual adjective, "fucking." He must be impressed, he thought.

Rachel Barrows entered with a smile and a flourish. She was dressed in a silk blouse and pants, and her makeup was as perfectly applied as it had been the previous evening. Devlin wondered if she ever wandered around in a bathrobe and fuzzy slippers.

"Gentlemen, I don't have much time," she said as she seated herself across from them, crossed her legs, and placed both hands demurely on one knee. There was a smile fixed on her face, but she looked slightly older now, the facial lines more distinct, and Devlin recalled that the lighting had been lower and softer for the party.

Grogan introduced himself and Devlin, whom she recalled from the previous evening. They had decided that any pretense, given the ongoing FBI interviews, was now useless.

"I didn't know we had a police officer present last night," she said. Her voice sounded as though her home had been surreptitiously invaded.

"I'm not a police officer," Devlin said. "I was once, but I'm retired. But I am a friend of Detective Grogan, and he asked me to help."

She offered an amused look. "You're young for retirement," she said.

"An injury," Devlin explained.

The woman dismissed the information and turned to Grogan. "So how may I help?" she asked.

Grogan sat slightly forward. "Like I told you on the phone, one of your guests last night was murdered."

"Yes, I know. Melissa Coors." She shook her head. "Terrible. I read about it in the newspaper. But, certainly, you can't think it involved anyone who was here."

"We have to check," Grogan said. "Did you notice anyone paying special attention to her? Following her around? Anything like that?"

Rachel Barrows laughed. It seemed somehow out of place. "You mean before or after she stuck her cleavage under their nose?" She turned to Devlin. "Certainly you noticed. She was being a bit slutty, wasn't she?" There was a slight edge to her voice. Disapproval, or perhaps concealed anger. She paused when Devlin didn't respond, then turned back to Grogan. "She did seem a little miffed with Vincent Richards as they were leaving. Or perhaps he was miffed with her. I really didn't pay all that much attention."

Both men waited, letting their silence play on her. It was a police technique that usually kept people talking, made them feel they had to say more.

"Actually, I think Umberto seemed a bit perturbed with her as well." She laughed again. "But he's such a prissy thing. The slightest thing perturbs him. And I think I heard her snap something rude at Brenden Brooks, as though he had said something that had made her angry. But there were several people nearby, so it might not have been him. All of this went on when everyone was saying their good-nights."

"What did she say?" Grogan asked.

The woman smiled, almost impishly. "I believe she said, 'Fuck off.'"

Devlin recalled the same words, only he remembered them being directed at Richards in the lobby. Perhaps he had missed them earlier, upstairs.

"Actually, I'm surprised our guest of honor wasn't upset with her. She put her breasts in his face often enough." The edge was back in her voice. Then she smiled again. Even more impishly, Devlin thought. "But then, Father Jim has a bit of a reputation, I'm afraid."

"What kind of reputation?" Devlin asked.

The woman's eyebrows shot up. "You didn't know? I thought everyone did. He had an affair a few years back. With an entertainer." She said the final word as though it explained itself, or somehow made the facts even more disreputable. "He was working at the arch-diocese at the time, a rising star in the clerical world." She laughed again, as though the thought of clerical stars in itself was ridiculous. "When they found out what he was up to, they booted him out. Put him in charge of bag ladies. Where he's done a marvelous job, I might add." Her smile widened. "And where there's very little temptation for anything else."

"I understand that Father Jim invited Vincent Richards," Devlin said. "Did anyone else call you and ask if they could come?"

"Yes, as a matter of fact, two people did."

"Who?"

"Well, Mr. Richards called to ask if he could bring Melissa Coors. I was surprised because Father Jim had called earlier to say he had invited him, and that he'd be bringing Ms. Mendez."

"The priest told you that?"

"Yes."

"Did anyone else call?"

"Yes, a short time later Brenden Brooks called and asked if he might come as well. But I'm certain there were no others. At least none that I can recall."

"A horny priest," Grogan said as they headed back downtown. "And maybe one who's got a psychological hard-on for women who tempt him. Women in the arts. Interesting."

"And who knew Adrianna was going to be there. Either from Vincent or somebody else. Did you ever ask Gabrielle whether she told him about the party, and about Adrianna going?"

"Yeah, I did," Grogan said. "She only knows him because of some work she does with homeless people who go to his shelter. Some of that freebie stuff I told you about." He took his eyes off the road; glanced across at Devlin. "She likes him; respects him. And she seemed a bit miffed when I asked her if she told him Adrianna was going to the party. Said she didn't discuss her patients with nobody."

"I wonder if she knows about his past," Devlin said.

"It sure don't seem to be no big secret," Grogan said. "Maybe we should ask her."

13

The child is in the bed. The door begins to open slowly. Then the figure is there, nothing but a black shadow against the dim light in the hall. It pauses. The rest of the house is quiet. No one else is there tonight, but still the figure is silent, cautious. It is part of the pleasure; the child understands this in some unspoken way, something that is instinctive, beyond any process of reasoning.

Now the door begins to close, cutting off the light, and the child hears the slow, soft, steady movement toward the bed.

"No. Please, no." The child hears its own voice, a whisper that trembles slightly. Somehow the child knows it is all right to speak tonight. There is no one to hear. It does not break the rule of silence that has been imposed.

There is a hushing sound from the dark, not harsh, but soft and gentle, intended to soothe, perhaps even to placate. The movement comes closer and the child hears itself whimper, then begin to cry softly. The hushing sound comes again, and the bed sags as the figure sits. A hand reaches out and touches one cheek.

"Shhhh." The sound is almost like an exhalation of breath, soft and steady. "You make me come. You know you do." The stroking continues, even more gently, one finger tracing an undulating line from under the ear, across the cheek. The words are whispered, so softly they are barely heard. "Now it's time." There is a sudden, sharp intake of breath, and the hand drops from the cheek and moves beneath the covers. "Yes. Now it's time. Now it's time to pay the piper."

Bolt upright. Sweat pouring from the face. The dream again. Only the dream. No, it's more than that, you know it's more. Across the room, hidden away in the back of the closet. It's there. The robe is hanging there, waiting. You have to put it on and go to her. She's like the others. It's not your fault. It's hers. Just as it was your fault long ago. Until you finally cleansed yourself. Two hands tighten into fists. But then you let filthy hands touch you, and you became dirty again. Sinned again. No, you mustn't go to her now. You're not ready. Not yet. Send the gift to her instead. Send it so the man can't keep it from her. She must see it and understand. Then she must wait and suffer. It's the way it's done. You know that. She must know the time is coming. Closer and closer and closer. And then she must wait for it. Yes, wait.

Devlin rolled over and forced himself upright. Adrianna was sitting at the foot of the bed, staring at him. He glanced at his watch. It was already eight o'clock.

"I didn't want to wake you," she said. "You were sleeping so soundly."

He ran a hand across his face. "Are you still mad? When I got back last night you were asleep. I didn't know if I should use the sofa or sleep here." He offered her a weak smile. "Since it wasn't pulled out into a bed, I figured it was okay."

Adrianna fought a smile. "Good guess," she said. "But I'm still going out today. Alone."

Devlin nodded. He had already made arrangements with Grogan. They would have someone outside who Adrianna had not seen before. The protection would be there. It just wouldn't be shoved down her throat.

"It's not a great idea. And I hope it won't become a regular thing."

Her hands twisted nervously in her lap, and he knew

she was already having second thoughts. But she'd do it, he knew. Just to prove she could.

"I'll be all right," she said. "And it won't be a daily event. I have too much work to do."

She moved up beside him and slipped her arms around his waist. "I won't be gone long. I just need some things I can't get at the art supply store downstairs." She laid her head against his shoulder. "Besides, Umberto is coming over later. He called last night, after I got back, and said he wanted to see those paintings we talked about."

"What time is he coming?"

"One," Adrianna said.

She moved along West Broadway, her steps quick and purposeful. There was a roll of canvas beneath one arm, and a large satchel hanging from her shoulder that was filled with the special paints she had just purchased.

The air was clean and clear and warm, and she knew summer would soon hit the city with all its brutal humidity. But she would escape it. After the show had opened, she would pack her things and head for Bridgehampton, and she would start the new work she had planned, and walk the beaches and forget everything that had happened. Her mind clouded momentarily. If, she told herself. If it's all over by then. If this maniac still wasn't stalking her.

She felt sweat begin to form in her palms, and she tightened her jaw, fighting off the fear that was slipping back. She had forced it away while she ran her errand. The streets had been crowded with people, and it had given her a sense of safety. Still, it had been difficult—perhaps it had only been a lie she had made herself accept—but she didn't want to lose it now. Not after all the effort it had taken.

The streets are still crowded, she told herself, and she forced herself to stare at the people moving in and out of shops, along the sidewalk. There was the usual mix of attire, from pseudo hip, to gaudy tourist, to the unwashed secondhand tatters of street people. She tried to think of the beach house again, and whether Paul would go with her. Only if it's still going on. Only if that maniac is still out there, she told herself. When it's over he'll go back to Vermont. Back to the life he's made for himself.

She stopped in front of a new boutique that had opened two weeks earlier, and made herself look at the clothing displayed in the window. The thought of Paul leaving had shaken her, and she wanted to drive it from her mind.

She started down the street again, then heard someone call her name. She stopped, turned, and saw Gabrielle moving toward her. There was a look of concern on her face, and she kept glancing back over her shoulder.

"Gabrielle, what are you doing here?" she asked as the woman reached her. She couldn't help but notice that Gabrielle was wearing makeup again, and that she seemed to have added some highlights to her hair. She looked good. Too good, Adrianna thought.

"I was coming to see Paul," Gabrielle said. She saw Adrianna's lips tighten momentarily, and rushed on with her explanation. "We had a disagreement last night." She paused, uncertain if she should continue. "About my work with him," she added quickly. "I thought we should discuss it."

She shook her head, as if it was now unimportant, then took Adrianna's arm and started her walking again.

"I was behind you, across the street. And I recognized you." She glanced back over her shoulder. "I think someone was following you. A man. He was keeping a steady distance behind you, and he stopped when you did." She looked back again. "But I don't see him now." She forced a smile. "Maybe I was wrong. Maybe it's all just getting to me too. Are you going home?"

Fear had crept back into Adrianna's eyes, and she

too looked back along the sidewalk. "Yes, I am," she said. She seemed to get hold of herself. "Look, please don't tell Paul about this," she said. "I don't want to listen to any lectures." She shook her head. "It was a dumb thing to do. Going out alone like this. But I had to."

"I understand," Gabrielle said. "And don't worry. It will be our secret." She glanced back again. "And I'm sure I was wrong now." Adrianna thought there was a lack of conviction in her eyes.

"I can't believe you're even suggesting such a thing." Gabrielle stared at Devlin, her look incredulous. "The man's a priest. And I know him. I've watched him work with people. If he were that unstable, I think I would have detected it."

They were standing in the hall outside Adrianna's loft. It was one o'clock, and Umberto was inside going through the paintings. Devlin and Gabrielle had discussed the tensions of the previous night, and had smoothed things over. Then Devlin had brought up the priest and what he had learned from Rachel Barrows. Now the tension was back in full force.

"It's just something we can't ignore," Devlin said. He watched Gabrielle shake her head, as though listening to the words of some foolish, recalcitrant child. "Why do you find it so objectionable?"

She hesitated, seemed to think about the question. "I suppose I'm just shocked by the suggestion. And it strikes me that you're going off in a direction that will prove so clearly unproductive."

"That's the way these things work," Devlin said. "Ninety percent of what we do will be a waste of time. But we can't overlook something just because we're pretty certain it won't work out. And I don't need you fighting me every time you don't agree." He was getting hot, and he fought it off and smiled, trying to soften the words. "I need you to give me whatever input you can. No matter what direction I'm going in."

Gabrielle leaned back against the wall and let out a long breath. "You're right, of course." She shook her head again, this time at herself, Devlin thought. "Perhaps it's my Catholic upbringing coming out. The idea of a priest being such a monster. But intellectually I know it's possible."

"Do you know anything about this affair he's supposed to have had?" Devlin asked.

Gabrielle shook her head one more time. "I didn't even know he had worked at the archdiocese. We never discussed his past. Our concern—mine and his—was limited strictly to the people in his care."

"Would it surprise you if it were true?"

Gabrielle stared at the floor for a moment. "I suppose initially. But not after I had time to think about it."

"Why?"

"Because priests are men, and the mere putting on of vestments doesn't change that fact." Her voice had grown slightly harsh, and she seemed to recognize it, made it softer. "What I mean is that they have the same normal urges, the same biological needs and instincts as any other man. They simply force themselves to suppress them. Are required to." She began tapping her fingers together. It was a nervous gesture Devlin had noticed before. She saw his eyes watching her and stopped, then eased herself away from the wall, and placed a hand against his chest. It was a delicate gesture. Affectionate. She was close enough now that Devlin could smell the faint fragrance of her perfume.

"Forced celibacy, even if it's taken on freely, can be an extremely difficult thing to live with," she said. "I've had priests and nuns as patients, and I know of what I speak."

"I suppose we'll have to ask him," Devlin said. "It could be an interesting conversation."

Gabrielle stared at him. "Don't expect him to be forthcoming with you. The Church, and its priests, are very reluctant to wash dirty linen in public. It's a inbred defense mechanism."

Umberto studied the canvas Adrianna had just completed. Devlin had come back inside and was off in one corner, reading a magazine—or pretending to. He was keying on the man's voice, stealing looks at his body language.

The gallery owner stood with his hands on his hips, head cocked at an angle. His legs were together, and one foot was set perpendicular to the other. "It's magnificent," he said after a lengthy silence. He pivoted, walked a few paces, then stopped. "I came here ready to be furious with you because there wasn't enough work." He placed two fingers against his lips and thought for a moment. "We're still a few paintings short of what we need," he finally said. "And I am getting just a bit nervous about that." He let out a breath as if resigning himself to his concerns. "But I have to admit, you've shown me today that the work is worth waiting for." He glanced back toward Devlin, and his lips pinched together. "Perhaps you could do with just a little less distraction," he added.

Adrianna's face broke into a wide, beaming smile. Like all painters—like most people working in the arts—public reaction to her work was limited to a few people and published reviews. It often left her feeling isolated and uncertain about what she was doing. When praise came it was like a balm to all her unvoiced fears, a justification for all the solitary hours spent before a canvas. She glanced back at Devlin, hoping he had heard. And she wanted to tell Umberto that without Devlin's presence, she wouldn't be painting at all. She would simply be too terrified to work.

"You don't know how happy I am that you like it," she said. "I wasn't sure. It's different from anything I've done before."

Umberto nodded, his eyes back on the painting. "Yes, it is. It's darker. Internally darker." He turned his gaze back on Adrianna. "I don't know what you're feeling—and I'm especially glad *I'm* not feeling it. But, frankly, I hope it continues a bit longer. It's drawing something out of you that I've never seen before. And, to be honest, well . . . it's wonderful." He spun away, walked a few paces, then turned back again. "Now, you must do something immediately," he said, suddenly all business again. "First, I want you to photograph the painting. Then, come over to the gallery and use our darkroom, and make me some prints." He brought his hands together and began rubbing the palms back and forth. "I want to include the photograph in the prospectus I'm putting together. As you know, I plan to take it around to potential buyers *before* the opening. And I think a number of them are going to drool on themselves when they see this." He raised a finger, as though indicating some stroke of inspiration he had just experienced. "I may also use it for a poster. I'm not certain. But suddenly it feels right to me."

Adrianna felt she might float out of her shoes. "Oh, God, Umberto, you're overwhelming me." She grinned at him. "Can we sell the posters?"

He took a step back and stared at her, wide-eyed. "Of course, darling. We don't do *anything* we can't sell." He took her arm, and walked her—a bit conspiratorially—away from the canvas. "Now, you must do those prints for me this afternoon," he said. He stopped and took time to stare into her eyes, lowering his voice as he spoke. "And, *please*, get rid of your friend," he said in a near whisper. "At least while you're working." He took a handkerchief from his pocket, made a face, then dabbed a spot of paint on her cheek. "And if you must have him around at other times," he added, "for God's sake, take him to a decent tailor."

When Umberto had left—flitted away was a better description, Devlin thought—Adrianna pointed at the just finished canvas. "I'm a genius," she said. She turned and did a little shuffle, grinning at Devlin.

He approached the picture slowly, taking in the wash

of colors, the mixture of light and shadow that seemed to flow from the canvas and dominate that small portion of the room. But the feeling it exuded wasn't a pleasant one, he decided. If anything, it was somewhat unsettling. It left him with a sense of inexplicable foreboding.

"I thought you'd just been cleaning your brushes on it," he said.

Adrianna elbowed him in the ribs. Hard enough to make him wince. "Philistine," she snapped. "Tell me if you like it."

He took her shoulders in both hands. "I like everything you do," he said. He gave her a slightly lascivious wink. "And if Umberto says it's wonderful, that's good enough for me."

"Very diplomatic," she said. She turned her head so she could better give him a sidelong glance. "Now, you better get out of here if anything else wonderful is going to happen for this exhibit. I can't wait to get back to work, and I still have to take those photographs and develop them."

"Fine. Eddie and I have to see someone uptown. And this time I'd like to send someone with you when you go to the gallery." He raised his hands, anticipating an objection. "But I'll tell him to wait outside for you. And to stay out of your way."

Adrianna's mind flashed to the man who might or might not have been following her that morning. "No problem," she said. The sudden surprise on Devlin's face almost made her laugh out loud. She was too happy now to worry about bodyguards. Too pleased with herself to allow anything to change the mood.

Devlin wasn't about to question the sudden change in attitude. He knew better than to push his luck with the woman. He turned and started for the door, then stopped and turned back to her. "By the way, what was all that whispered stuff between you and Little Lord Fauntleroy?"

Adrianna grinned at him. "Believe me, you don't really want to know." She pointedly looked him up and down, and began to laugh softly.

"Listen, the young man was sexually abused as a child. Sex—even the thought of sex, no matter how much he wants it—is painful to him. Give me pain. I want to see pain in your eyes."

Vincent Richards stood in the ninth row center of the orchestra, staring up at the young actor on the stage. He was wearing a bulky white turtleneck sweater that emphasized the flush in his cheeks.

Devlin and Grogan had just entered from the door that led to the backstage area. Richards glanced toward them and his irritation seemed to suddenly intensify. "What the hell do you two want?" he snapped.

Devlin and Grogan moved across the front of the theater, then up the aisle toward Richards. Seated in the row directly behind the director were Brenden Brooks and Fr. James Hopkins.

"Come at a bad time, did we?" Grogan chirped.

Richards collapsed in his seat, lowered his head momentarily, then looked up at the two men. "Every time's a bad time today," he said, getting hold of himself. "We're trying to rehearse, and we're trying to find a star-quality actress to replace Melissa. It's a ridiculous juggling act." He sat back, draped his arms over the adjoining seats, and sighed. "And now what do you have for me?" he asked.

"Actually, we're here to see Father Jim," Grogan said. "We went to his shelter, and they told us he was here. With you." Grogan shrugged. "So here we are."

Richards stared at Devlin, then back at the older detective. "You always bring a business writer with you when you question people?" he asked.

Grogan shrugged again. "Hey, you never know when you're gonna need good financial advice."

Vincent barked out harsh laughter, then turned his eyes on Devlin. They were far from friendly. "I don't know who you think you're kidding, Devlin. It's obvious what you're doing." He turned slightly in his seat. "I've had cops all over me since this thing with Melissa happened. And they're not just asking me about her. They're asking about Adrianna, and some other women I never heard of." He tapped one finger against his head. "So, brain surgeon or not, even I can figure out that Melissa's death, and the attack on Adrianna, and—somehow—these other women, are all connected." He gave Devlin a cold smile. "So, I ask myself where a certain business writer who smells an awful lot like a cop comes in. And the word bodyguard just sort of hops into my mind."

Devlin looked off at the stage. "What can I tell you, Vincent? Everybody's got to work." He turned back to face the man. "Right?"

The unpleasant smile was back on Vincent's face—residue from their near altercation the other night, Devlin decided.

"I suppose so," Vincent said. "But it must be dangerous work. I imagine that anyone who wanted to get to Adrianna would figure out pretty fast that he had to get to you first."

Father Jim followed Grogan and Devlin into the lobby, took a seat on the staircase that led to the balcony, and smiled up at the two men who hovered above him. Devlin had decided to let Grogan do the questioning—to squeeze whatever intimidation they could out of his NYPD shield.

"Some men came by the shelter this morning, and I told them what little I know." He offered the statement without being asked.

He was dressed in a bulky army fatigue jacket with a bright red T-shirt showing beneath, and Devlin thought it made him seem even frailer than he had at the party two days earlier. He wondered if the man ever wore clerical garb.

"What brings you here, Father?" Grogan began. He

was smiling down at the man, and the priest was looking back with what appeared to be complete innocence.

"When we saw each other a few nights ago, Vincent
invited me to come to a rehearsal. He said he and Mr.
Brooks wanted to talk to me about some more street
theater for my people."

"And have you decided to do some?"

"We really haven't gotten around to that yet," the
priest said. "I'm afraid it may have turned out to be a
bad time. Vincent seems to be a bit out of sorts."

Grogan bent forward. He was smiling, but his eyes
were cold, accusatory. "That happens sometimes," he
said. "Especially when your friend gets chopped up like
dog food."

The harshness of the words—or perhaps the image—
seemed to jolt the priest. "Yes, that was terrible. I
didn't mean to sound insensitive."

"Yeah, but you did, Father," Grogan said. "It kinda
surprised me." He squatted down in front of the man.
"But then, it shouldn't have, I guess. I used to be an
altar boy. Way back, a hundred years ago." He offered
another cold smile. "And I knew all kinds of priests
back then. I knew priests who were a bit too heavy
into the altar wine; some who liked the altar boys a
little too much; some who liked the altar boys' mothers
too much. You know what I mean?"

The priest stared back, his eyes taking on their own
hint of hardness. "There are frailties in all walks of
life, Detective. Even among those who serve Holy
Mother the Church."

Grogan's smile widened. He jabbed a finger at the
priest, as if he had just remembered something. "You
know, Father, that's just what I wanted to talk to you
about. Frailties. Ain't that funny. That you should think
of it too."

Father Jim seemed to twist a bit. "Frailties are my
job," he said. "How can I help you?" His pale blue eyes
had taken on a nervous cast now, Devlin thought. He
seemed slightly boyish, and the sandy hair that fell

across his forehead, combined with the thin, almost
gaunt face, only added to it.

"I understand you used to work at the archdiocese,
Father. Tell me about that."

The sudden change in subject seemed to unsettle
the man, but he fought it off.

"Yes," he said. "I worked in their public relations
office. Up until a little more than two years ago. Then
I was transferred to my present work."

"Quite a switch. You ask for this new job?"

"We all serve where we can," the priest said.

Grogan smiled again. Shook his head. "I heard it
kinda different, Father," he said. "I hear like maybe
you got caught dipping your wick into something besides the Holy Water font. And like maybe they tossed
your ass out of those nice digs over on Madison Avenue. Anything to all that?"

The priest's face paled, then flushed slightly; his lips
tightened into a thin line. "I don't think I have anything
more to say to you, Detective," he said.

He started to rise, but Grogan's hand shot out, the
stubby fingers jabbing him in the chest, forcing him
back to a sitting position.

"You fucking move when I tell you to fucking move,"
Grogan snapped.

The priest seemed overwhelmed with shock, disbelief. "You . . . can't do . . . this," he stammered.

"Yeah, I know," Grogan said. He motioned with his
head toward Devlin, who stood behind him. "But I got
a witness here who'll say I didn't have no choice. You
got that, padre?" He held one finger inches from the
priest's nose. "Now, I got some asshole out there who's
chopping women up. And the last one he chopped was
a broad who spent the night shoving her tits in your
face a few hours before she was killed. *Now* I find out
that you maybe had a little diversion a few years back
with the same kind of broad. One who worked in show
business. And that this little extracurricular gig of yours
kinda fucked up your life a bit. So it makes me curious.

And when I get curious, I need fucking answers. It's just the way I am. So tell me about this lady."

The priest's lips trembled—but now with anger—and his thin hands balled into fists. Grogan looked down at them, then back at the priest's face. Then he smiled again. The priest's hands opened and went to his knees, cupping them.

"I don't have anything to say," he said.

Grogan reached behind his back and pulled his handcuffs from his belt. "Hey, Father. We can do it easy. We can do it hard. We don't talk here, we talk at the precinct house. Up to you." He watched the priest's eyes fix on the cuffs. "Yeah, I know," he said. "The boys at the archdiocese are gonna be pissed at me, I take you in." He shrugged. "But, you know, they'll get over it. They'll figure I was just doing my job. And they'll even spring you, after a while. No question about it." Grogan let the cuffs swing a little in his hand. "But I think they're gonna be pissed at you too. They may even be pissed enough to find some other shithole for you to work in. Maybe one that's even worse than that fleabag you're in now."

The priest lowered his head until his chin was almost on his chest. His voice came in little more than a whisper. "The woman's name was Gail Collins," he said. "We became involved almost three years ago."

"And where is she now?" Grogan asked.

The priest shook his head. "I don't know. She left New York two years ago, and I haven't heard from her since."

"Well, that's okay, Father. I'm good at finding people. Now tell me about Melissa Coors."

Father Jim looked up at him. His eyes seemed haunted. Like someone who'd been through years of personal hell, and who suddenly found himself going back. "I never met her before the other night. At least I don't believe I had."

"She piss you off? The way she acted toward you?"

Father Jim's eyes hardened, flared with anger. "She embarrassed me."

"Embarrassed?"

"Yes, embarrassed." There was a sharpness in his voice, and Devlin knew Grogan had lost it, would get no more from the man.

Grogan sensed it too. He stood up. "Where'd you go after the party?" he asked.

"Straight back to the shelter. I live there," he said.

"You go alone?"

"Yes. No one else was going in that direction. I took a cab. By myself."

"Anybody there when you got home? You talk to anybody?"

"Everyone was asleep. It was late."

Grogan took a step back and stretched. "Okay, padre. That's great for now." He started to turn, then stopped. "I'll be back to talk to you again. In a few days. After I talk to Gail Collins."

They drove back toward Soho, fighting the usual traffic.

"You better check and see if the good father has a sheet," Devlin said.

"Yeah, I was thinking the same thing myself," Grogan said. "I'll run NCIC, the whole thing. And I'll dig around a little, see if I can find out where he comes from, then check to see if there's any juvenile record I can pry loose." He glanced at Devlin. "I'll do the same on Vincent Richards, this Brooks guy, and old Hubert Walsh, a.k.a. Umberto. Got any other ideas?"

"Not for now," Devlin said. "You think you'll get heat from the archdiocese on your little dance with Father Jim?"

"Naw," Grogan said. "I figure he's shit scared they'll find out somebody's poking around into his little dicky-dunking escapade. He ain't gonna volunteer that info. Not to people who can ship his ass to the fucking South Bronx." He tapped the steering wheel for a few moments. "But I do think the jig is up about you poking your nose around in this thing. Richards, or somebody—probably Richards—is gonna drop a dime about that. And that asshole Mallory is gonna know you're not just playing bodyguard."

"You expecting a forthwith?"

"Any fucking minute," Grogan said.

"What are you going to do about it?"

"Play dumb," Grogan said. "Blame it all on you." He grinned. "I'll say you and Adrianna used to be lovers, and she asked you to come play watchdog, and now you're getting out of control. I'll say I just found out about it when you showed up at the theater today, but figured there was nothing I could do." He jabbed a finger toward Devlin. "But they'll be on your ass. Cervone, those humps in the FBI, all of them. It should be interesting." He started to laugh. "Hey. Fuck 'em if they can't take a joke."

14

Eddie Grogan's words proved prophetic. Two hours after he left Devlin at the loft, a message came over his car radio. It was a "forthwith" to the chief of detectives office. Grogan glanced at his watch: six-thirty. Which meant Cervone was waiting for him rather than enjoying an evening cocktail with his political cronies. That fact alone told Grogan everything he needed to know.

When he arrived at Cervone's thirteenth-floor office fifteen minutes later, the chief's appointment secretary eyed him from behind his desk outside Cervone's private sanctum.

"I'm glad it's you going in there, Eddie. Instead of me," the secretary said.

"Hey, Charlie," Grogan said. "Into every life a little rain, right?" He forced a grin that was pure bravado.

The secretary stared at him for a moment, shook his head, then picked up his phone, pushed a button, and announced that Grogan was there. "You can go in," he said as he returned the receiver to its cradle. He watched Grogan step toward the door. "And, Eddie," he said, stopping him, "this isn't rain. This is a fucking hurricane."

The chief's office was surprisingly spartan. It held an executive-size metal institutional desk, a small vinyl sofa, and three upholstered metal visitors' chairs. Cervone was behind the desk, and the sofa was occupied by Matthew Mallory and Wendy Wilson.

M. M. and W. W. What a joy, Grogan thought. The

Fibbies and the head guinea prick. Maybe this isn't a hurricane, he told himself. Maybe this is a fucking typhoon.

"You sent for me, Chief," Grogan said. He stood before Cervone's desk, knowing he could not sit until offered a chair. He wasn't offered one.

Cervone inclined his chin toward the two FBI Behavioral Science Unit agents. "Our friends here have brought me a problem," Cervone began. His eyes were boring into Grogan. "But I think you already know about it."

Grogan remained silent. He had learned long ago to keep his mouth shut in situations like this—answer only direct questions and offer nothing. And when you did answer, you only told that part of the truth that helped you. There were a lot of ex-cops wearing square badges and patrolling shopping malls because they hadn't followed that simple dictum.

Cervone stared at him, knowing Grogan would wait him out. Like himself, Grogan had over thirty years on the job. You didn't last that long by being stupid.

"You ever hear of a guy named Paul Devlin?" Cervone asked.

"Sure," Grogan said. "In fact, I just ran into him a couple hours ago."

"Where was that, Eddie?"

Like you don't fucking know, Grogan thought. "Up at the Lenox Theater," he said. "I went there to question some people"—he waved a hand—"nothing special, just routine stuff. And, well, anyway, there he was. We sort of got there at the same time." Grogan mentally crossed his fingers and prayed that it was Richards or Brooks who had blabbed to the FBI. He was reasonably certain it had not been the priest. But if it had been, or if it had been Rachel Barrows, he was dead. He could dance around Richards or Brooks. But the priest or the Barrows woman would send him down like the fucking *Titanic*, he told himself. From now on he wouldn't be able to go anywhere with Devlin. Not if he hoped to stay on the case himself.

"Richards seemed to think you came *with* Devlin." It was Mallory, speaking through a typical smirk. Wendy Wilson's face had become dutifully severe. What a pair, Grogan told himself. He turned to Cervone, inclined his head toward the FBI agents and asked: "They doing the questioning here, Chief?"

Cervone's face darkened. He didn't like even the suggestion that someone else was in charge. Not here in his own domain. He shot a quick look at Mallory, then turned his gaze back on Grogan. It was not a friendly look. "No, I'm asking them. But answer the question anyway."

Grogan began his tap dance. He had been there to question Richards, he explained. But decided to put it off when he stumbled into Devlin. Instead he had taken the priest into the lobby and had asked him about the party, and about anyone who had paid any particular attention to Melissa Coors. Devlin, he said, had gone to the john, which was off the lobby, then had hung around to speak to him.

Grogan shrugged. "I didn't give a shit. I wasn't asking nothing I was worried about him hearing."

"Did he tell you what he was doing there?" Cervone asked. His eyes were hard, and Grogan knew he wasn't buying the story. It was time for a little truth.

Grogan nodded. "Yeah. Him and Adrianna used to be close. As in *real* close. And she asked him to come down from Vermont to play watchdog. And I think he decided to do a little poking around. That's probably why Richards is so suspicious. He's been dating Adrianna, and now, suddenly, Devlin is spending every night there. I guess he's jealous."

"And you didn't think to let us know," Cervone snapped.

"Chief, it was going into my Five tonight," Grogan said. He was referring to the DD-5, Supplementary

Complaint Report every detective was required to file on each new phase of an investigation.

"Yeah, I bet it was." It was Mallory again.

Grogan slowly turned to the FBI agent, but not slowly enough for Cervone to stop what was coming.

"You calling me a liar, you fucking empty suit?" Grogan knew his time for rage was limited, and he wanted to make the best of it. He immediately took his voice up several decibels, moving a step toward Mallory as he did. "Because if you fucking are, I'll throw your fucking sorry fucking excuse for a cop ass right out that fucking window." A finger jabbed at Wendy Wilson, whose mouth was a circle of shock. "And that little shit-faced fucking little law school graduate'll come fucking flying out right behind you."

"Who the hell do you think you're—"

Mallory had started to shout back, but Grogan quickly drowned him out. From the corner of his eye he could see Cervone on his feet behind his desk.

"I'll tell you who the fuck I'm talking to, you FBI fucking faggot asshole—"

"Eddie! God damn it!" It was Cervone screaming now.

". . . I'll punch your fucking face right through that fucking wall—" Grogan continued to scream at Mallory, his face beet red now.

"Eddie! Knock it off! Now!" Cervone's shout was enough to rattle the framed pictures of politicians on his walls. He turned his own red face to Mallory, and jabbed a finger at his face. "And you shut the fuck up too."

Grogan spun away from the two FBI agents and looked past Cervone, concentrating on the wall behind him. His face was still red, and his breath came in short gulps. He looked like he was about to have a stroke.

Cervone jabbed a finger at him. "Go outside and wait," he snapped. "And get a fucking grip on yourself."

Grogan spun on his heels and moved quickly to the

door. He pulled it open and stormed out, careful only not to slam it behind him. Instantly he could hear Cervone's voice bellowing through the room.

"Who the fuck do you think you are, coming into *my* office and pulling that kind of shit!"

All the feigned rage vanished from Grogan's face. He took a pack of cigarettes from his shirt pocket, lit up, and casually walked to a chair in the outer office.

Charlie, the chief's appointment secretary, stared at him incredulously. Then a slow smile came to his lips. He shook his head. "You are one fucking piece of work, Grogan," he said. He glanced back at the chief's door, listening to the continued shouts of his boss. His smile grew slightly. He was the chief's goon, but he was still a cop. And like all cops he held FBI agents only one step above defense attorneys. And it was a very small step indeed.

He looked back at Eddie. "You'll become a legend after this one, Grogan." Charlie's smile faded with difficulty. "But don't push your luck," he added. He inclined his head toward Cervone's office. "The man may be a politician, but he ain't no fucking fool."

Grogan kept a straight face. "Hey, Charlie," he said. "I was just defending the fucking honor of the fucking job."

Mallory and Wendy Wilson stormed out of Cervone's office two minutes later—Mallory red-faced, Wilson looking like someone had pulled her panties halfway up her butt. Mallory threw Grogan a look that said he wished he could shoot him where he sat. Grogan stared back, then raised his middle finger and held it there, giving the FBI agent a sustained bird.

"Grogan. Get your ass back in here," Cervone's voice bellowed from inside his office.

The chief was standing behind his desk, his weight resting on his knuckles. His face was dark, his eyes glaring. "What kind of shit you think you're pulling?" he hissed as Grogan resumed a position before him.

Grogan lowered his eyes. "I'm sorry, Chief. But that fucking hump—"

"Never mind that fucking hump," Cervone growled. "The only fucking hump you gotta worry about is me. Now sit down, shut up, and listen."

Grogan did as he was told, looking appropriately cowed and ashamed of himself.

Cervone stared at him suspiciously. "Now tell me about Devlin," he snapped. "And make it good, Eddie."

Grogan raised his hands in a helpless gesture, then let them fall back into his lap. "Chief, I heard he was around yesterday, but I didn't have time to do nothing about it. I know I should of told you, and I was gonna. In today's Five. Honest." He looked at Cervone as if to say: Please, Chief, don't come down on me on this one. "But, Chief," he continued, "what can we do? The lady's got a right to bring in anybody she wants to baby-sit her. She's fucking half crazy about this shit that happened. If I push her on this, she'll go bananas. She'll be down in the fucking *Daily News* office so fast, I'll have to give her a speeding ticket." Grogan shook his head, letting Cervone know he was between a rock and a hard place on this one. "And Chief, she's my dead partner's kid, for chrissake." He looked at Cervone. His eyes implored him to help. "And Devlin used to be on the job too. And he was a hero cop. We drive him out, and the papers ever catch wind of it . . ." He finished the sentence with another helpless shrug.

Cervone leaned back in his chair. "Devlin's nothing but a fucking cop killer as far as I'm concerned," he said. "And I want his fucking ass out of this. And I want it out now. *Capisce?*"

Grogan nodded. "All right, Chief. I'll tell him. And I'll tell him hard. But I can't guarantee what's gonna happen with Adrianna. You gotta understand that."

Cervone rocked in his chair, thinking for a moment. "No, on second thought, you stay out of it. I'll take care of Devlin. You stay close to the woman and keep her from doing anything stupid." He leaned forward.

"And you find this fucking killer. And you develop *any-thing*—any lead at all—you bring it straight to me. No-body else." He leaned back again. "I'll decide what this prick Mallory gets and what he doesn't get. This is *our* case. No matter what that nigger bastard in Gracie Mansion says." He stared hard at Grogan. "You got that?"

Grogan smiled. "I got it, Chief," he said.

When Grogan was gone, Cervone stared at his phone for several moments, then picked up the receiver and punched the intercom button. "Get me the head of the bureau's Behavioral Science Unit in Quantico," he snapped when his secretary came on the line. "If he's not in his office, get him at home. If he's not there, find out where the fuck he is and get him." He slammed the receiver down, then spun in his chair and looked out the window. That FBI prick Mallory had fucked up his whole evening, he told himself. He was already an hour late getting to his girlfriend's apart-ment in Queens. Now she'd be pissed and would keep her fucking legs closed for at least two hours to let him know it. And that would make him late getting home, and then he'd have to listen to his wife bitch about that. Somebody was going to pay for it, he told himself. And it was going to start with that asshole Mallory.

Adrianna walked to the sofa, holding a cup of coffee. It was barely light outside, and Devlin was still in her bed, sleeping soundly. She sat and looked across the room at him, a small smile of pleasure and satisfaction coming to her lips.

They had made love with abandon last night, both collapsing from exhaustion, then falling asleep in each other's arms. The smile faded. It seemed so right, so natural, and yet . . . She took a sip of the coffee, still watching him. She wondered how much of what she felt came from her fear, her need to have him there. She felt safe when they were together; she could put what had happened—the threat that still hung over her—out of mind. When he was away from her—except those times when she was deep into her work—the fear jumped out at her without warning and dug in its claws. She closed her eyes and let out a long breath. She didn't want to convince herself she was falling in love with him again. He was still a cop, and the way she felt about that hadn't changed. Not in ten years. And she didn't want him just as a much needed security blanket. She wanted it to be more, she told herself. She just wasn't sure it could ever be that way.

She looked away from the bed, allowing her eyes to roam the dimly lighted room. The new painting she had begun yesterday beckoned, but she lacked the energy to approach it now. Later, she thought. When he's gone and I need to fill my mind. Her eyes continued to move across the room, then stopped and tracked back. There was something under the door, but she could barely make it out. She leaned forward, half rising from the sofa.

It looked like a large manila envelope, and she squinted trying to be certain. Placing the coffee on the table before the sofa, she stood and walked slowly to the door. It was an envelope, and it had obviously been slipped under the door during the night or earlier this morning. She bent, picked it up, and moved to a small table. Turning on a lamp, she undid the metal clasp that held the flap, then withdrew a second envelope. It was black, the type used by photographers to hold prints and negatives. She used her thumbnail to pry open the second flap and removed several eight-by-ten prints. The backs of the prints were to her, and she turned them over. She froze.

Melissa Coors' body lay on a floor, a wash of blood covering her chest and stomach. Her eyes and mouth were partially open, and her legs were spread obscenely, so her vagina was clearly visible. In the mirror, above and behind the body, stood the hooded figure, the camera in his hands.

Adrianna's hands began to shake, then her arms, then her legs. She couldn't take her eyes off the photograph. She held her breath and forced herself to look at the others. They were all the same, taken from slightly different angles. All but the final one. It was a close-up of the woman's face. And it was the most horrible of all.

Melissa Coors stared up at her through half-opened eyes. Her partially opened mouth seemed about to speak.

And then the photograph began to fade.

"Paul!" Adrianna screamed. "Paul! Get up, Paul. Get up!"

Devlin flew from the bed, revolver in hand. He stumbled, righted himself, then hurried to the door, the weapon up beside his head, his left hand holding and steadying his right wrist.

"What is it?" He was turning slowly, looking in every direction for whatever threat had produced Adrianna's cry.

"The pictures, Paul. Look!"

He stared at the handful of photos in Adrianna's hands, then reached out and took one. It was a fast-fading blur, and he could barely make out the face of a woman. He grabbed another and stared at it. It appeared to be a figure on its back, but it was decomposing before his eyes, and he couldn't be certain.

"What the hell are they?" he asked. "And where did you get them?"

"Someone slipped them under the door," Adrianna said. "They were pictures of Melissa. Pictures of her *dead*." A chill went through her. "And the killer was in them. In the mirror. In his robe. With the camera in his hands." She stared at him, unable to believe her own words, realizing for the first time that Paul was standing there naked. She shook her head. "And then they started to fade. Right in my hands. Someone developed them that way. Did it so they would fade, disappear, right after I saw them."

"But how?"

"The fixing solution," she snapped. "If you don't use the right solution when you're developing the prints, they'll fade as soon as they're exposed to light." She picked up the black envelope—the one that had been inside the manila. "They were in this," she said, waving the black envelope at him. "So the light couldn't get to them until I opened it. And as soon as I did, it was too late. Nothing could stop them from fading then." She stared at him, her eyes imploring. "Could you see them? Could you make out Melissa in the prints?"

Devlin gave a rough shake to his head. More to clear his mind than anything else. "All I saw was a figure that looked like a woman. And a face. But it was too blurred to tell whose."

"Shit!" Adrianna stamped her foot. She began to crumple the remaining prints in her hands.

"Don't," Devlin said, taking them from her.

"But why? They're useless."

"We'll send it all to the lab. You never know." He put the pictures down on the table, then looked at the door. The sonofabitch had come again. Still playing his cat and mouse game.

Devlin turned and walked across the room to the telephone.

"What are you doing?" Adrianna called after him.

"I'm calling Eddie, so he can get his ass down here."

"But it's only six o'clock."

"Yeah, I know," Devlin said. "But I'm sick of this game. We've got to get some outside surveillance on this building. No matter who gets pissed off."

15

Father James Hopkins paced the bare wood floor. The small room he kept on the top floor of the shelter had a solitary window that opened onto a fire escape leading to a dark, narrow, and forbidding alley. The priest had used that alley and fire escape to enter his room at 4:00 A.M. Now he paced in a steady circle, staying little more than a foot from each wall. The small bed he used—really little more than a cot—was placed, oddly, in the center of the room, and the floor around the bed showed a scuffed, circular path, identical to the one he now walked.

The priest was naked from the waist up, and his bare feet—protruding from the slightly too long legs of his faded jeans—were smudged with dirt. His face held a film of sweat, as did his upper body. He had been pacing, intermittently, for hours, stopping every fifteen minutes or so to again try the telephone number of a person he was desperate to reach.

He glanced at the wall clock. Nine o'clock. Five hours. Again he went to the phone and dialed. Four rings later the call was answered.

"Thank God," Hopkins said. "I've been trying to reach you all night.

"What's wrong? You sound frantic."

"The police. They're digging into my past. They're going to destroy me." There was a note of panic in his voice, and he sounded as though he might be on the verge of tears. "God, I thought they were going to arrest me at the theater this afternoon."

"Why didn't you tell me right away? Why did you wait?"

"I was in a panic. . . . I didn't know what to do. . . . I just ran out of there when they finished with me." Hopkins drew a deep breath. "That man Grogan, he's vicious. And I know he'll never let up. He's going to hound me until he finds what he wants. And the other one. Devlin. He's even worse. I can tell. God, they're both after me."

"Calm down. And do as I say. Your past doesn't matter. It doesn't *mean* anything. I'll handle it."

"But if they go to the archdiocese, it doesn't matter what it means, or doesn't mean. . . . Oh, God, if they—"

"Shut up and listen!"

The priest stiffened, and his hand, holding the receiver, began to tremble slightly. Then more. And more. But he did as he was told. He listened.

Mario Cervone entered the commissioner's office promptly at nine o'clock. He had requested the appointment the night before, stating it was urgent he see the P.C. at his first available time slot.

Andrew Dalton seemed almost buoyant as he sat behind Teddy Roosevelt's old desk. He was anticipating news that an arrest of the serial killer who had plagued him was only hours away—news he could pass on to the mayor—news that would assure his next six months in office and guarantee the P.C.'s pension he so desperately wanted.

Dalton visibly slumped in his chair thirty seconds after Cervone had begun to speak; his Brooks Brothers suit seemed to wilt with him. Three minutes later, as Cervone finished the initial thrust of his argument, Dalton was becoming visibly angry.

"So let me understand," he began. "You called Mallory's boss in Quantico and made a formal complaint. Is that right?"

"Informal," Cervone said.

Dalton stared at the chief. He looked pleased with himself—content, almost chipper—and Dalton suspected he had probably gotten laid the previous night. He wondered when he himself had last looked that satisfied. Although with Cervone, he told himself, fucking Mallory would have had the same effect.

"And what happens now if the FBI decides to pull its people out of the investigation?"

Cervone's dark eyes almost glittered. "I can't think of anything that would be better for this department," he said.

Dalton pressed his thumb and index finger to his own eyes and slowly massaged. He looked up at Cervone. "Well, I can," he said. "Because that would accomplish two things, and two things only. First, it would greatly piss off a certain man who lives in Gracie Mansion. And second, it would guarantee that both of us would be out of work." He glared across his desk. *"Both of us."* He leaned forward, holding Cervone's gaze. "And neither of those things is going to happen."

Cervone's face remained blank, and Dalton knew he considered the threat as empty as the suit the P.C. now wore. The man truly believed that his friends at the archdiocese would keep him safe from all attack. And perhaps, just perhaps, he was right. Dalton also knew that the only people who would rush to his own defense were his wife and one daughter, who was blissfully spending his money at Sarah Lawrence College. And that would occur only when they each realized that his bank account was about to be infected with a terminal illness.

"So they stay," Cervone said, breaking the silence.

Dalton continued to glare at the man. "Oh, yes, Chief. They stay. Even if *one* of us has to get down on his knees and beg them."

Cervone's eyes hardened for the first time, and his square jaw seemed to become even more rocklike. He's telling you that one person won't be him, Dalton thought. But, dammit, it sure as hell will be. Even if

you personally have to hold a gun to his head to make
it happen.

The commissioner lowered his head and ran the fingers of both hands through his graying hair. Then he
looked back at the chief.

"And what, pray tell, are you doing about the real
problem? The fact that you've got a loose cannon sitting in the middle of what was supposed to be a very
confidential investigation?"

Cervone gestured with one hand. "I'm here to seek
your counsel on that."

Dalton leaned back, stared at the ceiling, and smiled.
"What you mean, Chief, is that you're here so, if the
shit ever hits the fan, you can point back at this office
and say you were following my instructions." The P.C.
sat forward again. "Which is the real reason you lodged
a complaint with the FBI last night. Which is the reason you drop every problem that arises in this case
right here."

The commissioner tapped the top of his desk with
his middle finger, and Cervone wondered if there was
any message intended in his choice of digits.

Cervone smiled. "Whatever," he said.

The commissioner returned the smile. Ice on ice.
"Just so long as we understand each other," he said.
"And now *you* understand *this*. You are to get Paul
Devlin out of this case. Out of this city. Out of this
state. And back to whatever God forsaken boondock
he floated in from. And before you ask: Yes, I will give
you that in writing. In fact, I'll make it a direct order.
And, if you fail to carry out that order, I will bring you
up on charges, even if it means I get tossed out of this
office on my ass. Because, you see, Chief, it won't
matter. Because if Paul Devlin, or anyone else fucks
up this investigation, I'll be out anyway." He watched
Cervone's eyes narrow, and offered up the same icy
smile again. "And I God damned don't intend to go
alone. Is that *understood*?"

*   *   *

Eddie flipped through the series of drawings Adrianna had made over the past three hours. It was her complete recollection of what the now faded photographs had contained. She had begun them as soon as Devlin had telephoned Grogan, and she insisted they were as perfect as she could make them.

"If I didn't know better, I'd think she'd been at the murder scene," Grogan said. He flipped back to one of the drawings. It was a close-up of Melissa's upper thighs and vagina. "This one really gets me. Even the blood pattern on her leg looks right." He shook his head, as if driving away a memory. "I'll compare them to the photos forensics took, but off the top of my head, I'll be damned if I can see anything that's out of whack with what I remember." He shook his head again, then glanced across the room at Adrianna. She was at her easel, back at work on her new painting. "I don't know how she does that," he said. "It must of shook her up. Shit, it shakes me up, just thinking how this creep stood there and took pictures of his handiwork. Talk about your pervert scumbags."

"Our friend Umberto has a darkroom in his gallery," Devlin said.

"You sure about that?"

"He mentioned it when he was here the other day. Apparently they do their own photography for the brochures and stuff they put together for their shows."

Grogan tapped his nose with one finger, then lowered his voice. "I think we better expedite our little break-in. I'd like to get a look at that darkroom, and we don't have enough shit to get a warrant." He paused a minute, staring off at nothing in particular. "You know there's something that always bothered me about this case. Everything I've ever read about serial jobs says the perp almost always takes something from the victim. Some kind of token that he wants to keep."

"They call it a trophy," Devlin said. "Sometimes it's even a part of the body."

"Yeah. Well, our perp doesn't do that. At least nothing obvious that's jumped out at us. But what if he takes pictures? What if he keeps his own little rogues' gallery? Shit, he did this time." Grogan paused and thought about his own premise. "And why didn't he send pictures to the other victims? Why *not* the others? Why only this time?"

"The others didn't know any of the earlier victims," Devlin said. "Hell, they didn't even know there were other victims. But Adrianna knew Melissa. So this had special shock value. A terror quotient, if you will." Devlin glanced back at Adrianna. She was still hard at work. "This was better than a letter or a phone call," he added. "And he knows I'm here. And why. And he wants to play with me too. Even to the point of sending a picture of himself and his handiwork. One that's going to disappear in my hands."

Grogan nodded. "Makes sense." He took out a cigarette, put a match to it, and blew a stream of smoke past Devlin's shoulder. "Shit. These fading photographs. This is one clever sonofabitch."

Diabolical, Devlin thought. Diabolical was a better word for it.

"But I don't know what we can do about outside surveillance," Grogan continued. "Especially now that Cervone is about to start chewing on your asshole. You hear from that guinea prick yet?"

Grogan had telephoned Devlin right after his meeting with Cervone. But Devlin had been unconcerned. Despite Eddie's promises when they began, he had known it was only a matter of time before the FBI and the bosses at the Puzzle Palace found out he was there.

"Not yet," Devlin said. "But I don't think it's gonna take Mario very long to find me and start chewing." He stared at the floor. "After that Ritual case, he wanted my ass bad. He even tried to block my disability retirement. The other bosses stopped him. They just wanted me gone. Like a bad memory."

Grogan understood; he knew the story. He hadn't

told Devlin about Cervone's "cop killer" comment. He knew the man didn't need to hear it.

Grogan looked at his watch. "What time is Gabrielle supposed to get here?" he asked.

Devlin checked his own watch. "Any time now."

"You really think more of this hypnosis shit will help?"

"Who knows?" Devlin said. "I just want to make sure there was nothing in those pictures that Adrianna missed." He took Grogan's arm and led him off toward a farther corner of the loft, well out of Adrianna's hearing. "I think we ought to check out our other people too," he said. "Richards, Brooks, and our little priest. See if they have any hobbies."

"Like photography?" Grogan suggested.

"Yeah, like photography. I think our killer may have a visual bent on things." He thought about that for a moment, then added: "And let's move as fast as we can on his woman Hopkins was involved with. She was supposed to be an entertainer. So have someone check with theatrical agents, booking agents, people like that. If she left town, somebody's got to know where she went, or where she's working. Something in my gut tells me Gail Collins fits into all this somehow."

The child sobbed against one hand, trying to keep the sound from being heard. The figure was in the bed now, and the child's head was pressed against one shoulder.

"You make me come. You know that's true, don't you?" The whispered question hung there. Then a pause, a moment of silence, awaiting a reply. A hand stroked the back of the child's head. The child's body was naked now. Flesh pressed against flesh. "But it's good that I come. It's good for both of us. You believe that, don't you?"

The child's body began to tremble, and it was suddenly pressed tightly against the other.

"You know that, don't you?" The voice was more insistent now, coming out in a low hiss.

The child gasped, fought for breath. "Yes . . . yes."

Gabrielle Lyons sat on the sofa, absently holding a cup of tea in one hand. They were alone—Adrianna had been taken to Umberto's gallery to review the plans for the prospectus and the poster—and Gabrielle, Devlin thought, looked particularly deep in thought. It was ridiculous, but it almost seemed as though she were sleeping with her eyes wide open.

"So there was nothing new that you were able to find," he said.

The sound of his voice seemed to startle her, and she looked quickly at him and shook her head.

"I'm sorry. I was thinking about something that came out under hypnosis."

"About the photos?"

"No. It was something else." She continued to stare at him, then smiled. "It wasn't something about this case. It was something else. Something I really can't ethically discuss."

"How does something else come out when you're asking questions about one particular thing?" he asked. Again he had not been permitted to remain during the hypnotic procedure. And again it had annoyed him that he had been excluded.

"Sometimes other things come out. It's a form of association. What I'm asking about produces a memory about something else. It's quite common." She looked at Devlin. It was a very firm look, he decided. "It's one of the reasons I insist about doing it alone with the subject. It removes any subconscious inhibitions. And in doing that, it also, occasionally, allows other things to come out."

"That's a little spooky," Devlin said. "But what about the photos?"

"Nothing additional, I'm afraid. But that's not surprising. Adrianna's an artist. She sees and thinks visually. And she has great powers of retention for the things she sees. If anything, I'd be surprised if she hadn't retained those images vividly."

"So we struck out," Devlin said.

Gabrielle didn't reply immediately. She seemed off again, as if running some idea through some mental hurdle.

"Paul," she said at length. "What did *you* see in those pictures?"

Devlin shook his head. "Nothing really. A figure. One that could have been a woman. A face. By the time I saw them everything was blurred, already fading badly. Why?"

Gabrielle stared into her tea cup. "Nothing. Nothing I can put my finger on right now."

"About the photos?"

"No." She hesitated. "Well, in a way. But nothing I can talk about without sounding like an idiot. Let me think about it. Then, if I think it's worthwhile, we'll talk."

16

It was midnight when Willie the Gimp slipped the blade of a thin putty knife between the windows and opened the latch. A steady drizzle beat down around them, making the Gimp's hands slick and slippery, but it had still taken him only a minute and a half to deactivate the burglar alarm. Now it took another two minutes of deft work with his lock picks to unlock the interior steel gate inside the sash. When he had finished, he swung the gate open, glanced at his watch, then grinned at Eddie Grogan. His large, uneven teeth were almost brown from the four packs of cigarettes he smoked each day.

"Just under four minutes," he whispered. "A new world's record."

The Gimp was a short, skinny, balding man who was pushing fifty. Years ago, Grogan had caught him inside a jewelry store, hiding in a ventilation shaft that had been small enough to give a cat claustrophobia. It was the only time, in thirty years of devoted criminal activity, that Willie had ever been caught. Oddly, it had made Eddie Grogan his friend for life. He was one of the few men Willie had found he could admire.

Grogan patted him on the head now. "You're a fucking artist," he whispered. "Now get inside and see if you can find a safe." He raised a cautioning finger. "But just open it. Don't take nothing. We ain't fucking thieves."

When Willie had disappeared through the window,

Grogan leaned back against the wall and grinned at Devlin.

"I hope Umberto don't have the safe wired with dynamite," he whispered. "It would be embarrassing to have to go to Willie's autopsy."

"It would be more embarrassing if you had to go to your own," Devlin hissed.

Ten minutes later, Willie climbed back through the window. He was grinning again. "It was in the wall, behind a picture," he whispered. "Very fucking original. And I didn't take nothing."

"I love you," Grogan said. "Now get lost, and get amnesia."

When Willie had disappeared, Grogan turned to Devlin. "You sure you don't want me in there with you?" he asked.

Devlin shook his head. "If it ever comes down to a search warrant, you may have to testify about what's found. I don't want you tainted. You stay across the street by that phone, and call if you see Sweet Cakes coming home."

"Okay. But watch that skinny Irish tush of yours. I don't wanna go to your postmortem either."

Devlin slipped through the window and into Umberto's private office, and began a search of his safe and file cabinet. Neither held anything of interest.

He turned to the antique partner's desk, searching one side, then the other. In the bottom drawer of the second side, he found two thick folders of photographs. He laid them on the desk and opened the first. It held more than three dozen eight-by-ten prints of women posed in various stages of bondage. Each were performing sexual acts with a male dressed only in an executioner's hood. He opened the next folder. The photos inside had obviously been taken at shows in Umberto's gallery. They were crowded scenes, but each had a particular woman as the camera's focal point.

Adrianna's image stared back at him from the photos. In most she was smiling or laughing. In a few others she was listening intently to cocktail conversation. In another she was hanging tightly to Vincent Richards' arm.

He turned back to the pornographic photos, turned one over, and noted the rubber-stamp logo on the back. They were professional. Posed jobs that had come from a sleazy mail-order house. Suitable for framing. He turned the photo back to its image side. It showed a terrified blonde in a particularly contorted pose. The executioner hovered over her, erection at the ready. He slipped it back into the folder, and looked at the adjacent pictures of Adrianna. Oh, Umberto. What makes me think you'd like to get her from that folder into this one? he asked himself.

He returned the folders to the desk, then, using a pen light, made his way to the outer storage area. He wanted to locate and search the darkroom, the basement, and finally the third-floor apartment. And he needed to finish before the Marquis de Sade got home.

One of Eddie's men had tailed Umberto to a dinner party uptown. It was in the home of an Italian diplomat, and his man had learned from a talkative doorman that the parties always ran late, seldom ending before two in the morning.

Devlin knew Eddie was in position next to a working phone across the street—one of the few left in New York. But the situation still made him nervous. The last thing he wanted was to meet Umberto coming up the stairs as he was leaving. Either dressed in a coarse brown robe or an Armani tuxedo. Just being caught like that would destroy the courtroom value of anything they might subsequently, and legally, find.

He located the darkroom with little difficulty, and searched through a file cabinet filled with prints. There were more than sixty folders, each containing photographs of paintings and posed portraits of the respective artists. Oddly, the folder of Adrianna's work was missing. But it could have been removed to prepare the prospectus and poster Umberto had spoken about.

Either that, or it was kept in a special place, for a special reason.

He searched the basement and found it surprisingly barren of artwork, which made him wonder just how stable Umberto's business was. Then he made his way up a rear staircase to the third floor, which suddenly took on the appearance of an opulent apartment building, with a richly carpeted hall, brocaded wallpaper, and delicate sconce light fixtures. He moved to a massive mahogany door and slipped the lock with a credit card.

The door led directly into a large, darkened living room, and off to the left were an equally dark open kitchen and dining area. He couldn't make out the furnishings, but the combination of the two rooms took up more than half the space of the entire floor, easily a thousand square feet, and equal in size to the first-floor gallery itself.

Off to the right were two doors, one closed, one partially opened. From the open door a shaft of light intruded into the living room. Devlin moved toward it cautiously, then froze as the distinct sound of someone humming floated from the lighted room.

Carefully, using the diffuse light from the room, Devlin moved quietly to the door. Inside, he could see a woman seated on a chaise longue, thumbing through a magazine that kept her face hidden. She had blond hair that hung to her shoulders, and was dressed in a sheer dress that flared out at the waist, revealing dark stockings, attached by a black garter belt. Her feet were encased in bright red stiletto heels. The only discordant note was the woman's bare chest, visible through the flimsy material. It was flat and covered with black, curly hair.

When the magazine dropped slightly Devlin got a clear view of Hubert Walsh, a.k.a. Umberto, and his meticulously made-up face.

Without warning Umberto tossed the magazine over his head and swung himself from the chair. He stretched, a lascivious smile spreading across his bright red lips. "Time to go. Time to go. Time to go," he sang to himself, then tottered toward a large armoire off to his right.

Devlin watched as the man withdrew a long black fur coat—mink, or perhaps even sable, he guessed. He turned quietly and beat a hasty retreat out of the building.

'Whadda ya mean he's inside?" Grogan said. Devlin was next to him in a darkened doorway across the street. "He left the joint at eight-thirty. My guy tailed him up to this apartment uptown, watched him go in, checked with the doorman, and took off. The sonofabitch is supposed to be eating cannoli with that fucking dago diplomat. And he ain't supposed to outta there until after his coach turns back into a fucking pumpkin." He shook his head. "I can't figure it. That dago ain't even supposed to serve dinner until eleven o'clock. Unless our little Mother Teresa got pissed off about something and left early. Shit, we're lucky you didn't get fucking nailed inside that joint."

Devlin stared at the entrance to the gallery, waiting for Umberto—mink and all—to emerge. Grogan's car was parked around the corner, and he wanted to follow the man wherever he went.

"I hope the guy you got watching Adrianna's loft is doing a better job than the mope who followed Sweet Cakes," he said.

Grogan let out a snort. "Hey, it ain't my guy's fault. He did what he was told." Suddenly Grogan started to laugh, thinking about the scene Devlin had described in Umberto's apartment. "Hey, so he had to leave early. Who could figure? Maybe he had to wash his hair, do his nails." The laugh turned into a low cackle, and he raised one hand, affecting a limp wrist. "It's a bitch keeping yourself up these days."

Devlin fought off a smile, then suddenly froze. Across the street Umberto was just exiting the gallery, the fur coat pulled tightly about him with one hand.

He moved quickly to the curb and began waving gaily at a cab headed up West Broadway. Devlin took Grogan's arm and pulled him from the doorway.

"Let's get to the car," he said. "I'll drive."

Grogan glanced back over his shoulder. "I think I'm fucking in love," he said. "Sweet Cakes sure got a nifty pair of gams."

They pulled out behind the cab, keeping a half block between them.

"You think he's going anyplace'll do us any good?" Grogan asked.

"Who knows?" Devlin said. "I just keep remembering what Juice told us about the guy who hired him. How he might have been wearing a false beard. Then I keep seeing Umberto with his wig and his lipstick."

"Don't forget the nail polish," Grogan added. "Although the color was definitely tacky." He rested his head back against the seat. "But, hey, I get your drift." He chewed on the end of his thumb, mulling over the possibilities. "This case is beautiful," he said at length. "A priest with a wayward dick, a Broadway director and playwright who are doing a show about a sexually abused kid, and a gallery owner who thinks he's fucking Marlene Dietrich. Wake me up when the talking horse gets here."

"I just wish I'd had a chance to get a look in Marlene's closet," Devlin said.

"Why, you running low on silk undies?"

"No. Coarse brown robes."

"I guess we'll have to go back in," Grogan said. "What the hell, it keeps the Gimp in practice."

"Let's just make sure Umberto's really gone next time."

"A minor flaw," Grogan said. "Besides, I kinda like the idea. Old Umberto's got a real nice set of pins on him."

Again, Devlin tried to hold back a smile but couldn't. "It's been a long time since you've gotten laid, hasn't it, Eddie?"

Grogan leveled a finger at him. "Not as long as you think. You just make sure you keep your pecker in *your* pants tonight. I don't want my godchild to get AIDS."

Umberto's cab headed west, then north, and weaved its way through a series of streets that held rundown tenements, warehouses, and an endless string of seedy bars frequented by merchant seamen. It turned into West Street, one of the few city streets that carried traffic in both directions, and finally pulled up in front of a bar set against a backdrop of the multilane West Side Highway.

"I knew it," Grogan said, staring at the neon sign on the squat, triangular-shaped building. "And I ain't going in there. Even if you hold a gun to my fucking head."

Devlin looked up at the flickering sign. The Hammer was one of the city's long established and more notorious sadomasochistic gay bars. He watched Umberto slide from the cab and totter toward the heavy steel door. He rapped lightly, then leaned his head forward as the door opened a crack. Finally it swung wide, revealing a hulking biker type who appraised Umberto's costume, then stepped back and allowed him to go inside.

"I see security hasn't changed on that joint," Devlin said. He had caught a homicide at the bar years ago—a performer in the "fist fucking" show that was the bar's main attraction. The bar—or club, as the patrons preferred to call it—was supposedly controlled by the Gambino family, along with the Anvil, the Strap, and the other clubs that dotted the West Side docks. It was part of a monopoly that included all the tits-and-ass joints frequented by heterosexuals trying to put some eroticism in otherwise stale lives. Together they gave the mob a firm grip on the underbelly of New York's sex scene, along with its control of pornographic bookstores, films, and sex shops.

The gay bars and clubs were said to be under the

tutelage of a mobster named Peter Rabitto—known in mob circles as Peter Rabbit—who was rumored by cops to be gay himself. Which, if true, Devlin mused, made the mob a more socially conscious employer than the U.S. military—more concerned about a man's ability to produce results than where he chose to place his magic wand.

"You going in there?" Grogan asked.

Devlin nodded. "I want to see who he's meeting." He reached down and unfastened his ankle holster and handed the weapon to Grogan, then reached into the backseat and retrieved a trench coat. Grogan was wearing a wide-brimmed hat against the rain, and Devlin snatched it from his head and put it on. "You have any sunglasses?" he asked.

Grogan pulled some from the glove compartment, then watched as Devlin struggled into his own makeshift costume. "You look like some fag Hollywood producer," he said. He grinned. "And almost good enough to eat."

"Thanks, Eddie. If you see me come flying out the door, walk over and pick up what's left."

The biker playing doorman eyed Devlin suspiciously. The club, like all its ilk, was regularly raided by the Public Morals Squad for putting on pornographic entertainment. After each raid the owners went to court, had the charges reduced or thrown out, tightened security yet again, and reopened for business. It was an endless game that only the cops seemed to enjoy, and Devlin had often wondered if it was done simply to increase the ante on the payoffs supposedly made to the squad commanders.

"I ain't seen you before," the biker said. He was shirtless, dressed only in a leather vest, leather riding pants, and motorcycle boots. There was a red bandanna tied around his head, and it was grease-stained from filthy shoulder-length hair. He was also big

enough to chew Devlin up and spit him out, and looked
as though he'd enjoy doing it.

"I'm from the West Coast," Devlin said in the light-
est voice he could manage. "A friend recommended
this place."

"The friend shoulda brought you," the biker said. He
took Devlin's arms, lifted them, and gave him a quick
pat down. Satisfied, he inclined his head toward the
interior. "You cause any trouble, I come to visit you,"
he said. "You turn out to be a cop, I'll fucking bust
your head."

The main room was as Devlin remembered it. Dark
and seedy and reeking with the smells of stale sweat,
bad cologne, and marijuana. Off to the right was a
free-standing bar shaped in a large rectangle. Behind
it two naked male bartenders raced about filling orders
for more than fifty customers. In front of the bar was
a dance floor jammed with unisex couples, and beyond
that was the small stage where the nightly performances were held.

Devlin scanned the crowd, wanting to be as far from
Umberto—a.k.a. Marlene Dietrich—as possible. See
and not be seen was the order of the night.

He spotted Umberto near the stage, talking with another drag queen. He seemed to be displaying the long,
false red nails that adorned each finger of each hand.

Devlin went to the bar and ordered a beer, which
was served in a can, sans glass. He would have preferred a stiff shot of Jack Daniel's, but had no intention
of touching one of the grease-covered glasses being
served up by the bartenders. The beer was five bucks.
Hard liquor was seven-fifty a pop. No one ever accused
the mafia of being a cheap date.

Devlin removed the sunglasses, kept his eyes on his
target. He felt rather than saw a man slide into the
space on his left.

"You should keep those glasses on. They give you an
aura of mystery," the man said.

Devlin turned and smiled. "I'm not lonely, and I'm not talkative," he said.

The man straightened. "Oooh. I love it when you talk butch." He winked at Devlin.

Devlin fought off laughter. The man was tall and thin, with neatly barbered, short hair and a precisely trimmed mustache. His eyes danced with merriment, and Devlin thought he'd probably be amusing company under different circumstances.

"I'm just getting over somebody," Devlin explained. "And I'm not very good company."

"Aren't we all," the man said. "Getting over somebody, I mean. My name's Gerard. In case you change your mind." He waved frantically at the bartender, who hurried over, his oversize penis swinging like the pendulum of a clock. "A Shirley Temple," Gerard said, then giggled. "Oh, you better make it Chivas. I'm depressed." He threw a sidelong glance at Devlin.

Umberto was dancing now—cheek to cheek with a man who looked like a pro football nose tackle. Off to the right a group of men stood in a ragged line.

"What's with the line?" Devlin asked Gerard.

"Oh, there's this sweet thing in the kitchen, giving out blow jobs like he was working an assembly line. It's so New York," he said. "You have to stand in line for *everything*." He turned to face Devlin. "There's a room downstairs, you know. Mattresses on the floor, soft lighting . . ."

"Not tonight," Devlin said. "I'm in mourning."

The house lights suddenly dimmed and spotlights illuminated the stage. Devlin hadn't seen the show before, but he had heard about it. He toyed with the idea of leaving.

The dance music ended in mid song, replaced within seconds by the sound of Ravel's *Bolero*. A young man, naked except for a silk scarf draped about his neck, danced onto the stage amid shouts and applause. He was painfully thin, with the body of an underdeveloped young girl, and hair cut in a long, layered shag that resembled an effeminate version of the style once worn by the Beatles.

He danced gracefully to the music as a trapeze was lowered from the ceiling. He moved slowly, teasingly toward it as two naked assistants moved out from the wings, grabbed him roughly by the wrists, and using the silk scarf, tied him to the crossbar.

Slowly the trapeze rose until the dancer's toes were three feet off the floor. The assistants took his ankles and roughly spread his legs, as the crowd began to murmur in anticipation.

As the drumbeat of the music rose, another spotlight illuminated the side of the stage. There, a hulking figure stood hands on hips. Devlin stared at him in near disbelief. He was dressed in a long, coarse hooded robe, a deep brown or black. He couldn't be sure. The front of the robe was open, revealing heavy chains crisscrossing the man's chest. The upper half of his face was covered by a black executioner's mask.

The executioner strode toward the hanging dancer, fist held high above his head. The crowd cheered, pressed closer to the stage. The assistants lifted the dancer's ankles, bending him in half, as the executioner approached him from behind. Slowly, deliberately, as the dancer wailed in simulated agony, the executioner inserted his fist into the proffered rectum, and slid his arm in to the elbow.

The crowd began to chant. "Two fists. Two fists. Two fists."

Devlin lowered his eyes. His fingers gripped the edge of the bar until his knuckles turned white. The executioner's hand had to be tickling the dancer's aorta, he thought. He remembered the homicide he had caught here all those years ago. Another dancer had died during a performance, in what proved to be the result of an epileptic seizure. During the autopsy the M.E. had marveled at the corpse's sphincter muscles, claiming they had been so distorted that the victim had obviously suffered from irreversible incontinence.

Devlin pushed himself away from the bar and turned to go. Gerard's hand took his arm, stopping him.

"There's more," he said. "The best is yet to come."

"Not for me," Devlin said, pulling his arm free.

He slid behind the wheel of the car, let out a long breath, and stared at Grogan.

"You fall in love?" Grogan asked.

Devlin closed his yes. "It's hell to discover that you're thirty-five years old and still innocent," he said.

Grogan's laughter filled the car. When it stopped, he told him about the robed executioner.

"You think maybe this is where our guy got his outfit?" he asked.

"I think we better check it out," Devlin said.

"Tomorrow. In daylight," Grogan said. "Whadda we do now?"

"We wait, and follow Sweet Cakes home."

The wait lasted until 4:00 A.M. The mafia might break every other law in the book, Devlin noted, but they abided by the legal closing hours. No sense in risking a liquor license in a seven-fifty-a-pop joint.

Umberto came out alone, as he had entered, and joined a queue for a line of cabs that had formed along the street. The hacks knew where the money was, and weren't shy about reaching out for it. Devlin wondered about the scenes they witnessed in their rearview mirrors. Or the familiar faces who at times provided them. One of them had allegedly been the late magazine magnate Malcolm Forbes, whose business conservatism was supposedly tempered by a love of rough trade.

"Looks like Marlene didn't score tonight," Grogan said. Like Devlin, he was slouched down in his seat, offering as little profile as possible.

Devlin suddenly rose slightly in his seat. "Jesus Christ," he said.

"What is it?"

Devlin pointed. Farther down the queue, and also alone, stood Brenden Brooks.

17

Two days had passed since the break-in at Umberto's gallery, and Eddie Grogan had spent most of that time hunched over a computer terminal or on the telephone, browbeating and cajoling people in five states and in Washington. He had a feeling time was running out. It was visceral, not something he could put his finger on. And it wasn't a question of the investigation. He knew time never ran out there. But it was running out for Adrianna.

He finally called Devlin mid-afternoon of the second day, and said he needed to meet. And he wanted everyone there, wanted as much feed into the information he had gathered as he could get.

They were in the living area of the loft, bright sunshine streaming through the windows. It was one of those rare days that New Yorkers rave about. Bright and crisp and clean. Days they want to believe are commonplace amid the endless assault of grit and filth. And it seemed incongruous to the things Grogan was about to discuss.

"First, we showed our boy Juice some pictures of our suspects. But it was useless," Grogan began. "The poor bastard's brain dead. But we did get the lab report back on the robe our little junkie was wearing. It was the same material that was found under Melissa Coors' nails. The same. Identical."

"But Paul had that robe. He took it away from the man *before* Melissa was killed." It was Gabrielle and she looked momentarily confused.

231

"That's right," Grogan said. He saw light dawning in Gabrielle's eyes, and grinned at her. "I'm gonna make a detective outta you yet," he said. He glanced quickly at the others. Adrianna seemed bewildered, but he could see Devlin's mind already racing ahead.

"So we got two possibilities," he continued. "Either a bunch of Capuchin monks are running around the city killing people or . . ."

"Or we have costumes all made for a specific order. From the same bolt of cloth." It was Devlin. He stared at Grogan. "Theatrical costumes."

Grogan nodded. "And I took a piece of the costume they use in the show at the Hammer. The lab tested it, and it don't match. Different material."

"Doesn't mean our boy didn't get the idea from seeing that one," Devlin said.

"No, it doesn't," Grogan said. "And I got people checking companies who do that kind of work. They're gonna go back five years on all special orders."

"But if they're theatrical costumes they could have been used again and again," Adrianna said. "I've been to costume agencies with Vincent. Sure, there are special orders, but most costumes are rented over and over."

"Yeah, that's true," Grogan said. "And it could be this guy rented two costumes—or got his hands on them somehow—that came from the same material. But I doubt it. It could also be somebody sitting at their little sewing machine at home, working from one piece of material." He shrugged. "But it's a shot. And we ain't had many of those so far."

"What's next?" Devlin asked.

"The pictures," Grogan said. "They were delivered by an all-night delivery service. You wouldn't believe how many pre-dawn deliveries are made in this city. Anyway, they were picked up from a security guard in a building on Wall Street." He looked steadily at Devlin. "A building that houses a lot of brokerage houses." He inclined his head to one side. "Something tells me our perp is playing a little game with us. Letting us know, he knows your cover is a scam." Grogan lit a Camel before continuing. "The security guard is no help. And there was a smaller envelope attached to the bigger one. With the fee inside. In cash. All prearranged."

"He needs to show you he's smarter than you are," Gabrielle said. "You've become a challenge to him. And that is extremely dangerous."

"It will be for him," Grogan said. "I've seen other perps play that game. They always lose."

"What about our list of people?" Devlin asked.

"That was next," Grogan said. He ground out his cigarette and settled back in his chair. "First, our party lady, Rachael Barrows. It's Dr. Rachael Barrows. She's a high-class gynecologist with a fancy office on Park Avenue. And guess what? Melissa Coors was one of her patients. Her name and office number were in Melissa's address book."

Devlin turned to Gabrielle. "Did you know she was a doctor?" he asked.

Gabrielle shook her head. "But that's not surprising. There are more M.D.'s in this city than . . ." She hesitated and smiled at Grogan. "Than cops," she added. "What does surprise me is that she doesn't flaunt the title. Most docs can't wait to let people know they have a medical degree. It's more important to them than sex."

"Anyway," Grogan said, "there's no indication any of the other victims were her patients. But we still have to check that out." He looked at Devlin. "It should be a priority, but there are some other goodies that may take precedent."

"Like what?" Devlin asked.

"Let me get rid of the easy one first," Grogan said. "Our priest. He has no criminal record, juvenile or otherwise. Shit, he was in the seminary at fourteen, never had time to get in trouble. And there are no new developments on Gail Collins, the lady he was sporting around with. I have found out she was a saloon singer, but I haven't dug her up yet. But I will." Grogan leaned forward again. "Now the good stuff. Our boy Richards for starters. Seems old Vincent directed Shakespeare in the Park about three years ago, and, according to his then wardrobe mistress, it was *Macbeth*, and he threw a shitfit about the costumes. Seems like the opening scene has three witches in it, and the costume company sent him these brown-hooded things instead of black like he ordered. The wardrobe lady said he was so pissed he just threw them out, and ordered new ones from another company. Apparently they had to pay for the ones he eighty-sixed, and it beat the shit out of her wardrobe budget. So she remembers it. Clearly."

"What happened to the costumes?" Devlin asked.

"Trashed as far as she knows," Grogan said. "But it seems he was also doing some street theater with our priest at the time." He shrugged. "There's nothing to show the priest got the costumes, and the wardrobe lady insists they were thrown out. But . . ." He let the sentence die. "Anyway, it's the only thing that even hints that the costumes might of gone to little Father Jim, and it's all pretty far out right now. And I don't think we could prove it one way or the other. Who's to say Richards didn't keep them, or somebody else didn't lift them out of the trash? So, unless somebody owns up, we got zilch on that."

"We'll check," Devlin said. He corrected himself. "*I'll* check."

Grogan nodded. "Okay," he continued. "Staying on our director. Seems his relationship with his soon-to-be ex-wife ain't as copacetic as he says. And not so soon-to-be, either. They formally separated five years ago, after she got a relief-from-abuse order against him, claiming he beat the shit out of her. He got her to drop the charge, and kept it out of the papers with a very healthy financial settlement and support payments that would choke a horse. And neither one of them's pushing for a divorce. He doesn't want her charges to come out, and she figures the court won't give her as much as she gets now if she pushes it. And any agreed-upon settlement would open up the whole financial thing to review later on, and not give her the opportunity to talk about the abuse. So she ain't throwing away her hole card. She's happy just holding onto his short hairs, and squeezing every time she wants something." Grogan made a face. "Could make a guy bitter about women," he added.

"Next we got Brooks. Seems like he's been down for a long time. Hasn't written anything anybody wanted until this new play. It's considered brilliant. And the talk is, it's also autobiographical."

"He insists the idea came from Vincent," Devlin interjected.

"Yeah," Grogan said. "And with the juvenile sexual abuse and all, it pretty much matches the FBI profile of our guy. Put that together with the fact that he plays at the Hammer, and—"

"Don't put too much weight on that," Gabrielle interjected. "I don't know how familiar you are with child abuse, but it isn't all that uncommon."

"Even for boys?" Grogan asked.

"Not as high as with females, certainly," Gabrielle said. "But still high. And performed by women as well as men, only to a lesser degree. And it rarely has an effect on homosexuality. It might make someone experiment. But homosexuality is genetic, not learned."

"What about the sadomasochism?" Grogan asked.

"It's a deviant behavior as common in heterosexuals as it is in homosexuals," Gabrielle said. She hesitated. "But it certainly could play a role in the type of person we're looking for," she added.

Grogan made another face, openly displeased that one of his points had been diminished.

"And now we got a final kicker," he continued. "Our boy Umberto is a twin." He waited, enjoying the looks on everyone's face. "He has a brother, Oliver. A dead ringer. Nobody's supposed to be able to tell them apart.

Nobody." Adrianna started to express her incredulity, but Grogan raised a hand stopped her. "It gets better," he said. "Seems Oliver got tossed out of the army about fifteen years ago. He was making a career out of it. Poor boy from the Bronx and all that shit. But with twelve years in, and sergeant stripes on his arm, he almost kills this sixteen-year-old Panamanian hooker. Testified at his court-martial that she fleeced his wallet, then started calling him a faggot when he caught her. Then came at him with a blade." Grogan shook his head. "The army didn't buy it. Seems there was a similar charge against him two years before that, but it was dropped. But the army has long memories, and they don't go along with this shit about inadmissible evidence. Everything's admissible. All the way back to the shit in your diapers."

"Where is Oliver now?" Devlin asked.

"Nobody seems to know. Seems to have disappeared." He grinned. "Except that his state tax returns list him as part owner of a Soho art gallery. Place called Umberto's."

Devlin let out a low whistle. He was thinking about the photograph in Umberto's office. The juvenile streetwalker eyeing the GI whose back was to the camera. "And there was a second door off the living room in Umberto's apartment," he said. "Maybe a second bedroom."

"Yeah," Grogan said. "And maybe my guy who followed Umberto up to that diplomat's party didn't screw up so bad after all."

Devlin nodded, more to himself than to what Grogan was saying.

"Thought you'd like it," Grogan said. "But I'll take Hubert and Oliver Walsh. That way it can just be tied to Melissa Coors. Adrianna doesn't come into it. And Umberto doesn't get pissed at her and maybe eighty-six her show. Right?"

"I'll go with you," Devlin said. "We'll leave Adrianna out of it. Just say I'm helping you on the Coors thing."

"Uh-uh. Cervone finds out we're doing anything together, I'll be working for you in Vermont. And I ain't
sure I can handle a cattle-rustling caper. Besides,
you're tied to Adrianna too tight. He gets pissed at you,
maybe he gets pissed at her anyways."

Devlin nodded. He hated to be left out of it, but he
knew Eddie was right. On all counts. And he knew
Grogan could handle it. "I'll take Richards and
Brooks," he said. "Later we can see the priest together.
We know he's not going to spill the beans. But we'll
wait until we know more about these witches robes.
And after we get more on our songbird Gail Collins."
He noticed Gabrielle staring at him. She was tapping
her fingers together. Her "comfort gesture," as she
called it. If that's what it was. "What do you think
about what Eddie's found?" he asked.

"Umberto fascinates me," she said. "The two Umberto's apparently. And so does Vincent Richards." She
shook her head. "But it's all too superficial right now.
I'll wait and see what you two develop."

Mario Cervone didn't take long to strike. Two men,
who had cop written all over them, boxed Devlin in as
he stepped from Adrianna's building later that day.

"I've got an appointment," Devlin said, as one of the
men flashed his gold shield.

"It won't take long," the detective said. "The chief's
in the car." He nodded toward a dark Chrysler sedan
parked at the curb. "He just needs a minute."

And he's going to get it whether I like it or not,
Devlin thought, as he walked toward the car. He had
not seen Cervone in almost three years. Not since the
aftermath of the Ritual case, when the chief of detectives was trying to have his ass drawn, quartered, and
fed to the fish in the East River. It was still too soon
to see him again, he told himself, as he opened the
door and slid in beside the chief. It would always be
too soon. They were alone in the car.

"Nice to see you again, chief," Devlin said. "But you've gotten fat. Must be the job."

"Fuck you, Devlin," Cervone snapped. "You carrying?"

"That's right."

"Give it to me."

"Fuck *you*, Chief. I've got a permit. Like all retired cops."

"Not any more you don't," Cervone said. "It was revoked. At my request." He held out one hand.

Devlin stared at it, then took his revolver from its ankle holster and handed it over. "Guess I'll have to call the Detectives Benevolent Association about this," he said.

"Call whoever the fuck you want," Cervone said. He hefted the revolver in his hand. "Shoot anybody with this?" he asked.

"Ballistics will check out," Devlin said. "It was only fired once. And you know when."

"Same piece you used three years ago, huh?" Cervone said. "Kind of attached to it, I guess."

Devlin glared at him. "Can't stop being a shit, can you, Cervone? It must be genetic."

The chief sat back and grinned at him, then stuffed the revolver in his jacket pocket, and gave it a light pat. He was enjoying himself, and Devlin wanted nothing more than to drive his fist into the man's face.

"I'll put this in the mail to you," Cervone said. "Tomorrow, when you're back in Vermont." He paused a beat. "If you're not there, I'm also gonna see you get a new physical, and I wouldn't be surprised if you got your ass called back to duty. Then you'll have a choice. You can quit, without a pension, or you can work for me. In whatever shit job I find for you." He grinned again. "And you wouldn't believe the shit jobs I can find."

Devlin returned the smile. "You don't have to hurry finding anything, Chief," he said. "Because by the time you get finished with the legal fight you'll get, you'll be an old man playing *bocce* in the park."

Cervone's grin faded, and he leaned closer, bringing his face only a foot from Devlin's. "Don't bet on it, tough guy. I'll get a city attorney's ruling that will put the order into effect while your little court fight is going on. And we'll make sure the case goes to a judge who'll uphold the order. Bank on it."

Devlin's retort was stopped by a tapping on the window. Both men turned, and found Cass Walker's smiling face staring in at them. She pointed a finger at Devlin, then at herself, then tapped her wrist watch before turning away.

"What the fuck you doin' with that bitch," Cervone hissed.

"Until a few minutes ago, nothing," Devlin said. "Now it's up to you." He held out his hand and stared Cervone down.

The chief reached into his pocket and withdrew the revolver, and handed to Devlin, making sure no one outside the car could see.

"And you better get that permit reinstated," Devlin said.

"This doesn't change anything," Cervone snapped.

"It better, Chief. Unless you want to see your ugly face on the tube. Along with Matthew Mallory's, the P.C.'s, the mayor's, and anybody else I can put there. *Capisce?*"

Cervone guessed that Devlin was bluffing, but he knew he couldn't risk being wrong. He leaned back and ran his tongue along the inside of his mouth, trying to imply as much bravado as he could muster. "You like power games, Devlin? We'll see how you like them when all this is over. I got a long memory."

"You also got a long fucking nose," Devlin said. "But that doesn't scare me either." He opened the car door and slid out.

Cass Walker was at his side before he could close it. She held it open and looked inside. "Anything in this meeting for me, Chief?" she asked. There was a soft, sensual smile on her lips.

Cervone forced himself to return it. But it was neither sensual, nor especially pleasant. "Just seeing an old comrade in arms," he said. He jabbed a finger at his two detectives, and one quickly closed the door Cass was holding open, then climbed into the passenger seat. The other jumped behind the wheel and immediately pulled the car away from the curb.

Cass turned to Devlin. "Chief seems to be in a hurry," she said.

"He's a busy man," Devlin said. "Places to go, people to see."

"Just stopped by to see if you had any good tips on the stock market, huh?" she said.

Devlin offered a helpless shrug, not unlike a schoolboy caught by the school principal. In reality, he felt like hugging the woman. She may have just inadvertently saved his butt from untold grief. "What can I say?" he offered. "I lied to you."

"That's what my little computer told me," Cass said. "I just couldn't figure out why. Hero cops aren't usually shy. In fact, most cops I know would kill to get their mugs on the six o'clock news." She was being coy with him, and she looked especially beautiful doing it. She was dressed in a red silk blouse that was buttoned in a way that made it plunge toward her cleavage, and gray slacks that hugged every curve of her hips and very tight bottom. He decided he'd let her lay out her game, and enjoy it as much as he could.

"A friend of mine downtown also tells me that the police computer spits up Adrianna Mendez's name. Seems she filed a complaint about a break-in and assault a week or so back." She inclined her head, giving Devlin a look of wondering innocence. "Made me think that maybe that was why you were squiring her around, beating off purse snatchers and all. It also made me wonder how it all tied in to Melissa Coors. Want to tell me about any of that?"

"You got me," Devlin said. "You're putting two and two together and coming up with five, far as I can see."

"And you just happened to be talking to Cervone, right?"

"Like the chief said, we're old comrades in arms."

Cass shook her head, then offered up another inviting smile. "You're a very sexy man, Paul Devlin," she said. "But you're a piss-poor liar." Her smile became more coy, a bit more suggestive. "Somebody once told me that good liars make the best lovers, because they always have to put on a good act. Since you're such a lousy liar, you could probably refute that idea."

"Only if I was the best," Devlin said. "That's a tough order for anybody."

"I'm sure you could handle it," she said. She looked him up and down. "But I've been fooled before," she added. She waited a beat, letting her words sink in. "You're not going to tell me anything, are you?" she finally asked.

"Nothing to tell," Devlin said. "Just a lot of coincidence."

"Don't believe in that," Cass said. She held his eyes. "Last time I saw you, I told you that I never give up. And that I always get what I want. That still goes, Devlin."

"I'm sure it does," he said.

18

Umberto sat behind his desk, precariously balancing an antique letter opener between his index fingers. The man seated across from him was as slovenly as he had ever seen—rumpled suit, soup-stained necktie. He wished now there was a rear entrance to the gallery he could bundle the man through. He was definitely detrimental to a rather hard-fought image. And besides, he was a cop. Umberto had despised their ilk ever since he was a boy on Shakespeare Avenue.

"Melissa was a bit of a tart," he said in reply to Eddie Grogan's question. "Of course, I always assumed much of it was simply acting—something to amuse herself. No one could be that much of a tart."

"So you knew her pretty well," Grogan said.

"Goodness, no." Umberto's lips pursed slightly, a feigned look of modest offense at the thought they might have been friends. "I'd run across her, of course. Occasionally at restaurants in the Hamptons, parties here in the city, fund-raising events, such as the one at Rachael Barrows' home." He grasped the letter opener in one hand and began lightly jabbing its point into the blotter. "You'd be surprised what a small town New York can be when it comes to the arts. The successful arts, I mean." He let out a small sigh. "And, of course, she was a star, after all. One tends to notice those people. But that doesn't mean one would invite them to one's home."

Grogan let his eyes roam the office, stopping briefly on the photo of the child hooker Devlin had mentioned. He glanced at the ceiling, waving one finger in a circle. "You live here, don't you?" he asked.

Umberto nodded.

"Alone?"

The man's eyes narrowed almost imperceptively, and Grogan could see his mind clicking. Trying to decide if he should lie or not, he decided.

"I've always thought that living with someone would be the precursor to Hell," Umberto said.

Grogan grunted, nodded. "I thought maybe Oliver lived here with you," he said.

Umberto remained silent for a moment, his eyes hardening. "What does Oliver have to do with anything?" he snapped.

Grogan offered a smile that failed to show any teeth, more a spreading of lips and squinting of eyes. "That's what I'm here to find out," he said. "So, Hubert—"

"The name is Umberto."

"Yeah, yeah." Grogan removed a notebook from his inside pocket, flipped it open, and glanced at it. "Hubert and Oliver Walsh," he said. "From Shakespeare Avenue in the Bronx. Both outstanding students at Music and Art High School. So good they get scholarships to college. Hubert to Columbia to study art history and business. Oliver to Bennington, where he takes up painting." He looked up at Umberto's reddening face. The letter opener was held tightly in one hand now, its tip pressed firmly into the blotter. "But Oliver mysteriously drops out after two years. Joins the army, and decides he likes the soldier's life." Grogan shrugged. "But the army decides it don't like him, and it boots his butt out after twelve years." His eyes moved back to the photograph on the wall. "That the hooker Oliver beat the shit out of?" he asked.

"I think this interview is over," Umberto said.

"No, it's not. It goes on here, it goes on at the precinct. Me, I don't give a shit. How 'bout you, Hubert?"

The man hesitated again as he tried, unsuccessfully,

to stare Grogan down. "What makes you think Oliver lives here?" he finally asked.

Grogan smiled again, looked at his shoes, and shook his head. "Hubert, Hubert, Hubert. You don't ask the questions here. I do. But this time, just to be nice, I'll answer you." He looked up, his eyes hard, boring into the man. "Oliver's tax returns. They say he owns half this joint." He waved one hand in a circle, taking in the building. "And they also give this as a mailing address."

"You're very thorough, Detective."

Grogan again offered his Buddha smile. "Hey, I only look like a slob," he said. "Just like you only look like an asshole." His voice hardened, matching his eyes. "Now answer my fucking question."

Umberto stared back at him, eyes equally hard. Then they softened. "Oliver's upstairs. Would you like to meet him?"

Grogan inclined his head to one side. "Hey, I'd be charmed," he said.

Umberto picked up the telephone and dialed an internal number. "Please come down to the office," he said.

Even forewarned, Grogan could never have prepared himself for the vision of the two Walsh brothers together. Except for their clothing—Hubert was dressed in a well-tailored Armani suit and tie, Oliver in a mauve silk shirt and tan slacks—they were more than identical. They were exact. Cloned reproductions of each other, without a hair out of place.

Grogan immediately wondered which of the two he had seen sashaying into the Hammer, and he was momentarily tempted to ask each to roll up his trousers to see which one shaved his legs. Shit, it don't matter if they both play Dolly Parton, he told himself. Besides, they probably borrow nighties from each other.

"Shocked, Detective?" Oliver asked. He had perched on the corner of the desk, one foot on the floor, the other dangling over the edge. "Are two Umbertos more than you bargained for?" There was a playful smile on his thin lips, and rather than being upset at discovery, he seemed to be enjoying himself.

"How come the little game?" Grogan asked.

"It works better for *us*," Hubert said. "We can divide up the work. Do that part which pleases us most. And never be overwhelmed by the conflicting demands of the business." He balanced the letter opener between two fingers again. "I, for one, prefer the business side. And I'm trained for it. Oliver likes dealing with the artists and their work. Something I despise. Something *he's* trained for." He shrugged. "It's rather simple, really. And rather convenient."

"And no one can tell you apart," Grogan said. It wasn't a question. It was a fact, one that was right in front of him.

Oliver laughed. "Not unless they see us naked," he said. He stared at Grogan. "My dick is bigger."

Hubert closed his eyes. "Don't be crude, Oliver," he said.

Oliver simply laughed again.

Grogan ignored the remark. "So which one of you went to Rachael Barrows' party?" he asked.

"That was my brother," Oliver said. "I prefer to stay at home, or when I do go out, move in my own social circle."

"Which is?"

Oliver shrugged. "Oh, occasionally I like to visit the Anvil, or one of the other clubs." He was grinning now, enjoying the look on Grogan's face.

"Like the rough trade, huh, Oliver?" Grogan asked.

"I find the club amusing," he said.

Grogan raised his chin toward the photograph on the wall. "You give up on hookers?" he asked.

"Women are more my brother's inclination," Oliver said.

Oliver caught Grogan's eyes darting between himself and Hubert. He laughed again. "You have a great deal to learn about homosexuals, Detective." He looked off to one side. "Although please don't ask me to teach you." He looked back. "But it is not a disease. It's in large part a genetic factor that's determined at birth. And, yes, siblings, even twins, can be of a different bent." He glanced back at the photograph. "I experimented, of course. There's a great deal of social pressure to be"—he raised his hands and used two fingers of each to make quotation marks in the air—"normal," he added. "But I found it decidedly unsatisfactory. Apparently, so did the army. Does that answer your question?"

"One of them," Grogan said. "Where were you the night of Rachael Barrows' party?"

"Here. At home," Oliver said. "I'd had a trying day, and I needed to unwind."

Grogan thought about Oliver's method of unwinding, but knew he couldn't pursue it. Not unless he wanted to confess to a B&E. "You here when your brother got home?" he asked instead.

"I was asleep," Oliver said.

Grogan glanced at Hubert. "You can confirm that?"

"No, I can't," Hubert said. "We have separate rooms, and we don't do bed checks on each other."

Oliver began to laugh. "It's hard, isn't it, Detective? Discovering which one has the Toni? Just like in the old television commercial." He continued to grin at Grogan. "And you'd never know if we were telling the truth, would you?"

19

Vincent Richards spread his arms, stretched, and rotated his head, as if relieving a crick. They were seated in the orchestra at the rear of the theater, turned to face each other, one empty seat between them.

"So how's Adrianna?" he asked. "I call, but she seems too busy to see me."

"She's working hard on the new paintings," Devlin said, wondering why he was making excuses for her, why he was trying—if he was—to ease the man's concerns.

"What's this all really about, Devlin?" Vincent asked. "It's no secret anymore that you're a cop, or used to be. And that you're playing bodyguard. It's obvious it has something to do with Melissa, and that it somehow involves that creep who attacked Adrianna."

"That's right. You were there that night, weren't you? Then you left." There was a touch of implied guilt in Devlin's words. It was intended. Designed to put Richards on the defensive. "I always meant to ask you if you had a key to her loft."

Vincent let out a soft snort. It was clearly derisive, but Devlin ignored it. "We were lovers, Devlin, but we hadn't reached the point of exchanging house keys," he said.

"I guess you just left the door open," Devlin said. "Accidentally, of course."

Vincent looked away toward the stage. "I suppose it's possible. But I really can't say if I did or not." He turned back to face Devlin. "Is this strictly a business—

or perhaps I should say, professional—relationship be-tween the two of you?"

"I'm trying to help," Devlin said, ignoring the broader question. "She's an old friend and she asked me to."

"So you're not a New York cop."

"I was," Devlin said. "I retired. Now I head up a police department in Vermont. I took a leave to help her out. Now how about you answer some of my questions?"

"Anything that will help Adrianna." He looked point-edly at Devlin. "I do care about her. Rather strongly."

"Tell me about Brooks," Devlin said, tossing out a sudden change of subject that he knew would throw Richards off balance. "And about his play," he added.

Vincent narrowed his eyes in curiosity, but took up the question. "Brooks is a brilliant playwright. What can I say other than that? And his new play—*my* play—is probably the best thing he's ever done."

"I understand he's had trouble writing lately. And some people say the new play is autobiographical. Some also say it's really your idea. *Your* play. The idea, at least. And that he only developed it."

Vincent laughed. "To say a writer of fiction only de-velops an idea is like saying an architect only makes blueprints of a house some bozo client has described to him. No, my friend. The writer—in this case Bren-den—creates the words, the emotions, the twists in plot. Everything." He hesitated for effect. "And in this case, it was his idea. Pure and simple. To imply any-thing less would be a cheap lie usurping the man's talent." He jabbed a finger at Devlin. "And, yes, he has had trouble writing lately. But all writers do. And some of his recent work hasn't been very good, and has not been produced. But you can't hit a home run every time, my friend." He raised his hands, palms up in a so-what gesture. "But now he has. And that's all that counts."

"So he wrote it himself. From the original idea on

through," Devlin said. It wasn't a question, only a confirmation of what Vincent was saying.

"Every bloody thought. Every bloody word," the director said. "And, yes, I suspect it is quite autobiographical. I base that on things Brenden has said over the years. Little hints here and there. And also from what I know about his past. *And* the fact that he can't handle women on a personal level." He smiled at the idea, as though it was almost impossible to conceive. "The man's gay. He doesn't make any secret about it." He gave a small shake of his head. "I imagine this play was very hard for him to write, which is probably why it's so damned good. Who knows? Maybe this will provide a catharsis for him. Maybe he's finally found a way to purge himself of his past."

Devlin remained silent, studying the man for almost a minute. He felt as though he was being pointed at Brooks. Deliberately? He decided to change tacks.

"I understand you did a production of *Macbeth* and threw out some costumes. Some brown robes. You know what happened to them?"

Vincent seemed startled by the question. But it could have been nothing more than the sudden change of subject. "Some idiot sent me the wrong costumes. So I got rid of them and ordered the right ones from someone else. What the hell is this all about?"

"The robes sound like the one Adrianna's attacker wore," Devlin said.

"Oh, shit," Vincent said. His tone was one of exasperation. "Christ, I don't know what happened to them. I got rid of them. Period."

"But why not return them? Why throw them away?"

Vincent leaned forward. The look on his face was one that might be used in dealing with a child. "Look, I direct plays," he said. "I don't return merchandise. I threw them out, and I fully expected the fucking wardrobe mistress to dig them out of the trash and send them back." He made his so-what gesture again. "It was an act of temperament—something theater people are known for. I can't help it if the silly bitch left them in the trash, and we got stuck with the bill."

"You didn't keep them?"

"Oh, for chrissake. Of course not. What for?"

"Is there any chance you or someone else gave them to Father Hopkins? For his street theater group. I understand you were working with him then."

"I never gave them to him. But who knows? Maybe he dug them out of the trash." he shook his head. "But, no. I saw his production. His people never wore anything like that. I would have spotted that. Probably would have gotten a kick out of it. A priest filching from our trash and all." He shook his head. "His actors were all playing what they were. Street people. They were dressed in rags. Probably their own clothes." He hesitated, staring at Devlin intently. "You can't be serious about suspecting the priest. What's all this about? The trouble he had with that bimbo singer a few years back?"

"You know about that?"

"Yeah, I know about it. Father Jim told me. We've become friends over the years. And so what? So he dipped his wick a few times. Big deal." Again he jabbed a finger at Devlin. It was starting to annoy him, and Devlin wondered how he'd like having it snapped at the joint.

"Look, I admire the guy. Not only does he do some damned good work, but he's also a good actor, believe it or not. Untrained but good."

"What do you mean?" Devlin asked.

"Just what I say," Vincent snapped. "He was in a couple of the street shows. I remember one in particular where he played an old woman. His walk, his mannerisms were perfect. If it wasn't for the theatrical makeup—seeing it up close like you did—you'd never know he wasn't a doddering seventy-year-old. And I know how hard that is. I played an old man myself once. And it is not an easy thing to pull off."

"You know where this woman he was involved with is now?" Devlin asked.

"I don't even know her name. *If* he ever told me that."

Devlin leaned back, ready to throw Vincent another curve. "Tell me about your wife," he said.

Vincent stared at him, his eyes suddenly hard, all the feigned cooperation quickly down the drain. "You too, huh?" he said. He leaned forward, mouth twisted in anger. "That clown cop Mallory was all over me about that yesterday. For over two hours. So I belted her once. So what? I've been paying for it ever since. And if she has her way I'll pay for it until I'm ninety." He jabbed a finger at Devlin, then dropped the hand to his lap when he saw his eyes narrow. "If I wanted to hurt a woman, she'd be the one I'd hurt. Not Melissa. Certainly not Adrianna. I told Mallory that, and I'm telling you. So lay off. Or else."

Devlin smiled at him. "Or else what, Vincent?"

"Just keep pushing and I'll show you."

Devlin rose slowly, still smiling. He stared down at the man. He was remarkably handsome. The good looks—almost perfect looks—of the actor he had once been. He was dressed in a gray turtleneck, with a red silk scarf draped around his shoulders, and it made him appear particularly arty and dashing. Devlin thought it would be very easy to pull it tight and choke the sonofabitch.

He smiled at the man. "Take your best shot," he said. "Anytime you're ready. Just don't expect to look the same after you do."

Brenden Brooks—as Vincent had said—was at home working on revisions. He lived on Central Park West, with a tenth-floor view that overlooked the park and the distant towers rising from the East Side. Devlin didn't want to think about what the co-op apartment had cost him. He didn't want to know the monthly maintenance bill. It would be too depressing.

"The priest?" Brenden asked. "Yeah, I know him. Mostly through Vincent. He's always hanging around." He offered up an elfin grin which added to that general impression of himself. "But I suppose that's his job. Or part of it. Staying close to people who can help him."

They were seated opposite each other in chairs set before a large window. The sunlight glinted off Brenden's balding pate.

"You ever see any of his plays?" Devlin asked.

Brenden shook his head. "I helped him with dialogue once. Vincent asked me to. But I never saw the actual performance."

The room they were in seemed in contrast to the luxury of the building. Books and manuscripts were piled everywhere. It had the feel of a hermit's hole. Brenden caught Devlin looking the room over.

"I write," he said, as if that explained everything. "It's all I do. All I want to do. I don't entertain, and I don't go out much. So I leave the place the way I like it."

"Tell me about your new play," Devlin said. "I hear it's brilliant. I also hear it was Vincent's idea. But he denies that." He waited a moment. "Some people also say it's autobiographical."

Brenden let out a long, sustained laugh. "First, it's not autobiographical. Not unless it's Vincent's autobiography. Because it's certainly not mine. And, yes, it was his idea, even if he denies it."

"Why would he do that if it's so brilliant?" Devlin asked. "I'd think he'd want some credit for it. He doesn't strike me as the wallflower type."

Again, Brenden laughed. "Oh, he certainly is not." He leaned forward, his bright blue eyes glinting mischievously. "I'd like to say it's because he wants all the credit to come to me. But I'm not that naive." He shook his head. "No, I suspect he's avoiding credit—or perhaps I should say culpability—in case the play flops. He'll take the appropriate bows later, if it's a smash.

Then the columns will be full of how it was his original idea. Although I doubt he'll say it was autobiographical—if, in fact, it is. Being abused as a kid is not something old Vincent could ever admit to. It would go against his image."

"Tell me about Melissa," Devlin said.

Brenden's face became suddenly sad. "Poor kid," he said. "You know I dropped her off that night. Her place was only a couple of blocks from here, and I didn't want her getting out of a cab alone." He twisted in his chair, as though uncomfortable talking about that night. "Even that few blocks away the neighborhood gets a bit shitty." he added. "And these cabbies we have today. Half of them are Pakistanis who don't want to know from anything once they get their fare. If they saw a mugger waiting they'd just figure it was his turn."

"Was Vincent with you?" He watched Brenden shake his head. "I thought you all left together," he pressed.

"The building, yeah. But Vincent lives on Fifth, right off Seventy-second. It was only a few blocks, so he decided to walk." Brenden hesitated for a moment, as if deciding whether to go on. "Besides, as you saw, he was a little pissed at Melissa. They used to be pretty hot for each other, and when she flaunted it the way she did that night, it sent him up the wall. Sometimes I think she did it just to see if she could make him crazy."

Devlin leaned forward, forearms on his knees. "Let's talk about you a little," he said. "Tell me about The Hammer."

Brooks stiffened momentarily; his eyes grew hard, then softened into something Devlin thought was sadness.

"That's none of your business, Mr. Devlin. And I don't think I want to talk anymore."

Devlin had decided to walk. He needed time to think, and walking had always worked for him, whether on city streets or on the isolated dirt roads of Vermont.

The day was clear and warm, the temperature had risen to nearly eighty degrees, and it was another bright, vibrant day. The sky was a deep blue, hardly a cloud to be seen, not the dull, forbidding gray that so often hung over Manhattan. And Central Park West was seldom crowded. It was purely residential, and except for the Museum of Natural History, farther to the north at 79th Street, there were seldom knots of people with whom a stroller had to contend.

He stopped at the corner of 72nd, the massive brown stonework of the Dakota rising to his right. He looked toward the entrance of the stately building, at the sidewalk in front, where John Lennon had been gunned down by a demented fan. He averted his eyes. He had enough murder to think about without conjuring up cases from the past.

He decided to walk to the subway station at Columbus Circle, thirteen blocks to the south, and to catch the IRT local to his next appointment. It was in an hour, still enough time to think, to decide what to do next. He was close to the killer now. He knew it, could feel it.

The figure watched him from almost a block away. The shabby raincoat was pulled tight, the old, wide-brimmed hat low over the eyes. The costume had been put on quickly, almost frantically, and the false beard had had to be adjusted several times already to make sure it was properly in place. But there was an urgency now. Devlin had to die; he had to die immediately. Despite all your efforts he's coming too near. And you can see now. See that you'll never get to her until he's gone.

The old man increased his pace. Not too quickly, he told himself. Not so quickly that you look like anything but an old man out for a stroll. The costume might already make you seem out of place, unusual. It was far too warm for the coat and nat, but there had been no choice, no time. But old people dressed this way. They were cold, always cold, unless the weather was positively stifling. It will work. You just have to get close enough. Then wait for a crowd.

A hand tightened on the long-bladed knife in the pocket of the raincoat, and power seemed to rise from the handle and into the arm. They don't know how strong you are. They think you're weak and frail, and they look at you with contempt. You've seen it in their eyes. All of them. Devlin. Grogan. Even the woman. That filthy slut who needs killing most of all. But first Devlin. Now Devlin. Then that slut.

Devlin stopped momentarily in front of the Conservatory, a quiet, unobtrusive restaurant he had always liked. He had often gone there with his wife, and he toyed with the idea of going inside now, having a drink or a cup of coffee, just to let the pressures of the day melt from his body.

He turned and started walking again. There was no time now, he told himself. Eddie had a man watching the loft, but he had to get to his other appointment and get back. He felt uneasy when he was away from Adrianna. He knew the killer would strike out soon, had no choice but to do so. Unless he decided to run. Or go on to someone else. But he didn't think that was going to happen. He was too fixated; the need was too great. He was certain that Melissa Coors had been an aberration, something caused by a momentary flaring of the man's madness. And he was certain now the killer was someone at the party. Someone he had already met, someone with whom he had already spoken.

Devlin darted through the traffic and made his way down the stairs leading to the subway. The smell rose to meet him, the dank, fetid odor that seemed to permeate the very walls. He smiled, thinking of the comic article he had once read. It had said that city workers cleansed the subways each day—with urine-scented disinfectant.

The old man entered the stairwell only ten feet behind Devlin. Hands fumbled in the pockets of the raincoat. There was no subway token. It hadn't been anticipated that one might be needed. Fool. Fool. Eyes far too young for the disguise watched Devlin push his way through the turnstile. The old man rushed to the token booth, a five-dollar bill clutched in a smooth, too young hand. He should have worn the gloves. But it would have been too much on such a mild day. It would have made the costume *too* odd. It would have drawn eyes he wanted to avoid. Perhaps even Devlin's own *too smart cop's eyes*.

The old man pushed through the turnstile, trying to decide which train he had decided to take. The IRT local or perhaps the faster Eighth Avenue Express. He raced to the stairs and plunged down toward the IRT platform. Slower. Slower. Don't attract attention. You're an old man. Too old to rush like this.

There he was. Up ahead. But the train was already in the station, and Devlin was moving toward the door, held up by a knot of people pressing in to board before the doors slid shut.

The knife came out of the pocket, held down alongside the leg. The old man hurried forward, eyes fixed on Devlin's back. Only five steps away now. Soon the knife would plunge deep into his body, slicing through vital organs. The old man knew just where to strike, just where the blow would bring certain death. There had been study. There had been learning.

A large black woman veered in front of the old man. Their bodies collided. She glared at him, cursing, then rushed toward the opposite side of the platform. The old man wanted to reach out and grab her, plunge the knife into her filthy throat, shut her disgusting mouth forever. He took two steps toward her, then caught himself. Devlin. He had to get to Devlin. The old man changed direction.

Devlin stepped into the train, his chest pressed against the people in front of him, his body barely far enough inside to allow the doors to close. They slid shut behind him. The old man slammed against the closed doors, his eyes wild with rage. He turned and saw a woman standing behind him. Her own eyes were wide and frightened, and she was staring down at the knife in the old man's hands.

Quickly the old man glanced over his shoulder as the train began to pull away from the station. Devlin had turned around and was looking out the door's glass panel. The sound of the old man crashing into the door must have alerted him. Their eyes met momentarily, and then the old man spun around and ran for the stairs.

20

Devlin looked down at his stomach and realized—
perhaps consciously for the first time—that it wasn't
as flat as it once had been. Bad, he told himself as he
glanced around the large, high-ceilinged room. Everywhere his eyes fell, trim bodies worked away on exer-
cise machines. There were stair-climbing machines,
running machines, Universal gyms that seemed to exer-
cise every part of the body, even an area with free
weights. And scattered among the machines, working
away like robots, were a collection of trim, sweating
bodies, all clad in designer workout clothing. He let
out a small sigh. Oh, there were a few fatties here and
there. But it was as though they had been stuck in as
a warning, just to let the others know what could happen if they failed to pay their dues. He watched a
particularly trim woman for several minutes as she
worked methodically on a stair climber. Her back was
to him, and her buttocks moved with a tight, mind-
boggling rhythm beneath a skin-tight body suit. Christ,
he told himself, fifteen years ago you would have
walked around this place with a woodie that would
have knocked down walls. And you're not *that* much
older. At least you don't feel as though you are.

"It would take you about eighteen months."

Devlin looked down at Gabrielle Lyons. She was
seated on some type of machine that required her to
open and close her legs like scissors. It looked excruci-
atingly painful.

"What would take me eighteen months?" Devlin asked.

Gabrielle inclined her head toward the woman on the stair climber. "To get your body in that kind of shape."

Devlin grunted. "That isn't what I was thinking about."

"I know," Gabrielle answered. "But it was what you should have been thinking about."

The woman had asked Devlin to meet her at her health club, claiming she had been cut down to one workout a week since she had begun helping with the case. Her muscles were becoming atrophied, she had insisted.

Devlin looked at her now and couldn't see any damage. Like the others, she was wearing skin-hugging tights, but had replaced the upper half of the costume with a T-shirt emblazoned with the message: A MIND IS A TERRIBLE THING TO LOSE. He had to admit she looked absolutely great. She wasn't as lithe and sticklike as some of the other women. Her body was firmer, chunkier. But there wasn't an ounce of fat anywhere, and her muscles looked harder than his own had been in the past five years.

Devlin let his eyes roam to a man in his early twenties. He was running in place on a treadmill, and sweat was pouring from his extremely trim body. But the way he held his arms and swayed his shoulders as he ran, Devlin suspected he would be more inclined toward Umberto's twin brother than any of the delicious women who surrounded him. Jesus, now you're making excuses. You're putting that guy down just because he looks better than you do.

Gabrielle sat forward on the machine and pressed a towel to her face. "God, that felt good," she said. She glanced up at Devlin, who seemed awkward and out of place in street clothes. But he looked good too, and she had found it necessary to fight off the attraction she felt toward him. "Sorry to bring you here," she said. "But the work load—yours on top of my own—is overwhelming me." She raised her chin toward a small, glass-fronted office that overlooked the workout area. "I got an okay for us to use that office," she said. "We can have it until five, when the night shift comes on."

Devlin glanced at his watch. It gave them an hour. More than enough time.

The furnishings in the office were spartan, a metal desk and two uncomfortable visitors' chairs. Gabrielle positioned herself behind the desk, and Devlin noted that she was taking charge again. But this time he didn't mind. He felt an urgent need for her input, convinced more than ever now that time was running out.

Gabrielle listened intently, jotting notes on a purloined pad of paper. Devlin had spoken on the phone to Grogan and now detailed what each had learned in their meetings with the four men they had collectively interviewed. Her eyes had widened slightly when Devlin told her—for the first time—about the earlier break-in at Umberto's gallery.

"The brothers fascinate me," she said when he had finished. "God, I'd love to have both of them as patients."

"You think they need help?" Devlin asked.

She smiled at him. "I think everyone needs help. But if you're asking if they're in desperate need of help?" She shrugged. "Who knows? But it certainly isn't your normal sibling relationship."

"But how does it play for us?" Devlin asked. There was a hint of impatience in his voice.

Gabrielle stared at him. "For this case," she said, "*if* they're involved, it plays scary for us, Paul. Very scary." She leaned back, put her legs up on the desk. They were exceptionally good legs, Devlin noticed. "Let's look at it." She clasped one finger in her hand. "If both of them are involved, and they're using their twinness to confuse the police, what we have is something that has escalated far beyond a sibling prank to something that is truly psychopathological."

Devlin looked uncertain. Gabrielle smiled at him. "What I'm saying, Paul, is that our killer is an obvious psychopath, which, put simply, is someone who manifests amoral and antisocial behavior in the extreme, i.e., kills or harms people without remorse; someone who lacks the ability to love, or form meaningful personal relationships; who is extremely egocentric, and who fails to learn from experience." She shrugged, indicating it was the best she could do. "What I'm also saying is that if both brothers are involved, we are dealing with the unique situation of two psychopathic twins who have allowed their sibling games to escalate into what we now are faced with." She gave a small shudder. "And that is scary."

"What if only one of them is a psychopath?" Devlin asked.

"Well, that's better, of course, but it also makes the psychopathic brother rather formidable."

"Why?" Devlin asked.

"Because he would be doing it right under the nose of not only a sibling but of a twin. And twins are noted for their closeness—even, in many cases, for their ability to sense what the other is feeling. Deception under those circumstances would indicate an extremely clever and manipulative individual."

Gabrielle watched Devlin let out a long breath. "Let me add something else, while I've got you in a sober mood," she said. "Our killer is a psychopath. That one fact is indisputable. And that means he considers himself God-like, unassailable. So anyone who attacks him, or threatens him in any way, has done the unforgivable. And he will hurt that person, destroy him any way he can." She gave a helpless shrug. "That, I'm afraid, includes us."

"Nice thought," Devlin said. "I'll hold on to it. Now let's move to Vincent Richards and Brenden Brooks."

Gabrielle nodded. "Let's take Brooks first, because he's the easiest. But only so because we know the least about him." Again she clasped one finger. "First, let's forget he's gay. It has no bearing on anything. He's a loner and, as you said, a bit eccentric. But that in itself also means little. The key point is this question of his play being autobiographical." She wagged her head back and forth. "But can sexual abuse as a child—even in the extreme—turn the victim into a psychopath?" She offered up a look of serious doubt. "Turn him into a sociopath—someone who has no sense of guilt, no sense of right or wrong? Certainly. But a psychopath?" She let out a long breath. "There are many in my field who believe psychopaths are born with a genetic imbalance, and that nothing, good or bad, will change that." She leaned forward. "Now, that is not to say that someone born with that genetic imbalance cannot also be abused, and that his psychopathic energies will not then be directed at a specific target, or those who symbolize that target."

She leaned back in her chair and began tapping her fingers together again. "But for me, given that scenario, Vincent is a much better candidate than Brooks."

"Why?" Devlin asked.

"First, he's egocentric. Little question about that from what we've learned. Second—as you've been told—he's a noted womanizer, someone who likes to use them for his own ends." She shrugged. "Not in itself a telling factor. If it were, in this society, we'd be up to our necks in psychopaths. But add to that the possibility that the play is autobiographical about *him*, and that the abuse he suffered produced a hatred of women, and we begin to have something. Even more, add the fact that he was physically abusive to his wife, and we have more." She removed her legs from the desk and leaned forward, almost to emphasize the point. "People who beat their wives or lovers are sociopaths. They feel no true remorse. They simply need to control and dominate that person for their own self-protection and gratification. And they will use any means to do so. Even physical violence. Now, control is the antithesis of love. They may tell themselves they are doing it because they love the person so much. But love has nothing to do with it. The two—love and control—have absolutely no correlation. They are, by nature, opposites." She leaned back and again began tapping her fingers together. "And while the reverse may not be true, all psychopaths are sociopaths as well."

"So Vincent is a definite candidate," Devlin said.

"Oh, yes," Gabrielle said. "I think he's a very strong candidate if all the factors are true. Especially the question of sexual abuse. If he is a psychopath, and if that really happened to him, it may have driven him to target a certain type of woman for his vengeance. Each one a symbol upon whom he must inflict his rage." Gabrielle leaned forward again. "What do we know about his estranged wife? What does she do?"

"She's an actress," Devlin said. "Or was, until she retired on Richards' money."

"Interesting," Gabrielle said. "Another woman in the arts. Perhaps even one he could never afford to harm. Not without opening himself up to a very real risk of exposure." She inclined her head toward Devlin. "One thing you must remember, is that psychopaths—though quite mad—are invariably extremely bright." She raised a lecturing finger. "I'm not talking IQ. I'm talking street smart."

Devlin digested that for a moment, his mind going over his conversation with Richards.

"There's something else you should know about Richards," he finally said. "I spoke to him about his involvement with Father Jim, and he jumped to the conclusion that the priest was a suspect."

"That's natural enough," Gabrielle said. "Given the fact that you're investigating an attack, and asking him about the man."

"Yes, but it's the way he did it. He assumed it was because of his involvement with Gail Collins. A singer. He made that point explicitly. That she was 'some bimbo singer.'" He paused for effect. "Don't you see?

A woman in the arts," Devlin added. "If that's what he was really getting at, it's something he shouldn't have known. That our attacker is after women in the arts."

Gabrielle rocked back in her chair. "You're right," she said. "yet it could have been coincidental." She studied Devlin a moment. "But I've never believed in coincidence."

She paused a moment, then continued. "You know, I still think you're off the money on Father Jim." She raised a hand, as if anticipating objections. "I know the man's reticence seemed suspicious to you, but you have to realize that he must be living in absolute dread of the archdiocese." She jabbed one finger against the top of the desk. "The men who run the archdiocese do not suffer embarrassment well, and Father Jim proved a great embarrassment to them." She sat back and tapped her fingers. More rapidly now. "Several years ago I did some counseling at the behest of the archdiocese. It involved a number of nuns, who were struggling with their identity in the Church. What it boiled down to was that they had suddenly awakened to the fact that they weren't simply little ladies in black habits, with rosary beads wrapped around their waists." She chuckled as if recalling the situation. "But there were those in the Church who thought they had simply lost their minds, or at least were suffering some kind of breakdown. To get to our point, I found the men who run the archdiocese to be a very unforgiving and self-protective lot. And those who break the rules, or who challenge the status quo, are not dealt with lightly. Oh, they're covered up for—for the good of the Church. But they pay. Personally. And I'm sure Father Jim has discovered as much himself. Hence the wish not to stir that pot again."

Devlin stared at her for a moment. "You're probably right," he said at length. "I guess we'll know for sure when we find Gail Collins."

As Devlin prepared to leave, Gabrielle took his arm, stopping him.

"The other day I mentioned something about the 'disappearing photographs' that was bothering me," she began. "Well, it's been eating at me, Paul, and I need to discuss it with you further."

"Sure," Devlin said.

They were standing in the office now, and Gabrielle began pacing back and forth.

"This is hard for me, Paul. Because, to some extent, it falls into the ethical area of patient/doctor relationship."

"How so? You were working for the cops. Right?"

"Well, technically, yes. But when Adrianna agreed to be hypnotized, I warned her that other matters might inadvertently come out. And I assured her that, should it happen, those disclosures would be held in the strictest of confidence."

"I'm confused," Devlin said. "Are you telling me you have a problem with the pictures, but can't tell me why?"

Gabrielle lowered her head, gave it a quick shake, then smiled. Devlin noticed how vulnerable the woman looked now. She stepped to him; placed a hand on his chest.

"I know it sounds foolish," she said. "But it's complex. Let me try to explain as much as I can." She looked up at him. "But you have to promise me that *you'll* hold what I say in confidence."

"Cops are good at keeping their mouths shut," Devlin said.

Gabrielle stared at him. The statement wasn't good enough by half, and Devlin knew it. "You got it," he said.

Gabrielle turned, walked to the desk, then perched on its edge. Immediately she began tapping her fingers together again. "During our sessions, and in some conversations we've had since, some emotional problems have come out that trace back to Adrianna's childhood." She stared at Devlin, her eyes pleading for understanding. "I *cannot* go into the details of those problems, or the incidents that caused them. But I can tell you they involve her relationship with her father, and that she's been trying to work through those problems—without help—for a long time now." She placed her hands on her thighs and began rubbing them up and down. "I want you to consider one thing, Paul. I want you to consider that the photographs may have been faked." She quickly raised a hand to ward off any objection. "I'm not saying they were, I simply want you to consider that possibility."

"That's crazy," Devlin snapped. "I saw them."

"No, Paul. You saw photographs that had already faded beyond recognition. You said as much. And Adrianna has the ability to make such prints. She's proficient in a dark room. We know that." Devlin was shaking his head in disbelief, but the woman ignored it and pushed on. "I also think you have to consider the possibility that the attack on Adrianna also did not occur. That it might have been something she fabricated—like the photographs—to get some response she needed emotionally."

"What?" Devlin was staring at her. The woman might as well be telling him that creatures from another world had just landed on Third Avenue. He shook his head. "That's crazy," he said. "To do that she would have to have known that other women had been attacked. And no one knew. No one was allowed to know."

"But she could have, Paul," Gabrielle insisted. "She travels in the same social circle as all of the victims. It is quite conceivable that she spoke to a friend of one of the victims, and learned about one of the attacks and scarrings." She gestured with both hands, imploring him to keep an open mind. "Oh, she wouldn't know the extent of the problem. If she had I'm certain she would never have tried to imitate it. If she, in fact, did. And, please, understand that I'm not saying it happened. Only that we must consider the possibility." She stood and took a step toward him, taking his arm with one hand. "And remember, Adrianna was *not* scarred. She is the only victim who escaped that." She hesitated, letting the words sink in. "Self-mutilation is a difficult thing," she added. "Even for a troubled personality."

"This is crazy," Devlin said. "What about the key we found in her lock? What about the junkie who was given that robe to wear?"

"Paul, that key could have been left there by any one, at any time. And what if someone is helping Adrianna perpetrate a hoax? Perhaps even for publicity before her show opens. And what if that person just happens to be our killer."

Devlin shook his head. "No," he said. "This just doesn't wash."

"I'm only suggesting we keep an open mind. I could be wrong, but I feel an obligation to put this before you. Please, Paul. Just don't preclude the possibility."

Devlin continued to shake his head, and Gabrielle could see her suggestion had produced a visceral, angry reaction. His eyes snapped to hers; held them. "You know, every time I bring up this little priest you admire so much, you tell me I'm wasting my time. Now, out of the blue, you come up with *this* off-the-wall crap."

Gabrielle's eyes hardened momentarily. She let out a long breath, forced her anger away. "I'm doing what I feel I have to do, Paul. And it isn't easy for me." She let go of his arm and took a step back. "And, perhaps, you're right. Perhaps I'm not looking at Father Jim with an unprejudiced eye. Perhaps even my childhood roots in Catholicism are getting in the way." She paused a beat. "Paul, perhaps each of us may not want to look clearly at something we don't want to believe." She paused again, a hard, level look in her eyes. "Tell me something, Paul. Are you sleeping with her?"

They had finished dinner and were seated on the sofa, Adrianna's head resting on his shoulder, her legs curled up in a nearly fetal position. Devlin had spoken to his daughter on the phone for nearly an hour, and had promised he'd be out to see her the following morning. Adrianna had listened to the conversation, had marveled at the gentle rapport he had with the child, his attentiveness to her words, even her childlike counsel and advice. She knew she was again falling in love with the man, and she wondered if that was really what she wanted.

Across from them, on the table set before the sofa, lay Devlin's book: *The Psychology of Pleasure in Killing.*

"Been doing some heavy reading?" he asked.

"Mmm. I hope you don't mind. I couldn't resist looking." She gave a small shiver. "That is one very disturbing book," she said.

"It's a very disturbing subject." He ran his hand along her shoulder and arm, feeling her warmth through the light pullover top she was wearing. "Did your father ever read books like that?" he asked.

She lowered her eyes and shook her head. "Not that I recall."

"I guess it was hard growing up with him? With an old school cop as a father." He felt a twisting in his stomach, and he immediately wished he had not raised the subject.

Adrianna was silent; her body seemed unnaturally still. "Yes, it was," she said at length. "Especially after my mother died." Again silence. "He seemed to expect me to take her place in some ways. Yet at the same time, he became incredibly protective. He watched me like a hawk. Almost as though he was afraid something would happen to me too. Or that I'd do something and it would be his fault it happened." Her voice had hardened. "And he was like all cops. They have power, and eventually it gets to them. Makes them think the rules don't apply to them, because they're the ones who enforce the rules."

"It wouldn't have been like that between us," Devlin said. "If we hadn't walked away from each other ten years ago." He didn't say it wouldn't be like that now. He didn't want to press the point.

"You ended up happy," she said. "And now you have Phillipa. You're lucky. You seem so relaxed together, and she seems to trust you so implicitly. I never felt that. Not with my father. Not with anyone."

"Did he hurt you as a kid?" He could feel his stomach tighten again, and rushed on. "Hit you? Stuff like that?" He felt her shake her head against his shoulder.

"If anything, it was just the opposite. Cubans are very affectionate toward their children. Especially fathers to daughters." She hesitated again. "But they're also very demanding. I think he was even more so. Because he didn't have Mom anymore."

"But you still loved him."

He could feel her breathing against him, feel her quiet again. "Yes, I did," she finally said. "But it was hard sometimes. When I was a kid I always felt his presence. Like he was always there, hovering over me. He was the first thing I'd face in the morning, and the last thing I'd face at night. And he was always questioning me. But he never seemed to hear my answers, never seemed to listen to my feelings about anything." She curled up tighter against him, almost as though pulling herself into a small, safe cave she had made of his body. "So, when I went away to school, I pulled away from him, and I never really allowed myself to be close again. And then, suddenly, he was dead."

He thought about questioning her further, finding some way to talk about it. But he knew that wouldn't work. He knew she would see through his questions. She had been a cop's kid, one who had been questioned too much already. Let it rest, he told himself. It's all bullshit. Just let it rest.

21

You must find out his movements. You must get to him, make him pay the piper. And you mustn't fail. Not like you did in the subway station. The figure sits hunched in a darkened corner. Depression seems to swirl about the room, flowing from every crack, every cranny. Only the corner is safe, and only as long as you remain hunched down, hidden. Across the room a closet door hangs open, revealing the robe and the tattered raincoat. On a shelf above are the old hat and the false beard, and all of it stares out now like an accusation. Oh, he thinks he's so smart. But you're smarter. Yes, so much smarter. He's discovered so much. But still not enough. And soon, when he's floundering like a fool, you can go to him, and you can kill him. Brittle laughter fills the room, then stops abruptly. Was that you laughing? Oh, yes. You're happy now. And after he's dead, you'll be even happier. So much happier. Because then it will be her turn. Her turn to pay the piper too. Yes, indeed. We mustn't forget her. Must we? So safe. So secure. How can anyone believe there is any danger? Does she believe? No. Not at all. Anyone can see that. Too safe and guarded and protected. *It must stop!* Shhh, you mustn't shout. Was that you shouting? But it can't be that way! Not if there is to be payment. And there must. There must. Nothing works without it. Nothing.

"No, none of the other women you mentioned were ever my patients. Only Melissa. What is all this about,

270

Mr. Devlin? When you came to see me before, you said you were a *retired* police officer. I don't understand."

Rachael Barrows sat behind her desk, looking mildly imperious. She was dressed in a white lab coat—a far cry from the elegance he had seen before—but the office they were in was every bit as plush, every bit as moneyed.

"The police think the person who killed Melissa may be stalking another woman. One I've been asked to protect," he said. "I think the other women I mentioned may be connected somehow. It's really that simple."

The woman eyed him a moment, then seemed to dismiss him. "I suspect it's not that simple at all, but it really doesn't matter. I never dealt with any of them, and I don't recall even having met them."

"What can you tell me about Melissa?" he asked.

"What do you want to know?"

"Anything that can help me understand her better," he said.

Rachael Barrows laughed. It made the lines in her face crease severely. He had been told she was in her mid-forties, but when she laughed she seemed older.

"She was an actress, Mr. Devlin. What can I say? She was spoiled, and self-centered, and totally self-indulgent." She paused. "Actually, that's not fair to actresses. There are a great many younger women like that today. They indulge themselves in whatever they wish, with *whomever* they wish, and then they turn to medical science to solve the resulting problems."

"Are we talking about abortion?" Devlin asked. "Did Melissa Coors have one?"

Rachael Barrows studied him for a moment, then shrugged. "I suppose, since she's dead, I'm not bound by any ethical stipulations." She gave him a level look. "But I'd appreciate it if this remained confidential. It simply isn't good for business," she said.

"Certainly," Devlin said.

The woman leaned back in her chair, and removed

the half glasses she had been wearing. "Yes, Melissa Coors required that kind of medical help. Twice, if I recall." She smiled derisively. "Oh, we don't call them that. We refer to it as a D and C. It involves scraping out the uterus. Although painful, it accomplishes the same result. And if the woman recognizes her pregnancy soon enough . . ." She shrugged again, then sat forward and began toying with a pen on her desk. She was wearing a large diamond ring, and the overhead light sent off flashes from the stone. Those D and C's pay for a lot of goodies, Devlin thought.

"I counsel them about the dangers," she said. "Venereal disease, AIDS." She let out a breath. "But some of them think they lead charmed lives. They're young, they're talented, and they have enough money to take care of themselves. So they think they won't be touched by anything so plebian as a sexually transmitted illness. And, of course, sooner or later they're wrong. Or at least some of them are."

"Was Melissa Coors one of the unlucky ones?" Devlin asked.

The woman shook her head. "Not that I know of," she said. "But it was only a question of time."

"You sound like you disapprove of the new sexual freedom."

The woman let out another long breath, then sat back in her chair. "I'm not a prude, Mr. Devlin. I just get weary of people who won't listen to sound medical advice." She offered up another smile, creasing her face again. "There are times when I feel like a trash collector," she said. "I seem to spend too much of my time cleaning up other people's messes. It is not what I trained so long to do." The smile and the creases returned. "But so much for disillusionment," she said.

Cass Walker was waiting in the lobby when Devlin stepped from Rachael Barrows' ground-floor office.

"Not feeling well?" she said. There was a playful smirk on her face.

"Bit of an upset stomach," Devlin said. "Are you following me?"

Cass ignored the question. "Just so long as it's not contagious," she said. The smirk had turned into a teasing smile. "Odd you should pick a gynecologist who just happened to be the hostess of Melissa Coors' last party. You have something for me, Devlin?"

"Just a smile. Maybe a kind word."

Cass cocked her hip and her head. It was a striking pose for her. Quite alluring, Devlin decided. "I've been doing some more checking," she said. "And it's starting to get interesting. A former hero cop comes down from his hideout in Vermont, and suddenly starts living with an up-and-coming young artist. Pretty tame," she said. "Interesting but tame." She let her tongue play along her upper teeth for a moment. "But then a well-known actress gets murdered, and the actress turns out to be connected with the artist's old boyfriend, and suddenly the hero cop is running around asking questions." She tapped her nose with one finger. "Curiouser and curiouser," she added. "So I start to smell a story. A very large, fat one that I very much want to have. So tell me. What gives, Devlin?"

He raised his hands in a helpless gesture. "I had a stomachache. So I went to see a doctor."

"A gynecologist."

"The pain was kind of low in my stomach," he said.

"You're cute, Devlin. And I really like cute men. But you're also fast becoming a pain in the ass." She stepped closer to him, and he could smell the expensive scent she was wearing. "Look, let's be friends. Maybe we could even help each other if we shared information."

"Let me think about it," Devlin said.

"You mean that?"

"No, but it's the only way I can think of getting away from here." He watched her eyes harden. "Listen. I'll think about it," he said. "No bullshit. I will. But not now. Not yet."

Cass nodded. With strained reluctance, he thought. "I'll keep in touch," she said.

"I'll like that," he said. "I've never been pursued by a beautiful woman before."

The smirk returned. "I doubt that, Devlin," she said. "I doubt that very much."

Mallory was waiting for him outside the loft, solid and square, from the top of his head, through his shoulders, and down to his oversize feet. Just looking at his wing-tipped shoes, Devlin would have known who and what he was. The FBI had an arrangement with the Bostonian Shoe Company that allowed its agents to buy three different styles of shoe at discount prices. They had had the deal for years, and it was almost impossible to find an FBI agent not wearing one of the distinctive shoe styles. Cops made jokes about it. The FBI slinking around, hoping the media wouldn't know they were there. And all of them wearing shoes that identified them as much as their badges did.

"I need to talk to you. Now." He wasn't being unpleasant, just insistent. It must be your day, Devlin told himself. He was starting to think he was leaving a trail of bread crumbs behind everywhere he went.

He glanced at the man's shoes again. "Nice shoes," he said. "What can I do for you?"

Mallory seemed momentarily confused. "I'd rather talk upstairs," he said.

"It's nice here. And I need the fresh air."

Mallory's eyes hardened. "That's what your girlfriend told me. Get some air." He paused a beat. "So that's the way it's gonna be, huh?"

"Doesn't have to," Devlin said. "We can be buddies. But let's talk here."

"You really think you're running your own show, don't you? You and Eddie Grogan."

"Grogan?" Devlin said. "I thought he was working for you."

Mallory offered an unfriendly smile. "And you'd swear to it in court, right?"

"On your mother's own Bible," Devlin said.

Mallory looked out into the street. "Someday I'm gonna find a cop who wouldn't perjure himself," he said.

"And someday I'm gonna find a Fibbie who isn't an asshole." Devlin watched Mallory's head snap around. He grinned at him. "Oh, wait. I found one once. But his bosses didn't like him. They shipped him off to Buffalo." He offered up a helpless shrug. "But who knows? Maybe today's our lucky day," he said. "Maybe we'll both be surprised."

Mallory squared himself on Devlin. He was an inch taller and about twenty pounds heavier, and he seemed to be trying to use it now. Devlin considered kicking him in the balls and getting the game over with. Quickly.

"You don't seem to understand something, Devlin. And it's that you're fucking up our investigation." He raised a mollifying hand. "I know you don't mean to. I know you think you're doing the right thing. But the bottom line is you're fucking it up." He moved a half step closer. "So, what I have is a deal for you. First, you go away. Second, we do what you people want." He inclined his chin toward the upper floors of Adrianna's building. "We throw a tight security net around the lady. An impregnable one."

"Didn't know there was such a thing," Devlin said. "Besides, nobody up there . . ." He paused and smiled. "Or down here, trusts you."

Mallory offered a wide, malignant smile. "Okay," he said. "Plan B. That's where we start pulling you in for questioning every day. And where we keep all protection off the lady for good. Zip. Zero." He hesitated. "Oh, and did I forget? Oh, yeah, we also have Eddie Grogan's ass shipped out to Staten Island, pulling a double tour. How's that plan sound?"

Devlin shrugged. "The press will love it. When's it

gonna start? There's this TV lady named Cass Walker I should call. I know she'll want to be there with a camera crew."

Mallory's face reddened, and he jabbed a finger toward Devlin's face. "You know that won't work, Devlin. If the press ever finds out this is a serial case, they'll be all over this street. They'll want to cover the next murder live. Shit, Oprah and Donahue and Geraldo will be tripping over each other. And our killer will just move on. But he'll come back later. Maybe in a year." He looked up at Adrianna's windows. "And then she's dead. So don't fuck with me, Devlin. Not if you want *her* to survive this."

The small scar on Devlin's cheek slowly lightened until it was only a thin white line. His voice remained soft, almost unnaturally so. "You ever get kicked in the balls, Mallory?" he asked. "I mean really hard. They tell me it hurts like a sonofabitch."

Mallory glared at him, then took a half step back. "You better think about what I said," he snapped. "You better think about it real good. Bad things can happen to you too, Devlin. Very bad things."

22

Eddie Grogan came through the door like a gleeful fifty-two-year-old bull who had just discovered cows did more than give milk.

"The computer just shit out the mother lode," he said, pulling a sheet of perforated computer paper from his inside pocket.

"You found Gail Collins," Devlin said.

"Oh, yeah," Grogan said. "But it's how I found her. That's the be-U-ti-ful part."

"So tell me," Devlin said. "Don't make me play Mahoodi the Magnificent and do some-mind reading act."

Grogan sprawled in a chair. He slapped the computer sheet with the back of one hand. "I've been running back five years, citywide. And I've been asking the computer to pull out anybody who was ever attacked and scarred on the left cheek." He grinned. "And bingo. Three years ago, a lady in Brooklyn Heights pops out. Guess who?"

"Gail Collins," Devlin said. "You don't mean it?"

"Gail Collins," Grogan confirmed. He was still grinning. "So I pull up the original incident report, and all the Fives, and suddenly I also got her real name and her Social Security number." He leaned forward. "Gail Collins is a stage moniker. Her real name is Martha Schultz, and, according to Social Security, she's lived in Philly for the last two years." He rubbed his hands together. "So I call her, and lo and behold, she knows our little priest Father Jim. In fact, she's the same

277

saloon singer who was playing patty cakes with him all those years ago. But she ain't saying no more over the phone. We wanna talk to her, we go there, and we show her some ID."

"So she was attacked and scarred the same way," Devlin said.

"You got it."

"And then she split and left no forwarding address." He looked up at Grogan. "What about her singing career?"

Grogan shrugged. Thought about it, then made a gesture with his thumb against his left cheek. "Maybe she don't look so good anymore. We wanna find out, we gotta go there."

Devlin stared at the floor for a moment. "So she disappears, and the perp never has a chance to go back." He looked up at Grogan. "He never has a chance to finish the job."

"Or maybe the fact that she ran away made him wanna be sure nobody else ever did that again," Grogan said. "But whatever. She's there for the asking. When you wanna go?"

"Now," Devlin said. "We can be in Philly in two hours."

"We'll take your car," Grogan said. "That department piece of shit I drive, it'll end up on a lift in some shitkicker's garage."

Martha Schultz, a.k.a. Gail Collins, lived in a walk-up in a somewhat battered working-class neighborhood on Philadelphia's South Side. As they stepped into the hallway, the odor of old cooking smells that had long permeated the walls assaulted their nostrils. It was an odor both men had smelled many times as cops—one of impoverishment and struggle—almost as though the walls held a reminder that only the meanest of plea-sures were to be found within. It struck Devlin immediately. This was the first place they had gone—the first person they had seen—where success and affluence wasn't commonplace. And, to the best of their knowledge, this was the killer's first victim, the first person from whom everything they had possessed had been gradually taken away.

Suddenly, Devlin felt he understood the killer for the first time, understood why he required a time lapse between the scarring and the murder itself. It wasn't just the terror it produced. Or the psychological torment of facial mutilation, coupled with the ever growing terror of what was still to come. It was a gradual destruction of the woman herself, a slow stripping away of every ounce of pride, every fiber of self-worth, until nothing was left but the shell of what she had been. And they had robbed the killer of that satisfaction with Adrianna. For the first time, Devlin understood how much the killer must hate them, how much he must hate Adrianna for protecting herself, and thereby withholding from him that ultimate, final pleasure.

As Eddie reached out to press the doorbell, Devlin delayed his hand. "You know, I think I'm just starting to figure out how big a monster our perp is," he said.

Grogan's eyes became uncharacteristically hard. "Like I told you at the beginning," he said, "I never wanted anybody like I want this prick."

When Gail Collins opened the door, the first thing Devlin saw was her mutilated left cheek. It was a vicious scar that moved in an undulating line from beneath her left ear to the corner of her mouth. The cut had been deep and, from the droop of her mouth, had obviously severed facial nerves and thwarted the talents of any surgeon. She had been disfigured with pure, wicked intent, and beyond any hope of redemption.

She turned her cheek to them as they sat opposite her on a creaky but well-kept sofa. "Ugly, isn't it?" she said.

Neither man knew what to say. Finally, Devlin pushed out some words. "It's been happening to other women," he said. "It's why we're here. We think it may be the same person."

Gail Collins' eyes became cold, icy. They were a beautiful deep blue, and from the unmarked lines of her face he could tell she had once been a strikingly attractive woman. Now there was slightly too much makeup—an obvious effort to diffuse the scar—and her longish blond hair had been poorly dyed, and the darker roots had been allowed to show through. And she was heavier than Devlin imagined she had once been. She had the look of someone who understood that efforts at self-maintenance would be wasted.

"I'm sorry for them. For the other women," she said. "But I'm sorrier for me." She stared at each of them in turn, as if awaiting some challenge to her remark. "But I hope you catch the bastard," she added. "I hope you catch him, and I hope you kill him and send him straight to Hell."

Devlin twisted in his seat. Despite all his years of practice, he wasn't good at dealing with the internal pain of others. It made him slightly nervous.

"We're particularly interested in your relationship with Father James Hopkins," Devlin said. "I know you may not want to talk about it. But it might help us a great deal if you did."

Gail Collins leaned forward and offered as much of a smirk as her disfigured mouth would allow. "Little Jim," she said, almost to herself. Her eyes darted to Devlin. "And I mean *little* in every sense of the word."

She barked laughter. At herself, Devlin thought.

"You think he's behind all this?" She shook her head. "The man who attacked me was a lot stronger than Jim." She thought about her words. "But I suppose rage can make you stronger. And Jim had every reason to feel rage toward me. I saw to that real good. The dirty sonofabitch."

"Tell us about him," Grogan urged.

Gail Collins sat back with a slightly bored sigh. "I haven't thought about him much." She gave them the crooked smile. "Except about once a day." She rubbed her palms together, as if warming them. "I was a pretty successful singer when I met him. At least I was on my way. One hit album and more nightclub offers than I could handle." She shook her head. "It looked good for me back then. Real good."

She sat forward, adding physical momentum to her story. "I was also a pretty ardent Catholic, and I did charity gigs whenever I was asked. Especially for the archdiocese." Again the crooked smile. "I was storing up chips to get me into Heaven someday," she added. "Well, anyway, Jim was working at the archdiocese. In their p.r. office. I never knew the Church had press agents, but they do. That's really all Jim was, a flack for Holy Mother the Church." There was a bitterness in the woman's final words, and Devlin suspected it involved more than an ill-advised affair with a priest.

She shrugged. "We worked pretty closely together. And . . . well, it's an old story. We ended up doing the beast with two backs gig, and little Gail got herself knocked up. And sweet, little, innocent Father Jim was the poppa."

"You got pregnant?" Grogan's voice was filled with incredulity. "I'm sorry," he quickly added. "We didn't know that."

"Oh, yeah," Gail said. "The whole bit. With child, as they say in the Bible." She laughed. "Well, Jim, he confessed his sin. He was scared shitless. And the boys at the archdiocese—the big boys themselves—well, they were in just a bit of a stew. Not only had one of their own been boffing a saloon singer, but he had gone and got her pregnant to boot. And a fair-haired boy right there in their midst. Not some priest hidden away in the boondocks someplace.

"Well, Jimmy boy's career was down the tubes. There was no question of repentance, or forgiveness, or any of that crap. He was shuttled off to take care of the bag ladies." Again she laughed. "No temptation there to let his little dick get out of control. And the big boys at the archdiocese took on the task of dealing with me."

"How did they do that?" Devlin asked.

She let out a snort. "Like the mean-spirited bastards that they are," she said. "That's how."

Gail sat back again, suddenly looking deflated by her own story, her own memories. "I pleaded with Jim," she said. "I begged him to leave the Church and help me raise our kid." She glanced at each of them. "You see, I loved the sonofabitch. I really did."

Gail fell momentarily silent, and they waited for her to continue. Finally the smile returned to her face, though it was clearly forced this time.

"Jim insisted he couldn't leave the Church, that he had to endure his penance and make amends for his sins. He told me the archdiocese would take care of our problem. That they'd help me get through it all. Our problem," she repeated, emphasizing the word. "The simpering sonofabitch wouldn't even let himself think of it as his child. Just his fucking problem."

"What did they do? The archdiocese?" Grogan asked.

"They assigned this monsignor, named Brian Duffy, to handle it. He was a real sweetheart. At first he suggested I go off and have the child quietly. For the good of Holy Mother the Church. He even asked me if I had insurance." She laughed again. "I think he was hoping they could avoid picking up the tab," she added. "But I was hot. And I was scared. I saw my whole life—my career, everything—coming crashing down around my ears." She shook her head. "Christ, there I was, thirty years old, and all by myself. I was scared to death, and all I wanted was for them to force Jim out of the Church. Make him marry me. Make him give our kid a proper name. When I told him that, Duffy just looked at me like I was some kind of crazy hooker or something." Her eyes hardened. "Hell, I was never an angel, and I grew up poor. But I was never a cheap slut, either. So I got mad as hell, and I threatened him. Said I was going to blow the lid off the whole thing, and that I'd start with the *National Enquirer,* and the *Star,* and all those other supermarket sleazoids.

"Well, that got the good monsignor's attention real quick. And he told me they had another solution. They'd help me out. They'd arrange for a 'very private' abortion." She looked at each of them, as if making sure they believed her, clearly certain that they probably would not. "And that's just what they did," she added. "And isn't that one for Ripley?"

Devlin and Grogan remained silent, each knowing they should not stop the woman now.

"So, anyway, I told Jim what I was going to do. You see, I was still hoping he'd do the right thing." She shook her head. "Well, he flipped out, all right. It was wrong, he told me. It was morally wrong. It was murder, pure and simple. And he refused to believe the archdiocese was part and parcel to the whole thing. Told me I was lying and begged me to reconsider. Shit, he even offered to let the child use his name. What a *generous* sonofabitch he was.

"Well, that did it for me. I told him to fuck off. I told him he was an asshole, and that he'd only been one of a dozen guys I'd been with, and that maybe he wasn't even the kid's father." She lowered her eyes. "It wasn't true, but I wanted to hurt the sonofabitch. Then I stuck the knife in, and I twisted it. I told him it was his kid, that there was no doubt about it. And I told him I was going to go ahead with what the Church wanted. And that he was equally responsible. That his kid was going to die because of him."

She fell silent again, and this time Devlin could see that she had worn herself out.

"So you had the abortion," Devlin said. He watched her nod her head. She didn't look at him. "Who performed it?" he asked.

She let out a short, derisive breath. "Oh, they were true to their word," she said. "It was very private. Very, very private." She looked up. "I was sent to this clinic way out in Westchester County. It was theirs—run by the archdiocese—and all the patients were nuns or priests. Mostly they were old, on their last legs. But some were younger, and I got the impression they did some alcohol counseling there. For priests who hit the sauce a little too hard. Stuff like that.

"But they did have operating facilities, and they wheeled me into one as quick as they could." She shrugged. "But they put me out as soon as I got there. And when I woke up, it was over, and I never even saw the doctor who did the deed." She looked at Devlin, her eyes no longer able to hide the sadness. "Christ, they treated me like I was a leper. The nuns who worked as nurses there, they acted like they shouldn't even touch me. Like they should run and wash their hands if they had to." Tears began to form in the corners of her eyes. "And it was their place. And they did it. It was what *they* wanted. *Them*, not me. *Them!*"

Devlin waited, giving the woman time to calm down. When he finally spoke, he tried to keep his voice as soothing as possible.

"How did Father Hopkins react to the abortion? Once it was over?"

She shook her head. "I never saw him afterward. Not after that last time when I told him what I was going to do." She stared into her lap, watched her fingers play against each other. "He was devastated then. Said he'd spend his life seeking redemption." She let out another short, derisive breath. "But he wasn't devastated enough to leave the Church and be a father to his child," she added. She looked up at them, each in turn. "You know, I wanted to keep that kid. And I would've been a great mother to it. But I was scared. I was just so goddamned scared."

Gail wiped the corners of her eyes and seemed to regain control of herself. "Anyway, I went back to work and tried to forget. Then, six months later, this creep breaks into my apartment—all dressed up in this hood and robe. And he does this." She brushed the back of her hand against her mutilated cheek. "And that's it for me. The doctors I went to said there was no hope. Just too much damage." She shrugged and offered a weak smile. "Nobody wants a saloon singer with a snake carved in her face," she said. "Nobody wants to hear a love song from somebody who looks like bloody Frankenstein. So I moved here. And now I waitress at the International House of Pancakes." She paused and smiled at them. "I bet you some priest would tell me it was God's punishment," she said.

As they drove along the highway headed out of the city—the dull gray ships of the Philadelphia Naval Yard off to their right—Devlin mused about what they now had, what their next step must be, and how difficult it would be to take. There was a motive now—a rock-solid one to build on. A madness spurred on by unre-solvable guilt. Unfortunately, it involved a priest, and Devlin and Grogan both knew that the bosses of the police department, and the politicians in the district attorney's and mayor's offices, would never condone an arrest, or even a heavy interrogation, until every t was crossed and i dotted. And the scenario also included the archdiocese and the involvement of two of its peo-ple—Fr. James Hopkins and Monsignor Brian Duffy—in an act that, rightly or wrongly, might shake the faith of every Catholic in the city. With the archdiocese in the equation, they knew the odds against them in-creased dramatically. The politicians who ran the city didn't call the Archdiocese of New York "the power-house" for nothing.

"So what do we do now?" Devlin asked as they moved into the bucolic scenery that spread out north of Philadelphia.

"We ain't got much choice," Grogan said. "We lay it on the line for Monsignor Duffy and sweet little Father Jim, and we see what shakes loose." Grogan stared at him for moment. "Or, I should say, you lay it out for them. One call to the P.C.'s or the mayor's office will cut me off faster than a ten-dollar hooker. So I'll start digging around to find out who did the abortion. And the first person I'll talk to is Rachael Barrows."

"You think she's the one?" Devlin asked.

"I dunno. But it sure would fit," Grogan said. "She seemed to know all about Father Jim's inability to keep his pecker in his pants. And I didn't get the impression that he was taking out ads in *The Times* about that."

23

The hands feel so rough and hard touching you there, and you can feel the breaths coming in short gasps against your neck. Soon the whispering will start, the way it always does, telling you how sweet you are, how very sweet. It's the reason the hands are there now, touching you, making you feel the way you know you shouldn't. But it's your fault. You know that. You make the hands come to you. It's something that can't be helped. You've been told that again and again. If only you weren't so sweet, so wonderful to touch. Then it would never happen. The temptation would be gone forever, and you wouldn't be able to make these things happen again and again and again.

Adrianna awoke suddenly, the sunlight streaming through the window, forcing her to turn her eyes back against the pillow. She reached out a hand and felt him lying there next to her, and she inched closer until she was against his back and could feel the heat of his body flowing into her.

He stirred slightly and pressed back against her, and her hand slipped around him, then down, and she took hold of him.

Devlin let out a low, soft grunt of pleasure as her fingers began to manipulate him, play with him.

"Hi, sailor," Adrianna whispered. "You looking for a date?"

Devlin reached his own hand back and began stroking her flank, then cupped the soft curve of her but-

tocks and pulled her even closer against him. He
glanced at the clock. The red numerals glared at him,
announcing it was seven. The others, he knew, would
arrive at eight-thirty, as they had agreed. He felt himself harden, felt her fingers play more vigorously now,
urging him on, or up, or whatever. He was reaching
that point where thought was becoming less possible,
where sensation was taking over and playing its own
music of action and reaction. He turned to her and
slipped his hand between her legs and felt the great
wetness of her, slick and soft against his fingers. Her
legs parted, offering more of herself, silently asking him
to touch her the way he had discovered she liked best.

"My goodness," he said affectedly. "What have you
been lying there thinking about?"

"Strong fingers," she said. "Strong and soft and gentle fingers." She leaned back her head, gave a short
gasp, then smiled at him. "I always wake up horny in
the morning," she said. "Didn't I ever tell you that?"

"No," he said. "But I'll remember."

She let out a soft moan as he found her clitoris and
began stroking it with the tip of one finger, feeling it
slick and hard against his touch. Her body arched
slightly, and then she pushed him back.

"I can't wait," she said. "I want more of this, but I
just can't wait."

She slipped her leg over him, then rose and maneuvered her hips until he slid just inside her. Her eyes
closed and her lips parted, and she began to lower
herself to him, slowly at first, then finally in a rush
that plunged him deep within her.

"Oh, God," she said as she began to rock back and
forth. "Oh, God. Oh, God. Oh, God."

They were seated in the living area: Gabrielle and
Grogan on the sofa, Devlin and Adrianna opposite in
separate chairs, afraid to be too close together lest their
hands begin touching each other with a will of their
own.

It was nine o'clock, and Devlin had just telephoned the archdiocese and made an appointment to see Monsignor Duffy at three. Grogan himself had just returned from using the phone.

"Rachael Barrows will see me at one," he said. "I said it was urgent, and she agreed to cut lunch short and fit me in before her first afternoon patient." He sprawled across one end of the sofa. "I had trouble getting somebody to keep an eye on this place," he said. "Had to ask one of the guys to do it on his own time. He'll be here at noon. Mallory's got everybody working on something. Claims he's close to nailing our boy."

"He say who?" Devlin asked.

Grogan shook his head. "Seems he don't need me. I think he's pushing Cervone to have me reassigned."

Devlin decided to remain silent about his little talk with the FBI agent. Eddie was a big boy, could take care of himself. And he didn't need to put Adrianna more on edge.

"I could arrange to stay here," Gabrielle said. "It would only take a few calls to rearrange my schedule."

"Uh-uh," Devlin said. "Nobody stays who isn't armed. Not alone. Not ever. We've done too well so far. I'm not about to change the game."

Gabrielle shifted in her seat. 'You're right, of course." She smiled at him. "But I hope I'm not detecting an attitude that says only men are capable of protecting poor, helpless females. If I am, we can try a little arm wrestling right now."

"Don't," Grogan warned. "She'll kick your butt, and then I'll have to tell all my buddies at the precinct that I know this hero cop who went to Vermont and got turned into a wimp."

Devlin glanced at Gabrielle. There was a coy, playful look spread across her face. "I saw her working out," he said. "Mrs. Devlin didn't raise any fools."

Adrianna watched the interplay. The woman was openly flirting, using some kind of macho weight-lifting nonsense to do it. And she was portraying *her* as some kind of simpering, helpless, witless woman at the same time.

"I'll be perfectly all right alone," she said.

Gabrielle turned toward her, eyebrows arched.

The doorbell ended the exchange. It was the bell on the upstairs door, not the buzzer for the downstairs intercom. They glanced at each other, and Devlin and Grogan immediately removed their weapons and moved toward the entrance.

When the door swung open, Devlin found himself facing a bemused Cass Walker. She glanced at the weapon he was holding down along his right leg, then at the one in Eddie's hand.

"I know the press isn't popular," she said. "But isn't this a little extreme?"

"How'd you get up here?" Devlin asked. They had begun making sure the downstairs door was locked as an added precaution. The lock could be slipped easily, but the noise would alert them.

"The mailman opened the door, and I just popped in." She grinned at him. "I thought he'd never come. And I knew if I rang the buzzer, I'd never even get this far." She walked past Devlin, took in everyone in the room, then spun back to face him. "Nice gathering," she said. "Cop, retired cop, department shrink. I suppose you're all here for a Tupperware party."

"Actually, we're kind of busy," Devlin said. "So—"

"Like you were in Philadelphia yesterday?"

Devlin stared at the woman, took in the self-satisfied smirk, and knew they were in trouble.

"Martha Schultz, or Gail Collins"—she shrugged—"whatever, is a very interesting woman to talk to, isn't she?"

"Maybe you better join us," Devlin said.

"Thought you'd never ask. Got anything cold? It was hot waiting outside. I think summer is definitely on the way."

"So you just happened to be in Philly yesterday," Devlin began when they were all seated together.

"Not really," Cass said. "It's a shame they don't teach you guys how to know when you're being followed. They should really add that course to the curriculum at cop school."

Adrianna watched the woman play her game. She too was flirting with Paul, and she was being a classic bitch at the same time. And she was doing it so well, she was forcing all the men to respond to her. Just the way she wanted. Adrianna noted the tailored linen suit the woman was wearing, and how her crossed legs raised the skirt a third of the way up her thigh, exposing beautifully shaped legs. She glanced quickly at Gabrielle, and from the look on her face, found that she too didn't like what she was seeing. She wondered if it was because she considered Cass Walker competition.

"So you spoke to Gail Collins?" Grogan asked.

"A long, heartfelt talk," Cass said. She glanced first at Devlin, then at Grogan. "She claims you guys told her that other women have been attacked here just the way she was." She leaned forward. "I think we need to talk about that." She tilted her head to one side. "And, please, no phony tales. I took the time to have some old incident reports pulled, and I have a list of names of women who've been attacked over the past two years." She nodded toward Adrianna, acknowledging her presence for the first time. "Including our rising young artist here."

"What's in it for us?" Devlin asked. He wanted to tell the woman to take a walk, and to take her information with her. But he knew he couldn't.

"Cooperation," Cass said. "I could do the story now. Especially the part about the abortion and the archdiocese. It would send this town into orbit, and me straight to the network. Maybe." She drummed her fingers against one knee. "But I think there's an even bigger story here. One that will get me everything I want. And if I'm right, I'm willing to wait for it. But only if I get it first. Twenty-four hours' lead time. Nothing less." She smiled. "Deal?"

"It doesn't sound to me like you've got too much," Grogan said. He was staring at the woman. It was the hard-cop stare that Devlin thought Eddie did especially well. Cass, however, seemed unimpressed.

"I've got enough," she said, with a sweet, false smile. "I can go to the archdiocese and to Father Hopkins, and I can put together what they say—or don't say—with the wonderful tale Gail Collins has to tell. Then I can put together the incident reports on other women who've been scarred, and just stir the pot." The smile returned. "Believe me, the scum will float to the surface. It always does."

Gabrielle stood, briefly smiled at the woman, then turned to Devlin. "Paul, I think we need to speak for a moment." She gestured toward the far end of the loft. "May we? Eddie too."

"Looks like we're in the soup," Grogan said when they had secreted themselves in a corner, out of view behind the easel that held Adrianna's latest canvas.

"I'd like to strangle the woman," Gabrielle said. "If she does what she says she'll do, and if our killer is Father Jim—and that's starting to seem more inescapable by the minute—well, she could send him into a frenzy. Just by letting him know what she knows. Just by raising the threat of exposure." She looked at each man. "And I mean a frenzy that will leave bodies scattered around."

Devlin nodded. "So what do you suggest?"

"You have to give her something," Gabrielle said. "Anything that will blunt her. Even temporarily."

Devlin nodded. "I think she's right. We have to have time to prove our case against him—if we can—and to throw a tight net around him so we can keep him under control. Otherwise, he's liable to run."

"Or worse," Gabrielle said. "It's impossible to predict *what* might happen."

"How much do we tell her?" Grogan asked.

"Just enough," Devlin said. "She apparently didn't do enough homework. She hasn't made the connection between the attacks and the killings. Nothing was ever released about Melissa's scarring. And apparently she hasn't put the other names together yet. The incidents—the scarrings and the murders in each case— were spaced far apart. And she hasn't connected them. She's a typical television reporter. She doesn't read the papers. She only follows her competition on television. So, we're in luck that way." He looked at each of them. "But once she starts talking to people, and when she puts her stuff on the air, somebody else will make the connection. And then we're dead."

"So we'll keep it to the attacks," Grogan said. It wasn't a question, more a need of assurance.

"You got it," Devlin said. He looked at Gabrielle. "Okay?" he asked.

She nodded. "I'd still rather strangle her, but it's the best we can do. But we have to keep her away from Hopkins and the archdiocese. That's crucial if we're going to keep Father Jim under control."

Cass closed her notebook and grinned like the Cheshire cat. She was delighted with the information, and even more at getting her own way. "But I can't wait forever," she warned. "If I even get a hint Gail Collins is talking to anyone else—or if I find out you guys are talking to anyone else in the media—the game's over, and I go with what I've got."

"We'll keep our end of the deal," Devlin said. "You just keep yours." He gave her as hard a stare as he could deliver. "And if you decide you're going with the story—for any reason—you tell us first. That's part of it."

Cass' smile widened. "You got it, Devlin," she said. "And we keep in touch. You and I. Don't forget that part."

When Cass had left, Adrianna ground her teeth, the woman's final words replaying in her mind. "Bitch," she said.

Gabrielle laughed softly. "Bitch and a half," she countered.

Rachael Barrows stared across her desk at Eddie Grogan. Her hands began playing with the pen that lay before her, and Grogan picked up on it instantly.

"This is all getting a bit sticky," she said. "And I think it's something I definitely don't want to be connected to."

"Can you just check your records and see if Gail Collins or Martha Schultz was ever a patient?" Grogan asked.

"I can tell you from memory that they weren't," she said.

"What about the archdiocese? You ever do any work for them? Charitable? Whatever?"

"I'm not even a Catholic, Detective. I'm a Jew."

"That don't answer my question," Grogan said.

Rachael Barrows let out a long sigh. "No, Detective Grogan. I never did any work—abortions or anything else—for the archdiocese. And I seriously doubt anyone else has either." She shook her head. "The whole thing is preposterous."

"Well, if the television reporter I told you about comes around, I hope you'll tell her that too," Grogan said.

"Believe me, Detective, if Ms. Walker shows up here, she won't get past my receptionist. I don't plan to have my practice dragged into this kind of mess. Professional suicide has never appealed to me." She twisted the pen between her hands, and for a moment Grogan thought it might break. "I'm sorry I ever mentioned Father Hopkins' little peccadillo to anyone," she said. "And had I known he had gotten the poor woman pregnant, I never would have."

Grogan stared back across the desk. "I guess you wouldn't let me look through your records, just to see if certain names you might have forgotten just might happen to pop up?"

"I certainly would not."

" 'Course I could get a warrant, I suppose," Grogan offered.

"Than you had better get one," Rachael said. "And be assured my attorney will fight it in court on ethical grounds."

"Never doubted it for a minute," Grogan said.

Monsignor Brian Duffy reclined slightly in his high-backed swivel chair. The telephone was clenched in one hand, and his wide mouth was now a tight line as he listened to the caller. He was a stocky man, modestly overweight, short in height but not in stature, a man who at fifty controlled a great deal of what went on in the Archdiocese of New York. He had neatly trimmed gray hair, the florid, puffy face of someone who enjoyed food and drink too well, and soft gray eyes that became steely when he was challenged or threatened in any way. In short, he looked like the business executive he was. And his eyes now had that steely quality that invariably made his subordinates uneasy.

"I assure you, nothing will ever get out about Gail Collins," he said. "And certainly not about your involvement. Not from anyone here, or from anyone at the clinic. Our people operate under a vow of obedience. And it is a vow we take quite seriously."

The monsignor listened again, his mouth returning to the tight, uncompromising line. "I understand. And I assure you that any further intrusions by the police will produce a telephone call to the appropriate parties. But not yet. Sometimes a complaint made too early can prove counterproductive."

He listened again, one finger roaming the rim of a coffee mug centered on his desk. It bore a legend—originally attributed to Nixon aide Charles Colsen—that intoned: "When you've got them by the balls, their hearts and minds will follow." It was something he left out only when fellow clerics were in the room.

"I assure you, it will be taken care of, and I promise to contact you immediately if anything unexpected develops." He paused again, listening. "I understand. I know you never got a release form signed by Miss Collins. It just wasn't possible if we were going to keep your name confidential." He paused again. "Yes, I know that could make it appear she did not act of her own accord. But we both know that wasn't the case, and I assure you the question will never arise. Certainly your name will never come into it, no matter what. You have my word on that."

Again he waited. "Yes, yes. I'll see to it. I must go now. God bless you."

Brian Duffy sat forward and returned the phone to its cradle. He briefly looked at the portrait of Jesus Christ on the wall and slowly shook his head. It was not the life you planned when you sat in the seminary all those years ago, he told himself. He took a cigar from a humidor on his desk, clipped it, and lit it. But this was the real world, and his job—his only job—was to protect the Church. And, unfortunately, the real world was not some fairy tale conjured up by monks behind cloistered walls. He recalled the words of Archbishop John Marcinkus and took solace in them: "You can't run the Church on Hail Marys."

"You certainly cannot," Duffy whispered to himself. "God, that you could."

He reached out and pulled his calendar to him. It listed his appointments, and he ran his finger down until he found the one at three o'clock. Paul Devlin, it said simply. A good Irish name, he told himself. Hopefully an Irish Catholic. He thought briefly about cancelling the meeting, but decided that might only urge the man on. No, we must scotch the snake, not kill it, he told himself. Whether from the Bard or the Bible, it was good advice.

But it didn't hurt to be prepared, he told himself. He picked up the phone again and punched out an internal number.

"Father Moore?" he said when the call was answered. "This is Monsignor Duffy, and I need you to check our files on a Paul Devlin. He's a former New York City detective, and I want everything we have on him." He waited. "Yes, as quickly as possible," he said. "I have an appointment with the gentleman in one hour, and I'd like to be fully prepared. God be with you, Father."

The monsignor sat back and allowed his eyes to roam his office. What he saw pleased him, as it had from the moment he had first entered the room so many years ago. What was it? Five years? No. It was six. He gave a small shake of his head, then looked around the office again. It was large by clerical standards, and the rich wood paneling gleamed under the light of the heavy brass chandelier that hung from the center of the ceiling. The desk was large as well. A highly polished mahogany that he kept clear of unsightly clutter.

His eyes fell on the solitary prayer kneeler that stood against one wall, under the portrait of Jesus Christ, and he momentarily questioned if he was guilty of the sin of pride in taking such pleasure from his office, from the specter of power it presented to those who entered it.

He hoped not. But he knew it was always a danger. He did not consider himself a particularly able priest, but rather an exceptional administrator. And the Church, he knew, needed those every bit as much as it needed its saints. And one served as one could. With the talents one had. He closed his eyes and offered up a silent prayer that God also saw it that way.

24

Brian Duffy was pleased with the information he had reviewed when Devlin arrived at the three o'clock meeting. The monsignor did not like surprises—and the dossier he had read had offered none. The man had been an exceptional detective, but he had dealt with his ilk before. His mood changed, though, with Devlin's first words. The man explained that the matter they would discuss in some way involved a woman he had been asked to protect. Earlier, on the phone, he had said only that it involved Fr. Hopkins, and Duffy had later learned that also meant Gail Collins. Now another woman was somehow involved. If it turned out that Hopkins had again failed to keep his trousers zipped, he vowed he'd have the man sent someplace that would make bag ladies look like Raquel Welch. *After* he strangled him with his own rosary beads.

"I think you better explain how all this involves Father Hopkins," Duffy said. He put on his most cheerful exterior, knowing that if eventually forced to take on a more severe demeanor, it would only add to the power of it, make it all the more authentic. In his six years of service to the archdiocese, he had dealt with many difficult problems, and he considered himself a master of the technique. "I must confess, I'm a bit mystified," he added. Just for effect.

Devlin began slowly, telling Duffy about the attacks on women over the past two years—women who were all young, who were all working in the arts, and who were each on the verge of major success before they were viciously killed. He detailed the women individually, beginning with the ritual scarring, the months of torment, then finally their brutal murders. He then took Duffy back to the first victim, Gail Collins, the woman with whom it had all begun, and who apparently had established the method for the other victims. He ended with Adrianna Mendez, and his attempt to find the killer before she too joined that growing list of victims.

Throughout the discourse, the monsignor's eyes grew steadily larger; his jaw dropped slightly, and his rather round body became unnaturally still.

"Are you saying you suspect Father Hopkins of having . . . of having . . . ?"

Devlin looked at him levelly. "Yes, I do, Monsignor."

Duffy stared at him for half a minute. "My God, man. You are talking about a priest. A Roman Catholic priest." The monsignor's already florid face reddened to the point where Devlin was suddenly concerned for him.

He lowered his voice, made it as gentle as he could. "Priests can become ill as easily as anyone else," he said. "Our evidence isn't conclusive, but it's strong enough that we need to take a very hard look at Father Hopkins." He paused for emphasis. "*If* we hope to help Adrianna Mendez. *If* we hope to keep other women from being scarred and killed. And to do that, we need your help."

The monsignor sat shaking his head. His color returned to its normal shade of red, and he appeared to have gathered himself, made himself ready for what lay ahead.

"How would you go about doing what you propose?" he asked.

"I need to look pretty deeply into Father Hopkins' past," Devlin said. "With your help, and the help of the police investigating the murders. And we need to interrogate him extensively." He pressed his hands together, almost in a gesture of prayer. "It would be best if that could be done without any formal charges, even without taking him into custody. Perhaps it could even be done at a facility of yours. That way it would be quiet. No one else would have to know about it." He held Duffy's eyes. "And we also need to search his belongings, and, to be frank, we'd be hard pressed to find a judge who'd let us do that." Devlin paused again. "There's no question of prosecution in this," he added. "If he's guilty, the man is ill, and no district attorney will try to circumvent that. There are no reputations to be made in prosecuting a priest. It would be more like political suicide."

The monsignor began drumming the fingers of both hands against his desk. "So, what you basically want is for the archdiocese to help you suspend Father Hopkins' constitutional rights. Am I right?" He looked across the desk at Devlin. "I suppose you also want to keep him under rather tight surveillance. Correct?"

"That's basically it," Devlin said.

"Mr. Devlin. I—the archdiocese—certainly want no harm to come to Miss Mendez. But we cannot just arbitrarily agree to the suspension of a man's rights—a priest, at that—on the basis of some very unproven conjecture." He seemed uncomfortable with the words, but then his resolve suddenly seemed to harden.

"I see no solid evidence here, Mr. Devlin. None whatsoever. No *believable* evidence that indicates Father Hopkins would have any reason to harm any of these women." He spread his hands. "Mr. Devlin, we are men of the world. We know that priests are supposed to be above temptations of the flesh. And we know, from time to time, that some are not." He let his hands fall and shook his head. "The Church has certainly experienced enough scandal lately involving priests who have had failings with women. Recently, there was even an Irish bishop you may have read about. And we've even had cases involving young children, God help us." Again he spread his hands in an all-encompassing gesture. "But you are talking about mutilation and murder. And there is simply no believable motive for such crimes."

Devlin leaned forward. "There's the question of Gail Collins' very private abortion," he said. "I believe you're familiar with that: where it was performed and by whom." He paused a beat. "We think it may have been the final blow that pushed a very devout, very sick man over the edge."

The monsignor was clearly shaken, and Devlin could see him calculating how much was really known and how much could be proven. But again he seemed to gather himself, and he suddenly became a sterner, harder man.

He leaned forward, across his desk. "Mr. Devlin, you are talking about something the archdiocese would vehemently deny. And if that ultimately became impossible, only one person would shoulder the blame." His eyes hardened. "And I assure you, sir, that person would do so gladly for the good of the Church. It would come down to a question of one man's failing. Nothing more."

Devlin's hadn't expected that reply. But he knew the man was right. Even he could not be certain if the archdiocese was involved in Gail Collins' abortion, or if Duffy had acted on his own initiative. And he doubted if anyone could ever know. He had thought of it as his trump card, and it had proven to be a pretty weak point of attack. There was simply no real pressure that could be brought with that issue. Except, perhaps, pressure on the man himself.

"Monsignor, that's an issue that should never have to be raised," he said. Again his voice was soft. "And, as I said, we are not dealing with the possibility of a trial where motive would come out."

Duffy sat back and stared at him. "But we are talking about scandal, Mr. Devlin. A scandal that would hurt the Church, and one that in the end would serve no one. Least of all the dead." He steepled his fingers and began tapping them together. "But let me try to put your mind at ease. We, Mr. Devlin, have ways of dealing with our own. Ways of helping them. We have the facilities to do so, and we have the authority over the people in our care and service. I assure you we will deal with Father Hopkins. We will get to the truth of the matter, and, if necessary, we will help him." His fingers became still. "And I assure you, if he is the person you suspect him of being, he will be cared for, and will never present a threat to anyone again."

Slowly the priest stood, indicating their meeting was over. "As to your requests, Mr. Devlin." He shook his head. "I'm afraid we cannot help you. And we will vigorously oppose any attempt to circumvent that decision." He paused again. "With all our strength and influence," he added.

Monsignor Duffy rose from his knees. He had been praying. In part for guidance and forgiveness, but also for comfort. He went back to his desk and picked up his phone and punched out an internal number.

When a voice answered he spoke curtly.

"This is Monsignor Duffy. I need to transfer someone. And I need it to be someplace desolate, and preferably out of the country. And I need to do it quickly. Please get to work on it right away, and let me know what the options are."

He returned the receiver to its cradle, and sank into his chair. And make room for another transfer if this doesn't work, he told himself. Absently he straightened the papers on his desk, then looked at the phone again. There was one other person he should call. One other person he should warn. He placed his palms together in a position of prayer, and lowered his face against them. God forgive me, he thought. He let out a long breath and wondered if He would.

25

Cass Walker never intended to keep her promise to Devlin. At the same time he was sitting across from Monsignor Duffy, Cass was being led toward the small, cramped office at St. Jude's Mission for the Homeless. She wrinkled her nose as she walked through the shelter, which was located among the grit and seediness of Ninth Avenue. The interior was clean enough, she told herself, but it held the overwhelming aroma of body odor, mixed with a lingering smell of stale, mass-cooked food. It disgusted her. If she hadn't already known better, she would have immediately categorized Fr. James Hopkins as a candidate for sainthood just for the fact that he worked there every day.

She had come to the shelter ostensibly to do a story about bag ladies in the middle of Manhattan's theater district. Father Jim, as he had told her to call him, had been delighted. Now as he ushered her into his cramped office, replete with battered, old wooden furniture, he was positively glowing.

"You have no idea what this means to us," Hopkins said as he dusted off a wooden chair and offered it to her. "Every time we get positive publicity the donations come rolling in, and we're able to do so much more for our people."

Cass smiled politely, then looked at the chair and wondered who—or what—had sat in it last. She shrugged inwardly, telling herself she had never much liked the suit she was wearing anyway.

Hopkins was still smiling at her, and she had to

admit he was a handsome man, although not really to her taste. He was too thin and seemed to vulnerable—the tragic poet figure—the kind of man some women always wanted to mother. But mothering held no allure for her. She liked strong, virile men who exuded power. They were a pain in the ass, and you could never trust them, but she liked being in their company—and their beds. She simply felt more suited to them.

Hopkins was dressed in jeans and a black cotton turtleneck, and she could easily envision him having a romp in the hay with Gail Collins, then skipping off to hear some teenager's confession, and counseling her to keep her knickers up around her ears. She had already decided she didn't like the man, and his pseudo-hip attire only confirmed it. He was a phony, she told herself. And she fully intended to prick *this* prick's balloon.

Hopkins dropped into a chair behind his desk, then extended his hands in a "here I am, I'm yours" sort of gesture. "So what can I tell you?" he said. His light blue eyes were gleaming, and there was a spray of sandy brown hair spread across his forehead. Any innocent young boy in his mid-thirties, Cass told herself.

"Why don't we start with something about you?" Cass said. She had removed a reporter's notebook from her purse for effect, and was tapping a gold Cross pen against it. A small, voice-activated tape recorder was already turning in her bag. "I'm told you used to work in the archdiocese. In their public relations office."

He grinned. "We never called it that, but it's pretty much what it is. Yes, I was there for four years. Right out of the seminary, in fact."

"Pretty good assignment," Cass said. "Your star was definitely rising. How come you left?"

What she thought was a flicker of fear passed across Hopkins' eyes, but he masked it well. He shrugged. "Frankly, anyone can do that. But please don't quote me, or I'll be in trouble. This"—he waved his arm, taking in the room and more—"well, this requires a bit more commitment."

Cass nodded, jotted a nonsense note in her notebook, then looked up, her eyes all innocence and wonder. "So what people say isn't true," she said.

Hopkins looked as though some stranger had walked up and kicked him in the stomach—all surprise and amazement, and just a touch of hurt. "What do you mean?" he said. Now there was clear-cut fear in his eyes. He tried to mask it with another smile, but this time he failed. "I don't understand. What are people saying?"

She maintained her own look of open-eyed innocence. She knew that it—together with being a woman—always made men think she could be easily bullshitted. Right up to the time she cut off their balls.

"They say . . . how should I put it? That you were sort of asked to leave. And then sent here. Right after the archdiocese found out about your affair with a singer."

Now Hopkins truly looked as though he had been kicked, and Cass thought she could almost see him suck in his stomach.

"I don't know where you heard that, but . . ."

"From Gail Collins, for one," she said. She stared at him, looking as though what she was saying was the most natural thing in the world.

Hopkins sat stone-like for almost a minute. Then his eyes slowly began to harden. "Where is Gail?" he asked.

"Uh-uh," Cass said. She fought off a smile. "She asked that I keep that confidential. I'm sure you understand."

Hopkins continued to stare at her, and Cass could feel an icy chill coming off the man. She fought off a shiver. "I'd like to speak to her," he said.

I bet you would, Cass thought. "Well, she's a little gun shy. Or maybe I should say, knife shy. Right after her medical treatment, someone took a knife to her cheek. There wasn't a helluva lot left."

"What medical treatment?" Hopkins asked.

His eyes were riveted on her, and his body looked like a coiled spring, ready to leap from behind his desk. Cass hadn't failed to note that he had registered no surprise about the fact that Gail Collins had been cut. Or that it had been a deep and vicious wound. He just seemed to know. She felt the chill returning, but fought it off.

"What medical treatment?" he repeated. His voice was a bit harsher now.

Cass adjusted herself in her chair and stared at him. There was no longer any innocence in her eyes. It was show time, and she'd be damned if she'd let this bozo scare her out of it. "The abortion, Father. The abortion she had after you got her pregnant. The one the archdiocese arranged at that little clinic they run up in Westchester."

Hopkins' hands began to tremble, then his shoulders and his chin. But it wasn't fear, she told herself. It was rage. Cass briefly thought she might have to make a run for it. Then the man seemed to gain control again.

"That never happened," he said. "It's a lie. It never happened."

"You don't think she had an abortion?" Cass asked. "It's not that hard a thing to prove."

"I didn't say that. I said the archdiocese never arranged it. That's a lie. They would never do such a thing."

Oh, sweetie, Cass thought. Have you got a lot to learn. "Why not? *You* let her do it. Why not them?"

Hopkins looked as though he had been hit again; his body actually seemed to move back under the blow. Then he seemed to sag. "I don't want to discuss what I did," he said.

Cass leaned forward, playing the big sister now. "Look, Father. It's no big deal. It was just a little . . . sex." She had almost said *fucking*, but had stopped herself. After all, the jerk was still a priest. "She probably just couldn't resist you. She—"

Hopkins jumped from his chair, and threw himself forward against the desk. For a moment Cass thought he was coming over it, and she jerked back in her chair.

"Don't say that!" he shouted. His eyes had become wild. It was as though she had pushed some hidden button that had triggered a bomb in his mind. "Who told you that? Who said I lured her into it?" His arms began flailing, and his face seemed haggard and beaten and lost. It was despair, Cass told herself, and it was the first time she had seen it written across someone's face.

"I sinned," Hopkins said, his eyes wider, wilder. "God understands man's failures. He must. And I have sought redemption." He began shaking his head, but his eyes never left her. "But I never lured her to me. Never! Never! She wanted what happened. She wanted our sin. She planned it. From the very beginning she planned it. And then she murdered the child. She murdered it." He leaned forward again, and again Cass thought he might come over the desk. "Have you ever seen a fetus? Have you? Have you?"

Cass got to her feet. Her legs were shaky. She backed away, holding her notebook out like a shield. "Whoa, Father. Just take it easy," she said. "I think we just better deep-six this interview." She reached behind her, feeling for the doorknob. "I'll call you, and we'll finish up on the telephone," she said.

She pulled the door open, spun, and headed down the shabby hall, glancing back over her shoulder as she hurried away. Hopkins was still behind his desk, but his words chased after her.

"Have you?" he shouted. "Have you?"

Hopkins slumped into his chair when the woman had left, and he barely heard the insistent ringing of the telephone. Finally the sound broke through, and he picked it up and mumbled something indistinguishable.

He straightened in his chair at the sound of the voice on the other end, his hand tightening on the receiver as he listened to the words flowing out at him.

"I'm afraid it's worse than you think," he said. "A television reporter, named Cass Walker, just left here. She knows everything. All about Gail Collins." He sobbed. "She says I made her do it."

He waited, listening. The words were stern, unforgiving, and the instructions were precise.

"Of course," he said. "I'll do as you say. And . . . and, I'm sorry."

He returned the phone to its cradle and sat staring at it. Now there was a call *he* had to make. There was simply no escaping it. He reached for the receiver again.

Cass sat in the living room of her Greenwich Village duplex. She was wearing a silk Japanese robe over nothing but a pair of very brief panties, and her legs were propped up on a coffee table as she reviewed her notes about Fr. James Hopkins.

The little prick, she thought. He had scared the living hell out of her. There was no question in her mind now that he had cut Gail Collins, had sliced her face open like a Thanksgiving turkey. She thought of the serpent-like scar on the woman's cheek, of Hopkins' priesthood, and of all the biblical bullshit about Eve and temptation. Oh, Christ, she told herself. You are not going back there alone. Next time you'll have a camera crew with you. The biggest, burliest guys you can find in the studio.

Her eyes scanned the room. The duplex was her sanctum, a place she felt safe and secure. She had made it so with considerable effort. And it was richly decorated—done by a professional—and even the paintings on the walls were originals. She had paid handsomely for them, allowing herself to be guided by that outrageous little poof of a gallery owner in Soho.

But it was all worth it. And soon, she knew, she'd be able to afford even better.

The sound of the doorbell jolted her, and she responded with a long breath. She had received a call from the studio a half hour earlier, saying a messenger would be by with an early morning assignment. *They probably want you to interview some fucking dog at the animal shelter, or make another trip to the goddamned Central Park Zoo,* she told herself. *But not for much longer,* she thought. *After this one breaks, it's network news for this lady. All the way to the top.*

Cass pulled the door open, a look of mild irritation fixed on her face. The brown robe surged forward, knocking her back, sending her sprawling to the tiled floor of the foyer. She lay there, gasping, the breath knocked from her lungs. The last thing she saw were the wild eyes and contorted face of her killer, and the flash of a large, gleaming knife.

Adrianna made two quick brush strokes, then stood back and appraised the evening's work.

"You like it?" Devlin asked from the sofa. He had been watching her for more than an hour. Watching her work like a demon—a woman possessed.

Adrianna grunted. "Yeah, I like it," she said. She picked up a cloth and wiped traces of paint from her hands, then moved to the sofa and slid down beside him, her head coming to his shoulder like a magnet. She blew a long breath up along her face, trying to dislodge a strand of rich black hair that had fallen across her eye. She finally surrendered and used the back of her hand.

"I've been thinking about your meeting today," she said.

"While you worked?"

"Yep."

"And what have you been thinking?"

"I'm just surprised you didn't expect what you got."

"You think I should have expected it?"

"Sure, I do."

"Why?"

Adrianna turned her head so she could see him out of the corner of one eye. "Because they're an organization, a kind of brotherhood. And they protect their own. And they only want to present one image to the public. And it has to be an heroic one, and squeaky clean. If anyone should understand that, it's a cop."

Devlin smiled. She was right on the money. "Cops don't do that," he said.

"You're cute, Devlin," she said. "But you're going to have a hard time selling that to a cop's daughter."

"What can I sell you?" he asked.

"Very little, hotshot. I may be a little Cuban girl from Brooklyn, but I've heard that jive before."

"Short on innocence, huh?"

"Since I was about fourteen."

"Tell me about it."

"No way, Jose. A little mystery is good for your cop's soul." She snuggled in against him. "Besides, I like to keep my tawdry little teenage memories to myself."

Devlin slipped his arms around her and squeezed lightly. She felt good against him. Perfect. The evenings they had spent like this had been good for him. He hadn't realized how much he had missed the companionship of a woman. It was even better than the sex, and that was amazing.

"I like the new painting," he said. "I don't understand it, but it sort of grabs me."

"It's supposed to," she said. "If it didn't, it wouldn't be worth anything, except maybe a cover for a calendar."

"What's it about?"

Adrianna smiled to herself. "You're not supposed to ask what it's about. You're just supposed to feel it."

"What am I supposed to feel?"

Her smile widened, and she shook her head. "It's called *Redemption*. You figure it out."

Before he could respond the telephone rang, and Adrianna hauled herself up with a grunt and went to answer it. After she had said hello, the silence made Devlin turn and look at her. She stood with her back to him, but he thought he could see her shoulders begin to shake.

"What is it?" he called as he saw her replacing the receiver. But he knew the answer.

Adrianna turned to him, and her face was pale and shaken. "It was him," she said.

"What did he say?"

"Just that you were next," she said. She stared at him from across the room. "And then me."

Eddie Grogan stared at Cass Walker's body. It lay in the center of the foyer, centered in a pool of drying blood. The Japanese robe she was wearing had been stained dark brown by the blood, and it lay open, exposing the slashes and puncture wounds in her chest and abdomen. Her panties were still around her waist, but the crotch had been cut free and pulled away, and there were bloodstains on her inner thighs. He looked at her face. Her mouth was open in shock, maybe horror, and the blue eyes that had made her so appealing to television audiences were filmed over, staring blindly at a ceiling she would never see again.

What a fucking waste, Grogan thought. What a miserable fucking waste.

He turned and walked into the living room. The circus was over, all the bosses who had flocked to the scene when they had learned a celebrity had been killed were long gone. Mallory and his crew were upstairs, going through the woman's clothing and private possessions. There were still TV crews outside, and print photographers and reporters, and Grogan knew they'd stay there until they got their shot of the body bag being loaded into the meat wagon.

He walked over to another detective, the first one to arrive at the scene. "You still got it?" he asked.

The detective nodded and handed Grogan the appointment book and miniature tape recorder he had found, and had slipped into an evidence bag, and then into his jacket pocket.

"Don't say nothing to Mallory or any of those other FBI assholes," Grogan said.

The detective inclined his head to one side. "I don't know what you're talking about, Eddie."

Grogan slid the evidence bag into his own pocket. He had read the appointment book before the FBI team arrived. He hadn't yet listened to the tape. He had given both back to the other detective for safekeeping. The way things were going, he wouldn't have put it past Mallory, or even Cervone, to have him searched.

Now he was leaving, and he was taking the recorder and the book with him. The book had one interesting entry, and right now he didn't want the FBI or Cervone to know about it. He didn't want to be told to back off, that someone higher up would handle it.

The appointment entry listed a three o'clock meeting with Fr. James Hopkins. And Grogan intended to stick it under Monsignor Brian Duffy's nose. This time he would take on that pompous Irish prick. Besides, Devlin would be busy running Father Jim to ground. And then beating the fucking truth out of him if he had to.

26

Eddie Grogan sat on the soft leather sofa, his thick body wrapped in an equally soft terry cloth robe. It was 7:00 A.M., and he had just replayed Cass Walker's tape for the third time that morning.

Grogan's apartment was a four-room affair on Riverside Drive. It was in an old, rent-controlled building and the rooms were large with high ceilings and an abundance of windows, most of which overlooked the Hudson River. It was far more space than he needed, but he had lived in the building for years, and the controlled rent was quite affordable, and he liked it.

It was also surprisingly well furnished and immaculately clean, something that always amazed those who visited him there. They viewed his rumpled exterior and his bachelor ways, and assumed he would live a slovenly, ill-kept life. But Eddie liked his comfort, and he had purchased furnishings to satisfy that inclination. And comfort, for him, included cleanliness, so he paid a cleaning woman to come in twice each week. She scrubbed, polished, and even buffed the apartment; she did his laundry and even took his suits to the cleaners. But that latter effort never seemed to work. No matter what Eddie put on, it was a rumpled mess minutes later. But all of it gave him the life he wanted, while freeing him to do the one thing he enjoyed. And that was being a cop.

There had been times when Eddie had missed the company of a woman and children. He secretly envied men like Devlin. But his friends had kids he could

313

privately enjoy. And a woman, he had decided—for all
the benefits—didn't add to a man's freedom, only to
his work. And after seriously studying the society he
had lived in for more than thirty years as a cop, he
had decided that women had been forced into one ever
present role. They were victims, and Eddie Grogan believed he already had enough victims in his life.

Eddie snapped off the recorder, then lit a Camel.
The priest was fucking bananas, he told himself as he
blew a stream of smoke across the room. The man's
trolley did not make all the stops, and that weight-
lifting nut case collector, Gabrielle Lyons, had been
right. The man had been thrown into a frenzy. And all
because an over-ambitious TV reporter had tightened
the noose too much, too soon.

He glanced quickly through his notebook. Cass
Walker's duplex had been as secure as she could have
made it. There had even been an alarm system on the
doors and windows. A good one—one even his friend
Willie the Gimp would have had trouble taking out.
So why had she opened the door? He wondered if
they'd ever know. But it had forced the perp to abandon his usual tactic of getting inside and waiting. He
had come through the door like a roller coaster and
had chopped her up then and there. Even the faked
intercourse had been different. This time he had used
the knife. And the ritual cut on her cheek had also
been deeper than usual, more like the ones adminis-
tered to Gail Collins and Melissa Coors. For some reason he had seemed to hate them even more, and he
wondered if that meant anything, and if they would
ever understand why. But none of it mattered. The
frenzy was there, Grogan told himself. Oh, yeah, it was
there full blast, and it was getting fucking scary.

He closed the notebook, stood, and headed for the
shower. But a certain self-satisfied monsignor was
going to carry some of the weight for this one. He
planned to be at Brian Duffy's office by nine o'clock.
He'd go there unannounced, with no time for Duffy to

make a preemptory call to the chief. And one way or
another, the man would see him. Old Eddie Grogan
planned to make fucking well sure of it. And he didn't
really give a fuck about the consequences.

Brian Duffy surprised him. Grogan was ushered into
the monsignor's office without a moment's hesitation,
and the detective found himself met by a smiling face
and an affable handshake.

"Grogan. That's an Irish name, isn't it?" Duffy asked.

"Yeah, Monsignor, it is," Grogan said.

"So I assume you're Catholic."

"Yeah," Grogan said. "But I don't practice it much
anymore."

Duffy spread his hands in a forgiving gesture. "Well,
we're always ready to have you back, Eddie," he said.
"Keep that in mind."

I will, Grogan thought as he watched Duffy move
behind his desk. When assholes like you stop running
the show.

Grogan didn't waste any time. Duffy's rump had no
sooner hit the seat of the soft leather desk chair than
Grogan let him know the subject would be Fr. James
Hopkins.

The affability faded quickly, and Duffy leaned back
in his chair and attempted to stare Grogan down. "I
spoke to a gentleman named Devlin about this yesterday," he said at length. "May I assume you're familiar
with that conversation?"

"Yeah, you can assume that," Grogan said. He knew
the time for pretense was gone. They couldn't afford
to play political hopscotch any longer. Hopkins had to
be contained, and it had to be done fast. And Grogan
knew the bosses would never allow it unless the archdiocese gave its blessing.

"Then you know our position," Duffy said. "What
makes you think anything has changed?"

Grogan took the tape recorder from his pocket and
laid it on the monsignor's desk. "I want you to listen

to something," he said. He pressed the play button before Duffy could object.

He watched the monsignor's face as the voices of Hopkins and Cass Walker filled the room. The man seemed startled, then concerned, then his features gradually began to show anger. When the recording was over he glared at Grogan.

"You bugged Father Hopkins' office?" he snapped. "How dare you do such a thing?"

"The recording was made by the reporter," Grogan said.

"So she surreptitiously recorded him, and then gave the recording to you? I fail to see the difference."

Cass Walker's murder had been discovered too late to make the early morning editions of the newspapers, and it was obvious Duffy had not listened to any radio or television news shows that morning. It gave Grogan the element of surprise, and he loved that kind of edge. He placed the appointment book on Duffy's desk, already opened to the proper page.

"Cass Walker met with Father Hopkins at three," Grogan said. There was no surprise on Duffy's face, and he could tell the man had already been told of the meeting. "We got the tape from her, but she didn't *give* it to us." Now there was some degree of surprise, Grogan noted. "We took it from her apartment. She was murdered last night. After she was marked. Mutilated just like all the other women Paul Devlin told you about."

Duffy fell back in his chair and stared at the detective. The man was shocked, but Eddie wasn't feeling kind.

"If you had listened to Devlin yesterday, we would have had Hopkins in some out-of-the-way place. And we would have been grilling him." He jabbed his finger into the top of Duffy's desk. "And this woman just might be alive today."

Duffy sat forward abruptly. "You can't know that,"

he snapped. "And you can't know that Father Hopkins did this horrible thing."

"Yeah, and maybe pigs can fly, Monsignor. But you're right. I can't know. Not for sure. And I'll never know until I'm *allowed*"—he almost shouted the final word—"to investigate him properly. But I can sure as hell make a pretty good, fucking educated guess that he was involved. And I think you can too." He fell silent, stared at the man, then lowered his voice as he continued. "So, you tell me. Where do we go from here?"

Duffy's lips moved soundlessly. Then he seemed to pull himself together. "I-I don't know, Detective." He sat straighter in his chair. "But I know the Church must not be allowed to suffer because of this."

Grogan glared at him. "The Church or you, Monsignor?"

Duffy seemed startled by the suggestion, then angry. "The *Church*, Detective. *Always* the Church."

"So you're not going to help us," Grogan said. "You're going to hide behind your political clout, and hope it all goes away."

"We'll help, Detective. But we'll do it in our own way." He leaned forward, again trying to stare Grogan down. "And yes, we'll use our political clout," he said. "And if that causes you personal harm, I'm sorry. But you leave me no choice."

"You may find it harder this time, Monsignor. If the press finds out that one of their own was killed because the archdiocese was playing power games, and that they're still trying to keep the cops from pursuing a major suspect, then even your buddies in City Hall might chicken out."

It was a bluff. Grogan knew it, and he could tell Duffy knew it as well. But still, it could happen. At least he had planted a seed of doubt.

"I'm afraid you have our answer," Duffy said. "We will help. But we'll do it in our own way. And the Church will be our first consideration."

When Grogan had left, Duffy again fell to his knees

and prayed. But this time the solace he sought wasn't there. He rose, went to the telephone, and called Mario Cervone. Then he called Delong Norris, and again reviewed with the mayor his meetings with Eddie Grogan and Paul Devlin.

"I'm not conceding these men are right about Father Hopkins," Duffy told the mayor. "But I assure you the archdiocese will handle this matter very quickly and very privately. And any danger, real or imagined, will be put to an end."

He waited as Norris asked how that would be done.

"He can be sent to a Church-run sanatorium for the mentally ill," Duffy said. "He won't be the first we've had to help this way, although admittedly for less serious concerns. But these men—Devlin and Grogan—have to be stopped. We cannot have an arrest and a trial. It would serve *none of us*." Duffy paused for effect. "Once Devlin and Grogan are removed, the matter can be handled discreetly. I hope the archdiocese can count on you, Delong. As you know you can always count on us."

Duffy listened, then briefly closed his eyes in relief. "Thank you, Delong," he said. "Your help won't be forgotten."

Several miles downtown, Delong Norris replaced his telephone. There was a look of disgust on his face, but it had been there before, and he knew it would be there again. Just so long as he remained in politics. He had three telephone calls to make now. The first would be to his police commissioner, who would then light a fire under Mario Cervone, even though he doubted that would be needed. The next two would be to Washington. First the FBI, and then the office of a certain senator from Vermont. It was the best he could do, and he only hoped it would be enough. You don't make a promise to the Archdiocese of New York, and then fail to deliver, he told himself. Not if you expect to keep your ass in this chair. And Delong Norris in-

tended to do exactly that. No matter what it cost, or
who paid the price.

Devlin was waiting for Grogan when he returned to
the loft. His face was tight and angry, and the scar on
his cheek had become a thin white line. Grogan asked
him what had happened.

"I went to the shelter, and he was already gone,"
Devlin said.

"Hopkins?"

"He left about six o'clock this morning, suitcase in
hand. The guy manning their front desk said he
wouldn't say where he was going."

"Did this guy say how he looked?" Grogan asked.

Devlin nodded. "He said he looked like shit. And
acted as if somebody he didn't want to see was hot on
his tail." He paused. "And don't forget what I told you.
Our boy called Adrianna last night, and said *we* were
next."

"Shit," Grogan snapped. He thought about what
Devlin had said. "Then it can't be the archdiocese
who's hiding him out. Not if he called last night, and
left at six o'clock in the fucking a.m. Even if you scared
the shit out of them yesterday, they wouldn't be yank-
ing him out then." He shook is head. "No, our boy is
running on his own. And we're gonna find his fucking
ass before they do." He stared at Devlin. "And then
we're gonna set him up and nail him in the act. And
then even City Hall won't be able to fuck with us."

Devlin nodded, considering the idea. "That'll be a
cute trick, Eddie," he said.

"Hey, I'm a pretty cute fucking guy," Grogan said.
"You just ain't been paying attention."

27

Mario Cervone didn't waste any time. By three in the afternoon Devlin was being ushered into his office. He had been literally kidnaped on the street by two detectives named Fucci and Cordino, hustled into a waiting car, and driven straight to the underground garage at One Police Plaza. A "forthwith" had also been issued for Eddie Grogan, but the thirty-year detective was among the missing. And he fully intended to keep it that way.

"I suppose you can't tell me were that fucking Grogan is?" Cervone snapped as Devlin stopped before his desk. Matthew Mallory was seated on the chief's sofa, and he was grinning.

"He works for you, Chief." Devlin said. "Why ask a tourist?"

Cervone's eyes became malevolent. "You'll be a fucking tourist before I'm through with you, Devlin. If you know what's fucking good for you."

Devlin folded his arms. "Let's cut the shit, Mario. Tell me what you want, so I can tell you to go fuck yourself and get the hell out of here."

Cervone jabbed a finger toward his face. "You got an appointment with a department doctor in thirty minutes, asshole. And the city attorney has already ruled that you're back on duty forthwith, pending any appeal you decide to file. Just as soon as the pension board revokes your disability." He offered up a smile to match his eyes. "And it just so happens they're having an emergency meeting this afternoon at five."

"Up yours," Devlin said.

Cervone half rose from his chair, then thought better of it. He sat back and smiled again. "Miss that appointment and I'll have your pension stopped like that." He snapped his fingers.

Devlin started to laugh, and it had the effect of erasing the smile from Cervone's face. Now the man just glared at him.

"Mario, in the worst of all possible worlds, you still wouldn't be king," he said. "Besides, I'm too sick to go to your doctor. In fact, I was just on my way to my own."

"What's his name?" Mallory asked from the sofa.

Devlin glanced at him, then turned back to Cervone. "You bringing your idiot relatives to work with you now, Chief?"

"You'll be getting a call from Vermont," Mallory said. His voice was silky and self-satisfied. "Then we'll see who the idiot is, tough guy."

Devlin ignored him. Instead he smiled down at the chief. "Set up the appointment by the book, Chief. Send the notice to my home by certified mail. Hell, I'll be happy to have a free physical." He shrugged. "But on thirty minutes' verbal notice? Gee, I just can't make it." He placed his hands on Cervone's desk and leaned forward. "So, fuck you, Mario."

Cervone looked as though he might explode, but he fought it off. "You'll get your notice, clown. Hand-delivered. And you miss the next appointment, I'll personally see your pension is stopped, forthwith."

Devlin grinned. "You like that word, don't you, Chief. Tell me, you use it with your wife when you want to get laid?"

Mallory could see the chief ready to blow, and he quickly intervened. "You could stop it all, ace," he said. "You could just pack up and go home."

Devlin turned back to him. "I'm on vacation," he said. "And, like the song says, I love New York."

"You may like it a lot less when you hear from your

bosses in Vermont," he said. "But it doesn't have to be that way."

Devlin turned back to Cervone. "Is that all, Chief?"

"No, it's not." Cervone extended his hand. "Turn over your weapon now. And that's official. You get caught wearing one, you'll spend the next month protecting your asshole out on Riker's Island. The prisoners out there, they'd just love to get a shot at your shit chute."

Devlin didn't hesitate. He withdrew the weapon from its ankle holster, unloaded it, and tossed it on Cervone's desk. "Never liked it much anyway," he said.

Cervone pushed the revolver aside. "Now, you go call anybody you want," he said. "The Detectives' Benevolent Association, the PBA, or any other group of assholes who'll listen to you." He glanced at the pistol, then back at Devlin. "You go out and find another one of these, I'll have your ass locked up so fast, you'll think you're fucking Son of Sam. Got it?"

Devlin just stared at him. "There's only one call I'm going to make," he said.

Cervone laughed. "Hey, make it. I heard Cass Walker isn't taking any calls today."

You cold-hearted, cynical sonofabitch, Devlin thought. He forced himself to smile. "She had a lot of friends," he said. "They find out she was killed because of your little cover-up, they might decide they don't love you anymore, Chief." He forced the smile back. "Hey, but you'll look good patrolling some shopping mall in Great Neck. The square badge will match your fucking head."

Cervone jabbed a finger at him. There was no fear in his eyes. He'd obviously been promised he'd live through any shit that came down. No matter how deep it got. "You won't even get work doing that," Cervone snapped. "Not when we're finished with you."

"You go ahead and do it, ace." It was Mallory again. "Hell, we'll live through it." He offered an exaggerated shrug. "The Bureau? We were just doing what the mayor asked." He inclined his head toward Cervone. "The chief here? He never liked it, but it was shoved down his throat." He grinned. "And the mayor? Well, he's a fucking master at covering his black ass. It won't be fun, but it won't be terminal, either." He casually crossed one leg. "But you know who won't survive it? Your cute little artist friend. And you know why? Because as soon as the story hits the streets, your perp is gonna dive under the bed, and he's not gonna come out until everybody's packed up and gone home." He traced his finger in the air, as though it were a knife. "And then he's gonna play mumbly-peg on that little lady's chest. You know it, and we know it. So take your best fucking shot, ace." He paused. "Just make sure Ms. Mendez knows who's gonna end up paying the tab for it."

Devlin felt his balloon begin to leak air, but fought off showing it. They were right about his bluff. He knew it, and they knew it. It was risky for them, but they were obviously willing to chance it. The heat must really be on, he told himself. And he thought he knew where it was coming from. But there would be time to even the score. Later. When he caught the perp. *If* he caught him.

He turned and started for the door. "We'll have to see," he said. "Maybe Adrianna will just have to pull a Gail Collins and move to another town." He kept on toward the door.

"Who the fuck is Gail Collins?" Mallory demanded.

Devlin turned and glanced back at him, a look of feigned surprise on his face. "The perp's first victim," he said. "I thought even you assholes would have figured that out by now."

He started for the door again, but was again halted by Cervone's shout. "You tell that fucking Grogan I expect his ass in here before the day's fucking out."

Devlin answered over his shoulder as he reached for the doorknob. "I got places to go and people to see," he said. "Get one of your *gumba* detectives to deliver your messages, Chief. *If* you can get one to take his nose out of your ass long enough to find anybody." He slipped through the door and was gone.

Mallory stared at Cervone. "What the fuck is he talking about?" he snapped.

The chief stared down at his desk. "It's just bullshit," he said. "Don't worry about it."

Cervone thought about his conversation with Duffy. The case was over as far as he was concerned, even if Mallory didn't know it yet. As long as Devlin didn't screw it up. "You think he'll go to the press?" he asked.

"He better not," Mallory said. "Or I'll be working in Boise next week." He hesitated and shook his head. "No, he'll listen. If he's not fucking crazy. The screws are gonna turn too tight on his balls."

Cervone stared at his desk, thinking. "That pension thing is gonna take two weeks, maybe three," he said at length. "I hope those assholes in Vermont move faster than that." He looked up at Mallory. "How did that nigger bastard in City Hall pull that one off, anyway?"

Mallory grinned. "He called in a favor from a certain U.S. senator from Vermont," he said. "And we offered him a little piece of cake to go with it." The grin widened. "So the senator decided he should call some people he knew up in the boondocks, and offer some favors of his own." Mallory leaned forward, as if offering some secret. "He was told the file we have on him just might make its way to his personal shredder if he played ball." He raised his eyebrows for effect. "The senator really liked that idea."

"What's with him? He like little girls too much?" Cervone asked.

"No," Mallory said. "The senator doesn't like little girls. Not at all."

The message was awaiting Devlin when he returned to the loft. The first selectman of Blake, Vermont, had called and spoken to Adrianna. Devlin was being ordered back to work, and was expected within forty-eight hours, or the town would be forced to find a permanent replacement.

"Did he say what the crisis was?" Devlin asked. He was smiling, and Adrianna couldn't understand why. The idea of him leaving terrified her.

"No," she said. "The message was just sort of: get back there or else."

Devlin stuck his tongue in his cheek. "I thought maybe a whole bunch of cows got loose, and started to burn, kill, rape, and plunder the town," he said. "Or maybe somebody blew up some farmer's manure bank."

Adrianna wanted to smile at the image, but found she couldn't. "What's a manure bank?" she asked.

"It's like a big oil tank," he said. "Except it's full of shit. Just like the rest of the town." He slipped his arm around her waist. "Let's go out and eat," he said. "I'm starving. You may be a great artist," he added. "But not in the kitchen."

"So you're not leaving?"

"I'm not going anyplace," he said. He could feel her body sag with relief.

"I didn't like that crack you made about my cooking," she said, fighting for some bravado now. "My mother was Italian. If there's one thing I know about, it's great food. See if I ever feed you again."

"That's all right," he said. "I live on the food of love."

"Oh, yeah?" Adrianna said. "You may be in for an unexpected diet, big guy."

28

They went to Forlini's, an Italian restaurant on Baxter Street, right on the dividing line between Little Italy and Chinatown. It was a place Devlin had frequented as a cop, and like most old-line Italian restaurants it had waiters and bartenders who had worked there half their lives, so he was remembered and greeted like a long-lost relative.

"Should I be impressed?" Adrianna asked as they were seated in an oversized banquette. She took in the warm, if slightly gaudy decor. At least there wasn't a photograph of Frank Sinatra, like the hundreds that seemed to find their way to the walls of most New York Italian restaurants. She mentioned it to Devlin, and he assured her there was one in the bar.

She laughed and tried to relax. She had avoided discussing the telephone call on the cab ride there, and she was still fighting off the nervousness she felt eating away at her. She repeated her claim that she was impressed by the reception he had received.

"You'll be impressed by the food," he said. "It'll be just like your Italian mama used to make."

"She taught me how to cook," Adrianna said.

Devlin winced. "Poor kid," he said. "Well, maybe she was just a lousy teacher."

"She also taught me to keep my legs closed," Adrianna said.

Devlin grinned. "See, she was a lousy teacher."

They ordered veal cardinale, on Devlin's recommendation, a variation of veal parmigiana, with added layers of eggplant and prosciutto ham. It came to the table in a casserole, the thick red sauce still steaming.

As they ate, he told her about the session with Mallory and Cervone, which also explained the call from his masters in Vermont.

"So what will you do?" she asked. She tried to keep the residual nervousness from her voice—she wanted it to be casual, unconcerned. She didn't want his decision affected by her fear. She wasn't sure she had succeeded.

"I'll pull an Eddie Grogan," he said. "When the town calls back, you'll say you haven't seen me and don't know when you will. In the meantime I'll play hide-and-seek with the clowns who'll be trying to serve me with a notice about my physical. When they finally catch up to me, I'll postpone it every way I can think of." He shrugged. "Then I'll take it, and they'll order me back to work. But that could take months," he assured her. "Especially if I get the Detectives' Benevolent Association involved. They'd rather see their wives and kids in jail than let anybody mess around with a cop's pension."

"You mean you'll pass the physical?" she asked.

"The department doc will give them whatever finding they ask for," he said. "Then the union and I will have to fight it, and eventually the city will give in. It won't be worth the trouble to them. Not with the union involved. But in the meantime—maybe for six months or so—I'll be pounding a beat on Staten Island, with my little gold shield pinned to the blue bag."

"And what about Vermont?" she asked. "What happens there when they figure out you're just hiding from them?"

He shrugged. "I'm afraid my bucolic days in the Green Mountains may be over," he said. "But I was getting bored there anyway. And Phillipa will do a cartwheel when she hears we're coming back to New York." He paused and looked across the table at her. "And I've found some new interests here," he added.

Adrianna felt a rush of warmth. "Even if I can't cook?" she asked.

"Who said you can't cook? You're a great cook. Especially that . . . what do you call it? The stuff with all the vegetables and tofu and straw and strained dirt in it."

Adrianna reached across the table and took his hand. "You'd be giving up a lot," she said. "And you won't be a cop anymore." It was the point where she was supposed to say he didn't have to do it—that she didn't want him to. She didn't say any of it.

"No, I wouldn't," he said. "But I took the job up there because I was bored. And I also wanted to make sure I could still do it. Especially after what had happened here," he added. "On my last case as a cop here." He raised one hand, palm up. "It was sort of a test. And I passed it." He looked across the restaurant. "And the pension thing will only be temporary, if it happens at all. In the meantime I've got a house up there I can sell, and some money in the bank. I'll be fine."

Adrianna squeezed the hand she was still holding. "You are fine," she said. "And thank you. For staying, and for not making me beg you to do it."

He smiled. "You would have begged me?"

"On my knees if necessary," she said. A coy, almost impish look came to her eyes. "And not just for the protection," she said. "You also happen to be a wonderful piece of ass."

They walked back from Baxter Street, arms around each other's waists, Adrianna's head occasionally resting on his shoulder. They detoured slightly, going along Houston, then down West Broadway, so they could look in the gallery windows and delay their time out alone together. They were alone in the loft, true enough, but despite the intimacy they had known there, it had still become somewhat of a prison to them. A place where they felt under siege, someplace they left only with a sense of guardedness.

It had been especially true for Adrianna, and she thought about it now as they stood before the windows of Umberto's gallery. She also thought of what it would be like if she were there alone, or with only Eddie to watch over her.

There was a light on in the rear of the gallery, and she wondered which of the two Umbertos was in the rear office or storage area. She had wondered the same thing that afternoon when one of them had called, suggesting they meet for a drink and discuss the show. She had begged off, and had sensed a degree of annoyance that she had. The same feeling had come through later, when Vincent had also called. He was pressing her to see him, and she knew she would have to do it sooner or later. Make a clean break in their relationship. Try to remain friends, although she doubted that would be possible. Vincent either possessed or he rejected, she told herself. And while he had never possessed her, there had always been the possibility. At least in *his* mind. She hadn't told Devlin about either call, had decided not to. Certainly, he didn't need any additional strain right now. And neither did she.

"Looks like Umberto is working late," Devlin said.

"Which one?" Adrianna offered.

"Yeah, it does become a question, doesn't it? Does it make you feel any different? Working with him? Or them?"

She nodded. Then shook her head. "I don't know," she finally said. "I guess it just feels a little spooky. And I know I'll always be wondering which one I'm talking to."

"Neither one's a prize," Devlin said. "Although Eddie thinks one of them has really nice legs."

Adrianna let out a small shudder. "Stop it," she said. "I don't even want to think about it."

They moved up the stairs to the loft, their arms still around each other. In the hall, Devlin stepped ahead of her, readying the key for the door. Normally he would have his weapon out by now, and would enter the loft with it in hand. Then he would search each crevice and closet, seeking out anyone who might be lying in wait.

But there was no weapon now. It was gone thanks to Mario Cervone. Someday, he hoped, he'd have a chance to place his fist right between the bastard's eyes. But it would have to be after Cervone retired. Otherwise he'd be living on Riker's Island, and he would be walking around with his back to the wall.

Devlin slipped the key into the lock, then instinctively ducked and spun around at the sound of Adrianna's scream. A robed figure was hurtling at him down the hall, the knife held out in front, slashing wildly.

Devlin pushed Adrianna behind him, then stepped into the attack, using his left arm to parry the first blow. The knife bit into his forearm, and he could feel the pain, the sudden flow of blood. The figure lunged again, and again Devlin batted the knife away, this time grabbing the robe and pulling the figure toward him as he fell back.

As he hit the floor, he drew his knee to his chest, placed his foot in the midsection of his attacker, and drove the leg out with all the force he could produce.

The figure flew back and hit the floor hard, and the knife fell away. A hand scrabbled for the knife, found it, just as Devlin was getting to his feet. But so was the robed figure, who turned and ran for the staircase. Devlin started to follow, but Adrianna grabbed his arm.

"Don't," she screamed. "Please, Paul, don't. You're hurt, and you don't even have a weapon."

He stopped and sagged against the wall. She was right, and he'd never catch the sonofabitch anyway. Not the way the blood was pouring out of his arm. He'd be too weak by the time he reached the bottom of the stairs.

"Shit," he said. He looked down at the arm. It didn't look good. "Let's go inside and clean this thing up."

"You'll need stitches," she said.

"We'll see," he said. "But right now, let's get inside before that bastard decides to come back." He bundled Adrianna through the door. That goddamned Cervone, he told himself. If he hadn't pulled his piece, then, one way or another, the damned thing would be over now.

He thought about that. He knew he had been frightened enough to kill, that the killer had taken a heavy risk. And he had to be running very scared to have done that.

29

His arm required stitches, and Adrianna also wanted
to call in the police and report the attack. But Devlin
nixed the latter. The call would only open the door for
Mallory and Cervone to send in people under the guise
of searching out evidence. And Devlin knew there
would be nothing of value to be found, and now he
wanted to keep them as far away as he could.

Instead they reached out for Grogan. They would
become an even tighter group now, and only use other
detectives whom Grogan personally trusted. And they
would use them to run Father Jim to ground, and then
keep him under surveillance until they could catch him
in an act of violence. That way neither City Hall nor
the archdiocese could thwart an arrest.

When Devlin returned from the hospital, they began
planning their course of action. His left forearm was
bandaged, the wound just below the deep scars on his
upper arm that had forced him out of the department
years earlier.

"This is starting to become a habit," he told Grogan.
"If I don't find work that keeps me away from people
with knives, I'm gonna end up looking like a quilt."

Grogan handed him his "throwaway" weapon. It was
a small .32-caliber automatic, a purse gun from which
the serial numbers had been removed. "Just don't let
Cervone's people catch you with this," he said. "And
if you shoot the sonofabitch, make it a head shot, and
make sure his fingerprints are all over it."

Devlin weighed the weapon in his hand. He wished he had had it a few hours ago.

"I got six men I can trust who've been working this case," Grogan said. "They're already working every snitch they got trying to find out where this little prick is holed up." His eyes were cold, hard. "At least we know he's still in Manhattan. Unless this thing tonight made him decide to put a couple of states between him and us."

"He's not going anyplace," Devlin said. "He was after both of us tonight—Adrianna and me. He's in a panic, just like Gabrielle said he would be." He paused. "*If* it's him."

The others looked surprised.

"You got doubts?" Grogan asked.

Devlin stared at the floor, then looked up at Eddie. "I don't know," he said. "He was a lot stronger than I would have expected him to be. And he used that knife like a pro, like somebody who knew just where to cut." He hesitated again. "I keep remembering that Umberto's brother spent a lot of years in the army." He shook his head. "But I also know that this guy's had a lot of practice with a knife, and that head cases can be unusually strong." Another pause. "Shit, I just don't know. Something about it just doesn't feel right. But I'll be damned if I know what it is."

"Were you able to see his face at all?" Eddie pressed.

Devlin shook his head. "The light in the hall stinks. And that damned hood he wears comes out about six inches in front of his face. All I saw was a shadow." He shook his head again. "I don't know. I just can't put my finger on it. And, Christ, it was over in ten seconds."

"Maybe we should let Gabrielle put you under. Shrink your head a little," Grogan said. He was grinning at Devlin, but he was only half joking.

"No, thanks. I'll work it out. The woman would make me cluck like a chicken when she had me alone. I know she would."

Grogan thought about what Devlin had said. About Umberto's brother. "I'll have one guy keep an eye on Umberto's place too," he said. "Just in case. What about Richards?"

"We can't spread ourselves that thin," Devlin said. "Not if we're going to find the priest. And he's still our best bet."

Devlin lay in bed, unable to sleep. Moonlight coming through one window spread across the floor, formed a patch on the lower part of the bed, then ended on the wall. It seemed serene, even romantic, and only the throbbing pain in his arm, and the automatic lying on the bedside table, kept reality in check.

He had given up trying to decide what about the killer bothered him. Perhaps it was a carryover of his concern that they were going only in one direction, with only one suspect—something subliminal to keep him from eliminating the others too quickly. But it was all there. The priest had motive, the opportunity, and after listening to Cass Walker's tape, the incipient, inexplicable rage that seemed to come out of nowhere, and for no plausible reason.

Except that he had felt trapped, cornered, Devlin told himself. And that his antagonist had been a woman.

As a cop he had often pondered why women were so often victimized by men. It wasn't just that they were physically smaller and weaker. If that was the primary criterion, there were certainly enough men, old and young, who also fell into that category. No, there was a hatred there. And a fear. He thought it had to do with their ability to bear children, that they were a man's only hope for progeny—society's only hope for perpetuation. It gave them an unerasable power, and even a man's hormonal structure was designed to recognize it, to respond to it. And they also had the power to withhold it. And that, Devlin thought, went against male instincts to dominate and control, and in some cases—more than most men would care to admit—it created a resentment and a bitterness and, yes, often an unrecognized hatred as well. And the less power a man had, the more he despised power in others; the more he sought someone weaker, someone more vulnerable to dominate. And women, rightly or wrongly, seemed to offer the easiest target.

But this case was different. Something in his gut told him that. The brutality that had been visited upon the victims didn't involve domination. It involved punishment. And he didn't think it was a punishment that found its roots in revenge. This was punishment for something he couldn't even begin to fathom. It was almost as though the women were surrogates of some kind. A type of woman. One the killer despised beyond reason. Or perhaps they were a representation of something that had happened in the killer's past. Something that had hurt him. Something that had twisted his mind beyond repair. He closed his eyes, deciding to fight for sleep. You'll never know, he told himself. You may discover part of it if the killer survives his capture. But you'll never know all of it. No one ever will.

It was five o'clock before Devlin finally found sleep. And it was six when the telephone began to ring.

Adrianna picked up the bedside phone, and mumbled a barely coherent hello. Devlin was still struggling with consciousness when she started to shout.

"You're a priest, God damn you. Why are you doing this to me? Why? Why? You're a priest!"

Devlin grabbed the phone and held it to his ear. Only the dial tone came back at him.

"He's gone. What did he say to you?"

"He said *soon*, in that horrible, garbled voice that makes him sound like he's talking from inside a tunnel. Then he said I was lucky tonight. And then he said *soon* again." She buried her face in her hands, then forced herself to sit up and look at him. "When I started screaming at him that he was a priest, and asking him why he was doing it, he said: *Not anymore.*

"What?"

"That's what he said. He said: *Not anymore*. Just like that. Like he was telling me he wasn't a priest anymore."

Devlin sank back in the bed, then pulled Adrianna to him. He felt her knees come up into a fetal position as she sheltered herself against him.

Not a priest anymore, he told himself. The attack, and now those words, confirmed that Father Jim wasn't hiding under any umbrella of protection provided by the archdiocese. He was on his own. If that was true, then they'd get him. They just had to keep Adrianna safe and hunt him down. And then the bad part would come. They would probably have to kill him.

30

The figure walked in a circle, the brown, hooded robe pulled tightly against the body by hands clenched into fists. The single bed that had come with the furnished room had been placed in the center of the floor, as had the painted dresser and shabby table that made up the room's only other possessions. The replacement of the furniture had left a clear, circular path the figure could use. Around and around, the pace quickening, then growing slow, then quickening again.

James Hopkins' suitcase lay on the bed, and alongside it his clerical garb lay torn to shreds. He would never wear those clothes again, and he had told Monsignor Duffy as much when they had spoken. That part of his life was over, and it was her fault, and he would see that she paid for what she had done to him. He only had to make sure there was time.

They were after him now—knew who he was and what he had done. And it was only a matter of time before they captured him. He understood all that. The voice who told him what to do had explained it all, had told him that he must finish his work quickly, no matter what the risk. He searched for the voice now and listened. Adrianna Mendez would be the last one. The last one he would mark with the sign of Eve, the sign of the temptress, the corruptor of man. He had tried so hard, and he knew there were so many more who should be marked, so many who should be punished for their sins. They came to him, one after the other. The voice told him so. Some had come to him in person. Tempting him. Trying to make him feel that it was *he* who had drawn them to him. That it was *his* fault. That *he* had made them come. Some of the others he had only seen in newspapers and magazines. But the voice had told him they were the same. And that it was only a question of time before they too tempted him, and tried to make him sin again.

But he wouldn't. He would never sin again as he had with Gail Collins. His purity would never again be tarnished. And never again would a child die because of him. No other soul would ever be snatched away from God's gentle hand because of his weakness.

He continued to pace, then suddenly stopped. He was being hounded by this man Devlin. And he was being kept from the final woman he had to mark. The voice had told him so, just as it had told him to hide now, to wait until he was told where to go next. But nothing could happen while Devlin remained at the woman's side. Nothing could be done until he was driven away. Or lured away somehow. Yes, the voice had said that could be done. If all else failed that could certainly be done. He walked to the window and stared out into the shabbiness of Tenth Avenue. A cold, steady rain was falling, and soon it would wash away all the filth and grime that had accumulated. Wash it away into the gutters and the sewers where it belonged. Once Devlin was lured away, then she could be his. And then, once and for all, just as the voice had promised, it could be over.

"We know where he is," Eddie Grogan said. "He took a room in some fleabag hotel on Tenth Avenue, only about five blocks from his shelter. The room clerk says he's there now, and I got him staked out tighter than a Boy Scout's asshole. Two men, in three shifts, around the clock."

"That uses up all our people," Devlin said.

"I know," Grogan said. "I'll try to find one more guy

to watch Umberto's place, but it ain't gonna be easy. And wait till you hear the name he registered under."

"What?"

"James *Richards*."

"You think that means anything?"

Grogan shrugged. "Who the fuck knows with this loony tune? Maybe it's just the first name that popped into his warped little head. The clerk said there was nobody with him when he checked in, and he ain't had no visitors. You think, I dig up another body, we should put him on Richards instead?"

Devlin thought about it. Every investigation he had ever worked always boiled down to the same thing. How to use your people. Who and what and where to watch. And when. He shook his head. "No, we'll roll the dice. Let's leave it the way it is. As long as Adrianna stays away from Richards, we're all right. And one of us will be with her."

"You wanna go up and check the place out?"

Devlin nodded. "Yeah. We'll send one of the guys down here first. I want to see the place, figure out just how he'll move when he leaves. Each team will have to have a car close by in case he grabs a cab, right?"

"Already taken care of," Grogan said. "And you better do your checking from a car. His room overlooks the avenue. He sees you, he's liable to bolt again."

Gabrielle arrived just as Paul and Eddie were preparing to leave. Devlin took her aside in the hall, explained what had happened the previous night, and what they were now doing.

Concern flooded the woman's face. "God help me for saying it, Paul, but be careful. Don't take any chances with him. He's over the edge now. And he'll be both enraged and terrified when you corner him." She gripped his good arm, her eyes urgent. "You have a beautiful child who needs you. Don't think of anything else. Only of that."

He put his hand on top of hers. He knew it was a

hard thing for her to say, and he was grateful for it. "I will," he said.

He started to go, but her voice stopped him.

"And, Paul," she said. "It's not wrong to kill. Not if the reasons are right."

Gabrielle and Adrianna sat talking about the last telephone call. Eddie's man was across the loft, watching the street from a window.

"How did his voice sound?" Gabrielle asked. "What did you perceive the stress level to be?"

Adrianna shook her head; her hands were twisting in her lap. She was dressed in a baggy, paint-stained T-shirt and jeans, and her feet were bare. Even that way she looked beautiful, Gabrielle thought.

"I don't know. I couldn't tell," Adrianna said. "He sounded like he was talking from inside a tunnel. It made his voice sound tinny and gravelly, like he was using some kind of machine to make his voice sound different."

Gabrielle nodded. "At least he's still thinking clearly enough to do that," she said.

Adrianna stared at her, confused by her words.

Gabrielle smiled, reached out and patted her hand. "He's still thinking protectively," she explained. "And that's good. It means he'll act with some degree of rationality. And that means Paul and Eddie will have a better chance of anticipating him. After the attack here the other night, I wondered about that." She smiled, trying to ease the effect of her words. "It must have been terrifying," she said. "But it's over. It won't happen again. They have him contained."

Before Adrianna could answer, the telephone interrupted them. She jumped in place at the sound, then rose slowly and went to answer it. The detective turned and started across the loft.

"Oh, yes, Umberto," she said into the phone. She glanced at the detective, and he turned and went back to the window.

Adrianna listened, twisting the telephone cord in one hand. "I know. I know we have to meet. But I can't just now. Maybe tomorrow, or the day after."

She listened to the man rant, and she wanted to scream at him. Tell him to leave her alone, to stop pressing her. She wondered which Umberto she was speaking to, and she had a self-destructive impulse to ask him. "No, it won't be longer than that. I promise. I understand how important it is."

Twenty minutes later, the telephone interrupted their conversation a second time, and again the sound made her jump. She hurried to pick it up and listened to the voice. Again the detective started across the room, and she looked at him and shook her head.

"It's good to hear your voice too," she said. She listened and again the telephone cord twisted in her hand. "I know, and I agree. I think it's important that we sit down alone and talk. But I just can't today." She waited, listening to his words, wanting to get away from them and the phone. "Call me tomorrow," she said. "I'll try to do it then."

When she returned to the sofa, Gabrielle's eyebrows were raised in question.

"It was Vincent," she said. "Having a tantrum about not being able to see me." She lowered her voice, glancing toward the detective. He was still staring down into the street. She lowered her eyes and let out a long breath. "He wanted to see me today. To talk about our relationship. Or what's left of it."

"Do you want it to continue?" Gabrielle asked.

Adrianna shook her head. "No. But I don't want to hurt him either. He doesn't deserve that."

Again, Gabrielle patted her hand. "It's Paul, isn't it?" she asked.

Adrianna nodded.

Gabrielle smiled. It was a very tight smile, Adrianna thought. "Well, *you* don't deserve the added pressure," she said. "Or need it."

"Vincent doesn't understand how terrified I am,"

Adrianna said. "Even though he should." She let out a small laugh. "I'm not sure it would make any difference if he did," she added. "Vincent tends to be a bit narcissistic. But I still want to be fair to him." She shook her head. "And, oh Christ, am I sick of all this protectiveness." There was a sudden edge to her voice.

Gabrielle nodded. "Then see him. Get it over with. Get it out of your mind. The added pressure is only going to wear on you. And you need a clear head now. Free from outside pressure."

Adrianna wondered briefly if the woman was suggesting it just to drive a wedge between she and Paul. But she had nothing to fear from her. She knew that now. She let out a long breath. Still, how *would* she explain it to Paul. She wondered if she should even try. They had the priest bottled up. She was safe from him. She only had to make herself believe it was true.

That night, Paul reassured her the net was drawn tightly about Hopkins, that two of Eddie's men were on him at all times, that Eddie himself would be there early the next morning, and would stick to the priest like glue if he left the hotel.

"He's in a box," Devlin assured her. "And he doesn't know we're there. When he thinks he's clear, and he gets his courage up, he'll move. And we'll move with him. All of us." He stroked her cheek and smiled at her. "If you see me racing out of here, you'll know it's over. You'll know we've finally nailed him." He drew her against him. "There's no way he'll get away this time. I promise you."

Adrianna's head was against his chest, and she closed her eyes. She felt surprisingly sorry for the man, for his illness. For whatever had happened to him to twist him into what he had become.

"Will you have to hurt him?" she asked, even though she knew it was a question Devlin couldn't really answer.

"I hope not," he said. He stroked her arm. "But that will depend on him. We'll try not to."

Adrianna drew herself up tighter against him. She believed what he said, felt safe and secure for the first time since it had all begun. It would be over soon now, she told herself. It would all be over soon.

She momentarily considered telling him about Umberto and the pressure he was exerting to see her. And about Vincent. She decided against it. It would be over. Maybe even by tomorrow.

Outside the hotel, Steve Miglioni and Sam Sherman—two of Grogan's men—watched an old man leave the hotel. It was 1:00 A.M., and another team had seen him enter at seven o'clock the previous evening, but had paid no attention to him. Neither did Miglioni or Sherman now. The old man was carrying a battered shopping bag, like so many of the urban refugees who prowled the city at night. Desperate old people, who lived in shabby hotels, if they could afford them, shelters or abandoned buildings if they could not. Forgotten people who roamed the streets collecting empty bottles and cans from trash bins to supplement their meager existence.

The old man scuttled down the street. He was hunched and frail, and he moved like some ancient crab, a walking victim waiting for some mugger to take the few cents he had out of his pockets.

Miglioni shook his head as he watched the old man's retreat. Where the hell are your kids? he wondered. Where are the people who are supposed to take care of you?

31

The hooded figure hovers over the bed, staring down at the child. The knife, held tightly in one hand, glimmers in the faint light that comes through the now open window. The child's arm is loosely draped about a doll, its glass eyes looking up at the hood-shrouded face. The words play over and over: I had to come to you. I had no choice. But it's not my fault. Not. Not. Not. You made me come to you. You know that. Everyone knows that.

The blade flashes as the hand moves. The other hand holds a cloth that gives off the sickly sweet scent of chloroform. A light, cool breeze filters into the room, and Phillipa turns in her bed, pulling the covers tighter about her. She mutters something in her sleep, and the figure leans closer, trying to hear what the child is saying. Then the hand holding the cloth reaches toward her face. It is 5:00 A.M. It's time. Now it's time to pay the piper.

Phillipa awoke as the cloth was clamped over her face. Her legs and arms began to thrash, and her eyes grew wide, bordering on the edge of hysteria, as she stared up at the hooded mass that loomed above her. The hand pressed down against her face, pinning her to the bed, and the hooded face came slowly lower until it was only inches from her own.

"I had no choice. You must tell him, I had no choice. He simply wouldn't go."

Gradually, raggedly, Phillipa's thrashing subsided as

the chloroform seized her mind. The figure rose and slid the cloth back into a pocket, then carefully pushed back the hood, revealing the twisted face of an old man. The knife was elevated before the eyes, then moved up and down, then across in a ritual sign of Christ the Lord. Then slowly—ever so slowly—it was lowered again. Back toward the child's now unconscious body.

Devlin slept fitfully, awakening every hour. Each time he listened to the silence to make sure all was well, then forced himself back to sleep. He had moved to Adrianna's side of the bed to be closer to the telephone. He wanted to be able to get to it quickly if it rang. If they called to let him know the priest was moving.

The phone rang at seven, and Devlin grabbed it. Adrianna didn't even stir. His sister's voice came across the line. It was pitched high, nervous, struggling for calm.

"Paul, everything's all right. I'm at home. Phillipa's been hurt, but she's all right." She seemed to gasp for breath, still fighting to remain composed. She couldn't manage it and surrendered to her own anger, disbelief. "Oh, God, Paul. Somebody broke in last night and they attacked her. I heard her crying this morning and went in to her. Oh, God, Paul. I don't know how it happened. The police are on their way. But she needs you. Please come. Please come now."

"How bad?" he said. "How bad was she hurt?" He could feel his heart pounding, his stomach lurching to his throat.

"Oh, God, Paul. I don't know. She's not in any danger. It's just . . . it's just . . ."

"Beth, I'll be there as fast as I can. Tell her I'm coming. Tell her everything will be all right."

"Oh, Paul, hurry. Please hurry."

He slammed down the phone and pulled on his clothes. His mind filled with rage and fear and concern

for his child. He looked at the clock. It was a little
past seven. He thought about getting Adrianna up, taking her with him. But it would take too long, would
delay him beyond any point he could tolerate. One of
Eddie's men would be there in less than two hours, he
told himself. They'd agreed to that last night. She'd be
all right. All she had to do was keep the door locked.
He stared at the automatic pistol on the table—the
one Eddie had given him. He reached for it, checked
to be sure there was a round in the chamber. He had
shown her how to use it, and he'd leave it for her.

He shook Adrianna's shoulder, jarring her awake. "I
have to go," he said as she struggled to comprehend
what he was saying. "Eddie's guy will be here soon.
Don't let anyone else in. No one. The gun's on the
table."

He headed for the door, almost running.

"Paul, is everything all right?" she called after him.

He didn't want to tell her. Didn't want to frighten
her. Didn't want to take the time to explain. "Just keep
the door locked," he called back. And then he was
gone.

Devlin reached the house at seven forty-five. Phillipa
was in Beth's room, sleeping. A doctor who lived a few
doors away had come and given her a mild tranquilizer.

Beth clutched his arm. "Thank God," she whispered
as she fell against his shoulder. "The bastard who did
this talked to her. He told her was doing it because
you wouldn't go away." She shook her head, fighting
unsuccessfully to keep the tears from her eyes. "I'm so
sorry, Paul. I'm so very sorry. Dammit. God damn it."

"It's not your fault." Devlin stroked is sister's slightly
plump shoulder. "What did he do to her?" The words
seemed little more than a croak in his throat.

Beth stared into her brother's face. His eyes looked
frantic, fighting for control. The small scar on his
cheek had turned white, and the muscles in his jaw
were dancing wildly.

Beth drew a deep breath. "Calm down," she said. "I'll show you. Then you have to go to her, and she'll need you to be calm."

He nodded, fought to get his rage under control. She led him to a sofa, where two uniforms were sitting. Between them lay Phillipa's doll, encased now in a plastic evidence bag.

Devlin picked it up and stared at the doll's face. A deep, undulating scar had been cut into its left cheek.

Phillipa lay in the bed. She looked small and frail, and when her eyes opened they were momentarily filled with fear. He went to her and kissed her forehead, then took her hand and kissed it too.

"How are you, honey?" he said.

"I'm scared, Dad. I don't know what happened. I woke up and this thing was there, and it put something on my face, and . . ."

He held her hand gently, one hand stroking the top of it. "Everything's okay," he said. "It's over, and you're safe here. I promise you, nobody will try to hurt you again."

A tear broke free and ran down her cheek. Her hand was shaking. She wasn't the tough, self-possessed eight-year-old he was used to. She was more like a terrified child of four or five. "Was it the crazy person you're trying to find?" she asked. "The one who's trying to hurt Adrianna?"

He nodded. "I think so," he said. "But we know where he is, and I'm going to get him now." He felt his gut ripping at the thought of leaving her, of being unable to stay with her as long as she needed. "Aunt Beth will be here," he said. "And there will be cops outside."

Her eyes widened. "Are you sure they'll stay?"

"Yeah, honey. I'm sure. I'm gonna call Eddie Grogan right now, and he'll make sure of it. I promise."

"Will they be real cops?" she asked. "New York cops?"

Devlin let out a breath and smiled at her. She had always referred to the cops who worked for him in Vermont as "make-believe cops."

"Yeah," he said. "Real cops. Not like the bozos who work for me."

She smiled at him. "That's good," she said. "But come back quick. Promise me you will."

"I will, honey," he said. She's such a smart little kid, he told himself. So quick. Sometimes she makes you forget how small she really is. "I promise," he said. He leaned forward and he kissed her again.

The two detectives had watched the hunched old man enter the hotel, then emerge a half hour later. It had been six-thirty, and they had been due for relief in an hour and a half, and the old man had held little interest for them. He had been dressed in a heavy top coat, his head pulled down inside the collar, and the shopping bag he had carried seemed heavy, and had caused him to list to one side. Steve Miglioni had thought again about the old man's kids, and had cursed them under his breath.

"Shit. Shit. Shit. That motherfucker!" Eddie Grogan thought he'd crush the telephone receiver in his hand as he listened to Devlin. "I don't know how he got out without our guys seeing him. But that little fucker will be back there now. He's got no other place to hide." He listened to Devlin, his own rage growing. "I'll meet you there," he snapped. "And I'll call the Flushing precinct and make sure the uniforms stay there. It'll take ten minutes. Stay there until they get the call from their boss. Then come to the hotel, and we'll go in and nail that cocksucker to the fucking wall."

Eddie disconnected the phone, then found the number for the Flushing precinct and placed the call. That motherfucker, he told himself. It was going to be a race to see who shot the sonofabitch first. Him or Devlin.

* * *

It was five after eight when Vincent telephoned. Adrianna had just dressed, and was waiting for the espresso machine to cough out a strong cup of El Pico Latino coffee.

His voice sounded strained, his words urgent, and had she not known him better she would have thought he was frightened.

"Please. I really can't explain," he pleaded. "But it's important. Really important. Meet me at the theater right away. The actors will be here for rehearsal, but we can find a quiet corner."

Adrianna glanced at the clock. "Rehearsal?" she said. "This early? You must have turned over a new leaf, Vincent."

"Please. Just come."

"Okay. Okay. Calm down. It will take me about half an hour. But I'll be there."

"Thank you, love. We'll have a chance to talk, and I'll explain everything. Half an hour."

"Okay," Adrianna said. "I'll bring some coffee."

She returned the receiver and stared at it for a moment. Vincent's sense for drama was getting out of hand, she told herself. And this new work ethic. Wow, she thought. But it was over now. She was free of the insanity for the first time in weeks. Paul had gone racing out of the loft to arrest the priest, and her life was returning to normal. She smiled. This is normal? she asked herself. Well, normal for you, she decided. She could afford Vincent's eccentricities.

The espresso machine finally hissed out its brew, and she poured some and took a quick sip. She looked at the clock. Eddie's man wasn't due for another half an hour, and she decided she'd leave the door open, write him a note, and tell him where she had gone. Then he could meet her there, and, technically, she wouldn't be going back on the promise she had made to Paul.

She jotted the note and taped it to the coffee machine, where it would jump out at anyone who entered the loft. Then she took another sip of the coffee, put the cup down, grabbed her red cape, and slipped it over her shoulders. God, it would feel good to go out without a bodyguard, she told herself as she headed for the door.

It was eight-thirty when Devlin's car pulled to the curb in front of the Tenth Avenue hotel. The crosstown traffic had been murderous, and Eddie Grogan was already there, waiting for him.

"My guys claim he never left," Grogan said as Devlin reached him.

"I don't give a shit what they say," Devlin snapped. "He was there. The fucker was there. Alone with my kid."

Devlin turned toward the hotel entrance, but Grogan grabbed his arm. "I called Adrianna's, like you told me to. There was no answer. I figured she was in the shower or something." He glanced at his watch. "My guy should be there any minute."

Devlin stared at him. "Call the loft again," he snapped. "Make sure she's okay. I'm going up."

"It's room four-A," Grogan called after him. He jabbed a finger at the two detectives. "Go with him," he said. "Don't let him shoot the sonofabitch. I wanna do that myself."

Devlin didn't hesitate. He put his foot to the fragile old door, splintering the frame and knocking the door off one of its hinges. The two detectives were still beating their way up the stairs, but Devlin didn't wait. He rushed inside, his eyes scanning the room. Then he staggered to a halt and froze.

Father James Hopkins was on the floor, his body propped in one corner. He was wearing the heavy brown robe, and his fingers clutched his chest. Devlin could see blood seeping between them. There was also blood on Hopkins' face—from the deep, undulating cut in his left cheek.

Devlin went to him, his mind racing with the

thought that the man had done this to himself. That an attack on a child, his child, had been too much for him to live with. Instinctively he looked for the knife as the two detectives entered the room behind him. There was none to be seen.

He took the priest's hand as he heard one for the detectives speaking to 911 on the telephone. His rage was returning, and he glared a the man. "How'd this happen?" he asked.

The priest only shook his head slowly.

Devlin reached out and took hold of the robe, just under Hopkins' chin. "Why'd you go after my daughter?" he growled. He felt one of the detectives place a hand on his shoulder, but he shook it off. "Why?" he demanded.

Hopkins shook his head again and struggled to speak. A thin trickle of blood oozed from the corner of his mouth. But it was the look in his eyes that held Devlin. The man seemed horrified.

"No," he said, his voice barely a whisper. "I . . . could . . . never harm . . . a child." He coughed, and a bubble of blood rose from his mouth. "I . . . didn't even know . . . you had a child." He struggled, forcing strength back into his body. "I caused one child to die. I . . . I . . . could never hurt another."

"But you cut those women," Devlin said. "You cut them, and then you went back and killed them."

Hopkins shook his head again. "I cut . . . them," he said, struggling again. "I had to . . . redeem myself. But . . . I never . . . killed them."

Devlin leaned in close to the man and urged him to talk to him, to tell him what had happened. The story spilled out of the priest, slowly, laboriously. He had sinned with Gail Collins, had caused their child to die. He had been ridden with guilt, and knew he had to redeem himself, to purge his immortal soul.

Then he had gotten help; had been shown the way; had been told what to do. He had to mark the women who were sinful.

"So you started with Gail," Devlin said.

The priest again shook his head. He raised himself up, as if fighting for strength. "No, I loved Gail. I could never hurt her. Only the others. Just them. Only the others." He fell back against the wall.

"But who?" Devlin asked. "Who cut Gail? Who killed the others?" He leaned closer as Hopkins whispered to him, told him the rest of it.

Devlin rocked back on his heels and stared at the man. Behind him Eddie Grogan burst into the room.

"Jesus Christ," he said, staring down at the priest.

"We found him that way," one of the detectives explained. "There's an ambulance on the way."

Devlin spun around. "Adrianna?" he snapped. "Was she at the loft?"

Grogan shook his head. "She was gone when my guy got there. She left a note saying she was going to the theater to see Richards."

"Oh, shit," Devlin said. "We've all been set up. She'll be dead if we don't get there first."

He pushed past Grogan and raced through the door. He could hear Eddie running after him, but he wouldn't stop.

"Wait," Eddie shouted. "We'll take the car."

"The traffic's too bad," Devlin shouted back. "We have to run, Eddie. Run, God damn it. Run!"

32

The stage door was open when Adrianna arrived at the theater, and she was smiling as she entered. She was anticipating the man who guarded the door, an old codger named Charlie, who was grumpy to everyone but managed a smile whenever she came. There was a paper bag in her hand, containing three cups of coffee—one each for Vincent and her, and one for Charlie, who drank the stuff as though it were mother's milk. But he wasn't in the small cubicle he occupied by the door, so she placed the container on the battered old desk he used. She never noticed the splash of blood low on one wall, or the narrow trail of smeared stains that led away from the cubicle, as if someone, or something, had been dragged through them.

Adrianna walked through the wings, then out onto the stage. The lighting was much dimmer here, and beyond the stage the house lights were down, throwing the orchestra and balcony into darkness. It was as though a play had already begun.

There was furniture on the stage—a sofa, two chairs, a table, and a clothing tree—but there was no scenery, and the bare brick wall behind the stage, crisscrossed with heavy cables, looked stark and forbidding, a place where some oversize spider had been hard at work.

She walked to the center of the stage, marveling at how battered and well used the furniture looked up close, so different from the image offered the audience with the benefit of lighting. The entire theater seemed deserted, and Adrianna wondered if the actors and the horde of stage personnel had simply not arrived yet, or if Vincent had simply told her a rehearsal would be underway to make her feel less reluctant about meting him.

She felt no fear either way. Vincent, she knew, liked to have things the way *he* wanted them, and was not beyond a bit of exaggeration to have them as he wished.

Adrianna stopped center stage and called his name, listening to the faint echo off the high ceiling. She could barely make out the first few rows of seats in the orchestra, the outlines of the balcony and the boxes along each side. The theater—the portion used by the audience—was elaborate and gilded, a sharp contrast to the starkness of the stage. It was like an undrawn line between reality and fantasy, between what was presented and what was truly there.

Adrianna turned and thought she saw a shadow off in the wings, stage left. She took a step forward and saw the faint outline of a figure. She walked toward it, but as she got closer she could see it was only a tailor's dummy, placed beside a rack of costumes and left there from previous fittings. She called Vincent's name again, then lightly stamped her foot when there was no reply, annoyed that he had apparently decided to keep her waiting.

Well, the hell with him, she told herself. She was ready to leave when she remembered the detective would be meeting her there. But she could wait outside for him, she decided. Rather than stand here like a fool, waiting for Vincent to show up in his own good time.

But the stage door had been open, she told herself. But that could just be Charlie, off to the loo, or doing some chore in another part of the theater. She shook her head, angry with herself for giving in to Vincent's urgent plea and now finding herself stuck. Waiting for him to make his appearance. In his heart, he was still a damned actor, she told herself, and entrances were important to him. And so was manipulation. It was at the core of his nature.

Reluctantly she decided to give him five more minutes, and hopefully get it all over with. She walked back onto the stage and dropped into one of the battered old chairs and began to tap her foot in irritation.

There was a rustling behind her. She pivoted and saw a figure standing not far from the tailor's dummy she had just left. The curtains along the wings were still swaying from the new arrival, and she stood and turned toward the figure, a look of justified annoyance fixed on her face.

"Vincent," she called. "If it's you, this is a bit much."

She took a step forward, then hesitated. The figure seemed shorter than Vincent, and she could tell now it was wearing a heavy top coat, and that there was a large shopping bag in one hand. Momentarily she wondered if one of the street people who permeated the theater district had wandered in, and she felt a sudden rush of fear at being alone and unprotected.

The figure stepped forward, and she could see that the collar of the top coat was pulled up, showing only part of a face under a broad-brimmed hat and shock of gray hair. But the face was somehow unnatural, and she suddenly realized it was altered by theatrical makeup.

A hand reached up and removed the hat and wig, and Adrianna recognized the altered face. She stared at it, confused, momentarily uncertain. Gabrielle Lyons smiled at her.

"I suppose I should have worn the robe and the hood," Gabrielle said. "It's in the bag. Would you like me to put it on?" She smiled. "Perhaps just this will do."

Her hand reached into the shopping bag and withdrew a long knife that glistened in the lights above the stage.

"It's time, Adrianna," she said. "It's time to pay the piper."

The paper bag fell from Adrianna's hand, splashing the stage and chair with a shower of warm coffee. She could feel her heart pounding, and she struggled to speak through the fear that suddenly welled up in her throat.

"Where's Vincent?" she suddenly managed, praying that he was there somewhere, that he would come and help her, help drive away this horror, this woman she had known and trusted.

"He's otherwise engaged," Gabrielle said. There was a rictus of a smile on her lips, and her eyes glittered with a mixture of malevolent merriment and pure, unmasked hatred.

"Why?" Adrianna pleaded, hearing the high, shrill sound of her own voice.

"Because you make them come," Gabrielle said. "So you make me come as well."

Adrianna tried to make sense out of the insanity of the words, and instantly realized that she never would. She quickly bolted to her right and ran as fast as she could, back toward the stage entrance and the street.

But Gabrielle was quick, almost cat-like, and she moved along the rear wall, cutting Adrianna off as she emerged from the wings at the right of the stage.

The knife was held out before her, and it flashed back and forth as Gabrielle flicked her wrist, almost as though she were toying with the weapon. Then her arm straightened, and she jabbed the knife at Adrianna's throat.

"That way," she hissed. "And very slowly, please."

"Where . . . where are we go—going?" Adrianna could hear the fear-ridden whine in her voice, and her eyes darted from side to side, looking for something she could use to defend herself, to attack the woman, even kill her if she could.

"It's no use, dear," Gabrielle said. "I'm much stronger than you. I could even kill you with my bare hands if I wanted to." The rictus returned. "But I don't want to do that. It's not the way the piper is paid."

The hideous smile turned into a glare, and the eyes became wild and cunning, almost feral in their intensity. *"Now, do as I say,"* she screeched suddenly. Then the voice softened again, just as quickly. "It will be so much better if you do."

Adrianna inched backward, moving in the direction indicated by the still jabbing knife. Gabrielle was only four feet from her, and she knew there was no way she could move around her; make it to the door before the woman was on her.

"I-I don't understand," she said. The words were spoken more as a defensive delay than out of any hope of revelation.

"And you never will," Gabrielle hissed. "You've led such a perfect little life. So beautiful. And so talented. It was so easy for you to make them come." Her voice suddenly rose again, and again she was shouting. *"Even though you never should have done it. Never made them come to you that way."*

"Who?" Adrianna pleaded. "Who did I draw to me?" There was a begging quality to her voice now, and she hated the sound of it, hated the pleading purr of the victim coming from her own lips. It wasn't her, had never been her, and she knew she couldn't allow this woman to turn her into something she had fought against all her life.

Adrianna's hands clenched into fists, and she took a step forward. "Stop it!" she shouted back. "Stop doing this to me!"

The knife flashed out, a slashing move across her body, and the edge caught her shoulder, cutting through the heavy red cape and into her flesh.

Adrianna jumped back, stung by the sharp, sudden pain, and she could feel a slow trickle of blood moving down her arm beneath her clothing.

A low, coarse laugh rose from Gabrielle's throat. "Don't be too brave, dear," she said. Her eyes hardened, gleamed with the intensity of madness. "You can die here. It won't be as convenient. And it won't be as interesting. *But . . . you . . . can!*" The final words came out in a fierce growl, and it sent a cold shiver coursing through Adrianna's body.

The voice softened again, became almost singsong. "I've been waiting for you for almost an hour. You see, I had to be sure you came alone." Her head tilted to one side, as if remembering something. "I worked so hard to get you here alone. But I couldn't be sure. I even went to Paul's daughter last night. Made sure he had to go to her. But I couldn't be sure he wouldn't take you with him."

Adrianna gasped. "You didn't . . ."

"Of course not," Gabrielle snapped. "The child is pure. I could see that, see it in her eyes the one time I met her." She glared at Adrianna. "*Not like you, you filthy slut.*"

The knife jabbed again, coming within inches of Adrianna's throat.

"Back!" Gabrielle snarled. Her voice suddenly became soft again. "Go down the stairs behind you. Into the basement. Yes, into the basement. That's where we're going. I was waiting for you there, and I'd hoped you'd come there, looking for Vincent." The eyes glared again, and the voice rose. "*But you didn't! And I should have known. I should have known you'd make him come to you. Make me come to you.*"

Adrianna staggered back, and turned into the metal stairs that led down to the area beneath the stage. She stared into the yawning mouth of the stairwell. Only faint light illuminated the brick walls and dirty concrete floor. Slowly, her legs shaking so badly she thought she might fall, she started down the stairs.

Gabrielle moved behind her, the shopping bag still in her other hand, bumping rhythmically against the iron railing, her feet striking each stair heavily, beating out a sound of inalterable determination as they struck each rung. Adrianna could hear the woman's breath, heavy with anticipation, behind her.

At the bottom of the stairs Adrianna was disoriented

by the sudden lessening of light, but Gabrielle pushed her forward, and she staggered ahead, stumbling past the wardrobe room and into the large, darkened area directly beneath the stage. She tried to slow herself, found she could not, and then her foot struck an object on the floor, and she fell heavily, scraping her palms on the rough concrete.

Sprawled on the floor, her legs still draped over the object she had hit, she spun onto her back so she could see Gabrielle's approach. There, on the floor staring back at her, was the lifeless face of Vincent Richards, eyes and mouth open in an expression of horror, throat sliced into a second gaping mouth that glistened with blood and gristle.

Adrianna screamed and scuttled back along the floor until her back struck the pointed edge of a solid mass. She spun away and looked back at the object, and found herself staring at a dust-covered mahogany coffin leaning on end against the wall. She screamed again and began to push herself away on the seat of her pants, when Gabrielle's foot slammed into her chest, pinning her to the concrete floor.

"You seem to be having a very bad day," Gabrielle said. Her voice was half hiss, half whisper. She began to laugh but stopped abruptly, which made it seem even more terrifying. "But your lover Vincent had an even worse day." She paused. "So far." Again the short, harsh, aborted laugh. "He was very reluctant to call you. Until I put my knife to his throat. And then he was quite eager. But so nervous, he could hardly get the words out." She sneered. "It was incredibly pitiful." She increased the pressure of her foot against Adrianna's chest, almost cutting off her ability to breathe.

Adrianna stared at the foot pressing against her. It was encased in a heavy work boot, with a steel toe, the kind construction workers wore. She was confused, almost mesmerized by it.

Gabrielle saw her staring at the boot, and again began to laugh. "It makes a wonderful weapon," she said. "And since I have some gifts for you that you definitely won't want to see—"

"But why? I don't understand why." Adrianna forced the words out. She had to keep the woman talking. Eddie's man should have found her note, should be on his way. He would stop her. Stop her before . . .

"You want to know why?" There was a sneer in the woman's voice, and her face was twisted. She was no longer attractive. Even the finest application of makeup wouldn't hide the madness spread across her face.

Her mood swung again, and she began to laugh softly. "It started with my little friend Father Jim," she said. "And suddenly I saw the tool, the weapon I had waited for for so long." Her lips spread into a wistful smile. "He was so easy," she said. "He was so shattered after the abortion." Again her eyes hardened. "The fool! The child was better off dead!"

Again the mood changed. "That's why I killed it." Why I performed the abortion." Gabrielle's head tilted to one side, as if recalling the event. "They came to me, those pompous fools from the archdiocese." Her eyes glared again. "They were always coming to me to treat their stupid nuns and priests. Those *people*," she spat. "They were never content with serving God. They always wanted more and more and more."

Gabrielle's breathing had grown rapid. Now it subsided just as quickly. Like her sudden switch in moods. It was like watching a roller coaster, rising slowly, then falling with ever increasing speed. Adrianna knew she had to gauge her words for the lulls.

"This time they wanted me to clean up their little mess," Gabrielle said. She laughed. "Most people forget that a psychiatrist is also trained first as a medical doctor. But *they* didn't forget. They wanted things done quietly. And they knew I could do that for them." Her head tilted to the side again, and her voice became almost girlish. "So I did," she said.

"And then I treated Father Jim for his depression. I made him understand that he had to mark other women. Women like the one who had seduced him. It was so easy. He was so sick, so trusting." Her eyes became momentarily confused, then filled with rage.

"No!" Gabrielle shouted. "It wasn't that way." Again her voice softened. "I told him how to redeem himself. How to help others. How to mark those women with the sign of Eve so other men would be warned."

Suddenly her eyes became amused. "He was so sheltered. He'd gone into the seminary when he was fourteen. A child. He had never seen life. And suddenly it had risen up and bitten him." She smiled, cocked her head to one side. "Why do they send them there so young?" She suddenly snorted. "And then everything he had believed in began to unravel, and the people he trusted turned on him, treated him like a pariah. Oh, it was so easy to make him see what had to be done. How those women, who were so much like Gail, had to be marked."

Her voice became girlish again. "And then, after he had marked them, I went and killed them." She began to laugh. "After I had let them suffer with what he had done to them, after I told them again and again what was going to happen to them."

She reached into her pocket and withdrew a small shiny metal box, slightly larger than a pack of cigarettes. She pressed it to her throat. "Do you remember this voice?" The raspy, hollow words seemed to echo through the room.

She seemed to swell with pride. "I gave them what they really deserved. And it was so easy. I used the police like stupid puppets. Talked them into involving me in their oh, so secret case." She laughed again. "They even let me hypnotize them. Alone!" She stared at Adrianna, letting her know she had been a fool too. That she had been manipulated as well. "And I planted thoughts in their minds. Added to their pain. Even suggested careless things they could do." She shrugged. "Sometimes it worked. Sometimes not. But in the end . . ." She allowed Adrianna to finish the thought.

"And I took keys from them while they were unconscious and made impressions. Oh, I was smart. So very smart. Yes," she hissed. "And they deserved it. All of them." She jabbed the knife at Adrianna. "Just like you deserve it."

"Why? Why do I deserve it?" Adrianna asked. She wanted to keep her talking, keep her occupied until help came. A man with a gun, who could stop her if he had to.

"Because they had *everything!*" Her voice came out in a long wail that rose into the theater above them. "They had beauty and talent and success. They had been *given* everything." Her eyes were wild again, and her head moved in a slow circle, rotating on her neck. "And they lived like sluts," she said, her voice dropping to a near whisper. "They tempted men. Made them come to them. Sinned with them. Oh, I saw them. I saw their pictures in newspapers and magazines. I even saw some of them in person, like that *filth* Melissa Coors. Hanging on their arms, laughing, taunting them, encouraging them with their eyes, with their dirty bodies." She suddenly held her head high. "Killing isn't wrong, you know. Those fools I studied with thought it was all an illness. And I agreed with them, went along with their stupidity. But it has to be done. People have to be cleansed." She glared at Adrianna again. *"Don't you see that!"*

"I see it," Adrianna said. "But how can you be sure who needs it?"

She shook her head back and forth. "Oh, I know, I *know*. I was a foster child, and I went from home to home. Oh, I was sinful then. I made men come to *me*. Oh, I was frightened when they did. But I *enjoyed* it. I knew that I *enjoyed* it. They even told me how much I enjoyed it." She fell into a crouch, her eyes becoming feral. "But I stopped. And I redeemed myself." She looked toward Adrianna, and her eyes blazed with hatred. "Oh, I tried to live like you. In college and in medical school I had men who said they loved me."

Her mouth twisted obscenely. "But they only wanted filth. Just like the ones who came to me when I was a child." Her hands began to tremble. "But you never suffered, did you? They never came to you as a child. They never used *you* like a piece of inanimate meat. Did they?"

Adrianna listened to her with a pitying sense of sickness rising inside. She listened to her mind move from victim to perpetrator, then back again, almost as though she could no longer understand the difference. And she couldn't, she told herself. Hadn't been able to for a long time.

"No," Gabrielle said, drawing the word out, her eyes still fixed on Adrianna. "Your life was perfect. Perfect!" She jabbed the knife at her again, then her voice dropped, took on a fatalistic tone. "So you have to pay," she said. "Just like all the other sluts had to pay. They had to pay for what they were given, and how they misused it. *All* of them. And now you. You have to pay the piper."

Gabrielle stepped back abruptly, then brought the toe of her boot crashing into Adrianna's temple.

A bright flash of light filled her field of vision, and she heard a distant yelp of pain. But she never became aware that she was hearing her own voice. Her mind clouded, as though her head had suddenly filled with cotton, and she lost consciousness, never hearing the sharp, brittle laughter that echoed off the brick walls of the basement.

Gabrielle reached into the shopping bag and withdrew a large, hard plastic dildo, out of the end of which a long needle-like blade protruded. She had made that modification to the device on the spur of the moment, just before she had killed Cass Walker. The filthy slut had deserved it. And she had enjoyed wounding her there so much, she had decided to make it a permanent part of her weaponry. She stared at the object. It was wonderful, she told herself. A true weapon of retribution.

Gabrielle lowered herself to Adrianna's body, and began unfastening her jeans. There was a sudden crash from above, and she froze and listened, her eyes going suddenly wide and wild.

Devlin raced down West 45th street. He had left Grogan far behind, and could no longer even hear the beat of his feet in pursuit. He cut into the alley that ran alongside the theater, and hit the stage door without stopping. It flew open and crashed back against the wall.

Devlin skidded to a halt, listening, his eyes instinctively darting in every direction. Then his eyes fixed on the floor in front of him, on the faint wet smears of blood. He bent down, touched one with a finger, and raised it to his face.

Without thinking, he reached for his left ankle, where his holster had been before Cervone had relieved him of his weapon. He muttered a silent curse, then moved cautiously forward, following the blood trail.

It led to the door of a small broom closet, and he carefully eased it open, dreading what he might find. The body of an old man lay stuffed in one corner, his shirt front a mass of drying blood.

He turned away, his eyes again darting about the backstage area, his breath coming in hyperventilated gasps. Then he shouted Adrianna's name, praying she would hear him—could hear him—could utter some sound that would tell him where she was. There was nothing but silence.

He fought against it, against the rage he felt inside. "Gabrielle, you fucking bitch," he shouted. "I'm going to find you and I'm going to kill you."

In the basement, Gabrielle stared back at the staircase, the blade-fitted dildo still poised in her hand. She threw back her head and screamed.

"Noooooooo."

Devlin raced to the stairs, then forced himself to

stop. He searched around him for some kind of weapon, finally spotting a short piece of two-by-four leaning against a far wall. He picked it up and returned to the staircase, then slowly descended into the dimly lighted basement.

At the bottom of the stairs, he put his back against the wall and waited, giving his eyes time to adjust to the light. He glanced quickly into the wardrobe room, then moved on to the large open area beneath the stage that lay ahead. As he stepped into the room, he saw Vincent Richards' body almost immediately. Then beyond it, a few feet from the coffin Grogan had joked about during their earlier search, he saw Adrianna. He rushed forward, dropped to his knees, and instinctively reached for her neck, searching for a pulse. It was there, still strong. He dropped the two-by-four, reached for her shoulder to lift her, and felt a warm, slick wetness against his fingers. Blood, he told himself, and his heart began to race again.

Adrianna let out a loan moan; then her head moved, and her eyes fluttered, then opened. She stared up at him, the whites of her eyes suddenly wide with fear. Then she recognized him.

"P-P-Paul," she stammered. "It was Gab—Gabrielle. She's st—still . . ."

He placed a finger gently against her lips. "I know," he said softly. "Do you know where she is?"

Adrianna's eyes suddenly widened again, and she began to gag as she tried to shout out a warning. He twisted his body and started to spin away.

Behind him the door of the coffin opened. It had begun slowly, moving only a few inches at first. Now it flew back, and Gabrielle rushed out, lunging, the long knife pulled back, already beginning to swing down toward his neck.

Devlin jerked to his left, and he felt a rush of air as the blade cut past his face, nicking the edge of his coat. He smashed his arm into hers, pushing the knife even farther out, then grabbed her heavy coat with his free hand and pulled her past him, throwing her body out and down to the floor.

Gabrielle hit the floor heavily, but rolled immediately and jumped back to her feet. She moved like a trained athlete, quickly, smoothly, and the knife was still in her hand. Now she was between Devlin and the stairs, and she crouched and glared at him.

Devlin looked from her face to the knife, then back at her face again. His training reasserted itself. He had to watch her eyes. Keep them there. Any sign of sudden movement, he knew, would show itself there first.

"You're good, Paul," Gabrielle hissed. "Faster and stronger than I thought you'd be. Especially with that bad arm I gave you." Her eyes flared. "But not enough." She made a quick lunge at him, forcing him to take two quick steps back. Then she stepped back herself and, deftly moving the knife from one hand to the other, shrugged out of the heavy coat.

Instinctively he started toward her, but the knife jabbed at him again, stopping him.

"That's better," Gabrielle hissed. "I wouldn't want to give you any advantage." Her body was swaying now, moving lightly from the ball of one foot to the other.

Behind Devlin, Adrianna tried to push herself up.

"Stay there," Gabrielle snarled. But Adrianna ignored her, staggered to her feet, then backed up against the wall.

The woman's eyes went wild with rage, then suddenly softened. A small, low laugh emerged from her lips. She was wearing a tightly fitted long-sleeved jersey, and Devlin could see the lean, hard strength of her upper body, enhanced by years of training with weights. He was momentarily uncertain if he could wrest the knife from her if she attacked again, and he silently prayed his damaged left arm would hold up if she did. His mind raced back to the day, years ago, when another knife coming out of the darkness had injured him so badly. Then he fought the image off.

"It's over now," he said, trying to both soothe and

distract her. "Everyone knows. And they want to help you."

The psychiatrist's head shook back and forth violently. "No one knows." Her voice snapped out each word. "No one knows *anything*," she repeated.

"Father Jim told us," Devlin said. "He's still alive. On his way to the hospital." The woman's eyes seemed momentarily confused. Then angry. Then surprisingly relieved. She smiled, and her voice became soft. "That's good," she said. "He's a nice man. A weak man. But nice. A good priest." Then her eyes sharpened again, and the animal cunning returned. "But he doesn't know either. No one *knows*." She drew the final word out.

She took a step toward Adrianna, but Devlin moved in front of her, cutting her off. She glared in hatred at him.

"I always knew I'd have to kill Father Jim someday. Just to protect myself." She glared at Devlin, and her voice became louder, harsher. "But now you've spoiled even that!" Again her face, her eyes, her voice, suddenly softened. "But it's all right," she said in the singsong voice of a child. She stared past Devlin at Adrianna. "There's still her. She can still pay the piper."

"Like my child had to pay?" He heard the rising hatred in his voice. "What was her sin, Gabrielle?"

The psychiatrist seemed momentarily confused. She shook her head again. "But I had to drive you away, Paul. It was the only way I could do my work. You were always *there*." She dragged out the final word, pointed the knife at Adrianna, and she seemed surprised that Devlin didn't understand. "I even told you things about her; tried to make you think she had been abused. That she was fabricating everything. That she didn't need your protection. That she wasn't really in danger from anyone but herself." Her eyes became glaring holes again. "But you wouldn't *listen*. She had already made you come to her. And that's all you could see. All you wanted to see." Her voice softened again, became reasonable, almost consoling. "I even tried to kill you. But you were so lucky. Always so lucky. So I had to go to your child. I had to show you. I had to get you away from *her*." Her eyes moved to Adrianna again. "Even if I could only do it for a few hours. Don't you see that, Paul? Don't you see?"

Devlin felt the hatred welling up. It was beyond control now. In his mind he saw Phillipa, her eyes filled with fear, begging him to keep her safe.

"No, you *fucking* bitch. I don't see that," he snarled. "All I see is a degenerate who could hurt a child. Who enjoyed hurting her." He stepped toward her. "I just want to choke the life out of your sick fucking body."

Gabrielle let out a shattering howl and lunged at him. Devlin used his forearm to knock the knife away. It struck her wrist and sent the blade clattering to the floor. But she spun back, moving into him, and drove the heel of her hand into his jaw, stunning him. Then she grabbed his coat and hurled him away from her, throwing him to the floor like a rag doll.

Devlin struggled to his feet, not believing the womans' strength. He saw her bending to pick up the knife, and behind her he saw Eddie Grogan moving into the room, weapon in hand.

"Stop!" Grogan shouted, his eyes squinting against the dim light.

Gabrielle screamed; she spun around and started toward Adrianna. Grogan didn't wait. He leveled his weapon. Fired once. Twice. A third time.

Gabrielle's body jerked with each hit, and she staggered forward, then turned and fell, a look of surprise, almost wonder, on her face. Her body lay half inside the coffin. Grogan fired three more times, and Devlin watched Gabrielle's body jump as each bullet plowed into her chest, driving her farther inside.

Epilogue

Six months later

The water crashed against the shore. A fine spray misted the air, and the surf swirled with foam as it ebbed back away from the beach. Devlin sat on the deck, watching the water, watching the gulls swoop down toward the retreating wave, searching out some bit of food left behind.

He had sold his house in Vermont, and he and Adrianna had bought the beach house in Bridgehampton. It was slightly rundown, and it needed work. But he was doing the work himself. They were living together now, and had even spoken about marriage. But neither was in a hurry to rush forward. Too much had happened, and they each needed time to live with it before they took any final step.

He thought about Gabrielle. He often thought about her. After her death the police had gone to her apartment. They had found photography equipment and pictures of each murdered women. Aside from that the apartment had been virtually barren—a solitary single bed, a chair, a table—not even a desk or a book in sight. A monk's cell. She had lived like a hermit, had had no contact with anyone outside her work or the few social engagements she accepted. No one knew her for herself. No one saw anything but the professional facade she presented. The good, caring woman who offered her time to those in need. And perhaps that was part of her, Devlin thought. Somewhere in her twisted, tortured mind, perhaps it too had been real.

He tried not to think about what had happened to her as a child. He wasn't sure he could easily live with the end result if he did. He still hated her for what she had done to Phillipa. What she had wanted to do to Adrianna. And he tried to put that out of his mind as well.

Phillipa was recovering from the terror of that night. She was seeing a psychologist, working her way through it, and she no longer awoke during the night, crying out in fear. And Devlin was working with her to erase emotional scars he feared might one day surface.

Adrianna's guilt over what had happened to the child—the way she had been brutally used to get to her—was also waning. And they were becoming closer each day. Adrianna was teaching Phillipa how to draw, claimed she had enormous hidden talent, although Devlin found it difficult to see.

The job in Vermont was gone. But he didn't miss it; he understood that it had served its purpose. And he was glad to be back. Adrianna still had the loft in the city, and they went there now for weekends, the three of them. Adrianna's show had been a success, and Umberto—both Umbertos, he guessed—were reveling in the financial rewards. And so was Adrianna. She was truly going to be an affluent woman, and she seemed to like the idea.

The case was over. Not as he would have liked it to end. But over, anyway. James Hopkins had recovered and been spirited off by the archdiocese with the blessings of the police and the politicians. He was in a sanitarium run by the Church, and there had been private assurances he would remain there indefinitely under their care. Monsignor Duffy was still in charge of the office of subtle, and not so subtle, manipulation, as Devlin now thought of it. But he was good at it, and Devlin didn't really care.

The mayor, Delong Norris, and his police commissioner, Andrew Dalton, had not fared as well. Dalton's resignation had been sought and received shortly after Gabrielle Lyons' name had been splashed across the tabloids. The scandal of a police consulting psychiatrist as a serial murderer had been too much, and Norris had sought to save himself by sacrificing Dalton. It had come only five months short of the time needed for Dalton to earn his pension. But he had yielded to pressure, and had kept his mouth shut. He was now in private practice, specializing in matters dealing with the city. Devlin suspected he was making a healthy living.

But the mayor had not survived in the long run. The attempted cover-up of a serial murder had ultimately brought him down. He had been challenged in the primary by Howard Silver, the borough president of Brooklyn. And he had been badly beaten.

Mario Cervone and Matthew Mallory had survived, though. Although he doubted either would view it that way. Each had tried to take credit for Gabrielle Lyons' demise, but Eddie Grogan—who, together with Devlin, had been ballyhooed as heroes by the press—had carefully leaked the facts to friends in the media, and the newspaper and television reporters had walked all over the chief of detectives and the FBI with spiked shoes.

And the new mayor, Howard Silver, had offered a surprise as well. He wanted Devlin to return to the Police Department, reporting directly to his office, and concentrating on controversial and "high-profile" cases, as he put it.

There was an unused rank of Inspector of Police within the department—an appointive rank that had been ignored for years—and Silver wanted Devlin to assume it. He had offered to temporarily suspend his pension by executive order for as long as Devlin held the post. It would be a position responsible to no one but the mayor himself, a position that neither the chief of detectives, nor any other chief, nor the commissioner, could impose his will on. It would drive Cervone crazy. And that fact alone was making Devlin give it serious consideration.

Eddie Grogan had promised to withhold his retirement and to work with him if Devlin agreed to take the job. It was a ploy, Devlin knew, an attempt to push him in that direction. Grogan had no intention of putting in his papers. The fifty-two-year-old detective, Devlin believed, wouldn't leave the department until he was driven away with a silver crucifix and a necklace of garlic.

So he was thinking about it. And he liked the idea, but he was in no hurry to decide. He'd wait until he became bored. And then he'd talk it over with Adrianna. He suspected that getting bored might take some time.

Adrianna and Phillipa bounced out onto the deck. They were both grinning.

"What's up?" Devlin asked.

"Oh, nothing," Adrianna said.

He glanced from one to the other. Finally, Phillipa explained. "Uncle Eddie's coming out for dinner," she said. "And he might stay a few days."

Great, Devlin thought. Pressure from a fifty-two-year-old hump who wouldn't be able to walk straight if there wasn't a pistol hanging from his belt. He smiled. It would be fun, he decided.

"Wanna take a walk on the beach?" he asked.

"Sure," Phillipa said.

"It's cold. Let me get our coats," Adrianna said. She turned and moved back into the house.

Devlin watched her go. Then he turned to Phillipa and smiled. It felt good, he thought. Just looking at them. Just having them both there.

Don't miss
William Heffernan's
other thrillers starring
Paul Devlin

Read on for a preview
of both exciting novels

RITUAL

Devlin and his partner, Stanislaus Rolk, find themselves hunting a bloodthirsty serial killer, whose method of killing resembles an ancient ritual of human sacrifice. Here, in the book's opening chapter, a shocking discovery is about to be made. . . .

Stanislaus Rolk stood quietly, hands thrust deep in the pockets of his overcoat, his body bent slightly forward. He was on a small knoll that looked down on what was left of the woman's body. He remained motionless, his lined face impassive; only someone who knew him well might recognize the pain in his eyes. To anyone else he would simply appear tired, or, perhaps, even bored. Rolk kept his eyes on the woman for a long time. The contours of the body were now flaccid in death, but there was enough to tell him she had been relatively young; enough to tell him she had been physically attractive, the kind of woman men would have looked at more than once. Of course, she could have had a homely face, but he would have to wait to be sure. Wait until someone identified the body and gave them a photograph. Or until they found her head.

Below, the crime scene had been cordoned off in a large circle and portable arc lights cut through the early morning darkness, giving the area the bright glare of midday. The section of Central Park was isolated, a small clearing surrounded by a copse of trees, yet located no more than three hundred yards from Fifth Avenue and Eighty-first Street. The two uniformed officers who had discovered the body had responded to a 911 call about a woman's clothing found at the base of Cleopatra's Needle. The clothing had been folded, the smaller garments placed in a trail that led to the body. The woman's purse—or a purse they assumed hers—had been left where the head should have been.

Rolk glanced at the two officers who were now standing at the inside edge of the circle, talking nervously to other officers assigned to keep reporters at bay. He had spoken with them when he had arrived an hour earlier and they were still green and sickly. But they were both young; in a few years the sight of human horror would no longer make them ill. And that, he told himself, was the unresolved sadness of the job they had all chosen.

Rolk's eyes moved back to the body and the tall, slender man who stood next to it jotting observations in a notebook. Paul Devlin was only thirty, a cop for nine years, and Rolk's partner in Homicide the last four. But Rolk knew the sight of this mutilated body would not disturb Devlin any more than it did him, and he wondered if that callousness, learned over time, was something to be envied or pitied.

As Paul Devlin closed his notebook and looked up at the knoll where Rolk stood watching him, a small smile played momentarily on his lips. Rolk was as rumpled as ever. His topcoat looked as though he had slept in it. His thick hair, streaked with gray, always seemed groomed with fingers instead of a comb. Rolk had a sharp, softly lined face. Not a cop's face, but the face of a bachelor uncle who appears for dinner every other Thanksgiving or Christmas, then fades from memory for the next year or two.

A hand touched Devlin's arm, and he turned to face a uniformed sergeant.

"The meat wagon just pulled into the park," the sergeant said. "The lieutenant said he wanted to know when it got here."

"I'll tell him," Devlin said. "Who's the assistant ME who caught this one?"

"Jerry Feldman. Doctor Death."

Devlin nodded. Feldman was probably the best pathologist in the medical examiner's office, but a man with such a morbid and cutting tongue that most cops avoided him.

"I can't wait to hear what he has to say about this one," Devlin said as he turned and started up the knoll toward Rolk.

"Me neither," the sergeant said to his back.

Devlin slipped the notebook in his pocket as he reached Rolk. At six-foot-two, he was three inches taller than the lieutenant, but his slender frame seemed to tower over Rolk's broader, more muscular body.

"The ME's just pulling in," Devlin said.

"Who?" Rolk asked, his eyes still fixed on the crime scene.

"Jerry Feldman."

Rolk nodded. "Any luck finding the head?"

"Nothing. Not in the immediate area anyway." Devlin glanced at his watch. "We should have sunrise in about half an hour, and they'll expand the search then." He gestured with his head toward the area behind Rolk. "The Emergency Service boys are checking in New Lake. It's shallow all the way across, so if it's there, they'll find it."

Rolk thrust his hands deeper in his coat pockets and started down the knoll. "Let's see what Jerry has to say."

The morgue wagon pulled up to the outer circle of the crime scene, causing an immediate rush of the press, whom uniformed officers fought to keep back. Television lights went on as Feldman emerged from the passenger seat, and camera crews jockeyed for position, drawing shouts of protest from members of the print media they tried to push out of their way.

Feldman turned and scowled, ignoring even those reporters and cameramen he knew. He was tall, vastly overweight, and red-faced, with black hair that had receded to the middle of his scalp. He had compensated for the baldness by allowing the hair on one side of his head to grow long, then combing it up and over the top, which only served to emphasize his lack of hair and make him look mildly ridiculous.

Feldman stopped at the barrier and slipped an oversized lab coat over his tan polo, then stepped through and walked casually toward the body. He patted the lab coat as he reached Rolk and Devlin. "Cashmere," he said, of the coat beneath. "Hell to get blood out of."

Getting no response, he dropped his medical bag and stared down at the body. "Shit," he began.

BLOOD ROSE

In a small Vermont town, Paul Devlin is the new chief of police, and his first case has all the earmarks of his previous one: a depraved killer, and a string of brutal murders. It's not until the second body is found that Devlin sees a horrible pattern emerging, and suddenly he's at the mercy of this diabolical killer. . . .

Devlin sat at his desk and reviewed the already growing file—photographs of the scene, the coroner's report, the interview with the farmhand who had discovered the body, and a list of almost nonexistent physical evidence.

There was still the possibility the coroner was right, that Eva Hyde's death had been an accident. But Devlin found himself unable to accept it. Eva had been 21 years old and had had the reputation of being the town pump. The locals fond of talking about such things were quick to point out that getting into Eva's knickers, or enjoying a blow job, or hand job in the back seat of a car on a first date, was equivalent to a good-night kiss from most other young women. Devlin doubted the veracity of that claim, but he also didn't give a damn either way. The young woman, he knew, had come from a brutal environment, a broken home of two equally abusive parents. So she had sought love and comfort and affection wherever she could find them. And that had led her to bars and roadhouses, and to men who were quick to provide any substance that would make her pliable to their wants.

"Born to be fucked." That had been Free's idiotic comment when the body had been found. And indeed she had been, by many people, in many ways. But Free was too stupid to understand what that meant.

Devlin looked at the photographs again. Eva's body had been found in an uncultivated meadow outside of town by a farmhand looking for a lost heifer. A sharpened stake had been driven into her chest. But the stake had had dirt on its blunt end, and it was possible she had fallen on it. At least that's what the coroner thought. The theory was that she had been cutting across the field to escape an amorous misadventure, had stumbled and impaled herself. But Devlin couldn't buy that scenario. The body had been savaged by animals, the entrails scattered and partially eaten. But Devlin thought he had detected the remains of an incision, although the coroner disagreed, and the badly mauled state of the body made it impossible to be certain. And then there was the matter of Eva's missing heart. Animals or a madman? Devlin could not be sure. And the dried red rose found some distance from the body, the petals brittle with age, as though it had spent years pressed between the pages of a book. Had it been closer to the body before the animals finished their work? Left as some sort of totem?

He turned to the report on Eva Hyde. The suspicion—his suspicion—that her death might have involved deliberate mutilation had, like the crushed rose he had found, been kept from the public, or at least he thought it had. With the cops he had inherited it was impossible to tell.

But they feel the same way about you, Devlin told himself. They resent where you came from and how you were brought in, and most of all that you're not one of them, and never were.

Yet he couldn't blame them. He had moved to Vermont to escape the past, to be alone with his 6-year-old daughter, and away from police work. Then the old chief had died, and town officials—aware of his past employment, as they seemed to be aware of everything about everyone—had come to him and asked him to take over. He had agreed, in part for therapy, in part to escape the boredom that had begun to gnaw at him. And it had worked, and when his reappointment had come around the following year, he had gotten it, much to the displeasure of the men who worked for him.

Fuck 'em, he said to himself, as he had whenever the thought crossed his mind. Life sucks, and the sooner his deadhead cops learned that basic fact the better.

The eyes follow the woman as she moves toward the door. The subtle sway of hips. Dark hair tossed over a shoulder in that unconscious gesture that was practiced and studied in her youth, a way to draw attention to her beauty, her availability; something that would bring her the filth she wanted, leaving behind only one possible ending. *Just like mother.* An image fills the mind—hearts torn and bleeding; broken by pain; pierced; rived; impaled; suffering. Oh, yes, suffering.

The hands close into fists and a slight tic develops at the corner of one eye. The woman disappears through the door, a young boy following close behind. The sound of a beating heart fills the mind, a rhythmic pulsing, soft, steady, unrelenting. The head nods, not to the rhythm, but to another voice, silent, unheard, speaking of punishment already begun, easing other pain.

But still the pain returns, again and again and again. And it will keep coming until you stop them. The beating grows louder, but only in the mind.

"Stop the men from coming." The voice, almost a hiss, the words drawn out, then again. "Stop them."

The figure moves toward the door the woman has entered, then hesitates, uncertain. Louder, a steady, constant, thumping beating. Fists open and close, open and close, open and close.

"Now. Stop them now."

Both *Ritual* and *Blood Rose* are available
wherever Signet paperbacks are sold

PULSE-POUNDING THRILLS
AND EXCITEMENT

☐ **WILD AGAIN by Kathrin King Segal.** A terrifying spiral of passion, insanity, and murder ... "A sexy, intense thriller ... holds you from the first page to the last."—Nelson DeMille   (402979—$4.99)

☐ **BLIND OBSESSION by K. Patrick Conner.** Liana was the girl Cahill loved, but had lost to someone else. Now he finds that she is his for the taking, *if* he does what she wants, *if* he is willing to follow her into an exquisite web of murder and deceit. Sexual attraction turns deadly in this chilling thriller of erotic obsession. "Steamy, high excitement ... strong pay-off!"—*Kirkus Reviews*   (174402—$4.99)

☐ **DROWNING IN FIRE by Thomas Metzger.** There are some killers you can't resist. There are some secrets you can't guess. There are some thrillers you can't put down ...   (173120—$5.50)

☐ **SAFELIGHT by Linda Crockett Gray.** One man wanted to kill Rikki. One man wanted to save her. But the only one she could trust was herself in this novel of a beautiful woman dazzled by love—and stalked by death-lust.   (173171—$4.99)

☐ **CUTTHROAT by Michael Slade.** The hunt for a savage serial killer—in a thriller that embraces man's darkest fears.... "Would make de Sade wince."—*Kirkus Reviews*   (174526—$4.99)

Prices slightly higher in Canada

Buy them at your local bookstore or use this convenient coupon for ordering.

PENGUIN USA
P.O. Box 999 – Dept. #17109
Bergenfield, New Jersey 07621

Please send me the books I have checked above.
I am enclosing $_____ (please add $2.00 to cover postage and handling).
Send check or money order (no cash or C.O.D.'s) or charge by Mastercard or VISA (with a $15.00 minimum). Prices and numbers are subject to change without notice.

Card #_____ Exp. Date _____
Signature_____
Name_____
Address_____
City _____ State _____ Zip Code _____

For faster service when ordering by credit card call **1-800-253-6476**

Allow a minimum of 4-6 weeks for delivery. This offer is subject to change without notice.

⊘ SIGNET   ⬤ ONYX   (0451)

HAIR RAISING THRILLERS

☐ **THE PLOT TO KILL JACKIE ROBINSON by Donald Honig**. When hot-shot, young, black baseball player Jackie Robinson signs on to play for the Dodgers, sportswriter Joe Tinker hears rumors that Robinson won't live to walk off the field. And, when Tinker finds the connection between these rumors and a Greenwich Village murder, he may be the only one of 25,000 fans to know that a sniper waits somewhere in the ballpark, dead-centering on Robinson.
(175840—$4.99)

☐ **THE ONES YOU DO by Daniel Woodrell**. Lunch Pumphrey was missing $47,000 and John X. was the one he was looking for. A lot of folks had debts to collect from John S.—and he needed more than his cue stick to keep from paying with his life. "Authentic, profane, chock-full of winning details . . . an irresistible narrative."—*Publishers Weekly*   (403851—$4.99)

☐ **PRIME SUSPECT by A.W. Gray**. A fall guy hunts a psychosexual killer on the dark side of Texas . . . a riveting thriller of big money, corruption, illicit sex, and murderous deceit. "Compelling!"—*Dallas Morning News*
(404262—$4.99)

☐ **THE LOVE THAT KILLS by Ronald Levitsky**. A shattering novel of lawyers in a web of sex, drugs, and death . . . "Compelling and provocative."—*Washington Post*   (403746—$4.99)

☐ **CORSICAN HONOR by William Heffernan**. The brutal breakneck Mafia thriller . . . "Terror, murder, intrigue, and treachery . . . damn good."—Nelson DeMille, author of *The Gold Cast*   (176286—$5.99)

Prices slightly higher in Canada

Buy them at your local bookstore or use this convenient coupon for ordering.

PENGUIN USA
P.O. Box 999 – Dept. #17109
Bergenfield, New Jersey 07621

Please send me the books I have checked above.
I am enclosing $＿＿＿＿＿＿ (please add $2.00 to cover postage and handling). Send check or money order (no cash or C.O.D.'s) or charge by Mastercard or VISA (with a $15.00 minimum). Prices and numbers are subject to change without notice.

Card #＿＿＿＿＿＿＿＿＿＿ Exp. Date ＿＿＿＿＿＿
Signature＿＿＿＿＿＿＿＿＿＿＿＿＿＿＿＿＿＿
Name＿＿＿＿＿＿＿＿＿＿＿＿＿＿＿＿＿＿＿＿
Address＿＿＿＿＿＿＿＿＿＿＿＿＿＿＿＿＿＿＿
City ＿＿＿＿＿＿＿ State ＿＿＿＿＿＿ Zip Code ＿＿＿＿＿

For faster service when ordering by credit card call **1-800-253-6476**
Allow a minimum of 4-6 weeks for delivery. This offer is subject to change without notice.

Ⓢ **SIGNET**   Ⓞ**ONYX**

INTRIGUING THRILLERS!

☐ **MITIGATING CIRCUMSTANCES by Nancy Taylor Rosenberg. National Bestseller!**
When an intruder invades the home of ambitious Assistant District Attorney Lily
Forrester and commits a savage attack against her and her thirteen-year-old
daughter, she decides to head out on a trail of vengeance beyond any law but that
of her own rage. A mother's worst nightmare, a woman's best revenge . . . "Riveting."
—*New York Newsday*   (176723—\$5.99)

☐ **FLIGHT by Fran Dorf.** After twenty years in a catatonic trance, a woman awakens
looking younger, slimmer, and more beautiful than she did as a girl of eighteen.
What she doesn't remember is her plunging from atop a two-hundred foot cliff and
the sensational trial in which her boyfriend was convicted of her attempted
murder. Love, betrayal and murder . . . a psychological thriller that is "riveting,
tantalizing, shocking!"—*Publisher's Weekly*   (176472—\$4.99)

☐ **DEAD EASY by Arthur F. Nehrbass.** A twisted psychopath turns a South Florida
housewife's sheltered life into a nightmare of violence and unimaginable terror.
"Gripping, fascinating . . . a fast-paced thriller."—Carl Hiaasen(177045—\$4.99)

Prices slightly higher in Canada

Buy them at your local bookstore or use this convenient coupon for ordering.

PENGUIN USA
P.O. Box 999 – Dept. #17109
Bergenfield, New Jersey 07621

Please send me the books I have checked above.
I am enclosing \$_____ (please add \$2.00 to cover postage and handling).
Send check or money order (no cash or C.O.D.'s) or charge by Mastercard or
VISA (with a \$15.00 minimum). Prices and numbers are subject to change without
notice.

Card #_____ Exp. Date _____
Signature_____
Name_____
Address_____
City _____ State _____ Zip Code _____

For faster service when ordering by credit card call **1-800-253-6476**

Allow a minimum of 4-6 weeks for delivery. This offer is subject to change without notice.